The
TEA
GARDENS

Fiona McIntosh is an internationally bestselling author of novels for adults and children.

Originally from Brighton, Fiona moved to Australia in her teens and went on to co-found an award-winning travel magazine with her husband, which they ran for fifteen years while raising their twin sons.

She now roams the world researching and drawing inspiration for her novels, and runs a series of highly respected fiction masterclasses. She calls South Australia home.

Also available by Fiona McIntosh

The Pearl Thief

The
TEA
GARDENS

FIONA McINTOSH

arrow books

1 3 5 7 9 10 8 6 4 2

Arrow Books
20 Vauxhall Bridge Road
London SW1V 2SA

Arrow Books is part of the Penguin Random House
group of companies whose addresses can be found at
global.penguinrandomhouse.com.

Penguin
Random House
UK

This edition published by arrangement with Penguin Random
House Australia Pty Ltd.
First published in the UK by Arrow Books in 2021

First published by Penguin Random House Australia Pty Ltd.

www.penguin.co.uk

A CIP catalogue record for this book is available from the
British Library.

ISBN 9781787466869

Typeset in Sabon LT Pro 9.41/13.7 pt
t. Ltd, Pondicherry

Clays Ltd, Elcograf S.p.A.

House is committed to a
or our business, our readers
s book is made from Forest
l® certified paper.

For Ian, with whom I share so many cups of tea.

Prologue

I didn't dare look at the palm of my hand for fear of seeing the bruising arc pattern of fingernails from the clenching of my fist moments earlier. Was it despair? Jealousy? Or was it plain shock to gaze upon him again, to feel his skin against my ungloved hand once more? Oh, dear heaven, I had to hide! I could not unravel now, after all this time having kept our secret so tightly wound inside. *Find a quiet spot,* I urged. *Act your normal calm.*

I half tottered, half strode, but grimly refused the temptation to look back over my shoulder, especially as I could feel my mind loosening while my treacherous body trembled like the late-autumn leaves clinging desperately to their branches. I spotted the park bench hidden behind a large oak and steered for its iron solidity to regain some balance. Meanwhile the banker, speaking so intently to my husband, was an unwitting ally; he'd happened along at the ideal moment to save me intolerable shame. They were deep in conversation but my husband would not wish to leave me alone for too long.

Had my darling husband registered my fluster, or had I covered the signals of guilt? Moments ago it was all I could do to breathe through the shock. Whichever series of decisions brought him to me today resulted in pain that undid me like a zipper.

I kept trying to convince myself that if only we had chosen to walk through Kensington Gardens instead of Hyde Park, this aching, twitching version of myself would never have emerged. Jove had gently insisted, though, claiming he felt like a change, but now I regret what his decision had cost me . . . may yet cost us. I recalled with loathing how my responses had come out hesitantly, and with aching politeness. I didn't respond to his declaration of yearning. He noticed. He forgave me. The awkward conversation heated my cheeks; was it minutes or just seconds? It felt like moons had waxed and waned while I tried to catch my breath at the sight of Saxon Vickery once again.

Is it wrong to love two men as I do? I can almost wish to split myself into a pair and exist in separate lives, but this is surely a pathway to madness.

I chose, although I had no choice.

But the yearning doesn't disappear. Instead it enjoys punishing me as it lazily ebbs – like counting the ticking seconds of every minute as an entire day passes from morning into night. I've been guilty of losing time in this way, staring out of a window from our house as if hoping to find the answer on the horizon. My heart feels as though it beats a minim slower each day, as though his absence has become the metronome of my life. My academic training convinces me this burden will lighten in time but the invisible wound suppurates its grief daily and I must work hard to keep the pain hidden, for to show it means bringing sorrow to my dear husband, who deserves nothing but my affection and happiness.

'Darling?' That lovely familiar voice.

'Yes, dear,' I gushed, a fraction too enthusiastically to cover the terror of exposure.

'Ralph over there is in a bit of a fix, my love. I was wondering . . .'

I didn't want explanation; I was just glad I might have a few more minutes to swim against the tide of shock. 'Go,' I said, genuine in my smile of affection.

'Twenty minutes . . . tops,' he promised. 'I said I'd have a cup of tea with him over at the kiosk. I don't want to, mind, but he needs my advice.'

'He looks rather anxious, actually, so help if you can. I'll meet you back here in twenty,' I said, amazed at how breezy I managed to sound.

He kissed my hand. 'Thank you. And Ralph thanks you too.' He turned and walked away with the banker towards the small café kiosk in the park.

It suited me. I needed to take control; settle my upset, draw back the scattering thoughts that had already raced treacherously towards the Himalaya and box them in again . . . and turn a key on that box's lock.

Sitting here, allowing my pulse to slow while distracting myself watching children at play, I knew the time approached when I would have to broaden my role as a wife and bless our marriage with youngsters. I suspected I would be pregnant soon and the moment I felt that child quicken within, it would be the moment to finally let go of selfish recollections of a single life.

So . . . perhaps if just to indulge myself a final time, I closed my eyes briefly against this sharp, winter sunlight and allowed the full memory of 1933 to engulf me once again.

The banker's pipe had caught alight, I noted, and I could just catch a whiff on the air of the burley of Kentucky. My father used to smoke a pipe too and had tried all the tobaccos while he searched for perfection. I shared each of his displeasures, this burley of Kentucky among them for being artificially sweetened, he claimed.

I looked away from my husband's retreating figure to recall the passage of time, as though I possessed one of those memories that remembers every word, every nuance, each colour and scene that the mind has encountered. It's true that my talent for reliable and detailed recollection now feels like a curse because it won't let me escape what I am trying so hard to run from.

I think it was a gentleman called Ballard who, just before the Great War, wrote of a type of memory processing called hyper-mnesia, postulating that memory of events is improved dramatically in clarity by the regularity of retrieving them. I have gone over these last almost three years so often that I am ashamed to face my dependence upon them, and my repeated retrieval has made these memories vivid enough that there are times I imagine myself reaching to trace the lines of his face. There are moments when I am so lost with him in memory that I can feel his breath against the skin of my neck as he kisses it, or his fingertips gently caressing my hands. 'Healer's hands', he called them.

Let me then open my mind, allow 1933 to slip back into full focus and permit me to remember the whole story, not in patches, but in its entirety. Maybe, after this indulgence, I might find my way out of this tunnel of dependency.

I

It was nearing Christmas and I was taking a stroll with my father through the sprawling royal park of Kensington Gardens to the north-east. The southern side near our house was home to museums and royal buildings, including the Royal Albert Hall and the Royal College of Music. We lived in South Kensington, which was both fashionably envied by the social climbers and yet perhaps not as highly aware of itself as Belgravia and Knightsbridge. I grew up in a small enclave called Kensington Gate. It was built originally by an importer of tobacco and meerschaum pipes, and became a favourite corner for men who roasted chestnuts on open braziers.

The developer had arranged two terraced groups of homes in the Italianate style that is not overtly showy but leanly elegant with stucco fronts. It was only the entrance porticoes, supported on Ionic columns, that added the lustre of grandeur. The terraces overlooked a central, closed garden, which was a private park for our neighbourhood. The end houses, of which ours was one, possessed an additional storey and my suite of rooms was on that highest level looking out through arched windows. It was the only home I'd known but it was graceful to my eye, and growing up I used to love stepping out on the small balcony that was attached to my mother's rooms. After her death my father suggested I move into her salon but not once did that feel comfortable, which I suspect pleased him, so the doors remain closed, locking in her perfume and scented talcs, her fragranced soaps and potpourri.

I probably believed we could maintain her memory with clarity by keeping her rooms as she had left them. This notion is still a comfort to two people who miss her brightness, which was like a sunrise to our quieter, sunset-like personalities.

On this particular winter's day, we were walking towards Kensington Palace, muffled up against early November's chill. The climate had been surprisingly dull and dry since autumn began gilding the landscape in her golden colours, and my father's mood had caught a similar disposition. He had been muttering about the pound being devalued but he had fallen quiet while my mind was busy with the news of the social visionary, Gandhi, who was on a visit to Britain and being received by our King.

I thought we were walking in an easy silence and so it came as a shock when my father suddenly said, 'Isla, we must discuss a suitable marriage.'

I'm sure my expression bore the same bewildered look as someone staring with disbelief at the arrow shaft poking out of their chest. It was a topic we had left well alone for years.

'You're nearing thirty now, my dear —'

He said this in a tone as if I needed reminding. 'And I have duly marked each birthday, Papa,' I replied, frowning.

He gave me a soft glare of admonishment and I knew he meant to have the conversation whether I cared to or not. 'I made a promise to your mother.'

'You surely made many,' I said, resuming our walk. It was easier to cope with this conversation if we didn't have to face one another.

'I did. Mostly about you and none more important than the two I made as she slipped away from us.' He paused, forcing me to do the same and to watch as he seemed to search for the right words. 'And the one about your marriage was agreed while she still had the strength to take a breath.'

I swallowed. My father was not prone to dramatics so I held my tongue.

'I promised her I would accompany you down the church aisle in your wedding gown no later than thirty-one.'

'So I have fourteen months,' I said, with a nuance that silently conveyed *plenty of time*.

'We can't be flippant, Isla.' The tenderness in his voice cut through to my heart more than any harsh words could. 'Your career is precious – no one understood that better than your mother, who I often thought of as a pioneer, cutting open a pathway for you bright youngsters to follow. But even she did not want your career to come at the cost of a husband and family.'

No, I had to say it. 'Papa —' I imagine my tone clued him in.

'Isla, my darling, I know it doesn't sound fair that your mother waited while she forged ahead in her research but there are too many complications – that you above all people should know – about older women and childbirth.'

I smarted at the suggestion that I was suddenly an older woman but his rationale was not incorrect. 'I lost your mother too early.'

'We lost her due to complications of her disease, not childbirth,' I said, as evenly as I could within the rising vexation.

'I disagree. The disease weakened her but so did pregnancy at thirty-five. In concert, that wretched TB and her carrying a child so late, with complications around your birth and the season of your delivery, played the perfect death march.' He held up a warning finger. 'She survived but not long enough. You didn't even have

7

your mother into your teenage years. I will not watch my only and beloved child follow entirely in her mother's footsteps. I suspect we have six months, my dearest, before we must commit to a groom from your many suitors; there is a reception to plan, vicar to discuss formal arrangements with, your gown to be designed and created, banns to be read, a suitable honeymoon to arrange . . .'

My vexation turned to clear annoyance, which rose like lava to the mouth of the volcano. 'Papa, who has been whispering in your ear? Is this Aunt Claudette again?'

He shrugged. 'Your aunt knows about the promise; probably made an identical one to her sister. We both love you deeply, Isla; as the only child in this family we naturally want what's best for you, but . . .' He gave an admonishing lift of one silvery eyebrow to stop the inevitable torrent and looked over the top of his spectacles at me. 'We intend to honour your mother's wishes.'

We'd paused at the back of Kensington Palace and my gaze scanned momentarily for any sign of the royals – a glimpse of Queen Mary, perhaps, restoring her mother's rooms, which we'd heard about on the radio.

'Isla, please understand that —'

'Papa . . .' I began, desperate to stop his discussion, which was sounding rehearsed.

'So I realise I can no longer expect you to choose someone, darling Isla, because you seem, well . . . shall we say, reticent?' He smiled with such affection I felt my heart give a little. He took the softening in my expression to be permission. 'Do you remember Jovian Mandeville?'

I blinked, bringing out of my memories a man I hadn't seen since childhood. 'How could I forget him, Papa? You know full well I had the most terrible crush on him when I was thirteen.'

'Used to amuse your mother and me how you'd blush in his presence and stammer whenever he spoke to you.'

8

'Which was hardly ever,' me said, sounding a fraction churlish. 'Gosh, I was so in love with Jove Mandeville, I kept telling myself if only he'd notice me for the woman I was inside and would one day be, rather than the flat-chested, pigtailed child standing before him.'

It was a joy to watch my father tip his chin to enjoy a genuine belly laugh. 'But look at you now: quite the eligible woman with beauty to turn any man's head.'

'Stop priming me, Papa. What are you up to?'

'I am now of the opinion that it's been those younger men's possibly arrogant dispositions that youth and wealth seem to generate that have turned you from them.'

I looked down to my two-toned suede leather boots.

'And I am further convinced that you would thrive in the company of an older man.'

I looked at him with helpless astonishment. 'Jove?'

'He's not at all like the others, Isla dear. He is now turned forty-two. Still dashing, and all that old money intact. Did I ever mention that his family hails back to the early Middle Ages? I think one of his forebears was the Constable of the Tower of London in the eleventh century. The family estates are around Oxfordshire, you may recall?'

I nodded. It was coming back to me now. 'Made their fortune in railways, steel, shipping, wasn't it?'

'Most varied, actually, including coffee importers, as I understand it. More importantly he's led an interesting life since those summer stays with us and with the means to be a frequent traveller, to be well connected and, although he doesn't broadcast it, I know him to be a noted philanthropist. For now you should know that he is returned to England, lives in Mayfair when Westminster is sitting —'

'An MP?'

He nodded. 'I don't know for how long. His constituency is somewhere in the Cotswolds. He has a country estate in Abingdon. I was delighted to be reconnected with him recently.'

Jove Mandeville! The name dredged up all sorts of fond memories, some awkward ones too; at the time, however, my girlish desire felt so real it was dauntingly powerful. He'd been in our lives as a young man for a few years – his parents close friends of ours – and then he'd begun to travel and I'd grown up, my mother had passed away, all those affectionate friendships were lost.

My father gestured to a bench and I sat next to him. We both enjoyed feeding the birds and it seemed like the best idea to keep us busy, even smiling, as the host of formerly hidden sparrows descended like a circus troupe on cue to flit around us, nipping at the breadcrumbs we tossed from small bags that we each carried.

'Surely he can find a suitable wife with all of that going for him?' I tried to sound polite.

'It's not a case of can't find a wife, darling. There are women all over England . . . America, even, who are more than keen.'

'Well, there we are. He hardly needs me.'

'The point is, it's not that he can't but more that he won't choose a wife from what's on offer.'

I frowned and finally looked into my father's kindly face, which was not unlike that of the old gorilla I'd seen in London Zoo. I don't mean for a moment that my father resembled a great ape – no, it was more the wisdom I'd recognised in those small, dark eyes of the silverback and the tender way in which he played with a recently born infant of the family. There was curiosity in that ape's expression but also a lifetime of knowledge.

I looked now at the pleading look in my father's eyes, which were the colour of distant heather-covered hills: a sort of smudgy purple blue. I'd inherited similar eyes – shape and colour – except his had already spent more than sixty years in the gathering of knowledge; he was one of the country's most celebrated physicians but it was his modesty and reserve I loved most about him. Actually, I lie. It was his adoration of my mother that impressed me most. His fondness for me required no stating but I sensed this was one of those moments . . . the passing of wisdom. My father's gaze implored me to pay attention this time, to heed his advice, to follow this course.

'Why won't he choose?' I asked and it was the right question, for my father became eager, tossing out the rest of the crumbs from his bag for our twittering friends so that he could turn and face me properly.

'Because, while he uses the excuse that he is likely the world's most boring man, who shouldn't foist himself on a poor female, I suspect the truth to be that his intellect and especially his joy at life are offended by the queue of sociably acceptable but, in his judgement, dull women who fling themselves into his path.'

'Shameful,' I said with a small grin.

He returned it. 'Well, some women are keener than you to be wed and are prepared to be more obvious in their overtones, but he refuses to marry for the sake of it. Has admitted to me he'd rather live alone than make a poor decision.'

'I agree with him,' I said, meaning it.

My father nodded with a resigned smile that said he knew he'd walked into that. 'Nevertheless, I want the two of you to meet up again. He is intrigued by what I've told him about that youngster who used to blush in his presence and be sure, my darling, that I've mentioned your reluctance to be married off.'

'Papa – I used to make such a fool of myself around him. Why would you suggest this? We're perfect strangers.'

'No, that's not true. I have come to a conclusion that you could be perfect marriage companions and you are *not* strangers. He really hasn't changed that much – leaner, greyer, wiser, but that boyish joy in simple pleasures has not left him. You'll recognise the Jove of fifteen or so years ago. Will you meet him?'

I sighed, standing to tip out my breadcrumbs, but my movement frightened the chirruping sparrows and we were alone again.

'You know I wouldn't put just anyone in front of you,' he assured. 'Jove always was a bit of a rare bird and it's the quirkiness, his lack of conformism, that I think you may find appealing – I also believe his age and reserve will match your maturity. Please say yes to a meeting. It will be like old friends reconnecting.'

I didn't agree. I had been a child and Jove a grown man when we'd last been together. I was playing with a skipping rope while he was lamenting to my father about the price of gold. He didn't even notice the adoration as I relentlessly skipped nearby. But I could see I had no choice. 'Yes, I'll meet him, for old times' sake, and for you and Mother.'

'Do it for yours, Isla. After I'm gone —'

'Don't,' I warned. We both knew his heart was failing. It did not need discussing.

He nodded. 'He's taking you for a drive.'

'So it's already organised?' My father gave me a look of tender sympathy rather than apology for the invisible hand pushing at my back. 'Can't we just meet in a hotel for afternoon tea or something?' Now I sounded churlish but I had to show my frustration somehow.

He shrugged. 'It was his idea to have a day out . . . away from London.'

I sighed, resigning myself. It sounded to me as though my father had already made up his mind and this meeting was close to being academic. 'I'm going to agree to this on one condition.'

He waited, watching me expectantly.

'If Jove and I find some common ground . . .'

My father sat forward, eyes widening.

'If . . .' I repeated for effect, 'then going ahead in any shape or form will be decided by me with Mr Mandeville. It is not for you or my aunt to make any decision on my behalf.'

'I agree!' He barely considered the careful wording of my proviso.

I nodded. 'Then let's hope he is every bit as interesting as you believe him to be.'

My father stood, a smile of triumph as he crooked an arm. 'This deserves celebration. How about a pot of cocoa at Claridge's? Let me hail a hackney.'

I glanced at my watch and winced with regret. 'I would love to but I've promised to look in on Mrs Dempsey before I start my rounds.'

'Ah, your lady with rickets? What's your course?'

I was glad to be back on safe ground, talking clinician to clinician. 'It's so painful for her to carry this child and she's been brave about it to date but I'm of the opinion that a caesarian section will be prudent: either tomorrow or certainly over this coming weekend.' I looked up for his approval, despite my confidence in my decision.

He nodded thoughtfully and gazed out across the lawns. 'The baby will need lots of help if that mother can't breastfeed successfully and perhaps even if she can,' he counselled. 'Even a wet nurse . . .' he offered, with a shrug.

The wisdom was sound but his old-fashioned protection could be circumvented with today's expedient measures. 'I was thinking about putting the baby under an ultraviolet lamp immediately. I know it frightens mothers but its effects are marvellous.'

He smiled. 'Medicine is going ahead so fast these days, I'm almost glad to be retired. Trust your instincts, Isla. You were talking about man-made vitamins last week.' He gave a soft sigh that was half dismay, the other half awe. 'I read up on them. I'm guessing you'll be planning on some of those too?'

I smiled. 'I will be prescribing some synthetic vitamin D; it can't hurt the child.'

My father gave a soft whistle. 'And there was I thinking cod liver oil.' We both pulled a face of disgust at the thought. He kissed my cheek. 'We'll have cocoa another time. Go look after your patients.'

'I might be late tonight. I said I'd do a special round on the ward for a couple of new midwives who've arrived at the clinic from India for training. Will you eat without me, Papa?'

'I can go to the club. I'll ring Mandeville from there.' He winked.

I gave him a glance of feigned warning. 'A meeting is all I've agreed to,' I reminded him as my father lifted his walking cane in mock surrender.

2

I wish I could say it was like any other shift at the hospital but Mrs Dempsey, and her imminent child, was only one in a queue of mothers who required my collective skills that day. It was as though I were being tested in my remaining working hours in London as a final precaution to ensure I was ready to head up a hospital department in Calcutta.

After leaving my father I had wended my way to the hospital via Bloomsbury, lingering in St George's Gardens, pondering Papa's new press towards removing my freedom. Oh, he didn't view it that way, bless him, but while he occupied himself with fulfilling the promise he gave my mother, he didn't know yet of my intention to keep an equally solemn promise. This was a silent oath I'd made as she had become so frail she couldn't lift her head from the pillow and her smile had become fleeting, often a grimace as she pushed through her pain. Towards the end even her precious but halting conversation came at a price.

As a child I wanted to strike back at the disease that was stealing my mother from me in small pieces and hurting her so much. And so I gave my word to the invisible listeners that I would find a way to take revenge. Mostly my wrath was directed at the country that gave her this disease. As I grew, though, I realised the best revenge was helping to eradicate any disease in India; this was what my mother was doing in her work and if I was true to her, I should continue that calling. In that juvenile mind, I couldn't foresee, as she lay dying, that my specialty would not be tropical diseases but obstetrics – the area of medicine that desperately needed more women doctors and where ultimately my tutors channelled me. Nor could I have imagined that my parents would strongly oppose me in following in my mother's footsteps, urging me, along with my tutors, into acquiring skills that promoted better health care for mothers and babies. My father's admission today was another piece of that jigsaw; until this morning I hadn't realised that my birth via forceps had contributed as much to her demise as the invisible disease.

'Well, if not in tropical diseases, I shall still keep that oath and practise in the tropics, as she did,' I told a busy blackbird fussing among the leaf litter. But how did I tell my father this plan? His heart had taken a long time to repair after losing my mother and here I was setting about breaking it again. If I'd been the doctor in charge of my birth, I could have saved my mother the internal damage of those forceps.

And now there was Jovian Mandeville. Another obstacle taking shape on that path I wanted to blaze along. His name spoken aloud again brought back so much mixed emotion. This was the first man, other than my father, who claimed an important yet unique place in my heart . . . he was the first love and the one who was the benchmark for all that followed. Any young girl's awakening into that first explosion of romantic longing is potentially more power-ful than at any other time. And I was no different: lovesick for Jove from thirteen until I was nearing fifteen. It had felt like a lifetime of unrequited passion.

And then he'd disappeared from our lives and I'd grown up and put his memory into a different place. Boyfriends had breezed into my life and moved on, a couple of suitors had mattered for a while and then my intensive study, training and now work had probably worn them down and we'd parted, one sadly, but we remain distant friends. I'd had one or two lovers that were never serious and those affairs had erupted and felt fiery and fun and then burned themselves out as quickly as they'd ignited. I was happy in myself, not looking for anything romantically meaningful since I'd hatched my plan for India, so the notion of seeing Jove again was unsettling. I didn't want anything, especially not romance, disrupting my course.

I thought about how my life would take shape if I hadn't secretly applied to that call-out for doctors to travel to India from Britain's medical journal *The Lancet*. I would probably be sucked into the range of worthy fundraising causes that would inevitably end up as gatherings for wealthy women gossiping and critiquing other people's tastes or choices. The notion of a life of unfulfilment terrified me; at least through this role abroad I could have an adventure that would deliver memories to recall over a lifetime, and India, well, from all accounts it was about the most challenging destination for any clinician. I wanted to be tested, stretched, put under pressure and prove I was as good at my work as any male doctor.

I glanced at the time and that made me hurry on into Hunter Street. The familiar four-storeyed red-brick building loomed to my right – my working home for the past few years. The clinic for the poor that I helped to run here could turn alarmingly busy as winter set in and so did most of the health problems, but I suspected the challenges in London could never fully prepare me for what I would find in India. I was grateful to the local women's charitable groups that continued to raise funds that kept us going – whether it was through recitals or garden parties – but I just didn't want to become one of those women.

Today was rare as I would be the most senior doctor on the mothers and babies part of the clinic, so I needed to clear my head of India and Jove. Normally Dr Dooley or Dr Hampton would be in charge but both were away at a special conference in the Midlands. My moment to shine.

I pushed through the door and my colleague and friend Ellen, a senior midwife, who was Anglo-Indian and on a special training visit from Bombay, was walking down the corridor to meet me. She was as slender as a sapling and moved lightly across the linoleum floor despite her struggles to master the lace-up boots she now wore and the chilblains that plagued her since moving to England.

'Last week or two, Isla! How do you feel?' she said, beaming.

'Excited, nervous . . . and weary for not sleeping due to its still being a secret.' I pulled off my gloves and scarf.

'You still haven't told your father?' Her disbelief was tempered by the resignation that followed. 'Why am I not surprised? Isla, how —'

'I'll find a way. I still have three weeks.'

I followed her into our clinic's back room and pulled off my coat and peered through the small porthole in the door. 'Already so busy in the general rooms,' I remarked, not genuinely surprised. I knew from experience that the waiting room would remain full all day, especially listening to the rumbling coughs and sniffles, and the wails of children who needed help in this coldest of seasons.

'Isla,' she said, pressing her hand, the colour of rich tea, against my pale skin, 'I'm a bit worried about Mrs Hill.'

I ran the names of the patients through my mind. 'She's due next month, isn't she? Is she here?'

She nodded. 'Came in yesterday afternoon looking terrified.

Her husband is recovering from a work accident so he's not much help at home.'

'And?'

She gave an expression that told me she was feeling awkward. 'I think she's in early stages of labour. But Dr Dooley believes it's phantom contractions of the first-time mother and told me to send her on her way. I'm not sure he sets much store by my opinion but as he's not here and she was too scared to leave, I thought I'd keep her overnight and wait for you to take charge.'

'Well, let's make Sarah Hill our first stop, shall we? What else is happening?'

'Mrs Jones began labouring yesterday afternoon.'

I blew on my hands to warm them. 'And all through the night,' I said with a frown. 'How far gone?'

'Only a couple of inches, I'm afraid.'

'How's baby doing?'

'Had been stoutly holding his or her own but —' she shook her head '— just a few minutes ago we listened and counted a slight drop in heart rate.'

'Caesarian section?'

She shrugged but it looked like she thought it would likely need to be. 'She's wearying . . .'

'All right. Go on.'

'Mrs Dickson has a nasty case of milk fever and she's refusing to feed this morning. She didn't feed through the night either. Her son is distressed because he's famished.'

'Right. Mrs Dickson first – that child needs his milk – then I'll see Mrs Hill, call in on Mrs Jones and explain what we think might be best for her, given the situation, and then we'll do the normal rounds with the team. Mrs Dempsey?'

'Doing well, resigned to the caesarean. Pot's brewed. Might catch it before it stews.'

'I wish you were coming with me, Ellen,' I said in a moment of weakness as I swiftly made myself a warming cuppa. 'I like the way we work together.'

She cut me a glance and hurried me on. 'I've only just got myself familiar with how to catch a bus in London! Besides, I'm learning plenty and need to keep learning so when I do get home I can make a difference and help a new crop of midwives.'

I nodded. 'And you will.'

'So will you. They're going to be queuing to be on your ward.'

'I'll make time for all of them.'

Her dark eyes were large, and if not for the white coat, the various shades of brown she wore would have made Ellen look like she'd stepped out of a sepia photograph. 'I'm trying to find the right word that describes what you're going to face.' She searched, shaking her head.

I frowned, smiling, and stirred in some sugar.

'It's not like here, Isla.'

I blew steam off the top of the mug and we pushed through the door to enter the ward's corridor. 'I know.'

She shook her head more defiantly now. 'No, you don't. Death is commonplace and people accept it. Children die, even as they're being born, and while you hide it well, you don't conceal from me just how emotional you can be.'

'Are you a palm reader in your spare time?' I said, trying to shake off her serious glare.

'All I know is that you are going to be confronted by sights and matters that upset you. What you must remember is that it's not your world. You will only be there for a short time so don't try to change anything; just make a small difference to a few while you're there. Don't let it become personal.'

'What does that mean?'

'I mean, come home without being damaged.'

'I'll do my best not to get emotionally involved,' I said obediently, to which she gave a soft glare. 'Come on, we have crying babies and scared mothers to help.'

———

I gave the woman a sympathetic nod. 'I know you're feverish, Mrs Dickson, but I want to assure you that you will not pass anything but goodness on to your baby. You must continue feeding him at your breast, no matter how ill you feel.' I stroked the infant's tiny head. He was only a few days old and loudly cranky that his mother was withholding food. 'Listen to that wail and let your milk down.'

'It hurts, Dr Fenwick.'

'I understand. It will pass soon and the fastest way to do that is to drain your breasts often. He'll do that for you if you'll let him. Have you named him yet?'

'It's Charlie, er . . . Charles.'

'My father's name.' I grinned. 'A good choice,' I said. 'He's so hungry and so tiny. Come on, promise me you'll grit your teeth and get through it. Start with the sore breast and put him in a position so the milk can flow easily down to him. I'll ask the nurses to give you some extra pillows. And you know, Mrs Dickson, if you have to go on all fours to feed because it means less pain, do it. No one's going to care and we can pull the curtain around you. Massage the area like this as you feed.' I showed her. 'You're encouraging the blockage to dissipate. It may take a few days of still feeling quite rotten but I promise it will pass quicker if you trust me.'

She nodded wearily. 'I'll feed him now.'

'Perfect. I'll look in before I go.' I turned to Ellen. 'Mrs Dickson will need cold flannels to the affected breast after feeding and do warm ones only sparingly, a few minutes before each feed. It will promote let-down. Make sure the nursing team ensures that Charlie is latched on properly too. Feed him more often so we can get him fattened up quicker – more regular feeds will help both of them.'

'I'll brief them shortly,' Ellen murmured. 'She'll do it for you but not for us.' We walked on.

'Just make sure she's doing it for him. Right, let's see how Sarah Hill is getting on.'

We found her bed empty. A harried nurse approached. 'Dr Fenwick?' I gave her my full attention. 'We've moved Mrs Hill. She's definitely in labour although Dr Dooley said he didn't expect anything for at least a few more days.'

I slanted Ellen a look. 'Let's scrub.'

We entered an attached room where the mother, barely past twenty-one, sweating despite the cold, was panting but seemed to be focused inwards. I took her hand. 'Sarah?' Her eyes startled open. 'You seem in a hurry to have this baby.'

She gave a wan smile but closed her eyes quickly, returning to panting. 'She's not giving me a choice. She's coming, with or without our permission.'

'You know it's a girl, do you?' I said in a light tone to keep all alarm for the mother at a distance. I moved around to lift the sheets.

'Only a girl would want this much attention,' she half wept, half growled.

Ellen's gasp was lost in Sarah's groans and I cut her a warning look not to frighten the mother, but the truth was my heart rate had just leapt from calm. It had accelerated to a pounding I could feel throbbing at my temple as all other thoughts fled and I could almost hear a click as my mind locked into gear at the sight of the baby's prolapsed umbilical cord. I'd only witnessed this once previously while still in training. I remembered then the senior obstetrician had warned to get the child out as quickly as possible.

His words came back to swirl in my mind now: *That's the concern. Don't wait for this to right itself, don't expect the baby to turn or that you can turn it easily. Every moment you hesitate is potential brain damage.*

'Get Mrs Hill into theatre and prepped for an emergency caesarean,' I said, my voice quiet and sounding as though it was coming from the other side of the room. All that was my life outside of the clinic had been pushed aside; only this mother and baby mattered right now. 'Who's on for anaesthesia?' My tone was brisk. This was now the ruthlessly professional voice of Dr Isla Fenwick and I had several gazes trained on me.

'It's Dr Stone,' someone answered.

'Fetch him immediately. No excuses. None!' I dropped my tone but Sarah Hill was no longer listening. 'This baby's in trouble,' I murmured to Ellen. 'We could lose it if we aren't fast and efficient. Keep her hips elevated, no matter how she protests. Go!'

Re-scrubbed, gowned and masked within minutes, I stood poised, scalpel in hand, with Dr Stone nodding at me. He had intravenously administered the sodium thiopental, a barbiturate that we loved in obstetrics for its swiftness as an anaesthetic. Sarah Hill lost consciousness within forty-five seconds and I could proceed without a second's further delay.

'Thank you, Henry,' I acknowledged. I began to talk – I did this to help Ellen and another midwife observing – but in all truth I spoke because it helped me to state aloud the procedure I had watched my tutor show me all those years ago as a quick response to this rare condition.

'There are so many problems to cord prolapse. We know this baby is arriving prematurely, so that's part of it, but the membranes could also have ruptured before their time, or this little one hasn't engaged because it's been lying in a strange position and that has allowed the cord to occupy the space below it.'

I steadied my breath and made the incision low and not too wide. This would be a small baby and I intended to have him or her out in moments with as little damage to Sarah Hill as possible.

'What's our main concern?' Ellen asked. She sounded appreciably nervous. To most this might have appeared a stupid question with an obvious answer . . . death. However, I silently applauded the midwives who asked questions.

'Our major worry is compression of the cord by the baby above it,' I answered. 'The pressure can cut the blood flow to the infant and that means potential brain damage and of course potential death to baby if you start debating the merits of forceps versus the operation.'

'How do we know . . . I mean, before it becomes such an emergency, especially if the mother is at home?' Another good question from Ellen.

My gloved hands were now in Sarah Hill's womb, trying to get a good purchase on her child. I could hear my voice was tight and I probably had a newly distracted tone as my fingers slipped and slid around the amniotic sac. I broke it deliberately. 'Listening to the infant's heartbeat is paramount. It's your clue to what's happening in here,' I said. 'The moment it drops, you should get the mother to a hospital . . . before the prolapse or a number of other problems occur.' A moment's pause. 'And here we are!' I finished triumphantly, lifting a steaming, tiny child from her mother's belly. We all gave soft sounds of relief as I handed the precious baby to be wrapped and gently wiped clean of her birth. I let go of my relief and relaxed further at the first cough and then a wail from the baby, in order to refocus on separating Sarah from what I hoped would be her healthy daughter.

'Everything as it should be?' I said to the room, not lifting my gaze from where I'd tied off the formerly wayward umbilical cord. The child was cut free and while Ellen and her colleague worked with the baby, I glanced to Dr Stone.

'Mother's strong,' he said, winking over his mask at me. I liked Henry. He had ten years on me but I appreciated his calming, supportive manner in theatre. He lacked the arrogance I encountered with most of the other male clinicians, which probably explained why Henry was never without female company.

'Baby's intact and strong lungs for such a little mite,' the other midwife called over her shoulder.

'Good.' I lifted the placenta free and into the dish that Ellen was holding out. 'Check it,' I said unnecessarily but out of habit, already turning to the nearby tray for my suturing equipment.

Two hours later, with Sarah Hill coming back to full consciousness and getting used to the idea of a tiny sucking infant at her breast, I was already midway through another caesarean section, this time for Mrs Dempsey.

The day passed in a blur of mothers in need, including one delivery where the baby was all but falling out of the extremely young mother at her first push.

Later, leaning against the side wall of the clinic, I let out a long sigh to Ellen. She was equally exhausted but I suspected she felt as exhilarated as I did. I could almost wish I smoked after so many continuous hours lost in my work. Women drawing back on cigarettes always looked so chic, I thought. 'What a day,' I said, sipping on another mug of tea, more to warm my hands, although the sugar felt reviving after toiling to bring four babies into our world. 'You were brilliant today, Ellen.'

She thanked me with a beaming smile. 'You should know that every day in India is going to be as challenging as this one,' she warned, eyeing me with sympathy.

'Well, I'm ready for it.' I grinned.

3

Jovian Mandeville had sent a telegraph apology that he would have to meet me at our rendezvous destination. A car and driver came to the house to transfer me to where my potential fiancé was waiting, the stopping place being kept secret. While I am not someone who likes surprises being sprung, I was comfortable with this arrangement for it meant none of the awkward small talk in the cramped space of a car. And if I am being honest, I must admit that the journeying to a secret destination was vaguely romantic and rather fun.

I worked out soon enough that we were headed south; at first I thought it might be to one of the pretty villages dotted among the rolling South Downs, that we'd meet in a country hotel or similar. But, no, we kept driving and it dawned on me that we were headed for the coast.

'Are we making for Eastbourne?' I asked the driver, trying to imagine the most conservative of towns of the south coast.

'No, madam,' he said and in such a final voice I didn't try any further suggestions.

And as we descended from the steep rise on one side of the chalky V-shaped valley known as Devil's Dyke, it was obvious that we were making for Brighton. Local folklore held that the devil had apparently been carving out a deep trench to allow the sea to flood the churches of the Weald. I learned this from my driver, who suddenly became animated as we crested the hill and I recognised where we were from previous trips to the coast.

We wended our way to the Hove seafront and its infamous Palmeira Square, which had once been empty land used for an ambitious project called the Anthaeum. I remember my mother telling me this fascinating tale. A botanist and horticultural writer had conceived a grandiose idea for the world's largest conservatory. He planned an elaborate indoor garden, which was to be topped by the largest glass dome on earth. It was eagerly awaited but on the day prior to its opening, the entire structure collapsed. And here's the final tragedy – the poor man turned blind overnight, supposedly from shock. As romantic as I was, the grown-up in me prompted a new belief that loving something, anything, to such distraction was dangerous to one's physical and mental health.

We headed east into Brighton, one of my favourite towns of the south with its massive, sweeping crescents of regency homes leaning around public gardens alive with narcissus and some early, hardy jonquils. These squares and crescents connected with their prouder cousins, the soaring seafront terraces painted in a pale custard colour, which were battered by winds carried across the English Channel from France. As a child I had often dreamed of living in one of these fine dwellings opposite my favourite promenade, and even in adulthood I held to the hope that one day I might have a home on a seafront terrace.

'I'm to take you into North Street, Brighton, madam,' the driver said.

'Oh.' I was startled by his interruption of my thoughts. 'Um, thank you. Where exactly am I alighting?'

'It's a tearoom, madam.' He sounded embarrassed.

I reassured him. 'I understand my journey is to be a mystery.'

Curiously, this playfulness made me like Jove Mandeville even more. It was returning to me now how much fun he could be.

We turned into North Street, which had the town's Queen Victoria Jubilee Clock Tower at its top edge. The wide street was lined with banks and insurance buildings but also the vast Hanningtons department store. I recall my mother buying a feathered hat from there when I was still young enough to hold her hand constantly.

We pulled to the kerb not far from this familiar building, which had expanded into East Street and looked even busier than I remembered. The driver moved swiftly from his seat to come around and open the door for me. The cold air rushed in and I shivered as I alighted. We were alongside a Lyons' tea house, a favourite with workers and crowded, if the view through its window was an indication.

'This teashop, I presume,' I said, knowing it was a redundant statement. I frowned, pulling on my gloves and shrugging my coat closer around my chin to scan the front more closely. I threw a smile of thanks to the driver before squinting over the distance from the car through the windows of the tearoom. Cakes, biscuits and pastries of every kind – dozens of them – filled the double-fronted window from a couple of feet above the pavement to almost the top of the shopfront. It was staggeringly colourful to see a multitude of cake stands. On them, pyramids of tarts oozing glossy raspberry jam and lemon curd the colour of sunshine vied for attention with sponges sitting on pillows of whipped cream, while small pink-and-green iced fondant squares and marzipan-covered fancies sat like a row of multicoloured gems. A shiny chocolate gateau with tiny pyramids of cream and strawberries captured my attention, but I peered beyond these treats into the background, which was busy with jolly patrons. I felt immediately conspicuous as a doorman in a uniform with polished brass buttons against his navy jacket nodded a welcome. Slightly panicked, I caught the gaze of the man from my childhood whom I believed I was in love with all those immature years ago.

Initially I'd looked up to the upper storey, where Odinot's Hairdressing & Shaving Salon promoted everything from manicures and chiropody to face and scalp massages, before I glanced to the right of the store. I noticed a neatly bearded gentleman regarding me intently. He was a study in grey; his mid-charcoal overcoat dropped halfway to his shins and was only marginally darker than the suit I could glimpse beneath. He removed his dove-coloured trilby with hands kept warm in gloves the hue of ash. He gave a small bow, like a street pigeon about to start a mating dance.

It was instantly disconcerting that he was more handsome than I recalled from my tender years. 'Jove?' I already knew it had to be him as I stepped lightly across the pavement, extending a hand but wanting to hug him, yet embarrassed by the thrill of warmth to my cheeks at a childish rush of pleasure.

He reached for it. Eyes, echoing argent, glimmered as though Jack Frost himself was sprinkling them with ice crystals to catch the low winter light. I recalled their pale beauty in a less lined face and one shaved so closely that his youthful complexion all but shone.

'Isla, good grief, look at you!' he said, his tone as buoyant as I remembered, but grittier; softer too. He paused for a heartbeat while our gazes fully connected. I readily admit to feeling a surge of pleasure that he addressed me so respectfully, and also a rekindling of that old candle that had once burned so brightly for this man. He briefly kissed my hand, heedless of people watching. 'I really should say hello, Dr Fenwick.'

Why I had anticipated a wrinkly fellow with a crusty voice and liver-spotted hands was beyond me. My father had certainly conveyed him as thoroughly likeable, yes, but somehow I had taken on the feeling that the target of my childish crush would now be wizened in his bearing. He defied that impression dramatically; he was as dashing now as he had been as a glowing younger adult – more so, perhaps, because I sensed an innate confidence that the years had blessed him with. He was tailored in a fashionable cut that sat with sartorial elegance upon what was clearly a lean figure, which spoke of restraint or plenty of exercise, or both. That's right – I remembered now that he had been quite the athlete, rowed for Oxford, among his sports, and looked good enough to lick in his tennis whites. *Did I really just think that?* I was slipping back to the silliness of my teens.

Nevertheless he appeared hale and his nut-coloured hair lustrous enough to defy his forty-two years.

He looked me up and down with affection that felt genuine and not at all inappropriate. 'Have you got that wretched skipping rope of yours tucked away in that handbag?'

I laughed. 'I was quite the champion skipper at thirteen,' I replied archly. So he remembered me that well; I was surprised.

'You were forever urging us to hold each end so you could show off your prowess in the middle.'

'And you were hopeless at it. Especially when it required two ropes to be turned at once.'

'Never could get the hang of it, no.' He shrugged, feigning shame. 'Would you consider a pot of tea welcome before we proceed?' I noted he didn't add a condescending 'my dear'.

'I would,' I replied, 'although now you have my interest piqued as to where we shall be proceeding to.'

He grinned and I glimpsed the neat, polished teeth I used to admire, and was pleased to see he'd taken good care of them. I took his elbow as he gestured towards the doors of the tearooms. 'Later all will be revealed. Shall we?'

I pushed away the immediate self-consciousness as heads

turned to glance our way and allowed myself to be escorted into the shop, which had appeared deceptively small from the street. Inside, its sizeable length was filled with patrons enjoying a mid-morning beverage, and plenty of food was being served too, I noted.

'I reserved a quiet spot over here.' He pointed and led me to a small booth. 'I hope it shall do?'

'Thank you,' I said, seating myself and slipping off my scarf and gloves, trying to appear relaxed. 'Although maybe I could have left the fur collar behind in London.' There – I'd already showed my insecurity; if he noticed, however, he didn't react.

'Why? I think you look splendid and I'm sure every man here is envious of me.'

'Maybe a little overdressed?' I smiled, hating how pathetic I must sound. Wasn't this everything he reviled?

'If you wish —' he began.

I raised my hand slightly to stop him. 'I'm annoyed I mentioned it. When you get to know me better you'll see that I set little store by what's appropriate or not.'

'I look forward to reacquainting myself with that precocious young thing who used to stare at me and make me stammer.' Mandeville leaned in and I could see darker motes of colour, like tiny shards of shrapnel, in his pale eyes. 'Incidentally, I thought meeting you here among everyday folk – all strangers – might relax both of us.'

I smiled. 'Most thoughtful,' I assured. 'You did have a slight stammer,' I gushed, recalling it now.

'All your fault. You were rather serious, and for someone so young, a bit prickly on occasion.'

I couldn't help the chuckle. 'Really?'

'Oh, yes. You had an awfully big brain throbbing away and it used to unnerve me at times.' He frowned. '"Do you know the capital of Turkey, Jove?"' he mimicked in a girlish voice. '"Because I do.

31

It's Ankara; used to be known as Angora. Most people think it's Istanbul because as Constantinople it used to be the capital of the Roman Empire in the East."'

'I never said such a thing!' I exclaimed.

'Yes, you did. You were terrifying.'

'I was trying to make conversation. My mother said I always acted rather strange around you and she was terribly fond of you and wanted me to be friendly.'

'I loved your mother.'

'We all did.' I sighed. 'Still do.' It came out sadly. 'Sorry.'

'Nothing to apologise for. She died far too young. I know that sounds clichéd but she was incredibly generous to me at a time when I was missing my own family.'

I'm sure we were both remembering the *Titanic* sinking in that moment. 'They died too young too,' I said, and reached for his hand to squeeze it.

'Thank you. But now let's not get maudlin. This is the happiest of circumstances to be reunited with you, Isla. And you're so accomplished. I hear you're the darling of the midwives.'

I couldn't help a smile but a sigh chased it. 'I saw myself as being more a physician . . . a researcher, even. I wanted to work entirely in tropical medicine but both my parents insisted that gynaecology was the significant area in which women doctors should really take charge. And it's true, new mothers, pregnant women, labouring women . . . they all respond better to another woman.' I smiled. 'I was a forceps baby and my mother suffered for that.' At his frown I explained. 'We're now so much more skilled with instruments but when I was born, they were just blundering around.'

I was glad he chuckled because saying this aloud for the first time could have made me feel guilty but his amusement allowed it to pass by.

'I dare say her encouragement of better handling of births is the major reason I find myself specialising these days in gynaecology and obstetrics. And so while I hanker to work in the tropics, I would be lying if I didn't admit to deriving enormous reward from being part of the team that has raised our hospital's record of successful deliveries by more than fifty per cent in the last three years.'

'So I hear. Your father is immensely proud of you.' He winked. 'I'm proud of you.'

It was a sweet moment and we both looked away after it.

'Tell me about your work. Yesterday, for example, describe it to me,' he said.

'Well,' I began, 'you couldn't have picked a more dramatic one.'

I told him of the events.

'Are you ever frightened by the responsibility?'

I shook my head. 'No, I've been trained by the best; I'm surrounded by talented people and, to be honest, there's no time to be fearful. A good clinician needs to be decisive . . . people are waiting on your lead so you'd soon earn a poor reputation if you hesitated. I think the important aspect to what I do, though, is to keep learning, keep broadening the knowledge base. My father made the remark recently that medicine is moving along so fast he can't keep up but the fact is, it's developing at such a rate with new skills, new ideas, new technology that all of us – even the younger practitioners like me – have to run to stay up with innovations. Only yesterday I watched our anaesthetist use a piece of equipment that only came into use this year – this was my first time to see it in action and it's set to change the world of anaesthesia.'

Jove sat forward, intrigued, so I continued.

'It may seem like a tame innovation to you but it's a cuff around the tracheal tubes,' I said, touching my throat. 'Used when a patient is under the influence of very strong drugs that keep her unconscious and pain-free while we cut her open to deliver a child, for instance.'

He winced.

'Sorry, it's rather unsavoury teatime conversation, isn't it?'

He shook his head. 'Go on, it's fascinating.'

'We need to keep that mother breathing safely and rhythmically, and a straightforward cuff – introduced earlier this year by a man called Arthur Guedel – allows doctors to control the ventilation of patients under anaesthesia.'

'Sounds simple enough.'

'The most useful instruments usually are. One can't help but wonder why we took so long to think of it.'

The crowded rooms, with the steam from tea and energy from the waitresses, created a cosy atmosphere around us. To be fair, apart from the initial moment of arrival, no one was paying us attention and I let go of my self-consciousness. I followed Mandeville's lead and slipped off my coat too. With smiling thanks he laid both across the arm of our waitress, who had returned with her pad. I'd already decided he possessed an eager smile that could warm up any chill. It flooded his eyes with its happiness and had an infectious quality that couldn't fail to ignite a similar response from whomever it fell upon.

The waitress proved my point, immediately grinning back. 'Welcome to the Lyons' tearooms of Brighton, sir, madam.'

'What's your favourite poison, Isla?' he wondered.

'I'll have a pot of your strongest tea, please.'

'Make that for two,' he said, 'and I think we should have a small slice of cake each, please. What do you recommend, Joyce?' he asked, reading her badge swiftly.

'The pound cake isn't iced but it is especially fresh and lovely today, sir. And,' she whispered, 'it's got a nice hum of brandy in it.'

He glanced my way, making sure I was happy with this by catching my nod. 'That will do us nicely, thank you.'

The young woman retreated and we were now left to finally confront each other. These early impressions would be lasting. We were, after all – and I was determined not to lose sight of this – sizing each other up for a lifetime together.

'You used to call me the Isle of Isla,' I accused.

'Because you were so fiercely independent and appallingly confident for one so young, plus you also had looks to match your pretty Scottish name. Nothing's changed.' His voice had a gentle, raspy quality that only added to his attractiveness. 'Are you still as difficult to navigate as the Hebrides from where it hails?'

'I do hope so. I'd hate to be a pushover.'

It was the right answer. He grinned broadly. 'Well, as we're on names, I struggle with mine.'

My eyes widened. 'What's wrong with Jovian?'

'I think my grandparents decided that as I was the first new male in the family it deserved recognition, without considering the consequences of forcing a little boy to grow up with such a burdensome Roman name.'

'If my classical education serves me right, isn't Jove an old way of referring to the god Jupiter?'

'The supreme god in Roman mythology.'

'Presiding over heaven and light,' I added.

'And the law of the land.'

'The protector,' I said, with a note of triumph.

His eyebrows lifted in pleasure, creasing his forehead.

'Well, for the record, I've always loved the name. I'm surprised you aren't aware that I was completely besotted by you when I was young.' It slipped out before I could censor myself; curiously, though, it felt amusing more than embarrassing to admit my crush.

'No!' he gusted, astonished.

I nodded. 'It's true. But a dozen or more years separated us and to you I was a mere child.'

'I had no idea.'

'Surely?'

'No. You must have covered it by being so intense around me.'

'You broke my heart.'

'Gracious. Let me heal it – cake is called for.'

We laughed delightedly and I admit to feeling thrilled at how relaxed I was in his company; it felt easy and familiar but also the ground had been levelled. We were two adults now.

'It was a little unfair to spring this place on you and with no forewarning. You've been a brick just clambering into a car with no idea of where you were headed . . . and towards a relative stranger. We could have gone to swankier establishments, but —'

'Between us, I'm impressed you chose it.'

'Really?'

I shrugged. 'Anyone of your standing who chooses a tea salon frequented by the everyday person suggests to me that you aren't so concerned with status . . . or money . . .' I was in the realm of vulgar mentioning his wealth.

'Or appearances?'

'Yes.' I shrugged. 'I could learn from that.' I could tell he appreciated my admission by the kind smile he gave me. 'It means you're not stuffy,' I continued, as usual offering my thoughts instead of carefully phrasing a reply. 'Actually, you never were that but when my father asked me to meet with you again I feared the years might have turned you conservative.'

'Perish the thought. And stuffy is definitely not part of my nature . . . neither of us have our laces tied too tightly, then.'

'I think we should drink to that,' I offered as our pots of tea arrived in simple creamware rather than the elegant porcelain that I'm certain we were both more used to drinking from.

The teapots and cups were laid out along with two quarter-plates accompanied by slices of cake studded with dried fruit, plumped from the bake. 'It's our best quality orange pekoe and well brewed, sir,' the girl said, but rather than wait for her, he gestured an offer to pour and I nodded for him to go ahead.

'Thank you, Joyce,' he said. 'This all looks lovely.'

She gave a small curtsey and disappeared.

'This is so much better than meeting in London,' I admitted. Jove looked to be enjoying himself serving me tea. I couldn't say I was used to a man being so domestic but then everything about Jove was a lovely surprise.

'Feels like we're playing truant, doesn't it?' He paused, with an expression of gleeful wickedness. 'I'll let you help yourself to milk and sugar. Please don't make me eat cake alone.'

'So, as we proceed I feel I must be myself . . . by that I mean my usual direct, precocious self without fear of giving offence,' I remarked.

'Isla, I'd be disappointed if you were anything but,' he reassured, and I noticed that he'd shown no inclination to talk down to me, despite him having many years on me. His maturity instead was showing itself in far more pleasing ways. I noticed the slightest feathering of silver at the curve of his ear where his hair was trimmed short, parted and combed tidily in a lush sweep across and away from a forehead that was a neatly spaced bridge to his dark, even brows. It was all symmetry from there on, down to the clipped moustache and chin that had surely been expertly shaved that morning.

We forked at our cakes. They crumbled pleasingly and I savoured the hint of lemon rind that sparkled on my tongue first.

'Mmm.' Jove groaned with satisfaction. 'Joyce didn't lie about the brandy. Delicious!'

I chewed politely on an almond sliver. Each bite was flavoursome, crowded with fruit or nuts. With our mouths full there developed a slightly strained pause between us as we both realised that a deeper dialogue was desperately trying to clamber its way out.

He cleared his throat. 'Isla, I'm a bit embarrassed, to tell the truth.'

I frowned, holding my tongue.

'You see, I find myself staring at you.'

I had noticed but I was surprised that I genuinely felt the need to lower my gaze; I could be rightly accused of fake modesty if I pretended my looks did not interest men. It was better to accept the compliment and move on.

'Look, I have no doubt you've been told countless times how pretty you are and I won't bore you with the fact that I find the adult Isla deeply attractive. I hope that doesn't make you feel uncomfortable, given our history?'

I lifted a shoulder. 'Not at all.'

'Good. But let's set that aside, shall we?'

I looked up, unsure whether I was disappointed he wasn't going to lavish me with sweet compliments or filled with delight that he was pragmatic. I chose the latter. 'Yes, let's.'

'So,' he continued, 'your father is keen to find an ideal partner for his daughter who, shall we say, measures up to her exacting specifications.' He pressed his lips into a sad smile and I realised that his general good humour hid the melancholy that seemingly lurked in his life. 'I readily admit that I have turned away from many a lovely woman because I've had this notion in my mind that she must be special beyond the shell that the gods have granted her. Good-looking people can't help but have an advantage in life and I would gladly debate it if anyone wished to contradict that idea. A beautiful woman has it hands down over a plain one – opportunities are more plentiful in every aspect of life, not just marriage. But I've come to the conclusion that beauty and attraction do not always add up to happiness. I have been guilty of falling for someone's looks only to discover that I am bored by her all too soon – finding little in common. And so now I've become cautious, reminding myself that I must be more interested in what makes her laugh, or feel sad, what her secrets and dreams might be.' He gave a small cough. 'That probably strikes you as odd.'

I shook my head. 'No, it strikes me as powerful.'

'Powerful?'

I reached for my tea and sipped, enjoying the brew that was the colour of toffee when first poured. I tasted the hint of its flowery richness from the large leaves that unfurled in the tea strainer and I sighed with pleasure. Sitting back, I weighed up whether he'd appreciate such an opinionated woman as I, but decided there was no point in hiding it. 'I take the view that men who deliberately court women on the basis of their beauty rather than their wit, intelligence or personality must surely possess a sense of inferiority, hoping these women will bolster their confidence in front of other men. You, by contrast, surely possess an innate sense of your own power – and you've already reached the conclusion that a wife who is considered beautiful by others is a compliment to her rather than yourself . . . but it has no bearing on your self-worth.'

He stared at me with astonishment. I could feel my neck warming with the rush of blood. I'd offered far too much. So there it was, another flaw on display – a major one. My father called it prideful. I would argue that I simply take a position on most matters.

'Good grief,' he uttered and I couldn't even take another sip of tea to keep my fingers busy because my throat felt as though it had shrivelled to let nothing pass, not even a gushing apology. 'I don't know what to say,' he added.

I pushed away the blockage with a soft clearing of my throat. 'You must forgive me, Jove,' I began, but he started to laugh softly. 'My father has warned me of airing my opinions too readily.'

'Isla,' he murmured, leaning closer as if no one else in the noisy tearoom mattered, 'there is nothing to be sorry for. I am going to hold that commendation of yours as the highest compliment.'

I spoke over his chuckling. 'I am impetuous; it is a failing of mine to speak my mind.'

'Also to have your own way? I seem to recall you possessed a clear vision of your desires and objectives from young.'

Honesty, we'd agreed upon. 'I know my mind and what I want. I haven't changed from that child you knew – I've just grown taller.' I smiled at the thin jest.

His expression had turned more thoughtful, fine creases appearing in his forehead. He looked at his teacup for so long I wondered if I should fill the gap with words. 'Again, I would want you no other way,' he said, finally meeting my gaze, all amusement gone. The curlicues of steam had dissipated and the space between us had shortened, filled by a new intensity stretching from him to me. 'My reluctance to marry is mostly because I don't want to spend my life with a woman whose conversation is tedious to me. I also don't want a woman who spends her life trying to please me all the time. That's just as numbing. I've become terrified of taking a vow to commit to someone so wholly and then disappointing a wife through lack of interest or even common ground. It just wouldn't be fair to bring a lovely woman into my life who ultimately will look upon me with bewilderment for how to behave . . . or worse, with regret.'

'Have you ever been close?'

'To marriage?'

I felt pinned down by his scrutiny. I nodded.

'No. I've fled in the other direction whenever I felt cornered.'

I didn't mean to grin but his wording painted an amusing picture. 'So why now?' It was out. We were finally discussing why we were both here in this tearoom at Brighton.

'I mustn't avoid commitment any longer. It's time to share my life . . . but I am determined to give love and to be loved back.'

'You know a couple of affectionate Labrador dogs will fill that gap, don't you? And they'll never answer back or bore you with tedious conversation.'

His gaze snapped back to me and, seeing the smile, burst into delighted laughter. 'Don't think I haven't thought of it!'

I couldn't hold back my laughter either and we shared a few moments of unbridled amusement. His modesty and honesty were charming me. Here was a man whom I knew from my father's information to be wealthy, with status and respect in his field. From my own perspective, while he was far from the 'old man' my father made him sound, he had the lines on his face that spoke of life's experiences and the knowledge won through them. He was a man who could move among the common folk without turning heads and yet his clothes were finely tailored, his appearance most carefully kempt. His amusement won looks from other patrons, perhaps with a little envy that we were having such fun. Our sense of companionship was immediate, a rekindling of the past, a genuine sense of connection via our families, and even if nothing came of my father's best hopes for us, I could envisage us becoming the very best of friends. Wasn't friendship vital for a sound union of two people who were going to spend their lives together, being able to find common ground on everything? That meant compromise. I wasn't adept at compromise but I sensed that Jove might be.

'I'm surprised we haven't seen each other over the years,' I admitted.

'I have travelled a great deal and I've been spending a lot of my time in my constituency —'

'Do you enjoy politics?'

'Only for as long as I can make a difference. I feel strongly enough about certain issues that I think it's no good nagging from the sidelines.'

'Stand up and be counted,' I said, making a fist and grinning.

'I suppose so,' he agreed.

'So tell me of an issue you feel moved to support,' I asked, sipping and watching him over the rim of my cup.

He didn't hesitate to take my measure and that impressed me. 'Indian Home Rule. I support the National Government's proposal, though with diehards like Churchill angrily opposed, you can imagine the difficult journey ahead for those of us who like to believe we're forward global thinkers.'

I didn't respond, letting him continue, quietly thrilled that India was part of our conversation.

'The grand old days of colonialism must be relinquished. I've seen it all firsthand . . . not just in India but on the African continent and elsewhere . . . don't let me bore you but our days as the ruling class, taking so much from these nations, needs to end. We can maintain great relations and be allies . . . friends . . . or, if we continue down this path, we can ultimately become enemies, as nationalist fervour will take much firmer hold. The Indians don't wish to be ruled by a sovereign in a country on the other side of the world.'

'I'd like to see India,' I admitted, surprised I was skimming so close now to my truth and where my real passion lay.

'Well, maybe we can travel together and I can show you the world,' he offered.

I didn't answer because I wasn't sure what to say; it felt affectionate and exciting to have his offer but I intended to see India on my own terms first. 'And when you're not party politicking?'

'I like to get away from London as often as I can – up to Scotland or into the Cotswolds. I've seen your father at the club occasionally but not as often as you would think.'

'It's odd, isn't it, that my father's thoughts suddenly landed on you after all this time?' I nibbled more of my cake politely.

'Not really. I'd been away for almost a year and then I became an MP, so it brought me back to London and we ran into each other at the club, then soon after found ourselves seated together at a fundraising dinner. He talked about you and I think he may have experienced some sort of epiphany when I sympathised with your attitude over a choice of marriage partner.' He smiled conspiratorially. 'Now, Isla, I didn't bring you all the way to Brighton simply to talk over cold tea at Lyons',' he said, touching the side of the pot. 'I have a little surprise for you.'

'Oh?'

'It requires braving the cold.'

'I'm game.'

'Drink up,' he urged.

4

The breezy walk from North Street to the seafront was having less impact than perhaps it should have. I was in a state of measured excitement because, try though I might to temper the feeling, I was beginning to think that my father and I might share common ground with regard to Mr Mandeville.

Setting attraction aside – and there was no doubting I was attracted to him, even more so as an adult – I was interested in his approach to life. His humour, his whole bearing, was as pleasant as it was intriguing to be around. He was striking me as a man of the age – modern in his thinking but without a desire to toss away tradition. The traditionalist overtones I could pick out – his background, education, elevated manners, language – and they were desirable rather than detracting. What did this all add up to? Well, as we walked and he talked animatedly about Brighton being his favourite place in England, I decided that the years of not even laying a glance on each other had been good to us; we were more alike than I cared to admit and I found myself enjoying this man very much, even admitting aloud to my long-held secret desire for a house on Brunswick Terrace.

'Technically that's Hove, of course.'

'Splitting hairs, Jove,' I warned, as we moved through the Old Steine Gardens.

'Just keeping you honest.' He winked. 'Brunswick Terrace is delightful – have you got one picked out?'

I enjoyed him indulging my daydream. 'Of course. Number fifteen would suit me perfectly. It's near the middle, not too close to Waterloo Street but close enough to the Brunswick Square Gardens.'

'Where you'd take the two Labradors for a walk, of course.'

I laughed. 'Yes. But only in winter. That's the best season to be down here.'

'When all the daytrippers have fled?'

'Exactly! And our drawing room has a clear view over the stormy grey sea and we wonder – even worry – when the tide is in whether the waves breaking over the top of the promenade could flood us.'

Did he hear me say '*our*' drawing room? It was a slip of the tongue but I pretended I hadn't made it.

He grinned at our smooth banter. 'And we can taste salt on our lips when we step out.'

'I can taste it now,' I gushed, making a show of licking my bottom lip briefly.

'Queen Victoria and Prince Albert were no fans of Brighton,' he said, helping us to move on swiftly. I appreciated his discretion.

'How come?'

'I think the Queen once famously levelled the words of "indiscreet and troublesome" at the people of Brighton.'

I shook my head, perplexed.

'Well, Brighton has always been so liberal, so daring in its attitude, and the Prince Regent led quite the high life down here,' Jove explained. 'Our Queen hated the outrageously extravagant folly of the Royal Pavilion, of course, and sold it to the town of Brighton for a song.'

'I see. So that's why she used Osborne House on the Isle of Wight as her palace by the sea.'

'Precisely. Quite the opposite of fashionable Brighton and no prying eyes from daytrippers.'

We were passing through the Steine Gardens, with the main Brighton promenade directly ahead of us. The long wrought-iron finger known as Palace Pier reached out into the Channel, pointing at Dieppe in France.

Jove was cleverly picking out relevant, interesting titbits. But what he probably couldn't guess was how much I also enjoyed the sound of his voice. 'The fishermen of old used to lay out their nets here when we used to call the region Brighthelmstone.'

'I thought these gardens were an extension of the Royal Pavilion?'

'All of this is relatively new. The tide used to come up to just below the cliff we're walking on.'

I looked impressed.

'Marine Parade was built as protection and Madeira Drive leads off to Black Rock. The colonnade below us with all of its novelty shops was there for the original chain pier that acted as a staging point for the cross-Channel ferries.' He paused, appeared suddenly embarrassed. 'Enough of all that, though; it's simply an introduction as I thought we might visit Palace Pier.'

I gasped, genuinely surprised by the childish delight that rippled through me. 'But it's closed, surely? The piers don't open until later.' I glanced at my watch before scanning the firmly shuttered gates. 'Oh, what a pity – that would have been fun.'

'Do you like the pier?'

'Enormously.' This confession prompted a smile so I gave him more. 'I like to think that once I step through the turnstile I'm crossing an ethereal threshold: from land to sea.'

Jove chuckled. 'Where magic is possible, especially during the equinox.'

'And we hover between those two worlds as the sun crosses the celestial equator,' I replied, matching his playful tone.

'Marvellous. A girl after my own heart,' he said, walking closer to the pier.

I remained still. 'But . . . ?'

He stepped back, leaning close. 'I may feel comfy among the working classes, Isla, but I am not ashamed of having the money that allows me to pay for Palace Pier to open one hour early so that my exquisite companion and I might have a quiet stroll upon its board-walk with no other people to dodge and a private conversation of the utmost importance.' He crooked an elbow again. 'Will you join me?'

Helpless gushing followed. As a doctor I'd learned to keep my mood even, emotions in check, but this felt like childhood fun of yesteryear. 'What a treat! Yes, I would love to join you.'

It was a working winter's morning so the majority of pier-goers would likely land tomorrow and probably in the afternoon, which was promising a milder temperature. I didn't feel in the slightest guilty that we were cheating anyone, but even so it felt like a naughty pleasure to slip through the turnstile, past a ticket seller at the counter who nodded, clearly expecting us.

'Jove, this feels a fraction wicked.'

'I agree, and there are not enough simple but wicked pleasures in our all too serious lives. Enjoy!' he said, making a sweeping ges-ture. 'I'm afraid the concert band only plays in the summer and the theatre is not yet open but the rest of the amusements await us. What shall we do first?'

I still couldn't believe the pier was ours for a full hour. 'I'm astonished.'

'It would have been fun to be alone on here at night to see the thousands of illuminated light bulbs across all these arches.' He pointed to the nearest tall curves of iron and steel. 'The whole look of the place, with all of its oriental domes and majesty, was meant to mimic the Brighton Pavilion and John Nash's oft-thought ridiculous pretension at an Indian Mogul's palace.'

The second mention of India felt prophetic. I took it as a sign that I could share more about the dream I held . . . the one I was yet to approach properly with Papa. Talk of marriage was adding a new obstacle I hadn't seen coming.

I realised I wasn't paying attention to Jove, who was still lost in his pleasures of the pier. '. . . the onion-shape of the domes.' He looked at me and I quickly gathered my thoughts.

'Er, well, I think of them more as iced swirls on a birthday cake,' I said, admiring the top of a minaret-like flourish that adorned several of the pier's structures.

'One day I'll bring you to see this in the evening – it's glorious. But a morning expedition it is for now. Come on.' He led me across the boards. 'We have nearly two thousand feet to walk out to sea. I used to love going to the tearoom. It faced out to France and its menu had a more French than English tone. Coffee was *café noir* but I used to order *café au lait* simply because I enjoyed saying it, plus they called their cold cuts *viands* . . . Marvellous!' he said.

'Did a man used to ride his bicycle off the end of the pier, or was that West Pier in Hove?'

'No, no, it was definitely here. Professor Reddish was his name. I was among the crowd in 1912 that watched him "Fly the Foam", as he used to call it. Hilarious.' I laughed as Jove mimicked sitting astride a bicycle. 'He'd ride at speed and just shoot off the end of the pier.'

'Ridiculous, surely?'

'Oh, but so much fun. The crowd would be laughing long before he plunged because it really was so very silly and thoroughly English, don't you think? Which other nation laughs at itself as we do?'

I shook my head to say I couldn't think of one.

'And the Brighton Air Race used to pass overhead here. I watched Hamel winning in his monoplane. I told my aunt who had brought me that he was waving to me. That's how it felt, anyway.'

'How old were you?'

'Ooh, about seventeen, I think, but I was one of those youngsters who could be termed a dreamer.'

I smiled at him. 'I like that.'

'I was completely in love with Zoe Brigden too,' he continued.

'Someone from school?'

'Only in my dreams,' he scoffed gently. 'No, Zoe Brigden was what they call an aquatic entertainer. She used to give diving exhibitions from the West Pier jetty and then swim to Palace Pier. Her most famous dive was called the "wooden soldier". We'd all hold our breath as she'd leap into the sea from the pier, head first, arms by her side, and hit the waves like a spear. It must have felt like concrete. I was quite captured by her in her bathing costume. Heaven only knows how she got all that curly dark temptress's hair into her rubber hat!'

'Which teenage boy wouldn't be charmed?' I added archly.

'My point exactly.'

I began to feel warmed by Jove's company and his amusing, self-effacing manner. 'I think I would have been frightened rather than entertained by her antics,' I added.

'Then I think I should do the test of strength first to reassure you to never be afraid of anything when I'm around.'

The declaration was made softly, intently; there was a deliberate message being conveyed. He knew his way around the pier, threading us in a looping stroll various amusements and the Winter Garden that had been designed as a miniature Crystal Palace. He offered further titbits of information as we passed by.

'His Royal Highness the Prince of Wales was patron to the Palace Pier Follies who performed here,' he said.

'Follies?'

'A small troupe of men and women: singers, dancers, general entertainers who had three shows a day; they were good too – I saw them in 1923. I'm sorry I can't show you through the Winter Garden itself – it's rather lovely, with its central fountain and lace-work in iron. The theatre, too, is considered a triumph in acoustics and is very beautiful inside, lavished in royal blue and gold. I was here recently to see a pantomime as a treat for a godson. *Mother Goose* – great fun.'

'Care to demonstrate your muscle power to the young lady, sir?' the man holding the hammer said in his best funfair voice.

'Indeed. I do hope you've rigged this contraption to ring that bell no matter how puny I am,' Jove jested. 'I mean to impress this wonderful woman.'

'Oh, you will, sir. You look a likely one.'

I was chuckling even before Jove took off his hat and overcoat to get a good swing and we were all rewarded by a loud gong of the bell. Our trio gave a small cheer.

'Madam, you will have no problems with this very strong man carrying you over the threshold.'

I was surprised that neither of us felt awkward at the man's innocent remark, although we seemed to take an age choosing our prize, perhaps unable to meet one another's gaze. I settled finally on a jar of cinder toffee and we strolled on, arm in arm again. We decided against the helter skelter but took one brief ride on the ferris wheel, which made me feel as if I were flying with the gulls that wheeled and hovered overhead.

Back on the ground, we strolled on, feeling exhilarated from the chilly air at the top of the wheel.

'What are you reading and enjoying at the moment?' I said, keen to keep our conversation going so I could learn as much about

Jove as possible before we parted. We skirted the other side of the Winter Gardens.

'I'm always reading – lots of contracts and documents, newspaper reports, but I've just finished a novel called *The Last September*.'

'Oh, by Elizabeth Bowen?'

'I can't admit that I enjoyed it.'

'Too feminist?'

'Not at all. Actually I found that aspect of it revealing . . . the idea that modern women may be regarding marriage as potentially futile is something we men should not be dismissive of.'

'In what way should men consider it?' I was impressed but didn't want him to know this yet.

'Well, I suppose in how we approach marriage today. It's a contract, after all, and gone are the days of women meekly agreeing to their parents' choices.' He gave me a meaningful glance. 'Today, while financial suitability still rules as a major concern, I am certain daughters now have a lot more say. They are looking for love, for romance, for integrity of the promises being given. For example, "I make solemn oath before witnesses to you that I shall be this or that". By the same token you also grant me certain promises.' He waved his hand as though he didn't need to state the obvious of what those may be. 'But I think there is a case to be answered by too many men who marry because it's the right thing, or the done thing. It gives them the woman they need in their life – that is to say, to *be* in a state of wedlock.' He drew a small tick sign in the air with a finger. 'Then there's the brood of children bearing their name: more ticks in the right place. Meanwhile those men go on having their affairs, or carousing, or simply neglecting their solemnly sworn oath . . . the promise to love and cherish.'

I would be lying if I said I didn't feel stirred by his words. 'Women are just as cunning, of course.'

He nodded thoughtfully. 'I have no doubt. But if the right choice is made – both parties with high affection for one another, romance alive and well in their relationship – then disappointment need not enter that marriage.'

'I love your sentimentality, Jove. It is inspiring.'

He gave a small bow of his head in thanks.

'So how do we recognise the right partner, then?'

'Ah, and there we have the age-old question. My take on it is that we should all look for someone who can grow alongside us and mature at a similar rate, and be keen to develop and be open to change and enrichment of all kinds. The danger is stagnation. A woman marries, has children, becomes content if there is sufficient money and status. The man marries, has children, begins to realise his wife is distracted by household duties, raising the family, keeping up with friends and acquaintances . . .' He put a finger to the side of his mouth. '*Keeping up* with friends and acquaintances in the worst of ways too, and the husband feels he's queuing now for all that former attention that was lavished on him.'

'And he strays?'

'He strays, he finds other amusements, reasons to work longer hours, and suddenly the happy couple feel mismatched, no longer in tandem. I've seen it repeated in several marriages of colleagues . . . even close friends. Their union turns stale, predictable. It's all about the children, the right schools, the right house in the right neighbourhood, attending the right parties but having little to say to each other that makes them throw back their heads in delighted laughter. As for intimacy, it becomes routine.'

'Oh, gosh, Jove, now you paint a bleak picture of marriage.'

'It's not my intention. My point is it doesn't have to be that way!' he said, rounding on me, keen to make his point. 'It begins with the right choice and for all the right reasons. That's my position and why, until now, I haven't married.'

'I truly understand your reluctance.'

Our gazes held in agreement.

'You and I are not so different. I'm sure you desire the same. Let me leave it at this: if women are turning away from marriage, then we men have ourselves to blame. I doubt very much that women are turning away from men. Quite the contrary – women have never been more sure of themselves.' He nodded at me as if I were his point in question. 'As to why I didn't enjoy *The Last September*, I think it is a lonely story and I felt maudlin after reading it.' He shrugged. 'I prefer my novels to be uplifting. How about you? What are you reading?'

I laughed. 'I'm nose-deep in books on tropical medicine, actually.'

'That sounds daunting.'

'An important subject.' I smiled. 'To me, anyway.'

'Will you tell me why?'

'Only if you can shoot all these ducks,' I said, as we found ourselves at the shooting gallery. I needed to think through how and what to say, for this would have to be the crux of my agreement to marriage.

'All? I'm not that accurate, I fear,' he bleated.

'Let's make it six, then.'

He took the small air rifle that was loaded with metal pellets and the man behind the counter winked at me. Jove shot carefully but missed all but three of the ducks that travelled along a small track from eight feet away.

'I am no lover of guns,' he admitted, handing the man back the weapon. 'I was never invited to hunts at country manors.'

I relinked our arms. 'I'm glad. I've never grasped the pleasure of killing animals for sport. I find it desperately cowardly.'

We gravitated to the pier railings to look out across the sea, back towards Hove, further still to Shoreham. The breeze was picking up. We wouldn't be able to stand here long and yet I was in no hurry to leave.

'Soon the anglers will be racing down the boards to find the best spot. There have been sharks spotted off this pier,' he said.

'None caught, I bet.'

He grinned, shaking his head. 'My granny used to tell me the marine fairies were riding white-maned seahorses all the way to shore,' Jove remarked, pointing at the gently white-capped waves rippling towards the shingle beach.

'Both you and your granny were romantics, clearly,' I chuckled.

'I still am,' he said, turning to face me, fixing me with that look of his I was finding increasingly addictive. 'Despite my poor aim, will you still tell me why you're reading about tropical medicine?'

This was the moment, then. 'I should admit first that I fear my father discovering it.'

'He's forbidden you?' He sounded concerned.

'Not in so many words. It's just taken as granted that I will not.'

He blinked, frowning his consternation. 'Your secrets are safe, and perhaps the burden is halved?'

The truth is I was keen to share my dilemma. 'All right, but we should get out of this wind or I shall lose my hat,' I said, reaching for my velvet cloche as France did her best to blow it off my head from twenty miles away.

We moved to sit on a bench in the colonnaded section shielded from the wind behind the theatre.

'I am building up to telling my father that I wish to practise medicine as my mother did in India.' He waited, sensing there was a reason I was so hesitant. 'My mother died of the complications of tuberculosis.'

'I didn't know that was the reason. I can understand why your father would not want you involved in the same pursuit.'

'So can I. But that doesn't make me any less determined to practise medicine at the toughest coalface, as she did.'

'It killed her,' he reminded.

'I don't plan to let it murder me. And if it did, frankly it's preferable to death by hosting coffee mornings or afternoon teas, garden parties, jamboree fundraisers, elegant soirees and piano recitals, which is where I might be headed if I don't keep pushing for my career.'

The darker humour and sarcasm worked. He smiled, knowingly. 'Even so, your father's concern is justified and perhaps that's part of his urgency for you to marry.'

I looked down to see him take my hand. His was ungloved and I could feel the warmth passing through the suede covering mine; it was reassuring, made me feel safe. Old synapses must have connected in my brain because suddenly I was thirteen again, staring at the man who used to make that teenage heart race.

'I'm guessing you've made a deal?'

I nodded. 'I've been working at the Royal Free Hospital School of Medicine.'

'That's not far from St Pancras, near St George's Gardens?'

'Hunter Street,' I said, nodding absently. 'I was enchanted by the legend surrounding it that the founder, a surgeon, found a girl collapsed on the steps of St Andrew's Church. She was clearly dying of disease but mostly from hunger and yet none of the nearby hospitals would offer help to her. She died and William Marsden was so moved that he set up a small dispensary for the poor who were sick. After a cholera outbreak – epidemic, actually – Queen Victoria granted a royal charter to extend the clinic that helped so many of the patients into a hospital. It became the Royal Free Hospital for people of pitiful means.'

'Now there's a fellow to admire,' Jove murmured.

I recalled my father had mentioned a number of social welfare projects that Jove was privately involved with: *He uses his own coin. He asks for and seeks no recognition for his support but there are several worthy causes that would collapse if not for Mandeville's funds.* I waited for Jove to say more, perhaps mention his special charities, but he was instead waiting for me to continue.

'The bargain I struck with my father was that I did not remain close to patients with tuberculosis beyond two years. Furthermore, not to practise solely in the same area as my mother. I have kept my side of the former promise and stopped working in the TB wards six months ago.'

He inhaled, the air whistling lightly through his nose. 'But you're flouting the promise regarding the latter?'

'I do intend to follow in my mother's footsteps as to where she did her best work and sickened. And that's because I'm a wicked, defiant daughter. That should surely give you sufficient insight to steer clear of me. I'm nothing but trouble, Jove.'

He curled his surprisingly long fingers to encase my hand. 'The contrary: I admire you. I am a sucker for an independent woman who knows her mind and treads her own path. So you'll move from obstetrics into tropical disease research at the hospital?'

I smiled sadly into his understanding gaze. 'No, the plan is far more dramatic.'

'You might as well tell me. We're conspirators now.'

'I want to practise in India.'

I watched the light of amusement dim in his eyes. 'Oh.' He paused. 'That's dangerous, surely.'

'Plenty do take care of the sick without getting sick themselves.'

'I can't imagine your father would let his only child go to the colonies.'

'Now you know the heart of my secret. I live with constant vexation over it.'

He stared at our linked hands, nodding. Finally, he stirred. 'Well, that is a conundrum. I think we have two choices.' He held up a finger. 'Either I take you to those tiny bumper cars we passed that are called the Dodge-ems so you can smash into me and take out your frustration. Or —' he held up a second finger '— we can consult the Lady Palmist for a reading.'

'The Lady Palmist?' I was grinning now in spite of how gloomy my confession had made me.

'Oh, my word, yes. She's the high oracle. So smash around in bumper cars, or have some insight into your future?'

'Definitely the Lady Palmist!'

Jove looked delighted with my decision. He stood, urged me to follow and led me to one of the many slot machines. We passed 'What the Butler Saw', 'The Execution of Mary Queen of Scots' and 'The Haunted House'. These were more for titillation value. I'd seen a couple of them over the years: fast-moving photographs that gave the viewer a brief visual drama to share. These vignettes suggested more than they actually showed, with a theme that was usually sexual or violent in nature.

We stood before the slot machine. It was as wide as a door and deeper than a bookcase. Inside was an illuminated scene of a decadently furnished sitting room replete with marble fireplace, oriental rug, wall hangings and plaster busts. Within the tranquil, Victorian-style scene stood the doll of a woman; she was dressed in dark velvet, wearing a serene expression as if in contemplation, awaiting her next client. The machine proclaimed that the Lady Palmist would answer any questions that I may desire to explore with her.

I laughed gently as Jove pointed to a circular brass plate with a pointer that could pick out any of the twelve set questions.

'Just a penny will earn insight into your future,' he said in a grave tone, reaching into his waistcoat pocket to pull out some copper. He held up the penny and then put it in my hand, folding my fingers over it. 'This is highly private business. I shall go in search of some light refreshment for us while you consult the Lady Palmist.' He didn't wait for my reply.

I scanned the series of questions, which ranged from *When Shall I Meet My Beloved?* to *Is My Friend True?* I felt ridiculous and cast an embarrassed glance around me but no one was present, and so to humour Jove I twisted the dial to *How Will Our Courtship End?* It seemed the most appropriate question for today.

Slipping the penny into the slot, I waited while the machine gave my query some thought. The prediction appeared in the fireplace, turning through answers to finally reveal its decision: *Rest Content, Happiness is at Hand.*

The machine gave another guttural sound as wheels and cogs moved and, to my left, from another slot, a card appeared, which I was apparently free to take. The card told me that the person I was courting was true and that our love would 'transcend all worriment and dilemma'. It was ludicrous to feel relief and yet I definitely felt a loosening within that a funfair machine was signing off on Jove's suitability as a life partner.

I tucked the card away into a pocket of my coat and was still grinning to myself when I rounded the corner and nearly bumped into Jove. He was carrying fairy floss the near-luminous colour of tooth tincture in one hand and a glistening toffee apple in the other.

'I didn't know which you'd prefer, and the fairy floss man was just getting his sugar machine cranked up for the day.'

He really was the kindest fellow. 'Well, you can break your teeth on it as I reserve my toffee apples for Bonfire Night but that fairy floss is most welcome,' I said.

He handed me the stick and the breeze bent its top-heavy cloud of pink. I had long ago learned not to chew directly into the floss as it often resulted in a face full of the sticky confection and instead pulled off a chunk of the wispy sugar strands.

'One final amusement,' he promised.

How could I deny him? 'Last one before I should be wending my way back to London. Will you be joining me?' I asked, as he escorted me towards a small roofed enclosure. I chewed on the sugar, and its texture turned almost immediately into a sweet, liquid swallow. I was flung back to childhood and a feeling of security. The pleasure flooded me with joyful memories as I walked. I could hear my mother's laugh – when genuinely amused she lost control and sounded like she was being frantically tickled; I could hear my father talking gently to me as he dabbed antiseptic on my scraped knees, the singing of our canaries and the low growl of my mother's lap dog whenever someone came to our door.

'If you'd like me to, I should be delighted. The car is already waiting.'

I had to think about Jove's words before I realised he was responding to my previous query.

'Yes, I thought I glimpsed it when we were on the ferris wheel. So, what last surprise do you have for me?'

'Follow me.' He'd deliberately led me in from a side entrance so I couldn't see the hoarding on the small building proclaiming what fun it held inside. And as we entered I realised we were in some kind of maze.

'A hall of mirrors,' I breathed.

'With a difference,' Jove assured and urged me in deeper to where I confronted my reflection, which was so distorted I exploded into delighted laughter.

Jove stood by my side, and we both regarded our mirrored images that had us standing on legs that were ridiculously tall while our trunks were compressed to one quarter of normal size.

He kept me moving while I ate my fairy floss and he the toffee apple and the convulsive laughter continued. It was truly helpless and delicious to laugh with such abandon, and without having to be aware of others, or good manners.

'This is how I used to laugh as a child,' Jove admitted, 'carefree and uproariously.' He stretched, holding his ribs. 'Oh, gosh, laughing hurts, doesn't it? I'd forgotten that bit.' He took my floss stick and threw it with his half-eaten toffee apple into a nearby rubbish bin.

I was wiping away tears, dabbing my face with a handkerchief and then the hilarity hit me again when I caught sight of a barely two-foot version of myself. My cloche had been flattened atop a wide head that was now barely inches in depth, with all my features squashed. It was both a hideous incarnation of me and side-splittingly funny. I pointed and convulsed again. 'Jove, you look like one of the seven dwarves!'

'And you're my Snow White,' he said. I thought his legs were buckling from the laughter but he was lowering himself to his knees.

'Are you all right?' I said, still laughing distractedly.

'I'm perfectly well, deliriously happy.' He withdrew a small black polished leather box from his inside pocket and snapped the lid open. Nestled in the velvet cushion sat a ring of diamonds.

My breath caught and the amusement died in my chest, allowing my heart's beat to fill the void with a thump so suddenly loud it was like a drum beat that I could swear in that moment an army could hear and march to.

'Jove —' My voice was small, choked.

'Let me speak, Isla,' he said from his knees. He glanced at the curved mirror and couldn't help a small snort of laughter. I should not have looked but I followed his gaze and then we were both holding on to each other, off again into the hilarity of how squat and ridiculous he looked in that kneeling position.

'You look like Rumpelstiltskin,' I admitted through watering eyes.

'And here I am hoping to look back at this moment as a profound one of my life,' he moaned, but we both knew he had deliberately chosen this ridiculous situation, this moment of unbridled hilarity, to ask me for my hand.

He stood. 'Let me try again . . .'

I wanted to deny him, stop him asking; it was too soon surely, and we'd only just rediscovered each other. Even so, the whole day had been joyous, designed with every intention to entertain me, and I do believe that Jove was also testing me. I remain convinced that he chose the location of sharing tea and conversation in plain surrounds and a morning on the pier to see how comfortable I might be without all the usual status symbols around me that our families' wealth and position afforded. He wanted to know that I liked him for the glimpse of his pleasure into the ordinary rather than his access to the extraordinary. And I suppose most of all he was testing that I found him agreeable, attractive, with a sense of fun – even that I may find him desirable.

I sensed all of this in a few of those pounding heartbeats. I knew what he was saying without him having to explain and it was this point, perhaps – my realisation that we communicated so well without words – that made me finally fall back in love with Jovian Mandeville.

'Isla, I know it's a cliché but as a child I found you challenging and thus interesting. As the adult I loved you on sight. I couldn't take my eyes from you once we sat down – I'm sure you're aware of that . . . watching your lip pout as you sipped your tea, those eyes of yours, with their copper-sulphate colour that remind me of a glacier I once encountered on my travels. Their unflinching gaze penetrated the shield I've built around myself; it looked within and found me.' He shook his head. 'But I mentioned that looks are not enough for me. And so it's your heart, Isla, that I love most. It's pure; you're looking to help others rather than to follow the easy path of wealthy indolence. It's honest too. You're looking for love of the most romantic kind rather than the wealthy kind, and I swear I will never look away from you, never let you down, and never take you at my side for granted.' He lifted a finger. 'Wait. This must be said. I am older, much older, and there will come a time when you will have to care for me, indulge my deafness, my grunts from arthritis, my general tetchiness at the young, my —'

'Stop!'

He did.

'Jove, you're only a dozen or so years older.'

He nodded. 'We must consider your future.'

'You see that in itself is a revelation. It's that you care how I might feel in twenty years that endears me to you. But, Jove, by then I shall be nearing fifty and I assure you that men age better than women. I should be asking myself about how you'll cope with an old maid at your side.'

He took my hands in his. 'Cope? I should be the luckiest man in the world if you were still at my side when you were nearing fifty. Be my wife, Isla, and I will give you no cause ever to regret it. I know it may seem odd, even creepy, dare I say, that I used to push you on the swing or turn your skipping rope. But there have been a lot of intervening years – you grew up and I grew old. And I feel like not much has changed for me – I still find you fabulously interesting, unnerving, demanding, challenging and hugely intelligent. I couldn't want for more in my life.'

I swallowed, glanced left and saw two dwarfed versions of us holding hands, and I loved him for this hilarity around something so serious.

'Walk with me,' I urged, for fear of derailing this important moment. He followed me outside and I discovered the wind had turned brisk. Little whips from an invisible icy hand slapped our faces and were determined to remove my hat. I looked at my wrist-watch. 'We don't have much more time to ourselves, do we?'

'You're right,' he said, lifting a small but heavy-looking gold watch from his waistcoat pocket. 'The pier is no longer ours in two minutes.'

'Come with me,' I said.

He frowned but moved in step with me. 'To where?'

'To a bridge between spiritual planes,' I said cryptically, leading him to the point of the pier where it crossed from beach to sea. I looked down and stood on the line that my gaze assured me was the meeting point of land and water. A place of magic, if one subscribed to the ethereal world. I watched Jove look down, smile and follow suit, adopting a similar stance with his toes facing mine. 'Now, in this spot of great power, I shall make a pledge to you.'

He said nothing but I sensed the tension held in his chest, making the space feel small in his body as it pushed against his ribs in anticipation.

'I have a condition.' I waited for an objection but it didn't come. His silence nearly threw me but I was on my path now; I was saying yes to marriage, about to throw my father into a situation that would tear at his emotions, because while I was giving him what he most wanted, I was also, in the same breath, going to give him what he least wanted. I was already convinced he wouldn't know whether to celebrate or argue with me.

And so suddenly my future, my happiness, my desire to live my life on my terms rested on the decision of a man. Perhaps one day I'd look back at this and consider it amusing that the very reliance on men that the modern woman in me demanded I cast aside was to be my crutch in this most important of moments.

'Jove, my condition is that I be allowed to travel to India – to Calcutta – and to help in a hospital, so that I don't feel my study and life's work to date or the legacy of my parents has been wasted.'

He didn't speak immediately but held me prisoner in his stare. Finally he blinked. 'Will you be working in the area of medicine forbidden by your parents?'

I took a breath. 'It is not my intention to deliberately flout my parents' desires. I will not search out wards or patients with TB but I have no doubt – in all honesty – that I will meet people suffering from the disease and I will not turn away from them if I can help.'

He nodded. 'I suspect that is a conversation, then, that you must face with your father. I just want you home safe and walking down a church aisle with me.' He smiled softly.

'You'd let me go?' I murmured in disbelief.

'It is not for me to "let you go", Isla. It is for you to decide to go in spite of all the best advice. I shall not make it any harder for you to follow your heart, because if it leads you back to me, then my heart is full and who am I to deny you the same?'

Every ounce of me poured into the beaming smile I gave him. 'Then, yes, I shall marry you, Jovian Mandeville.'

He stopped me leaning in to hug him, gently lifting a palm and lowering it quickly so it didn't appear domineering. 'I, too, have a condition.'

'Oh, yes?'

He nodded. 'Mmm, and it is that we set a time limit on your absence.'

I didn't see this coming but at the same time it didn't strike me as unreasonable, given the generosity of his stance. I frankly couldn't imagine another suitor who would allow me such scope and freedom on the back of a marriage proposal. 'What are you suggesting?'

'Go whenever you can but be home by the fall of the first leaf,' he said with finality. We were stuck in our fairytales. 'I shall give you until September. If it takes you several months to organise your affairs, that is not my concern, but I'm guessing that you can probably be on a ship to India faster than I can take off my hat and gloves.' He smiled fondly. 'Your stumbling block is not me, Isla, it's your father. Now that I've found you and fallen in love with you in a single morning, you have my unhappy blessing to ruthlessly leave me.' He paused. 'But I shall now make plans for an early winter wedding in 1933. We are agreeing that you shall return in September next year and that we shall become man and wife in November 1933 . . . a white wedding all round, perhaps. Do we kiss and seal the deal on that?'

Not quite a year, but long enough. It felt like a lifetime as much as a lifeline being fed out in front of me. Mild-mannered, marvellous Mandeville – I couldn't help the alliteration or the admiration for the man I would be calling my husband in a year's time.

He undid the box again and held it towards me. 'May I put this on your finger?'

I nodded, tearing up, surprised by the emotion I was suddenly feeling. 'I would be honoured to wear your ring, Jove.'

'Isla,' he said, just once, his voice choked, and we took a step into an embrace, straddling worlds, sealing a promise with a fleeting, gentle kiss.

We barely heard the distant but clearly delighted applause of the pier staff or the slow, crunching draw of the surf over shingle to the irresistible pull of its tide.

5

We pulled up nearby one of London's grand neo-gothic buildings along the Embankment in Whitehall Place. My father's interest in architecture had taught me this long, magisterial building was constructed by Archer & Green with links to the Royal Horseguards and was used by our Ministry of Defence during the Great War. It always looked to me like a grand French chateau and formed one of our landmark sights on the city skyline.

'You don't mind?' Jove checked again.

'I promise you I'm capable of travelling alone in this motor car with William —' I nodded towards our driver '— all the way to Kensington for the next fifteen minutes,' I added, making it sound like an interminable trek. 'So this is where your club is?'

He nodded. 'The National Liberal Club. I'm also a member of your father's.'

'Club man, eh?'

'With a difference. This one is about liberalism in everything, from politics to art.'

'I'm relieved to hear it. How about women and the club?'

'Welcomed happily as members . . . always have been – that's one of the key reasons I joined it.'

I was delighted at this news. 'You are a surprise, Jove. Well, it's a splendid setting and I can see how easy it is for you to skip across to the House of Parliament . . . or even to the Palace if you get knighted.'

He made a scoffing sound. 'Lady Isla Mandeville has quite a ring to it, though.' He grinned. 'May I come over later and see your father?'

I nodded. 'I think you should. Why don't you join us for dinner? We can celebrate.'

Jove leaned back into the car, took my hand and laid a soft kiss on my newly bejewelled finger. 'I still can't let myself believe you said yes.'

'Neither can I, but I will never change my mind about you.'

His expression lost its lightness, his brow knitted itself into a frown and he stared at the ring, as though he couldn't risk looking me in the eye for fear of seeing a lie. 'Promise?'

Realising he still felt insecure about today, I made sure my grave tone reflected the enormity of the decision I'd reached and the pledge I'd made. 'Look at me, Jove.' He lifted his gaze. 'I will keep my promise to return by September and in November we shall be married.'

'You don't want one of those fabulously large society weddings, do you?'

'If you'd agree to elope I would run away with you at the end of next year, but we both know that's not fair to family and friends. Nevertheless, the smaller the better for me.' The relief that slackened his expression made me smile. 'I'll put together a list of people who matter in my life and they're all I'll need. We can talk more tonight.'

This time he leaned further in and risked an affectionate touch to my lips but I pulled him closer and kissed him harder. I could swear I felt him tremble. My own delight at this sense of romance swirling into my life meant I forgot that William was trying not to look in his mirror at us, and frankly all other sounds disappeared. Suddenly the horns of traffic, the clank and rumble of carriages, voices of drivers and barrowmen muted while the new world of Isla and Jove built itself around us.

'See you at seven.' I touched his cheek.

'I shan't need my car. I could float over.' He unselfconsciously blew me a small kiss as he allowed William to close the door. 'Back to Kensington,' he said to the man. 'Slowly, William. You have my most precious cargo inside.'

'Yes, sir,' William replied, and I caught the wink and understood these two were likely friends.

I lifted a hand to wave goodbye as we eased back into traffic. Thin sunlight fired flaring sparkles in the diamonds that now encrusted my ring finger. I couldn't fault Jove's taste; the central stone had to be tipping the scales at three carats. It was cut in the European style to show off its seemingly endless facets, which caught the light and split it into rainbow colours across the ceiling of the car. I decided as I looked down at the ring that its shape was akin to the planet Saturn, the large orb at its centre flattening out with smaller diamonds and oblong bevel-cut sapphires so brilliant they echoed the gassy rings of the planet. It was a stunning piece that flashed and caught my attention no matter how hard I tried to look away. And for someone who set little store by possessions – or so I thought until this moment – I realised I was helplessly smug at the glittering pile on my hand that proclaimed me as belonging to Mr Jovian Mandeville.

Curiously, I didn't mind this notion; I always imagined I might resent any man who laid claim to me but suddenly it felt right to belong to the very first person I had fallen for romantically. My ardour for Jove in those early days of adolescence had felt all encompassing; I had been his prisoner – emotionally – for probably three years and then he'd left and I grew up. Even so, the rekindled feelings had caught fire quickly over the course of today and, frankly, if I had to marry, why shouldn't it be to the man whom my romantic instincts had first woken up to?

I looked again at the ring. Despite all of its glamour, it didn't feel heavy or awkward. It was easy to live with, as I suspect the man who gave it to me would be too. If early impressions were the most important, then he fitted around me lightly. I didn't feel squeezed; there was nothing overbearing in his personality that I could pick up, and I knew my father trusted him implicitly, and would have already checked into any wrinkles of character or his past. No, given that there was a certain amount of pressure in both our lives to make a marriage decision, this really was a sound match; our families were close and I could see myself easily falling in love with Jove all over again . . . this time as the adult and on equal terms.

I mentally hugged myself as we skirted around Green Park, heading east down Constitution Hill, away from Buckingham Palace, and towards Hyde Park Corner.

I thought absently that this road took its name in the 1600s when King Charles II enjoyed his constitutional walks along it. More recently Sir Robert Peel, Britain's prime minister, had been tossed from his horse on this wide road and had died from his injuries. And I would let Mr Archibald – my history teacher – down badly if I didn't recall that there had been several assassination attempts on Queen Victoria along this path too. And here, right now, I was equating important historical events with my engagement. But this was a most important milestone for our family; my mother – if she were watching over me – would be smiling, nodding in that quiet manner of hers. And if she were alive, waiting for news behind the doors of our home, I think she might even give a soft squeal of delight. She was not prone to emotional outbursts but the promise of her only child and daughter's marriage to a good man with a fine family history and no dark secrets was likely every mother's sighing pleasure. Plus, she had always held a soft spot for Jove. I knew my father wouldn't be able to keep himself from the cellar to drag out his finest French champagne and get it chilling, or open his very best claret to breathe, or both, to celebrate.

We passed the Palace on our left and before long turned into our square. I could see Nanny Rosie from No.8 with her three charges taking the air in the gardens, and old Mr Bodlington was strolling with Muscavado, his dark golden Labrador of equal vintage. And there was Dr Radcliffe, eminent surgeon, off for his late afternoon walk – I could set the time by the doctor's ritual.

Home. Would I miss it when I travelled to India? Would I miss it when I left to live in the Cotswolds with Jove? Handy to know he had the place in Mayfair down the road but, even so, my life was about to change dramatically. But first, I had to deliver what would be unwelcome news to my father about Calcutta. It would be overshadowed, I hoped, by what would likely prompt deep happiness at the announcement of his daughter's engagement.

––––––––

My father poked at the fire. I knew he was torn between disconsolation and jubilation; I was waiting for the latter to win out. So I remained silent in my armchair, coincidentally upholstered in a colour to match the olive that floated equally patiently in the martini I was supposed to be sipping. I admired this room for the umpteenth time as a way of remaining quiet. It had taken me two years of stealthy haranguing to get my father to agree to redecoration. Two Christmases ago our sitting room had been claustrophobic, albeit in a comfortable way, but it was nevertheless melancholy because it was decorated to my mother's taste at the time of her marriage. It reflected her era of heavy furnishings, which included a fascination for the Orient, marble pedestals and silver on display. She possessed fine taste: I noted all her choices were made with an exquisite eye for bold detail but also, mercifully, some restraint in terms of volume. My broomstick of change was not just about dragging No.1 Kensington Gate into the era of *style moderne* but also sweeping away the overbearing sorrow that this room inflicted upon us. *New beginnings*, I'd said. *Let's make this room into a fresh space*, I badgered my father, and finally won through with a budget and four burly men to carry away his wife's treasures into storage in the cellar.

Gone was the fleck wallpaper and brocade curtains, the massive sofas and her beloved Persian carpets. I began by painting the room in a colour that resembled a pale mushroom newly emerging from the earth; the symbolism was purely accidental but the hue of rich cream with just a vague whisper of pinkish warmth was not. The painter and decorators called it 'Ivory cherub' and I loved it on first sight on our walls. It remained softly bright with daylight flooding through our tall windows, but by the evening's glow and as lamps or firelight came on it slipped into a warm, blushing richness against the pastel-coloured Aubusson rug. New indoor ferns introduced a fresh, rather than gloomy, green. Neat bookshelves added to coves, occasional and much smaller, finer-made furniture promoted space and allowed a sense of light in. My father said I'd littered the room with lamps and in some respect he was right; on petite French oak sideboards sat electric candelabras held up by figures fashioned in bronze with shell-coloured silk lampshades. I'd finally settled on achieving a vaguely French look to the room, with practical yet elegant side tables within easy reach of the sofas and armchairs, either of pearwood or mahogany, another with a marble surface and a tray-like rim of laced iron, bronze in colour. All my mother's decorative paraphernalia was boxed in storage, save the silver-framed photographs of the family and some of my father's favourite portraits that I had rehoused in gilded settings. It had become a feminine room, but my father had not seemed to mind. I suspect he privately celebrated the relief of change and the release from our former sorrow when he entered. Our last two Christmases in here had been far more lighthearted, with lights winking from our fir tree that took up residence by the main window overlooking the park.

The carriage clock chimed eight times. I knew it to be a couple of minutes fast, which meant Jove would be here any moment. My father knew it too.

I looked up at his sigh. 'Isla, you've managed to make me the happiest father alive and yet the most traumatised in two sentences.'

I gave him a sad smile to say I understood. 'Can you not focus on the first sentence? Papa, I not only approve of your choice of husband but I believe Jove and I are sufficiently well matched that we shall find love and happiness together. Isn't that everything you and Mama could possibly have hoped for?'

He moved from the fireplace in a couple of steps to sit beside me on the sofa, leaning towards me with an earnest expression. No, it was more than that – it was a look of genuine fear. I sat upright, refusing to be intimidated by his concern. I knew my decision to travel would bring only worry to my father but I assured myself that if I showed only confidence, maybe I could soothe him into trusting my calm determination.

'Papa, I *must* do this, or I will live with interminable regret. Don't you see, this is my way of setting things right with the world . . . my world? Don't punish me for hearing the calling that both of you also did. She became sick because of her work in India. It wasn't just the disease, though; we both know it was the conditions and the lack of knowledge of the times. Allow me to take revenge against this killer, to find peace in my heart. India needs more skilled doctors. If we can teach its new clinicians about modern methods, we can not only save patients' lives but also help the doctors who live and work there permanently. I'm asking you to let me go for not even a year – seven or eight months at best – so I don't waste the training and knowledge and all my study into tropical medicine. Please, Papa. Imagine trying to tell Mama she couldn't come with you all those years ago.' I was playing on his guilt and sorrow, but the sentiment was no lie.

He dropped his head with defeat.

'Papa? If we succumb to fear, how can we call ourselves doctors?'

'You could die. And then I've lost you both. And Jove has no wife and then I might as well die too!'

'Don't be melodramatic,' I said, clasping his hands. 'I could die tomorrow for any number of unforeseen reasons, from fever to a motor accident, but I have no intention of dying in India when I have you and Jove to come home to. I am choosing to answer my calling to work in Calcutta but I promise you my genuine mission is to help teach a new batch of midwives who can make such a difference to the mortality rates. The position is specific. I can make a difference. It's why we take up our oath.'

'No TB wards?' he qualified.

It felt like the sun was rising in my chest . . . I could feel hope like a lightening horizon beginning to show itself. 'I will not be officially working the TB wards. I will work with pregnant women and mothers with new babies.' I wasn't being clever in my choice of words; I just wanted to ensure I couldn't be trapped in a lie. I had no intention of seeking out tuberculosis patients but I couldn't predict if I'd come into contact with some.

'Nevertheless, you'll almost certainly be confronted by the disease.'

'I could pass someone on a London street with it. Let's be honest, we are both running the risk of exposure to contact with TB patients most weeks, surely? And no, I can't avoid it entirely in India and if they need my skills, I'll give them . . . gladly.'

'Yes, but we're better equipped here in England.'

'As I intend to make sure we are over there. I have a responsibility to help. We can't just invade someone's country and not give anything back for all that we've taken and enjoyed for a century; my mother would understand. Besides, healing and caring for the sick – that's what you and Mama are all about. I spent an entire childhood roaming around your laboratories or kicking my heels in hospital corridors waiting for you to finish with this patient or that, with this test tube or that analysis. How can you not take some of the blame for why we find ourselves having this conversation?'

I didn't enjoy making my father squirm and he looked uncomfortable sipping his aperitif, his mouth twisting in exasperation as if the sherry were bitter, while fighting words that wanted to fly out and exclaim, 'Oh, but it was different for us.' Papa knew better, though, and kept his counsel, so I pushed a little harder.

'As clinicians you took an oath, the same one I did. But I don't want to leave without your blessing.'

'And Jove is going along with this?' he murmured in fresh dismay.

I nodded firmly. 'We've made a pact. Until next September is the time I have to get myself posted, travel to Calcutta, do my work and be home in time to plan our winter wedding. I'll be back before you can even miss me.'

'That's not true,' he assured. 'I shall mark off each day on a calendar until your November wedding.' I smiled. 'Is it enough time, darling? What about your gown, the reception, the —'

'Let Jove and me worry about that. You just say yes to everything, all right?' I stood and kissed his head. We heard the doorbell sounding. 'That will be him.'

He gave an unhappy shrug. 'Well, the final decision is your fiancé's.' I refused to bristle at this. For all his attempts at modernity, he was still a man born just after the middle of the previous century. 'I'd better have that champagne cork popped because I refuse not to let this be a happy occasion.'

'Good for you, Papa.'

Jove brought the cold air in with him, chilling my face with his affectionate hug as he pressed a kiss to both cheeks; the fire, too, guttered in protest at the draught as he arrived in the sitting room.

'Jovian,' my father welcomed, wrestling with a champagne cork, genuinely pleased to see him. They were clearly friendlier than I'd assumed. 'Well done, old fellow. I am delighted to hear that congratulations are in order. Ready for a toast?'

'Certainly today I am.' He risked taking my hand in front of my father, who didn't seem to mind in the slightest as my fiancé kissed it. 'I am the luckiest fellow on the planet.'

'I'll say.' The cork popped, exploding across the room, and I squealed as foaming champagne frothed onto the rug. 'No harm done, darling,' my father assured, laughing.

He tipped the sparkling wine into champagne bowls he'd readied and then handed us each one. We were all still standing and my father obviously wanted to mark this moment so I didn't interrupt.

'So, forgive me that I feel some words are necessary. This is an important moment for me to mark.' He held his glass out. 'To my darling child. Isla, you've made me proud all of your life but today you've made me exceptionally happy with the news of your engagement to a man I admire.' He shifted his attention to my fiancé. 'Jove.' He cleared his throat. 'I know you will treat my precious Isla with relentless care, and take joy in her achievements. I hope that you will love this girl forever and as much as I do.' We waited, sensing he had more to say. 'Isla, I know your mother will be smiling somewhere, delighted by this decision. Here's to both of you wonderful people; give me grandchildren to jiggle on my knee and keep me occupied in my dotage. Welcome to the family, old boy.'

I smiled at Jove, knowing my eyes were damp from holding back the emotion as I watched my father make his toast. We clinked glasses and each took a silent sip. I was able to swallow back tears as the champagne slipped down with a deliciously dry sparkle at my throat as Jove nodded his thanks and made to respond.

'Even Professor Reddish toppling off the Palace Pier that we visited today can't make me smile as much as I'm smiling inside and out right now,' he murmured to me. 'Thank you, Charles. I promise to cherish Isla as you have and do. And come next winter, I'll see what I can do about those grandchildren.'

I gave a soft gasp of feigned indignation for their benefit and my father found this enjoyably risqué, tapping his glass against Jove's again.

'Let's sit,' I said. 'I thought we'd eat in here as we don't entertain often and, when we do, never so cosily for one. I hope you like beef Wellington?'

'I eat everything, never fear,' Jove said, holding out a seat for me.

'He eats like a bird, darling. You'll have to get used to that.'

'Modesty in everything, Charles. That's my motto.'

'So my apple crumble is wasted on you?' I asked.

He gave me a look of pretend horror. 'Never!' Jove frowned. 'You've cooked for me?' He sounded genuinely surprised.

I nodded. 'I enjoy it. We have our dear Lottie who comes during the week and does a bit of everything. She helped me this evening with our meal,' I readily admitted. 'Being in the kitchen diverts me,' I added.

He waited, wanted to hear more, a look of query encouraging me.

'After a day like yesterday something as simple and domestic as cooking is usually the perfect balm.'

'Your work is so far from the yells and hoots and conniving of Parliament.'

'Oh, don't be so sure. The caterwauling of a mother in delivery can make your ears bleed sometimes,' I said with exaggeration in my tone.

'But you have something to show for your work. All we do is bluster and plot against each other.'

I stood to answer the soft knock at the door.

'Do you look forward to having children?'

I wasn't ready for the question and took a moment to open the door and smile at Lottie, who was waiting for the signal to serve. I nodded for her to go ahead and returned to his question and my seat around the table. 'I must admit that knowing how complicated the most natural act for a woman can become, it can be unnerving but, yes, of course, I look forward to being a mother.'

'And in the meantime I shall enjoy your fine food and hearing hospital tales.'

'Isla has her cookery bible and she makes a mean sponge cake from it.'

I smiled fondly at my father. 'There's a tome called *Mothers Cookery Book* published about six years ago that my mother used to buy and donate to maternity wings of every hospital or clinic she came into contact with – not that she was working in obstetrics. It's focused on infant welfare, as after the war and so many lost husbands, women were still living on frugal incomes. I like to give a copy out now to regional clinics wherever I visit.'

'She set a fine example.'

I nodded. 'She was generous in every way and never liked a fuss.'

Lottie had placed hot plates piled with beef Wellington, gravy and mashed potato in front of us. 'I'll bring the vegetables,' she said with a grin.

'Yes, it's why I loved your mother. You'll discover that I loathe fuss, so thank you for this.' Jove unceremoniously tucked his napkin into his collar to make me smile. 'I create a headache of laundry for my housekeeper or the club if I don't,' he admitted.

Lottie emerged once more with a platter of vegetables, glossy with butter and sprinkled with pepper and salt.

'Tuck in,' I urged.

Jove's first mouthful of my pastry-encased beef with mushroom paste prompted sounds of rapture. 'Isla! This is heavenly. It's surely better than the recipe at Claridge's!'

'I should hope so,' I dismissed, disguising my delight with admonishment. 'Baking especially brings me peace and it's when I'm calm and distracted that I can work out problems.'

'Like how to tell your father of your plans to go to Calcutta?'

Clever Jove. I knew what he was doing; we needed this tangled issue to be out in front of us so together we could tease it out.

'Yes. Now, Mandeville, have you really signed off on this plan of Isla's? Surely you have reservations?'

'Charles, you and I both know that nothing is going to stop Isla if she sets her mind to something. I am not going to order her to do anything other than come back to me, although Isla understands I am setting some conditions.' It was only now he turned to look at me with a different cast to his expression. Amusement did not lurk in it. Jove was pushing his flag into the ground and marking it as the line that must not be crossed. As much as I thought I was a woman who would resist any sort of bullying I found this new quality charming because he made it feel like a fierce protection, part of his overwhelming love. I also hadn't missed that his early 'condition' had suddenly become plural.

'Let's hear them,' my father said.

'I am in agreement that Isla will pursue her important work in tropical medicine, and particularly her desire to help the women and their babies of Calcutta.'

I nodded but held my tongue.

'Of course, you as her father will have your own view on this but in terms of her agreement with me, we have pledged that no matter when she leaves for India she will return during September with November the month of our wedding.'

It was plainly laid out; I sensed no guile to trap me. 'I am agreed to this,' I said firmly. It was likely unnecessary but I needed my father to hear it.

My father sighed and blew out his cheeks. 'I suppose Isla has spoken of her mother to you?'

'She has, Charles. She knows this contradicts your promise to her mother but it's fair to presume that neither of you could entirely know Isla's mind or her determination at the time of . . .' He gave a soft sound of sadness that allowed him to avoid saying the words. 'I'm sure you sense her determination to bear out her fine pedigree in medicine and I shall not be the one who even attempts to deny her that longing. I believe it may settle something disruptive within her too.' He flicked a glance my way. 'Forgive me for speaking about you as though you are not present, Isla, but I am laying out my thoughts for both of you to hear.' He returned his gaze to Papa. 'Charles, I fear that if we make this difficult for Isla, then her marriage to me might bear the brunt of her unhappiness. I think she is entitled to the same dreams and goals that either of us might be. The fact that hers frighten us is irrelevant; they don't frighten her. If she were your son you'd likely be clapping him on the back for his adventuresome approach to life. Frankly, I'm drawn all the more to Isla for her temerity. She's perfectly capable of making her own decisions and I support her in this.'

I felt the urge to fling myself into Jove's arms for his generosity but also for how quickly he had understood what drove me, and he seemed to capture the spirit of my dream faster and more eloquently than perhaps even I could. I flicked my attention to my father. It rested on him now but I was wrong; there was more.

'I feel I must make one other condition, though,' Jove spoke into the silence, 'and perhaps it bears airing now before your father gives us his blessing.' He looked at me, perhaps noting the surprise before I could hide it.

'Go on,' I said, realising I was twirling the new ring on my finger, which suddenly felt heavy.

'When you come home to me, Isla, and you take holy vows to be my wife, that is you leaving India behind; I want you to put our marriage, this family,' he said, gesturing towards my father, 'and definitely *our* lives first.'

'Of course —' I began, slightly indignant, but my response was hasty for him and I noticed how his neat fingers splayed slightly as though he was fighting the urge to raise a hand to stop me speaking. I stopped anyway, the breath of words backing up in my throat.

'Let me explain fully. As my wife, I anticipate you wholly involved in *our* life, not just yours.' He put fresh appeal in his voice, his palms open to me as he continued. 'You're a doctor in your own right, a woman to be admired and sought out. I don't want your work once we're married to ever take precedence over our relationship. Your father is my witness that I will never disrespect or take for granted that you have agreed to be my wife. I will put you first and I will include you in all decisions that relate to our family life – from where we may travel to where we shall live, to the schools our children go to and when. You are my equal in our marriage.'

I swallowed what felt like a ball of emotion that had risen to my throat at his stirring words but I knew what lay in them was his warning. I needed to pause, pay full attention to what he was actually saying rather than hearing only the cautionary note in his voice.

'While I would never ask you to give up your work as a doctor, Isla, I will be asking you to leave behind all future thoughts you may entertain for working abroad once you become my wife. So, to this end, I think you should leave England without wearing my ring.'

I gasped but he gently raised a hand to quieten my anxiety.

'I don't wish it back, just returned to its box and left with your father until you come home to claim it. I want you to go to India without encumbrance.'

'Why?' I frowned.

'Because – and you must forgive me if this sounds in any way condescending, although it comes with noble intention – you're young and you don't know what the future holds or how you may feel. I will not break faith with you, darling Isla. In ten months you will return and all that will be on my mind is making you my wife, but we don't know how India might affect you.'

I frowned deeper.

'Travel broadens lives . . . it introduces you to people and cultures, to ideas and experiences that you'd never thought possible. I know through my own travels how I've been changed.'

'It will not change how I feel about us or our marriage.'

'Nevertheless, I want you to have the complete freedom to experience all that this adventure offers, without guilt, and to return home to me without burden. Get India out of your system, Isla. Enjoy it to the full and then return to England freely and genuinely ready to become Mrs Mandeville. As long as I breathe, you will never go abroad again without me and I plan to be travelling far and wide with you. Icescapes in Alaska, the great red desert of that vast continent of Australia on the other side of the world, the massive rift of the Grand Canyon in America, the jungle of Africa, Bethlehem in Palestine, the pyramids of Egypt . . .' He stopped himself, but his eyes continued to sparkle with memory. He caught himself and shrugged, smiling.

I applauded his directness, even if I wanted to rail against his presumption that India would change me; it wouldn't.

'You not wearing my ring abroad is to prevent putting either of us in any danger of a broken engagement and the tarnish that brings.' His expression shifted into his melancholy smile, the one I glimpsed in the tearooms. 'It's also a protective measure, for to love you too deeply, believe you're to be mine and to lose you would break me. I know it.' He held my gaze and I saw only tenderness and plea in it.

That couldn't have been easy for him in front of my father. Watching him deliver his impassioned speech, pewter-coloured eyes softened by emotion, made me feel deeply wanted and, above all, enormously special. Men had tried before and failed. What was it about Jove?

I took a slow, visible breath and in that moment it was as though time slid to a pause. I relaxed my shoulders finally. 'I accept your conditions on the basis that they're made with a sense of care for my wellbeing as much as yours,' I replied. I laughed as my father gusted a breath of relief. 'I want to marry you, Jove. I'm looking forward to being your wife.'

'Oh, my heavens, let's drink to that,' my father said, reaching again for his glass of champagne, still fizzing merrily. 'To the future Mr and Mrs Jovian Mandeville. I hope you're watching, Clara!' he said, raising his glass and looking to the ceiling as though he had a private channel open to my mother.

6

For the last few weeks in London my heart felt as light as a hot air balloon on a summer's day, although I'd been convinced I would look like a simpleton if I allowed this sense of ridiculously elevated happiness to show through. I could swear the colour of London had magnified itself, as though I had entered a special tunnel that could only be accessed by the newly engaged, or those freshly afflicted by romance in their lives.

Love, if I'm honest, remained a fearful word. It was used so casually and yet I felt it carried with it so much force that I didn't utter it to Jove. He lavished me with it and didn't seem perturbed that I wasn't responding in kind. He took instead my laughter as proof, together with the physical affections – the smiles, the moments he caught me gazing at him, the kisses. I found these so much easier to give him as a demonstration of my growing fondness. And there's no doubting that after that last month together, as we had hurtled towards Christmas, I couldn't remember a happier time in my life. I was far too much of a scientist to turn sudden philosopher, so I was content to leave love as an elusive emotion I shouldn't question. All I can say is that I had been waking with a new sense of myself. There had arrived a novel warmth within, despite the chill of dawn; helpless smiles when normally there might have been a grimace at having to arise in the dark of a winter's morning; and a sense of pleasure and anticipation and even – I can't believe I admit this – a sense of belonging to someone. As important, though, and I couldn't say this to anyone, was the knowledge that I was finally filled with my purpose. It was no longer a secret. My childhood dream was becoming a reality.

We slipped over into a new year and I finally left English shores in the midst of a winter in which a deep depression near Iceland dominated the weather over the British Isles. I floated away from our dock while the country was experiencing widespread snow with hefty gales to the west and north. The two men I loved were rugged to their noses, hats pulled down over ears as they braved the freezing afternoon dockside to wave our ship farewell. I was glad I could blame a lot of my sniffling on that deep climatic depression at Reykjavik.

However, not even London's Covent Garden on a busy market day or the glimpse of the surging humanity of Bombay's Ballard Pier could prepare me for the new 'jungle' of unnerving strangeness that confronted me as I stood slightly dazed on one of the two dozen or more railway platforms at Howrah Main Station in Calcutta.

Suddenly the crossing of oceans that had felt daunting all those weeks ago when I kissed my father and Jove in a teary farewell from London, bound for Brindisi in Italy, now seemed simple and straightforward. I had people to help me, guide me and see to my needs. In Italy I had moved with a party of Londoners whom I'd attached myself to and together we joined our ship as a large and jolly group to be feted with glamorous evenings of dining and entertainment, a never-ending supply of food, constant amusements and parties. And as we sipped cocktails and discussed everything from Denmark abolishing capital punishment to the calling of the general election in Ireland and the fire onboard the luxury ocean liner *L'Atlantique* that destroyed it and two hundred and fifty-five souls, we tried not to show how that tragedy unnerved any of us. The enormous project of the Golden Gate Bridge won much discussion, as did the romantic gangsters of Bonnie and Clyde unleashing their form of terror in the United States, while we were all amazed by an Australian making the first commercial flight of over twelve hundred miles between Australia and New Zealand with passengers. Flying instead of sailing captured our imaginations and one entire night of dinner conversation, which also included the loss of British aviator Mary Bailey during her solo flight to South Africa. England defeating Australia in the third test claimed most of the conversation over brandy and cigars later. Meanwhile, the landscape, when we glimpsed it, as we moved across oceans and called into increasingly exotic ports, began to change dramatically from all I'd known. As we were docking in Bombay and my voyage came to an end I remember feeling a momentary sadness that I couldn't continue all the way through to the other side of our planet to Australia.

Thomas Cook representatives swarmed to help passengers into taxis and off to hotels while they took care of the transshipment of luggage. I shared a taxi journey with a couple of wives bound for Victoria Station in Bombay and was quite taken aback by its Gothic beauty. I suppose it had not occurred to me previously that India would have such glorious English-style buildings, and it felt as though we were arriving before a majestic church. But given how important India was to Queen Victoria's reign in particular, I privately admonished myself for a lack of foresight that India was likely crowded with British-built edifices such as this. I had to hurry on from my gawping at the ornamentation on the building's exterior or risk holding up the other ladies waiting for me. I had worked hard throughout our journey from England to make the necessary small talk to fall in with the other women. Shipboard life, however, was becoming a fast-retreating memory as I clambered aboard our train, which I was assured was the most luxurious steam train in the world. We were about to make a grand journey that would take us nearly two days to cross this enormous continent of India into West Bengal.

The Imperial Mail Train – known to these regulars as the Blue Mail due to its painted carriages – had to be booked in England and it timed itself to the P&O Line voyages such as the one I'd sailed on. I had been surprised to discover that the train only accepted first-class passengers, and at a premium. My father had organised my journey from London so I had no idea what he'd paid, but going by the fact that my fellow travellers included the Governor of Bengal 1st Viscount Waverley plus a band of senior British diplomats with their wives and various military men – none below the rank of brigadier – I hated to imagine the cost.

The outrageous fee paid meant we were spared the indignity of anything but the finest, cleanest, most hygienic experience available on the Indian railways. I didn't envy the passengers alighting from our ship at Bombay and going on to Rangoon via steamer. I'd certainly had my fill of ocean travel despite the romantic-sounding journeys that so many of the passengers I met were keen to discuss at length. In fact I was the happiest I'd been in more than a week to finally set foot on *terra firma*, sensing the destination of years of longing was finally at hand. One more journey, I told myself, although fourteen hundred miles to cross the breadth of India still felt daunting.

My father had entirely indulged me, it seemed, as I discovered I was to travel in a single compartment, which felt like a balm after all the socialising on the ship and shared accommodation with two other chatty, newly married women on their way out to join their military husbands.

Although the dark wood of my private room felt vaguely claustrophobic, it also seemed to cool it and a strategically placed fan at one corner of the ceiling kept the air moving. It was a finely equipped space – nothing I could complain about – from a single, surprisingly comfy cot with cool, starched linen to a pair of cane chairs with satin cushions, and plenty of overhead luggage space. I was also spoilt to have my own basin and large mirror so I could freshen up in private facilities. I remember how I shut the door, closed its louvres and felt as though I had cordoned myself off from outsiders for a while.

I let my world narrow to what I could see from my window as we snaked our way across India. I gathered it would be an electric locomotive to a place called Igatpuri and then steam all the way to Howrah in Calcutta. The butler taking care of my carriage informed me in excellent English that the only stops we would make would be to take on water and coal, but no passengers. I sighed with relief that I only had to make conversation at mealtimes with perhaps thirty others, maybe fewer, if the train wasn't full.

'You may keep the windows open, madam,' he assured. 'No steam until Igatpuri.'

I smiled my thanks and remember feeling relief as we finally jerked and then surged out of the Bombay terminal to cross a narrow coastal plain. It wasn't long, though, before we had to negotiate the Western Ghats mountain range, which in some parts required us to climb to just under five thousand feet. The terrain was like none other I had ever confronted previously and I imagined how pleased Jove would be when I wrote home about this jungle-like landscape as we cut through valleys on our ascent to the Deccan Plateau and our access to Northern India. While on our arrival Bombay's climate had felt like midsummer in England, perhaps seventy-five degrees, it was much cooler up here – almost chilly – but we were travelling through bright sunshine that warmed us from clear skies. I wanted to pinch myself to remember this virgin mountain forest. In London it had been impossible to imagine anywhere like this existed that wasn't peopled. The lush landscape began to thin as we ascended over the next hour or so, and became less vegetated and drier; green turned to brown as the Malabar Coastal Plain became separated from the rest of India.

We were warned that the stop at Igatpuri would be less of a pause and more of a wait as we changed over from electric to steam locomotive. As we took on water and fuel I strolled out with my fellow passengers onto the platform to stretch our legs while we waited. I was astonished to see that the coal was not only carried by women – coolies, according to my fellow passengers – but transported on their heads in huge bundles. I could already imagine what this work was doing to their spines, not to mention their chests with the inhalation of coal dust, but held my tongue. No one else seemed anything but vaguely entertained and instead appeared mostly bored by what was clearly a familiar sight.

From here on there was not much memorable about the scene beyond my window: mostly a characterless plain dotted by the odd jungle village. The monotony was broken by an exquisite afternoon tea served by my butler in my compartment as I'd chosen not to join the restaurant car. I knew it was antisocial but I had no intention of befriending these people even though I could hear Jove's voice in my mind berating me softly for being short-sighted. Some of his final words to me had been about making friends wherever I could because life would be challenging and lonely enough without isolating myself with only work. I had assured him I would be open to some of the social offerings and I hoped I hadn't lied to him.

With no passengers boarding or departing, the stations we stopped at were quiet – almost deserted – although I noted the workers were so well kempt that any English railway station manager would have been proud.

Another unsavoury experience was witnessing locals, more railway coolies presumably, taking their ablutions in plain sight of the station. My fellow travellers turned away but not with any look of horror; neither was it out of politeness – more about having seen it all so many times before. In the meantime my mind raced to the threat of disease and the ever-growing challenge ahead of me for life and hygiene in the hospital.

By dinnertime I was smartly reminded about the divide between us and the everyday person of the land we had colonised; all of us diners were in full regalia for the evening meal. The team of staff were no slouches either, clad in immaculate outfits; our dining manager was impressive in a black dinner suit, pristine white shirt and bow tie. His mission was to make sure our every whim was attended to with as much obsequiousness as one might anticipate in a top dining establishment in London or Paris. His bearers, meanwhile, were kitted in starched, long coats of white – known as *chapkans*, I was told by my dining companions – together with green trousers and brass buckled belts. Their turbans were white or green to match.

I had anticipated getting my belly used to Indian food but not on the Blue Mail. Here it was five-star silver service all the way, with traditional fare that could only be described as straight from the menu of a swanky European hotel.

'Home from home,' as one gentleman diner said; I seem to recall he was a major general visiting Fort William in Calcutta. He tipped a crystal goblet of claret in my direction as we all considered the *pigeons truffée a la perigord* or the *cochon de lait*. The light, reflected against the crystal glass, fractured to fling rainbow shards around the ceiling and that same light bounced off diamonds on the ladies' fingers and warmed the pearls at their throats. We were not just the rich in this country, we were the super-rich, and somewhere deep I found it all vulgar as I remembered the women squatting at their ablutions.

As neither pigeon nor suckling pig was suddenly to my taste, I chose the mutton served with risotto Milanese and shook my head against a first course, although I noted my fellow diners tucking into bouillabaisse or mullet in mayonnaise. Even oysters were on the menu, which I found astonishing. More surprising was how most diners found room for a slice of gateau, while I once again politely declined but sipped a coffee and nibbled on a bite-sized petit four that was exquisitely frosted in pink icing to look like a tiny gift with ribbon. All of this on a train in the middle of a country where squalor was all around us and poverty a way of life for most.

I kept my own counsel, though – a rare moment, perhaps, of enlightened discipline at not airing my opinion or stirring conversation from the banal to political. Instead I forced myself to consider this an interlude in my life of forty or so hours and tried not to question too much of what I was part of. This was merely a journey from A to B, and B was all I needed to focus on.

———

Finally I stood at point B, our destination of Howrah Station, Calcutta. We had arrived at last and I was feeling flushed and excited that I was on the brink of fulfilling that promise made so long ago. I looked around me, both fascinated and daunted at once. The building itself, I felt, was impressive enough in its cathedral-like vaulted ceiling to rival Bombay's admired Victoria Station. But the people! Many hundreds of them; it felt as though the entirety of a small English town moved in all directions, although giving me a wide berth. This was the same for all of us Europeans alighting from the train. I forced myself not to give in to the feeling of mild panic because I knew where it would lead if I entertained the thought that I was alone here with my wits, unsure of every step ahead now. I reminded myself that this was the adventure I'd craved and if the person meeting me didn't show up, then I was an adult – a doctor – and perfectly capable, surely, of hailing a taxi?

Taxi . . . Did such a vehicle exist? Would it be oxcart? I imagined trying to haul myself into an open wagon. Sensible outfit notwithstanding, suddenly even the simplest task that I took for granted at home felt like a challenge to fear. Just looking out across the sea of curious faces – the whites of their eyes standing out so clearly against skin ranging in colour from coffee to the deepest of chocolate – made me realise that even crossing from the platform to the main station was going to be an obstacle course. I took a breath and smiled, feigning lightheartedness, as Mrs Bourne-Hughes bid me farewell.

'Oh, darling Isla, I hoped I'd catch you before we all lost one another to the madness of Calcutta. Now, you will come over for an afternoon tea as soon as you're settled, won't you?'

'Of course.' I hugged her. 'Is it always like this?'

'Mostly worse,' she groaned. 'And out there —' she pointed towards the grand entrance and exit where the main stream of people flowed '— it can be quite the assault with these mostly savage people. At best it's tiresome.' She gave a clucking sound like a hen laying. 'Don't get me started, dear.'

I wanted to repeat my general query to most on the ship, perhaps more strenuously, as to why on earth she was here, then, if it was so taxing, but in that moment I didn't have the strength. Elmay Bourne-Hughes was not the problem and was actually a most decent person; she was simply part of the tapestry of British India. Some of it I gathered was brilliant, like the train we'd recently stepped off, and some of it was shameful . . . calling its nationals 'savages' was not the way forward.

'Isla, why are you standing here alone? Can I have my driver come back for you or something?'

'No, no,' I assured, wishing I could just say yes and leap into the car that was obviously waiting outside for this memsahib returning from Christmas in England. 'I am being met.'

'Only if you're sure, my dear?'

I nodded and hugged her again. 'We shall meet again soon.'

She disappeared into a swarm of people, her entourage of porters hauling trunks and countless items of baggage as she hurled threats over her shoulder if they weren't careful of her expensive luggage.

I took a deep breath and looked around me. I was being regarded by dozens of pairs of brown–black eyes. I averted my self-consciousness by looking up towards the sloping roofline that echoed the grand stations of England with their lacework of iron and elegant archways.

'Dr Fenwick?'

My gaze snapped to the slender woman who stood before me, serene-faced, her smile genuine and enquiring.

'Yes!' I gushed. 'Are you Senior Nurse Lilian Patton?'

'I am.' She held out a hand. 'Please call me Lily, though. My grandmother is Lilian and she is a fearsome lady.'

I laughed with her.

'I am so pleased to meet you, Dr Fenwick,' she said, large cocoa-coloured eyes crinkling at the edges in delight as I shook her hand with equal parts relief and pleasure. 'And this is Dipali, one of my colleagues, training to be a midwife. We call her Dip.'

'Dipali,' I repeated and nodded at the petite woman wearing a silken sari so richly pink I was reminded of fresh cranberry juice. She wore her draped gown effortlessly pitched over one shoulder and I wondered how it ever stayed there. The glimpse of flesh beneath her rib cage as she moved was both shocking and exciting. I couldn't imagine walking around showing peeps of my body and yet I envied her the freedom to do that. She looked like a perfect doll. Not one of her glossy hairs was out of place; they were scraped back off her oval-shaped face and plaited down her spine to her waist. I remember being impressed in school physics lessons to learn that in the visible spectrum, black is the absorption of all the colours we know. No visible light, we were taught . . . and yet Dip's hair was so dark it looked polished, reflective. I imagined all the jewel-coloured saris in India being absorbed into one to form the colour that was Dip's hair. Gold gleamed in her lobes, on her wrists, and glimmered from the border of her outfit. Dip smiled humbly as I appraised her; she too seemed to be taking stock of my plain, sensible linens that were meant to be airy and cooling but made me feel like the ugly duckling from the literary tales of Hans Christian Andersen.

'Please,' Lily offered, digging out a flask from the basket she carried. 'You may like to sip some water. It's boiled and clean.' She held it out. 'Very safe. But I took the precaution of filtering it over charcoal too.' She touched her belly. 'Your tummy must get used to the assault that's coming.'

I didn't mean to but I know I smiled weakly, trying not to think about what those simple words conveyed. I took the flask gratefully, though, and unscrewed the top to sip from it. I anticipated it would taste tainted somehow but it gladly answered a thirst.

'Drink water all day long,' Lily urged. 'Even when you don't think your body is parched. Rule number one for Calcutta.'

'Thank you. Er, my luggage is —'

'Do not worry. Dip will see to it and there's hardly anything,' she said, sounding surprised. 'We are used to the English arriving with an array of trunks so we have brought men.'

I only realised now that there was a small troupe of silent, khaki-clad men awaiting our pleasure. They didn't strike me as brawny enough to carry more than my hand luggage; in fact they looked as though they could all use a good feed and lots of exercises to strengthen spindly legs. Lily must have guessed my thoughts because she smiled.

'They are so much stronger than they look,' she assured and then nodded.

I followed her line of sight and saw a boy – he couldn't have been older than twelve – moving in the near distance carrying what looked like a bundle of rags on his back. The size of the bundle was, to my mind, not that much smaller than a heifer and while he staggered beneath it, he kept moving. I knew I was staring, perplexed, watching him progress down the platform as Lily turned to her colleague and exchanged some fast instructions, in their native tongue, I presumed.

'I'm only in India for months. There seemed little point in bringing much at all,' I finally said, looking at my two modest trunks.

'Come,' Lily said, in a proprietorial way. 'Let us get you out of here.'

I allowed myself to be led, not even caring to check over my shoulder at my belongings. 'I noted you admiring Dip's sari?' Lily offered in conversation as we pushed through a tide of people moving against us. 'This is called a Baluchari sari – and Dip's family is originally from the region of Baluchar. The raw silk from the cocoon is boiled before being dyed and a curious method of stretching the yarn is used to make it crisp. Then begins the process of making the motifs for the edges.'

I shook my head. 'I've never seen anything like it.'

She smiled. 'It's a long process and these saris were considered worthy only of the aristocracy – they tend to depict scenes from the lives of the Nawab. This one she wears – in your honour to welcome you – is called *swarnachuri*. They are the most gorgeous because they're woven with gold and silver thread to illuminate the pattern.' She shrugged. 'That's just one form of sari, though.'

I sighed dramatically. 'Lily, this is terrifying. I've barely set foot on Calcutta soil and I'm already daunted by how much there is to learn. What language were you speaking just now?'

'Simple Bengali,' she replied, cutting me a grin of sympathy. 'You'll pick up what you need fast – instructions for nurses, bearers, all the helpers. I had to.'

I swerved around a line of people balancing outrageously large bundles tied into blankets and balanced atop heads.

'What are they carrying?' I couldn't help myself.

'Their possessions. They're travelling. You carry luggage, so do they, except they don't have porters or people to help them . . . or leather trunks.'

I don't think she meant it to offend by accusing me of being privileged; I genuinely think Lily was trying to help me understand the world I'd entered. 'It's clever really. By carrying everything overhead they don't cramp the space around them.'

'It's not just clever, it's a feat of athleticism,' I said. 'But it's like all their chattels – look . . . pots and pans are swinging off that one.'

She shrugged. 'It's how the people move around.' But I could see from her expression that she enjoyed the compliment. 'I used to carry fruit and vegetables from the market on my head for my mother when I was growing up.'

'What a skill! Where are you from, Lily?'

'My mother's originally from a village on the outskirts of Bangalore but she married my father, who was English. He worked on the railways and died when I was a teenager but he was determined I study and encouraged me to go into nursing.'

'Was it hard to leave her?'

'It was hard to leave all my family – my mother, sisters and aunts, all my cousins – but I've always wanted to nurse and there is more opportunity up here in the old capital.'

'So you're Anglo-Indian? Is that the right term?'

'That's right.'

'You sound so English.' I felt instantly idiotic for the remark and wanted to drag back the condescending words.

Dear Lily seemed to take no offence, though. In fact her pleasure shone in her expression. 'Thank you. I was very well educated, Dr Fenwick. I studied at Bishop Cottons All Girls' School in Bangalore.' I knew I was meant to be impressed and so I gave back a look of soft awe and understanding. 'And I've been nursing now for four years but I want to specialise in midwifery. I can't wait to learn all the latest techniques and care coming out of England through you. I hope I'll visit one day.'

'We're setting up a program for nurses from India's north to study in London – Anglo-Indian women from the south are already travelling to Britain to learn. You should apply.'

She looked at me with fresh delight. 'Oh, I would definitely put up my hand for that, Dr Fenwick,' she said, sounding excited as we emerged from the shadows of the station. I blinked against the startling sunshine. The space in front of the building was more peaceful than I'd anticipated but beyond the concourse of Howrah Station I saw more people moving than I could ever imagine in one place. London was no comparison to the road outside this major Calcutta intersection. It was, indeed, the jungle that Elmay had griped about – an entirely different sort of bewildering landscape to London and momentarily overwhelming. Just for a second, I felt unsteady.

'Dr Fenwick? Are you well?' Lily's hand clutched gently at my elbow.

'Yes . . . yes, of course. I was just drinking it all in,' I said, hoping to divert her, but my voice was breathy and gave away that I might have just swooned slightly. I couldn't believe how weak I was allowing myself to appear but Lily had me in hand. 'Who is this gentleman?' I asked, to deflect attention, and gestured towards a man busy behind a counter at a kiosk. He appeared calm among the frantic activity surging around him.

'This is one of a dozen chai *wallahs* at the station.'

I tried to repeat the word, frowning.

'*Wallah.*' Lily laughed as she said it again. 'It means seller.'

'And chai is tea,' I said, nodding with understanding. 'I learned that word on the journey here.'

'Bravo. Chai *wallahs* have a special pride of place at all stations, and throughout India, to be honest. None of us can get through a day without our tea. If you take one of the regional trains, the chai *wallahs* serve drinks through the window yelling *Chaa-ye . . . chaa-ye.*'

I grinned. 'And so it tastes like the tea I drink at home?'

She shook her head. 'No, but please be assured that anyone who waits on you here knows how to make a good English brew. At home I only drink English-style tea – I was raised on it. However, the chai is delicious – it's spiced milk tea and very sweet, as the Indians prefer. Recipes vary, of course, from place to place, but it comes from an ancient Ayurvedic beverage of the royals.'

'What was that word?'

Lily laughed. 'Ayurveda is a form of healing . . . a way of life too because it consists of many disciplines relating to diet, herbal medicines, physical exercises, various therapies, and spiced tea was one of them.'

'Gracious! What's in this tea?'

She shrugged as we walked. 'Oh, good black tea from Darjeeling helps, plus additions like clove, cardamom, ginger, cinnamon, of course . . . And a large lump of sugar,' she added archly, gesturing with her forefinger and thumb to exaggerate the size of the sugar lump. 'I know some chai *wallahs* add peppercorns for extra heat. I suspect that is a special Himalayan recipe as they are always fighting the cold.'

I nodded thoughtfully. 'I can imagine that would definitely be warming to the belly. I'm intrigued to try it sometime.'

'Not yet and not here. You must be overtired from the journeying. You need rest, food, sleep,' she said, in the tone of a woman used to being listened to by people in care. I enjoyed her slightly singsong way of speaking; there was no mistaking her part-Indian heritage but her diction was precise, echoing her sound education. It was impossible not to fall under Lily's spell, which was a mix of charm, respect and constant delight. She was capable of giving instructions to porters with a beaming smile, sending away the inevitable beggars who shuffled in our direction with a few tiny coins and some soft words so that they never fully confronted me, and signalling our driver all at once, it seemed. 'Ah, here's Banshi,' she said. 'The medical director suggested we pick you up in the hospital car we use for dignitaries.'

I sensed either my father or, more likely, Jove was behind the use of the car but said nothing. I smiled and thanked her while we got in. She spoke on, gently calling my attention to sights as we rolled by slowly, parting hundreds of people milling around the station concourse, inching around bullocks that lay in the road, ignoring the constant ringing of bicycle bells and the odd horns of ancient buses rumbling alongside.

The assault of new smells captured my attention. I'd always possessed an ability to tease out flavours, whether I was sniffing at them or physically tasting, and right now I needed to make sense of my surrounds because everything smelled so foreign. I could latch on to a gritty taste of dust in my throat as well as a generally more earthy flavour all around me, and then it changed, becoming a more unpleasant savoury reek. There was no point in trying to hold my breath or avoid breathing through my nose. This was to be home for the next six to seven months; I had to force myself to confront the reality of my decision and get on with it . . . Breathe it, taste it, live it.

I could smell men, their sweat pungent, and animal droppings clashing against the bright notes of fruit – orange particularly – and something I didn't recognise on the stalls that had a fresh, apple-like quality in look and texture. I watched men expertly slice through these mottled green fruits but not before dipping their fearsome knives into a red dust.

'They're guavas with salted chilli,' my companion explained, noticing my frown. 'You must try this fruit in this way but only when I'm around to make sure it's not too fierce for you . . . and the knife is clean.' She laughed.

I'd never heard of a guava. I didn't even know how to spell it but I remained confounded that anyone would want their fruit dusted with a hot spice to burn the tongue, but this was instantly forgotten at seeing a man driving a cart that was being pulled by a zebra! Back home we paid to admire beautiful zebras at London Zoo. Here it was being used like any other mule. I must have made a sound of exclamation, pointing as I did so.

'That is unusual, I'll grant you,' Lily admitted, 'but anything goes in Calcutta. You need to be prepared for dozens of strange sights.'

Smell gave way to the impact of sound and I became increasingly aware of the constant noise that we were nearly yelling over. Dark hands were regularly thrust into the windows of the car as it paused for bullocks or people or both. These hands belonged to children standing roadside in wait for cars like ours and, like a tiny horde of highwaymen, they'd rush into the fray of traffic, dodging bicycles and animals to offer us all manner of trinkets or foods. On each occasion Lily would calmly send them on their way as I found myself lost for the right words or tone. I felt churlish shooing at beggars and yet I wanted nothing of what anyone was selling.

'You can't be well mannered,' Lily said, reading my concern. 'But no need for rudeness, I say. Too many newcomers —' I heard instead her masking the word 'British' '— are unnecessarily unkind, I feel. But in this situation if any of these waifs so much as spots a coin, you'll be mobbed. So I say no to all and make donations instead to places where I know people can be fed or helped.' She smiled kindly. 'Sometimes, if there aren't too many of them, I'll give children a few *annas* as I did back at the station but you have to be careful, Dr Fenwick, or you'll attract a crowd very quickly.'

It sounded like sage advice.

'This is the Howrah pontoon bridge we're about to cross,' she continued. 'There is constant talk of a new bridge – a beautiful architectural cantilever structure has been spoken about since the turn of the century and we're assured construction will begin in a year or two. The traffic on here is always congested and they have to unfasten it to let the bigger ships through. It's quite lovely here at night actually,' she admitted softly. 'You see all these lights we're passing?' I nodded at the lampposts she pointed towards. 'They're lit in the evening and people come out to walk across the Hooghly River.'

'Is this part of the famous Ganges?' It was out before I could consider it. 'I'm sorry, I'm a good doctor but I'm rubbish at geography,' I admitted.

'Don't apologise. It's confusing, I know. The Hooghly is a distributory of the Ganges but this water has made a very long journey before it reaches us here to stretch more than two hundred miles along the Bay of Bengal alone.'

I gave a sighing sound of awe to make her grin.

She toggled her hand in the air, a gesture I'd seen given by some Indians in London. 'I won't even try and explain all the other statistics that we learned in school but I think only the great rivers of South America and Africa have more water flow . . . but of course, the Ganges is the lifeline for so much of northern India and its people. It is the holiest of waters for Hindus.'

'What is your religion, Lily?' At her sideways smile, I baulked. 'Forgive me – is that rude?'

'No, not at all. I suspect we follow the same spiritual path, Dr Fenwick. I was raised in the Church of England. My mother's people converted from Hinduism when she was an infant, so she was raised in the Anglican faith. After she married my father, we children knew no other, although both our parents taught us to respect Hindu spiritualism and culture.'

'How marvellous,' I breathed but was interrupted by Lily pointing.

'And there you see the embodiment of the river's holiness to Hindus. People bathe in its waters in homage and Hindus believe it can cleanse you of sin. Watch them. They'll cup their hands to lift the sacred water; do you see that group of women doing just that?' I nodded. 'And watch how they let it fall back into the river. Ah, and there you see!' She pointed, redirecting my attention. 'Someone is scattering flower petals on the surface and sometimes you'll see them floating tiny oil pots with wicks that are lit at night.'

'Why?'

'Any number of reasons. Perhaps they're giving thanks for something good that has occurred in their life, such as the birth of a much-desired child, or possibly they are atoning, or most likely they are revering their dead by remembering them with offerings of rice or seeds.'

'One of the Indian women who was training with me in London told me about Varanasi being the most holy of places. I thought it was called Benares but as she came from near there, I deferred to her. It sounds fascinating.'

Lily nodded, waving away a persistent hand offering a fistful of petals not far from her face by a person selling garlands. The cooling scent from the bright flowers was welcome in the stale air of the car and the heat I was feeling increasingly wearied by.

'I haven't travelled the world,' Lily continued, 'but I doubt there is anywhere like Varanasi. It's the spiritual centre of our continent. The great cremation ground is a difficult place – not the easiest of sights to witness. In my teenage years I accompanied a friend from school in a pilgrimage with her family to Varanasi. They were cremating a treasured uncle of hers. Perhaps it's not so hard for a doctor such as yourself, or even a nurse as I am, but most visitors – especially the British and Europeans – would struggle to look upon the dead and not feel confronted.'

'But they're being treated with such respect, as I understand it.'

Lily lifted a shoulder. 'It's the sheer numbers, Dr Fenwick. That's what is so overwhelming.'

I made a mental note to write to Jove about this place as it sounded like just the sort of adventure he might chase after. 'Gosh, I don't believe I've ever felt this hot before,' I remarked, sitting forward, as I realised my flesh was sticking not only to my clothes but to the leather of the seats.

'And this is only February. By early March you'll think this was positively cool.'

I cut her an appropriate look of dismay. 'Then I had better make the best of February.'

'These are the Calcutta flower markets.' She pointed as we finally crossed the river and rumbled off the pontoon bridge. 'Welcome to the city of Calcutta, Dr Fenwick,' she said with triumph.

But to my sensibilities it was more of the same. In truth it was a crush of maybe three times more people jostling against wheeled vehicles, four-legged creatures among a new press of crowded streets and buildings that overhung narrow lanes.

'We're going into the older part. The European section, just entering Chowringhee. It's quieter there.'

I couldn't imagine it, but I also couldn't wait for some peace.

7

It was true I was weary. Whether it was a combination of being overtired and overwhelmed, I wasn't certain, but I was confident I wouldn't sleep and I was even more sure that I didn't want to be alone immediately. So I'd accepted the invitation passed through Lily to join some of the English staff of the hospital for drinks.

'You'll be there, won't you?' I asked her.

She gazed back at me and I thought I noted embarrassment. 'No, Dr Fenwick. I've . . . I've got some paperwork to ready for tomorrow and as I've missed much of today —'

'Yes, of course. Well, thank you so much for meeting me. How could I have possibly got here without your help?' I said, gesturing around the new apartment that would be home for the rest of this year.

'This is a lovely place to live,' she admitted. 'You can hardly do better than "just off Chowringee".' She smiled. 'And you can ride the tram to the hospital with ease on wide streets. Or take a taxi . . . they're cheap.'

We'd opened up the painted shutters to reveal tall double windows that overlooked a narrow road. It was a quiet street, tree-lined, with gracious buildings opposite and surrounding my building, which stretched around the corner into busier, cosmopolitan Chowringee. I felt fortunate that this was a large, airy apartment, flooded by light once the shutters were pulled back, and I could smell from the polish that everything had been recently dusted and cleaned through the large bedroom and three other little rooms.

'Thank you for the fresh flowers,' I noted.

'Matron thought it would be a pretty welcome into a daunting world you probably couldn't imagine from London.'

'She is right,' I admitted in an arch tone.

'Well, I hope you'll be very happy in this lovely space. And this is the hospital phone number. I'll leave it here,' she said, putting a small chit on a sideboard. 'The telephone is on the ground floor.'

'Thank you.'

'Are you sure you'll be all right? I can stay longer?'

'No, really, Lily, you've been wonderful and I think I'll just take some time to get my bearings here, unpack a little – thank you for organising the luggage,' I said, nodding towards my trunks and belongings sitting in the corner.

'Drinks at five in the Palm Court of the Grand Hotel.' She pointed out of the window. 'Don't be confused. Opposite you is the Great Eastern Hotel – you'll enjoy it, I'm sure. But the Grand is around the corner. Step out of your building, turn left, turn left again on the main road of Chowringhee and then you can't miss it. It's the huge, glamorous and colonnaded building where all the main shops reside. The horses and carriages will be queuing for space to drop off or pick up people.'

'Most convenient,' I said in a breezy tone. I hoped it would reassure Lily and permit her to leave without any guilt or sense of abandonment.

'Tomorrow morning, someone will collect you, Dr Fenwick,

just so that you can get used to getting to and from the hospital . . . get your bearings properly when you're not so tired.'

'What time shall that be?'

'I believe it's arranged for eight. Probably the same driver you'll recognise. You can breakfast near the hospital and then after tomorrow we can help organise provisions, but I've ensured you have some tinned milk, tea-leaves and bread and cheese in case you feel hungry. Boiled water is in the small refrigerator. You'll need to boil water daily.'

'I'll get myself into a routine, I'm sure. I'll see you tomorrow.'

'Good afternoon, Dr Fenwick,' Lily said, just short of curtseying. Her deference was unsettling and I was unhappy with myself to feel a slight rush of relief when I finally closed the door behind her. The release was fleeting, however, for now I was instantly isolated: finally alone in Calcutta, far from every aspect of life I knew or had taken for granted. Every sight would now be unfamiliar so I knew even in those first alarming unaccompanied moments that my life raft would be my work. Although conditions might be vastly different to what I was used to, the situation of pregnancy was happily familiar. I had already been confronted by so many variations that I didn't feel intimidated about the work ahead. If I lost myself in my role as medical consultant to the pregnant women or mothers with new babies who came to the clinic, then I could embrace this new life.

Making a sound of resolve that seemed louder than I meant as it echoed around the empty room, I straightened, even nodded to myself that I was finally in motion, achieving the oath I'd made to myself as a much younger person watching my mother die from the disease she acquired here, in India.

Would I break my promise to my father and deliberately seek out the sick and needy suffering from TB? I didn't trust myself to answer that question so soon after arrival. If I could immerse myself entirely in the obstetrics wards, I was sure there was more than enough work to keep me fully occupied for the next eight months.

Seven months. Just twenty-eight weeks. Not even the length of a pregnancy.

Jove had a few old contacts that he'd leaned on to help me organise accommodation from long-distance. We'd come the closest that Jove's mild manner would permit him to an argument over this topic. I'd discovered that my fiancé avoided confrontation, instead finding methods of negotiation to reconcile both parties' viewpoints into common agreement. He was good at it too and I had begun to fully appreciate his diplomacy skills and why he was clearly a popular representative in Westminster for his constituents. And yet those skills began to fail him when it came to the topic of my home in Calcutta, and his calm manner had become almost heated. He was certainly impassioned. He was determined that I stay with an English family of some standing while I remained stubborn about avoiding just that scenario.

'But why, Isla?' he'd pleaded.

'Jove, I'm not a child. I refuse to be treated as though I'm helpless.'

'Heavens! Who would dare suggest such a thing?'

The sarcasm was not lost upon me and I bristled. 'And still I get the feeling that you believe I need to be supervised, or within the bosom of a nurturing family that can spy on me.'

I remember how he'd stood up, frustrated, then sat down immediately to take my hand and press his point.

'What are you talking about, Isla? Spying? Don't be ridiculous. If I wanted to spy on you, you certainly wouldn't know about it, and what's more I'm offended that you consider me that insecure.'

'I don't. I'm sorry I said that.' My contrition was written across my face and in the slump of my shoulders. I felt genuinely ashamed at the childish response. 'I'm nervous, Jove, but I really do want to do this my way, not the cottonwool way that you want.'

My apology softened his expression still further. 'You need to understand how hard this is for me that you're going to such a far-flung place. I've become stupendously needy, I think, now that I've found you.'

He was so generous the way he took the blame upon himself.

'My darling Jove,' I remember saying as I stroked his cheek. 'I'm not going into the Kalahari, or the jungles of Borneo —'

'You might as well be, as far as I'm concerned. You are gone from me and so far away that I cannot reach you easily and I cannot protect you.' He held up a hand to stall me. 'Uh . . . and before you jump down my throat, I realise you feel you don't need protection. And, Isla, I know you see yourself as a pioneer but you're still a lone, unmarried woman, travelling without escort into a region that is fraught with incalculable dangers.'

I shook my head and could see from his flattened lips that this irritated him. 'No, I don't accept that. I'm betrothed,' I said, perhaps unnecessarily waggling my ring before him. It was due back in its box but I was enjoying wearing it until I left British shores. 'What's more, I'm a doctor with a job to do at the hospital. I positively refuse to be attached to the household of a chortling woman, married to some dignitary who is going to drag me to endless rounds of Pimm's parties and vacant talk.'

He sighed out his exasperation and then laughed sadly. 'Can you not allow that there may be some women of your status with a similar attitude in Calcutta?'

'All right, I'll accept that, but you and I both know how the society types seem to find one another in the colonies, Jove. I've been to enough events with expats newly returned from Africa or India, the Levant, even the Orient, to find them often tedious. My time is short – I will not give it up to parties or feel obliged to attend events. I don't want to have to dress for dinner or make small talk. I am there to research, to practise medicine, to heal, to learn, and I want to come and go as I please.'

'What if you get lonely?'

I laughed. 'You are jesting, aren't you? I'll be at the hospital every waking hour, be sure of it. With such limited time on the ground in India, I have to make every day count. I will not be making time to play.'

'And you can't do that by living safely, setting my mind at peace, by living within the comfort of a family home?'

'No.'

'I won't force you,' he finally said.

'You made a good fist of pretending you were about to,' I risked.

'No, I can see there's no point . . .'

I can still feel the warmth of his hands as I cupped them in mine and kissed them. 'You mustn't worry so much about me. This is 1932 and there are women who have suffered through the previous century to earn me the freedom I now enjoy. Don't take it away.'

I hadn't meant to appeal to his political ideals but I could see I'd ignited a spark. His eyes flared with shame. 'You're right.'

I'm sure I surprised him and indeed myself by playfully moving to sit on his lap so I could kiss him long and tenderly. He was hesitant to respond at first, probably thinking of my father, or our housekeeper or any number of other reasons why in this moment two people engaged to be married shouldn't be caught kissing in private. All I could think of was relief and how he tasted so deliciously of raisins from the sherry.

'What was that for?'

I grinned lazily. 'To show you that I adore you all the more for your concern and that I'm not ignoring it; I just want to feel free of other people's rules while I follow this dream briefly.'

He nodded. 'I can't deny you anything. I love you so, so much, I'm going to let you go and I hope that's a measure for you of the depth of my feeling. I put no constraints on you, except one.'

Another condition. I stiffened slightly. 'And what's that?'

'That you never sit on my lap again and kiss me unless we have a bedroom to move to.'

Now the housekeeper could certainly have heard my squeal of laughter.

I could hear it now echoing in my memory as conversation floated around me in the Grand Hotel. Perhaps I was smiling to myself; I was definitely lost in my thoughts deliberately because I was trying to avoid the party small talk. I'd made sure to say hello to everyone on arrival, share a few words, accept their welcomes and good wishes, repeatedly go over my journey, the weather, the food, the inevitable upset belly I could look forward to and my promise not to forget to boil the water I consumed.

'Dr Fenwick? Everything all right?'

I blinked my attention back to the present and the enquiring look of one of the doctors from the hospital, Miles Baird. He was younger than me, I reckoned, with a nervous smile worn on chapped lips, ears that stuck out like jug handles from beneath a shock of flame hair, and he spoke with the soft brogue of the Scottish borders.

'Yes, just trying to acclimatise.'

'This is hardly the real Calcutta,' he admitted, turning to look over his shoulder at the salubrious surrounds, lush and green, where I could guess the city's elite gathered.

It was a Sunday and apparently this was the main day to gather at the Grand. Pale, delicate-looking women dressed in various shades of ivory didn't seem at all bothered by the oddity of sipping what looked to be strong beer. It was obvious I had been staring.

FIONA McINTOSH

'There's plenty of claret downed too,' my companion said, noting my interest. 'The beer is actually quite good for the constitution out here,' he said, seemingly unaware of his patronising tone.

'Yes, I suppose it would be,' I admitted.

We were standing in the gallery that ran along the rim of this cavernous room and we were able to look down upon the merry-making.

'A lovely nurse called Lily met me today,' I continued.

'I know Lily. Anglo-Indian. Pretty girl.'

I contrived a puzzled expression. 'Why don't I see her here?'

He looked at me. 'Generally someone like Lily wouldn't come to an event in a hotel like this.'

'I see,' I said, not understanding any of it. 'Someone like Lily . . . as in her skin colour, you mean?'

'I don't know if it's written down anywhere,' he said, his freckled skin flushing slightly at my scrutiny. 'But the Anglo-Indians tend to keep to their own.'

'But we are their own. Lily has a full English father, is a Church of England girl, went to an Anglican school, is highly educated . . .' I could hear how bossy I sounded.

He raised his hands in a plea for mercy. 'I don't make the rules, Isla. May I call you Isla?'

I shrugged. 'We're off-duty.'

'For what it's worth, there are no rules as such, although somewhere like the Bengal Club is only for whites.'

I blinked at how disgraceful that sounded in this day and age.

'Personally, I'm very happy to mix with the Anglo-Indians in the clubs or gatherings like this. I have many Anglo-Indian friends,' Miles eagerly added.

'That's good to know,' I said, tempering the sarcastic tone as I gathered that he was feeling accused of something that was not of his making. However, it explained Lily's awkwardness earlier. 'Is it always like this?' I said, nodding towards the merry crowd.

'They call this "Palm Sunday",' he said with a soft chuckle. 'Happens each week.'

I smiled politely at the jest and that we were surrounded by palm trees.

'Have you been to Paris, Dr Fenwick?'

'Indeed I have.'

He tipped his head towards the various groups of people below us. 'In the evenings, the Palm Court seems to reorganise itself into the Grand's Café Royal society.'

I frowned.

'It's extremely popular at interval time with the theatre-goers from the Empire. This place is strategically situated between that and the Globe Opera House. All terribly French.'

'Good grief.'

He thought I was impressed but my exclamation was over the fact that my apartment was almost equally strategically placed to the fashionable social centre.

'And they're all owned by the same family,' he added for intrigue. 'The acquisition was begun by one man, he was a jeweller, originally from Persia and barely out of his teens when he arrived poverty-stricken in Calcutta.'

I smiled, enjoying him more now that we were not making small talk and he had relaxed into his storytelling.

'Sounds like you admire him.'

'I admire his ability to make money.'

I had to admit that this honest glimpse into his character caught me by surprise.

'How long have you been here, Miles?'

He blew out his cheeks. 'Nearly three years. Always surprises me when I say it aloud.'

'Do you miss home?'

He shrugged. 'Not really. This is a very good life for a bachelor and you can probably tell I enjoy the history of this place.'

'No prospects for a wife?' I don't know why I asked that. I was probably feeling suddenly a little too relaxed from the sparkling wine and the convivial atmosphere and my general fatigue. I wished I could take it back.

'Always looking, Dr Fenwick.' He glanced at my bare ring finger. 'Is there a lucky man in your life?'

'Soon to be and he is lucky, let me assure you,' I said, hoping the flippancy would amuse. He obliged. 'Jovian Mandeville and I shall be married at the end of this year.'

'He let you come here?'

'He didn't *let* me do anything, Miles. I make my own decisions.'

'Forgive me. I meant —'

I touched his arm. 'I know what you meant and it's sweet. But I hope to take every advantage of this next seven months and make a difference.'

'Oh, you will, you will. We need your expertise here and especially more women doctors because a lot of the local men won't let their wives come to hospital.'

I looked at him, astonished. 'But it's free, isn't it?'

He gusted his disdain. 'It's not about money. It's about religion and, please, if I may offer some advice, do your best to avoid caste issues. Make sure you have a good understanding about the latter because it's going to crop up in much of your dealings with patients.'

My father had mentioned this briefly but we'd both waved the topic away as though it was something to be learned about later. But it seemed later was now, as Lily had referred to it once too on our journey into the city but I hadn't paid much attention. 'So what happens to the women whose faith won't allow hospital care?'

He lifted a shoulder as if helpless. 'They go without medical care, consult local female healers or family, friends . . . So another woman doctor on the staff is a boon. You are most warmly welcomed.' He raised a glass and I followed suit. 'How's the champagne?' he asked. 'You know we're all here to honour the arrival of two new doctors and a midwife.'

'I only gathered that as I arrived. I'm flattered but I'm also weary and perhaps I was a little overenthusiastic to meet my colleagues.'

He nodded. 'I remember how I felt when I got off the ship and took that long train journey.' He noted me putting my glass down, lifting my small bag from a nearby table. 'Would you like me to escort you home, Dr Fenwick?'

'No, no, I'm perfectly fine, thank you.' He looked dubious. 'Honestly, it's probably not even a hundred steps away,' I lied. It had to be two hundred, but the point was being made.

'How did you manage that?'

'Jove is much too well connected, I fear.' I laughed. 'So, are these all the main staff?'

He cast an eye over the gathered. Bursts of laughter erupted from below while our group chatted jovially on the balcony, the champagne slipping down easily, I noted. I hoped no one was on an early shift.

'Well, there are some very senior people missing but your main colleagues are present,' he said, smiling at me. His round-shaped head really did look like a novelty mug with those marvellous ears of his attached either side. 'Oh, except one, of course, and he's rarely missed on these occasions.'

I wrapped a shawl around my shoulders. 'Oh, yes?' I said absently, not really interested.

'Mmm, the great man himself.' He sounded tense suddenly; his tone had become oddly cutting.

I looked back at him in enquiry. 'Not someone you like, I'm guessing.'

'Not someone any of us particularly like, I suspect, but I'd prefer it if you didn't repeat that.'

I shrugged to say it meant nothing to me.

'And not someone who cares about being liked anyway, so it's an even equation.'

'You called him "the great man" as though you admire him.'

'I do. We all do. He's brilliant. But entirely detestable, and if I might dare to give you a single piece of advice —'

'A second piece of advice,' I qualified.

He grinned. 'Yes, but you'll be glad I did.'

'All right . . .'

'Give Saxon Vickery a wide berth.'

The name meant nothing. 'Another doctor?' The question was redundant because it was obvious to me we were discussing a clinician but I was wearying fast and needed to make my polite escape.

'He's a genius, some say. Professor. His research into tropical medicine in this part of the world has no equal.'

'Oh, well then, no matter his personal disposition, we love Professor Vickery because we need him.' I flicked the tail of the shawl over one shoulder, clearly flagging my intention to leave in the next minute or so. 'Does he deliberately avoid social gatherings, then?' I felt my heart reaching towards a kindred spirit, despite the cautionary note from Miles.

'He's in England, returning in a month or so last I heard. We've all been sharing the load in his absence and the good of it is that the hospital is a happier place. The disadvantage is that all we can do is keep disease at relatively slow numbers. He alone seems to be able to fight it and achieve the decrease. He has remained in England longer than we anticipated. I don't know whether to be thrilled or worried.'

I couldn't appreciate his sentiment. I didn't know the man or the situation, so I turned to the banal: everything I hated about petty conversation. 'Well, he's missing the best weather here, I gather, and into the worst that England offers.' Did I really just start discussing the weather? I loathed my hypocrisy in that moment.

'True, it's only going to get worse from here on as it turns tropical; the heat and humidity send some people quite mad. A lot of the Europeans take to the hill stations.'

'Sounds charming.'

'His family has a property in the north, around Darjeeling.'

I frowned. 'Whose family?'

'Saxon Vickery's,' he said, as though I should have known to whom he referred.

'Miles, I think you have a crush on the professor,' I teased and he joined in, making a scoffing sound.

'It's true I'd love to work with him, learn from him, but he's brutal.'

I gazed back at him, perplexed. 'Oh, come on, Miles, where's your spine?'

'No, really. He bludgeons his staff. He moves through nurses at the speed of a disease. He's loathsome and cruelly blunt. Please don't repeat that. I think the champagne has loosened my lips.' He put his half-full glass down on a nearby small table, as if he dared not drink more.

'Heavens! How old is he?' I imagined a man my father's age or older, terrifying the medical fraternity with his brusque attitude.

'Late thirties, I suppose.'

I snapped him a surprise glance. 'And already such a curmudgeon? Well, I won't be around long enough for him to beat me into submission. And our paths will likely not cross that often,' I assured. 'Goodnight, Miles, thank you for your company this evening.'

'I'll look out for you tomorrow. Hope your first day isn't too daunting. It's not like an English hospital,' he warned.

'I'd hate it if it was. Where's the adventure otherwise? I promise you, I won't sleep for the excitement,' I assured, already in motion, giving him a small wave.

On the short walk home, dodging stray dogs and the odd beggar, two of whom were shooed away by helpful Europeans out for their evening stroll, I couldn't help but think on the warning to avoid Saxon Vickery. Despite what I had said it seemed highly unlikely that anyone with my interests was going to deliberately avoid a 'genius' in tropical medicine research. No matter how scarily Miles painted him. Nevertheless, I would try. I'd made a promise – a grave one – and I would do my best to keep it.

8

April 1933

India was luxuriating in its spring. To a local – and perhaps even to a European who had acclimatised – it was bearable because they knew worse was to come but to this newcomer a day hitting ninety degrees felt like I was living within a furnace. I'd been in the country nearly nine weeks but I imagined it would take at least until I was leaving India before I ever got used to such heat. Despite all the right precautions, departing for the hospital in the ethereal twilight between night and just as dawn was breaking, and setting out for home most evenings after sunset, I still found the heat claustrophobic. Already I yearned for a traditionally frosty English spring and I used this longing to reassure myself that it would be easy to leave India and its cloying heat behind in about five months.

That gripe aside, my deliberate looping route as I walked to the hospital from Chowringhee was one of daily marvel at the breadth of palatial buildings that Calcutta boasted. It didn't matter whether it was a hotel, municipal building or something historic like the awe-inspiring Old Writers' Building, the edifices were vast, mostly classically designed, and it was little wonder that this region was known as the place of the palaces. The hospital was attached to a medical college and even this building was something of a land-mark in Calcutta, known to everyone in its short form of MCH. It was a grand piece of fine architecture of Roman Doric style that would cosily fit any fine capital in Europe.

As would the torrent of invitations that began to arrive weekly from the anticipated round of social gatherings that kept this part of British India ticking. I hoped the polite enthusiasm to 'do the right thing' by the new female doctor would wane . . . I was still waiting nearly two months later as my ability to craft creative excuses began to desert me. With the arrival of this season came the all-important spring racing carnival that seemed to occupy most conversations beyond medical. Poor Miles had tried several times to escort me to various outings and it seemed he wasn't getting the message.

'But the Calcutta Turf Club is part of the fabric of our society out here, and the Derby sweepstakes in Calcutta is one of the rich-est in the world. It stops the city. A year or so ago the prize pot was more than one million pounds. A million pounds!' he repeated in case I was hard of hearing.

I had smiled and lifted a shoulder in silent apology. 'I've never much been one for horse-racing carnivals.'

I wasn't being entirely honest with him. I attended the races frequently at home and enjoyed the meets . . . I just didn't want to encourage Miles, who was taking a more proprietorial interest in me than I thought wise. Nevertheless, I refused to hold myself responsible for his feelings – I had told him of my betrothal within minutes of meeting him; any problem, as I saw it, was now his, not mine.

On balance, though, I was enjoying my new working life at the hospital. The Medical College of Bengal, I learned, was the first institution to teach Western medicine in India. We taught in English and the hospital emerged out of the British East India Company's need to look after the medical needs of the Europeans in India's north. I must admit to being impressed by the number of female students being admitted to train as nurses and doctors via the college itself, which was quickly growing up around the hospital. In the previous century, I gathered, this hospital was essentially run to treat the fevers that the Europeans suffered, including a special diphtheria ward, but it now encompassed general medicine and welcomed all patients. I was working in the western end of the main building concerning itself with women's health and mostly maternity needs.

I would be lying if I didn't admit that my days were full, varied and entirely rewarding. I genuinely loved the work. Perhaps it was because I knew my time was short here that I was so interested in everything about hospital life that affected me and I barely noticed the first few weeks passing by so swiftly. I was blessed with having no labours or births to date that were so dramatic I didn't know how to guide the team of midwives through. If I could have slowed down time, I would have, but the workload felt vast and my role was to teach, as much as to provide clinical support, so I rarely walked the hospital hallways alone. Invariably I had six or seven students trailing in my wake like a mother and her eager ducklings. The students learned on the job as I moved from patient to patient. I didn't mind; I encouraged them, taking the view that this was surely a key reason I was here – to stimulate the bright local minds, show them the way forward towards better women's health and instil a desire for research and, especially, for unrelenting hygiene.

I'd pinned signs in English and Bengali, helped by Dip, that read *Wash your hands!* at the entrance to each ward and to the nurses' station and exiting the wet rooms. Lily had taken it further, writing out more signs and attaching them to each bedstead. We were now plotting the incidences of cross-contamination between patients so I could have some statistics to quote to the other doctors that repeating this mantra verbally wasn't enough. I believed we had to make this simple step of hygiene so easy for everyone to observe, as automatic as breathing for all the medical staff. And I encouraged reminders everywhere they looked so it was imprinted in everyone's daily routines.

Over the last fortnight, feeling more confident in my workplace, I'd managed to slip into a happy, quiet routine on the ward. The autonomy I had been given was impressive – I was essentially in charge of the main women's ward, although my notion that I would be entirely involved in obstetrics was quickly abandoned, for I was seeing women with health needs that clearly came under general medicine. Only women with contagious situations were sent elsewhere in the hospital but otherwise we had patients with all manner of conditions presenting, from women in labour to someone who was having a broken bone fixed or suffering a slipped disc. I enjoyed the variety and, ignoring apologies from the nurses, I shrugged and got on with it, not thinking too hard on the whys or wherefores.

And this afternoon was arguably the most exciting birth I'd ever been involved with – perhaps might ever participate in. We were expecting a routine delivery from a young mother about to give birth to her third child. She was not fearful because she knew what to expect, and the only reason she was in hospital was that she'd fallen, broken an arm badly, and was likely to need some help in the early days. She was a favourite with us because she was always so cheerful and had helped some of the newer mums with their fears, and so it wasn't surprising that all the nursing team today had decided to look in on Parni and help welcome her child into her life.

I was present merely as a precaution and Lily thought it would be good for the midwives to watch what looked like being a text-book birth, but one that would probably have a long labour.

I was standing back, keeping an eye on Parni's expression as she panted her way through another contraction. She'd been in labour now for eleven hours. At the last check I decided it wouldn't be long before she'd be pushing. All was going well.

'Given that this is a straightforward labour, Dr Fenwick, what might we be concerned about with a similar situation if we were helping to deliver without so much expertise around us?'

I liked Yvonne, another Anglo-Indian midwife who was ever-curious and sponge-like in how she soaked up as much knowledge as she could at every opportunity.

'Well, even the most unremarkable labours can go wrong at the last minute,' I said, moving closer to the group so I could speak softly. I didn't want Parni being spooked by talk of complication. She was doing beautifully. 'Post-partum haemorrhage is a great fear and you must be focused on that with every birth; watch the mother's blood . . . her pressure, how much loss – there'll always be some – whether she's swooning if she moves and so on. These are all early vital clues. Actually, Lily, let's schedule that for next week's Monday lecture to discuss latest techniques in this area.'

Lily nodded.

'I had a mother with a cord prolapse at the beginning of this year and that's always confronting. Again, premature babies – and we get a lot of those in Asia – are susceptible.' I explained my recent experience and their need to react swiftly. 'All of you need to learn about a baby presenting in breech. We've done two of those now together but I want each of you to practise with the model we've set up. We're going to have each of you take a turn with each breech presentation to know how to do some of the manoeuvres. As most of you know, we have Genie with her baby presently in the breech position. Hopefully the child will right itself over the course of the coming fortnight but if not, Genie will need our help. This is especially important if you ever find yourself alone at a delivery so please don't miss it. Eclamptic seizure – we worked on that in my second week. Everyone recall?' I received a collective wide-eyed nod. 'What are you looking for with that complication?'

'Nausea and vomiting.'

'Jaundice,' someone recalled.

'Shallow breathing?'

'Shortness of breath, yes,' I qualified. 'Good to all of that and remember, please, these symptoms don't conveniently occur together or even just prior to birth. These signs could be shown far earlier and you need to be thinking about all of their possibilities, not dismissing symptoms because it's months away from delivery. What else?'

'Bleeding?'

I nodded. 'Possibly.'

'Blindness?'

'Yes, it's more a confusion and a sense of darkness experienced by some; convulsing, of course. And what steps should you have already taken?'

Hands went up. They were a smart bunch and they'd paid attention, remembering all the boxes I'd lined up that needed to be ticked to be sure a mother was not presenting as a known risk for this complaint. 'Do this research nice and early. If there's a family history, you need to know that from the first day you meet her.'

'Yes, Dr Fenwick,' they said in unison.

'I'm impressed,' I beamed and as I did so, Parni let out an anguished wail. 'Action stations,' I said and this always seemed to bring a round of delighted chuckles from my students.

Lily stroked Parni's head. 'Whenever you're ready . . . you push.'

'We're looking for your son, Parni,' I called softly from over her knees. 'This one is the boy your husband wants.'

She managed to cast me a fleeting smile through the big contraction and then Parni was lost, riding the wave of pain that she knew she must stay on top of until it broke at the shore of momentary relief. It was always at this point I felt a strange swell of envy. It's not that I wanted the pain; it was more that I couldn't fully imagine it, having not been a mother. I wanted to share it but for now all I could do was listen, watch, encourage. It wouldn't be long – Parni was perfectly dilated and we were ready for her child to be born.

Too many people talking or touching I knew could be distracting so I gave a look that quietened the nurses and had them gathering silently behind me. The only sound remaining was Parni's groans.

The head of the baby crowned and all the younger women gasped. I was instantly annoyed to see one of them looking faint. 'Take Sharni out, please.'

She waved away help and gave me a pleading look that said she was fine.

'If you insist on remaining, don't you dare faint in here, Sharni,' I warned. 'Now, everyone, hush!' I snapped as Lily came around to see from where she'd been at Parni's shoulder.

She opened her mouth but no sound came out.

'What is it?' she whispered.

I was equally amazed to realise I was tearing up. It was my first. 'This is a baby being born *en caul* . . . a French expression meaning shrouded or veiled.'

The women around me looked fearful.

'It's nothing to be scared of. The sac will probably break on its own. Push with the pain, Parni, use it,' I urged, my hands ready for the slippery mass that I was certain would slide out faster than any of us could imagine due to the translucent bubble that held the baby enclosed. 'Be ready.' I motioned at Lily and my tone seemed to snap her out of her stupor.

It was confronting but it was also the most beautiful sight I've ever beheld as Parni's baby was born complete in its unbroken amniotic sac. I wanted to pinch myself but there was no time to dwell on my surprise and delight. A couple of the girls wept. I know they were frightened but it was truly superb to witness Nature's special protection for her young. The infant squirmed within, magnified slightly by the thin veil that separated it from our world. Parni's baby was still unaware it had left its mother's belly.

Parni was desperately trying to see. I nodded at one of the mesmerised midwives in training. 'See to our mother, please. Parni, give us a moment and we'll put your baby in your arms.'

'Distract her,' I urged another.

Then I looked to Lily and smiled. 'I've never done this before,' I said, hearing the awe in my voice, 'but I have read about it.' I gently poked a hole into the surprisingly robust bubble that enclosed our new infant and as the fluid ran away I used a fresh muslin to gently dab away the veil of tissue. 'They say a baby born *en caul* will never drown. And . . . that it brings supreme good luck to the child and anyone who has its caul.' I held up the muslin. 'Midwives of the middle centuries in Europe used to sell these great rarities, particularly to captains of ships, for enormous sums of money. The sailors believed it kept them safe from the waters.'

We rubbed the child tenderly with the softest of cottons and he let out his first cry, drawn from the breath of our world. Helplessly, the women around me clapped, alarming the infant, and I truly couldn't help a tear escaping. I doubted I would ever be fortunate enough to participate in an *en caul* birth again. 'It's a beautiful, special, magical boy, Parni,' I said, putting her precious bundle into her good arm, crooked and ready to hold him.

Lily quickly translated and helped our magical child to feed at his mother's breast.

Hours later, wearied after a long day but nonetheless still walking the clouds from the theatrical arrival of Parni's precious son, whom a few were claiming was now somehow divine, Lily and I were in the small nurses' station just outside the ward. We had our heads bent over the file of a patient, Genie, and we were planning the various scenarios for the birth due in a week or so. I was fighting the urge to switch off the small desk fan that was determined to disrupt the sheets in the file but knew I'd regret it within seconds. Irritation nibbled on the rim of my mind.

However, the roar of a man's voice coming down the corridor made us both startle. Lily actually jumped, whereas I, annoyed to be disturbed so viciously, leapt to my feet and swung around to confront our intruder in the passage before he could reach our ward.

A man, taller than most I knew, with broadish shoulders and a slim-hipped frame, strode towards me with thunder in his expression. Above it flopped bright hair that could only be described as a golden yellow that was darker beneath its top layer, suggesting to me it would naturally bleach to be tow-headed in summer. It had been allowed to grow in an unruly way about his ears, adding a careless unkemptness to his untidy mood. I wondered at the shadow on his face – whether his beard grew fast or he had simply not shaved today.

'Stop!' My voice had a growling quality and while I'm not sure where it came from, it worked so I didn't question it. He halted, frowning beneath grey–golden brows.

'Who the hell are you?' he demanded.

I deliberately didn't answer immediately but held him with what I hoped was the intimidating glare my father accused me of possessing. 'Students will quake beneath it,' he once said. 'Make sure you reserve it only for the right occasion.' I hoped that moment was now.

'Will you please keep your voice down, whoever you are!'

'Dr Fenwick?' It was Lily by my side, speaking tremulously. 'Er, this is Professor Saxon Vickery.'

He didn't bother with polite acknowledgement. Clearly he was no longer interested to discover more about me. Instead, the stormy gaze from eyes of the Portland blue of Wedgwood's Jasperware now glared down at Lily.

'You! It was you, wasn't it? You meddling half-bred, half-baked —'

I stepped between them. 'How dare you speak to one of my midwives in this manner!' Now my ire was up to full power. They could surely hear me all over the ward . . . across several wards probably.

'You're as bad. Another well-meaning *memsahib*, no doubt.'

I didn't have time to let my hackles rise; I shifted one step as he loomed closer and stood over both of us.

'You've probably only been here hours and no doubt already meddling. Bugger me. Why and where do they keep finding you women to —'

I don't know what came over me. Some sort of blood rush to the head, but suddenly my hand was on his chest and I shoved him. Because he wasn't expecting it, he tripped over himself, lurching backwards. I was convinced if he'd been ready for me, I couldn't have pushed him half an inch in any direction. In that single touch I realised he may have a slim build but he was rangy and muscled, his body agile enough to regain a cat-like balance.

His shock turned to laughter. 'Well, that's certainly a new type of manners they're breeding into the misfits who find their way here.'

I tried to mask the horror I felt at my unbecoming action by sounding as indignant as possible. It was my only escape. 'Speak for yourself, sir. Now, I don't care whether you're a professor or the bloody Viceroy of India himself. But on this ward and in my presence you will show respect to me and my staff. And then you too will be accorded the same measure of respect you feel you deserve. Lily is my midwife and under my duty of care.'

'You and your precious Lily can both go and —'

'Professor Vickery?' It was the matron. Now, there was a formidable figure to walk any hospital corridor and I felt nothing but relief to see her. I could feel Lily trembling at my side. 'Dr Fenwick, good afternoon,' Matron said matter-of-factly but taking in the scene quickly and deciding the innocent could be dismissed. 'Lily, off you go; be about your business.' Lily cast me a glance of anxiety but at my nod hurried away. 'Now,' Matron said. 'Whatever is the matter here?'

We both bleated at once, hurling accusations at the other like children. We watched our elder blink, deeply vexed. I stopped talking first and Saxon Vickery's words petered out not far behind mine.

'. . . just not interfere,' were his last words. He forced himself to breathe slowly while I glared at him.

Actually it was hard not to look at him. If Apollo had decided to pay us mortals a visit from Olympus, this was likely how he might look. His bared teeth during his sneering rage were large and polished white, sitting within a jawline that men, I imagined, would give their only spare arm for. What a pity that he lived up to the popular opinion that he was contemptible. As with so many handsome men with status, he carried a shoulder-load of arrogance around with him.

Matron looked at me with appeal and I heard the unspoken request to hold my rage. 'Professor Vickery, can you please explain, in as few words that aren't angry or insulting, what exactly has happened?'

I gathered from how he dipped his eyes that he liked his elder, as we all did. 'Matron, I have likely got an entire village out there about to suffer an outbreak of tuberculosis because one of your high and mighty Anglo-Indian nurses, getting above herself, decided that a patient could leave the hospital without my say so.' He turned to regard me as one would an insect pinned to a display board. 'She's that nurse, by the way,' he said, jutting forward the square-angled jaw towards the corridor Lily had fled down.

'I'm sorry,' I offered politely, feeling weakened for having to offer up what I'd thought was the high ground only a few moments ago.

'I fully question whether she should even be around the maternity wing while poking around in the tropical diseases unit.'

'So would I, normally,' Matron said, leaping in, 'but as you well know, Professor, Lily hopes to move fully into the diseases wing by mid-year.'

That had slipped my mind. Lily had mentioned her desire to learn more about caring for the patients with tropical diseases but she'd said it so casually I'd all but forgotten, plus most of that first week was a bit of a blur.

I decided it was easier if I offered peace here rather than waiting for Matron to navigate us to an amicable truce. I extended my hand, which clearly surprised both of them. 'Professor Vickery, good afternoon. I am Dr Fenwick and new here. I'm sorry we haven't met but I gather you've been overseas.'

'Er, yes, I have,' he said, definitely taken aback. I noted he hadn't accepted my handshake yet so I deliberately kept my palm open between us. Now he'd have to be rude to my face in front of Matron and lose the ground he'd won and the apology I was making. Or, he could relent.

'Well, it's lovely to finally meet you,' I continued, sounding untroubled by his horrible manners. 'My mother had an intense interest in infectious diseases for all of her career, particularly in TB. It took her life in the end, and far too young. I think we're lucky to have your expertise here and I'm sorry that I misunderstood the situation.'

He opened his mouth to speak but I hadn't finished. I needed to set my own parameters on my ward.

'But I'll be damned if I let you raise your voice once more to me or any of my staff in the way you did just now. If you step onto my ward again, it had better be when you're calm. Then I shall extend the help of any one of my nursing staff, the stretcher/errand boys, even myself if you require me. It's unprofessional for anyone in our supervisory positions to be anything but level of mood. Otherwise we set entirely the wrong example; I'm sure you agree.'

He watched me carefully and I refused to quaver beneath the chilly glare. And then he surprised me by smiling impossibly wide and annoyingly bright, accepting the handshake. His hand was warm and dry, firm but gentle, reflecting the change that came over his persona, which was remarkable in that moment of relenting. Deep, vertical lines connected through dimples from mid-cheek to jaw to frame his grin. It felt like the sun had suddenly broken through a storm as he let go of the anger.

'I've behaved badly but then if you consult Matron, this is not uncommon, and it's why they keep me incarcerated in the far wing, well away from the more delicate personalities.'

Matron sighed. 'I don't think your father smacked you enough as a child, Professor Vickery.' The affection in her glance was unmistakable.

'He never touched me.' I heard beneath the words his disappointment and that what he was saying to Matron was different to what he meant. Was I the only one who caught the other meaning?

'Why don't you and Dr Fenwick share a cup of tea together, Professor Vickery? That might be a way to show your contrition.'

'Thank you, Matron.' I was glad for her involvement, which had snapped us both away from turning an ugly scene into a circus.

She withdrew, leaving us both standing uncomfortably in the corridor.

'Professor?'

'Right,' he said, immediately awkward. 'Tea?'

He was doing his best, I presumed, and for me to turn him down now would be churlish, but I'd already capitulated and didn't feel like making the necessary small talk that would inevitably have to take place.

'Well, actually I am a bit —' I was about to beg off but there was an invisible demon, I was sure, standing at my back and shoving me into the pathway of anyone and anything to do with the study of tuberculosis. My father and the promise seemed suddenly a long way away.

'Too busy?' he offered and I heard only hope in his tone. He wanted me to turn him down!

'I was going to say thirsty,' I lied, enjoying watching his expression falter. 'Of course, if you're —'

He scratched his head through the untidy flops of hair. 'No, no. Matron will kill me. Let's have some chai, shall we?'

I could tell it was taking an enormous effort for him to remain patient through this chore and curiously it made me take an uncharacteristic pleasure in his discomfort.

Dipali arrived, eyes turning wider and slightly fearful to behold the professor. 'Good morning, Professor.' She could barely look at him.

I wasn't having any of that. 'This is Dipali.' It forced her to regard him. 'She's going to be one of our best midwives,' I introduced, determined he not ignore her.

He nodded, but his gaze slid away towards the corridor she'd walked down.

I smiled at her for him. 'Dip, can you hold the fort for fifteen minutes while the professor and I swap some notes?'

'Of course,' she said, cutting him another worried glance as though expecting a blow.

I nodded thanks and had no choice but to follow his long stride because he was already in motion, on his way out into the hospital gardens.

———

We sat as far apart as two people sharing a tea break could, on a bench conveniently situated beneath a huge banyan tree, and I suspected we both shared relief that no one else was using its shade. It might have meant being seated closer. Heavens, but he was awkward . . . or was it me?

I sat straighter, angry with myself for feeling so unnerved. I knew how to make conversation, how to put people at ease, how to host and entertain; it irritated me that I was acting as uncomfortably as he was. Well, he was looking up to the sky, ignoring his role, so I suppose I would have to lead the way and get us through the next ten minutes and then I'd never spend time with him again. My early excitement about meeting the professor came tumbling down around me like blossom from a tree during a good blow in spring. Miles was right; the man was detestable and not even his eye-catching looks could overcome his unpleasant disposition.

'Pardon?' he enquired.

I must have made a grumbling sound or certainly a noise of disgust. 'Um, I was trying to imagine how you all learned to cope with this heat?' I began, hoping to trigger some sort of discussion into the cheerless silence.

He shrugged. 'I don't think about it.'

'So just pretend it's not there?' I teased.

His brow puckered as he considered my notion. 'You surely knew it was going to be uncomfortably hot in India?'

FIONA McINTOSH

I nodded. 'I did. I suppose the thought of something rarely lives up to the reality.'

He frowned deeply, then shook his head at what he presumably found inconsequential. Fortunately for both of us the bearer arrived with small tin mugs of steaming tea. I knew it would already be sweetened and I preferred fresh to the evaporated milk that the hospital served but I dared not complain.

'Shall I cool it, madam?' the bearer said.

Although I loved watching the tea makers pour their beverages, one arm outstretched so there was perhaps a yard of air between both receptacles and a lot of skill to allow that air to cool the hot liquid as it flowed from one cup to another, I didn't think we needed that theatre in this moment.

'No, thank you, Parth.' I took the proffered cup and smiled a dismissal before beginning to blow gently on the liquid.

Vickery was already sipping his. 'Do you know everyone's names here?' It sounded vaguely like an accusation.

I nodded. 'I made a point of learning as many as I could in the first week. It's polite, don't you think?'

'I don't even know Matron's name. I just call her Matron.'

'I suspect you're fibbing. She seemed to treat you most kindly?' I queried, hoping he'd let me in.

'Matron's a good woman, that's true, and she deals with everyone in that generous way.'

I think we both knew he was skirting the issue and he cleared his throat, vaguely self-conscious of being trapped in evasion. It was meaningless to me, though. I had no burning desire to know more about him as I had never been an overly curious person. It was a regular complaint from friends that I was no good at gossip. Frankly, I was purely being polite now and if I could have walked away in the next moment without being insufferably rude, I would have.

'How long have you been here?' I continued. The chai was good enough to keep me anchored. Curiously, while the ginger warmed internally it didn't overheat the drinker; in fact, I knew it would likely help alongside the black pepper that Parth favoured to dissipate heat through light perspiration. It was the cinnamon that captured my pleasure – the professor probably wondered why I smiled in that heartbeat; I wasn't going to explain that the cinnamon made me think of Christmas and that I'd be with Jove by then . . . married even.

'Six years, near enough,' my companion answered.

'I shall only be here through to September.'

'Why's that?'

I explained as succinctly as I could, already imagining he probably wouldn't tolerate a long story, and it was comforting to talk of home and of Jove, whom I realised I was missing more than I cared to admit. We wrote each week but I would write to him tonight again and surprise him. Vickery sipped as I spoke and his attention began to feel much weightier now that he turned his shoulders so he could watch me as I told him my tale. I found his focus unsettling, especially as it gathered in intensity, holding me as tightly as if he'd wrapped his arms around me and then dared my eye contact to waver. I began to lose sense of the activity around us, the sound of birds, the distant hum of city life. We must have appeared to an observer as if we were locked in a staring competition. I was awkwardly lost in us for those two minutes and then, suddenly and acutely uncomfortable, I dragged myself out of his spell by abruptly falling silent. There had been more to say but I didn't care to speak for longer.

The professor didn't so much as blink at the sudden pause, still holding my gaze as though he owned it. 'Is it worth it?' He punctured the invisible bubble that had wrapped itself about us, much like Parni's baby's caul, with his candid query and instantly the immediate world roared back to life around me. I could hear a bull-ock complaining in the distance and the sound of laughter of some nurses, probably coming off a shift. In a nearby building someone dropped a tray of pans and the shrill clattering echoed from one of the hospital wings. 'I mean, really, is it worth it?' he repeated. His straightforward enquiry cut quickly beneath my armour.

'It is to me.' I probably shouldn't have sounded as wounded as I did. It showed him my weakness and that was the last thing I wanted to reveal to this unpleasant colleague.

He snapped his attention from me to drain his cup and there was a curious feeling of bittersweet release. Although I had desper-ately wanted him to look away, I bizarrely felt instantly lonely, toppling from the cocoon he'd created. 'It's a long way to come for a matter of months and somehow I suspect this is not so much about midwifery as your mother's death, leaving your own mark.'

I found his directness painful in its accuracy. I cast my gaze down, unable to bear looking back into his eyes that had seen and judged far too much in a short time. 'You may be right,' I demurred. It seemed easier to let him score that point but perhaps he heard the slight tremor as I spoke. I thought I'd masked it.

'I am right,' he insisted. 'I can hear it in your voice,' he added, answering my fear. 'You're here to take revenge on the disease. I can help you!'

'No, I'll let you take revenge. Find a cure!'

He gave a sneer of embarrassment. 'I'm giving it my all, Dr Fenwick. Why don't *you* help instead of playing with babies?'

I had to inhale deeply, silently, to prevent myself from snap-ping. 'Saving lives is hardly playing, Professor,' I replied, pleased by how even I sounded. 'And I've already told you why.'

'It seems to me that you came here deliberately to break that promise to your father.' He raised a hand. 'Don't waste your breath denying it. Besides, your private life is of no consequence to me but

I desperately need a bright mind like yours on my side that has some experience in tropical medicine.'

I shook my head to deny him, angry but determined to keep my composure. He threw more fuel onto the fire of my building rage by smiling; I think he'd worked out already how it infuriated me. He loaded his mocking expression with intrigue and challenge. 'You can do both, of course. Run your ward, teach your midwives; I mean, frankly, Dr Fenwick, dear old Mother Nature has already equipped women with the internal mechanism and inherent knowledge for childbirth. Let's face it, it's not as though the mother has much choice – she simply has to lie down or squat. Nature does the rest.'

'Only a man would simplify it like that.' I couldn't hide the disdain.

'I disagree. Even you would concede that by the time a woman reaches term, she's pretty much prepared for the inevitable. Nature is an amazing force; it would have been getting her ready emotionally and physically for the entirety of the pregnancy for the very moment of birth.'

'And what if the baby presents in the breech position, or the umbilical cord is looped around its neck, or the —'

'Any number of complications, yes, yes,' he said, waving my protest away as though it were academic. 'And that's when you and your midwives play their role, but if saving lives is what you're after, Dr Fenwick, I doubt you can find a more worthwhile wing than mine. I simply can't get enough help. Even the nurses are scared of TB. I doubt you are.'

'I'm not,' I assured. 'But I have a job to do in maternity. The dangers of childbirth aside, I learned yesterday that there are pregnant women and babies dying who are not allowed to come to the clinic because of family pressure.'

He didn't look surprised. 'And why does that affect you? Be assured that the Muslim families will not change on this; husbands will not permit their women to undress, not even unveil, anywhere where men might be.'

'But —'

'Dr Fenwick, one of the first important wisdoms of working here successfully is respecting the rules of the local people. I do hope someone has explained the caste system to you too. That's vital if you're —'

'Would you stop lecturing me, please?'

He laughed as I bristled. 'There are so many do-gooders here in India, all trying to change the *poor savages* and show them how to live like proper Westerners.' The sarcasm struck like poison. I knew he was right. Just on the journey alone I'd listened to the dismissive way that the English spoke about their hosts but I wasn't going to admit that to him.

'Well, I'm not one of them,' I responded lamely.

'You are, you know. Actually, you're worse. They might be rich with impressive titles and important connections, but they're nonetheless ignorant, believing everyone but their own kind is inferior. You're far from ignorant but you've come on a selfish mission – a grandiose daydream to change the world, to somehow reverse time, show your adoring Daddy that darling Mummy didn't die in vain. You want to return home triumphant that you not only solved crises in midwifery but can bend someone's faith to suit your clinics . . . and maybe even cure TB as you pass us by . . . all in a matter of months, of course! Meanwhile, all the other *memsahibs* are just too self-centred and impressed with themselves to notice there is any other way than their —'

I didn't put much of a swing into it; I suppose because I've never taken to raising my hand to anyone previously. The sound of the slap died quickly against his cheek, so the effect was really more of a thud but it achieved the desired outcome and his tirade ended immediately.

The professor nodded. 'Congratulations, Dr Fenwick, your communication skills are succinctly honed. Matron might feel we haven't made much progress today but I think we understand each other perfectly.'

I took a ragged breath, genuinely appalled at my behaviour and angry that I was the aggressor. 'Professor Vickery. I'm really rather hoping our paths don't cross in the coming months. Can we both try to achieve that please?'

'I can't promise, but I shall avoid you if that makes it easier on your tendency towards histrionic behaviour. Drink your tea, Doctor; you should know that chai has immeasurable soothing properties. It will help to keep those female emotions of yours under control.'

I don't think I could have been angrier in that moment. If I'd even tried to hurl back a rebuke, it would have come out as an explosive stutter and I prided myself on having the presence of mind as white anger flashed through me to stay still, stay silent.

I stood, desperate to be the one to walk away this time.

'Before you go,' he said.

I halted, only out of a sense of shock at the full realisation that I had just hit someone, but I didn't turn to look at him.

'Take one piece of well-aimed caution and do *not* interfere with the ways of the locals.'

It was time to leave and I was going to have to tell Matron our little chat over tea did nothing but worsen my opinion of the professor and brought on violence that I had never thought a part of me. Breaking my hope that I could walk away without so much as sharing another word, I swung around on my heels.

'You have no jurisdiction over me, Professor.'

'I'm not claiming to have any. What I am doing is giving you solid counsel.'

'I didn't ask for it.' I sounded breathless from the exertion of not raising my voice.

'Yes, but you need to hear it, Dr Fenwick. You need to under-stand that you're dealing with faith now. And faith is far stronger to these people than our medicine or any of your clinics. And when it comes to caste that provokes terrible repercussions if the rules are flouted. Don't risk it.'

'Women and babies are dying unnecessarily,' I repeated and could see how it prompted only fresh disdain in that gaze I wanted to escape. 'I can and will save them . . . or have you forgotten the oath you took as a doctor?'

'No, but I'm rational enough to know when to exercise that oath. You will not save a woman from her family's wrath if she con-travenes the tenets of her religion. Husbands would rather kill their wives than break with their faithful traditions. Do *not* come between them and their ways. It is a pathway to danger and you're here but for a blink in their time.' He stood, eyes glittering with the passion of this warning but also something else . . . I couldn't tease it out in the moment our gazes met angrily. 'When you've calmed down and can see reason about what I say – even if you do despise me – maybe you'll visit the TB ward. You are most welcome, and be assured, Dr Fenwick, I've said that to so few people, I could count them on one hand. Good day to you.' He placed his cup into my hand and strode away.

I was so livid that he not only had the last word in such a superior, calm manner but that he'd stolen the march and stomped away before I could. I helplessly watched him, mouth open in aston-ishment at his nerve to treat me like one of his staff . . . worse, like one of his cringing servants. I looked down at his empty cup and it was only my upbringing that prevented me from hurling it against the tree we'd been sitting beneath.

9

The following day I was still fuming but the rage had dulled to fury at myself for being so easy to manipulate. I was a doctor, supposed to be objective, able to guard my emotions, and yet I'd acted precisely how he'd accused – a woman with a histrionic personality. My morning lecture walk around the ward – as the nurses liked to call it – lacked its usual humour. It was fortunate that Parni had given them so much to be in awe over and to discuss in great detail.

'Hold that memory, ladies, because perhaps none of us will ever witness such a birth again.'

They gushed on, one admitting she kept a tiny piece of the linen that had cleaned away the infant's caul.

'My husband is away at sea. I want him home safe,' she explained. The others laughed and I didn't have the heart to tell her that the luck was supposedly passed on to the sailor, not his wife, so he was the one who needed the linen.

We moved through our rounds, pausing while the midwives went through their checks of each mother in the ward.

'Up until even as recently as the Great War, your role was known collectively as "handywomen" and you did everything from attending births to laying out the dead in a local community. But we've come ahead in great leaps since then, and especially since the turn of the century, when it was made illegal for anyone uncertified to attend a woman giving birth.'

I could hear how stilted I sounded. There were nine pairs of eyes watching me, their mostly Anglo-Indian owners supposed to be hanging on my words, learning from each wise sentence I spoke, and here I was giving them a history lesson that had no bearing on their role today in India. I glanced at the frowning Lily and tried to shake myself out of my distraction. It didn't help that even though so many hours had passed I swore I could still feel precisely where my hand had connected with Professor Vickery's face. At the point where my fingers connected to my palm I had touched jawbone, hard and unyielding. My skin had scraped against a darkly golden beard, where he'd not shaved since the previous day. It was surprisingly abrasive for such a fair man. Now I came to think of it, his hair was blond but his skin had that olive, Scandinavian tone that tanned easily.

'Dr Fenwick?' It was Lily. My words must have petered out as I became lost once again in the spell of Saxon Vickery. This realisation only served to vex me further and I stopped myself just in time from snapping at my loyal head midwife.

'Er . . . sorry, everyone.' I gathered my scattered thoughts. 'What I'm trying to say is that you now own a measure of respect that has been well and truly earned. By the time you help a mother to deliver a child alone, you will be fully certified, well experienced in all aspects of delivery, including *en caul*.' They murmured a collective chuckle. 'You'll know when to get the doctor or when to simply hold your nerve, remain patient and guide your mothers-to-be through what is the most natural of processes.' I dared myself to say it. 'After all, Mother Nature has prepared her women well for the inevitable journey that is giving birth. She's been readying them for nearly ten months. And should something go wrong, I mean to ensure you're well equipped to lead your mothers through other procedures that may well involve the doctor, surgery, special care for their babies after delivery and so on.'

I dismissed thoughts of touching Saxon Vickery's face and found my rhythm.

'So, today, I want to concentrate on being able to judge the position of the baby simply by gentle touch on the mother's belly. Hello again,' I said, nodding at a heavily pregnant woman who was sitting up in the bed we'd all begun to cluster around. 'It's Gamini, isn't it?'

She smiled shyly and looked towards Dipali, who nodded. Gamini gave me the gesture I learned as the *Anjali mudra* – a special and polite greeting. Dip had explained in my first week that because I was a teacher, the *mudra* would be offered at chest height from students and probably from patients too. I gathered that if Gamini, for instance, were to give greetings to a god in her local temple, then she would make that identical gesture of palms placed flat against each other, fingers neatly pointing upwards, above her head out of fearful respect. It occurred to me to wonder whether Professor Vickery instructed his staff to make the *mudra* above their heads whenever addressing him. I bit my lip to force my thoughts back to where they were relevant; I was allowing Vickery far too much playtime in my head.

This time I succeeded and was able to lead my group through a helpful, valuable session that had begun to cover fundal massage, which would help them enormously for reducing bleeding and cramping of their mothers post-birth. 'You all need to be able to do this and we'll have a practical demonstration tomorrow if we have a birth and I suspect we shall,' I said, grinning towards Gamini. 'Any questions about what we've talked about this morning?'

One of the women raised a hand and I nodded.

'Dr Fenwick, can you give us some guidance on how to talk a mother through the delivery? I mean, there's a lot of pain clearly,' she said, looking around embarrassed, and I presumed this was because she'd not had a child of her own. 'I'm gathering it's up to us to get them through sometimes. What troubles me is that the women want to squat, not lie down.'

'This is true, Jennifer. A most valid point too.' I took them through the modern-day mild sedative pain relief we offered and about the new idea to use gas and air – not that it was available in India – but then moved step by step across what might be plausible for this ward, with mothers used to letting Nature take her own course. 'Warm and cold flannels, back rubbing and good old moral support remain our best weapons against pain that simply can't be avoided. Anyway, with Gamini due, we can tackle the topic more practically through her labour. Although it's not a mathematical equation – her baby will come when it and her body decide it's time.'

Jennifer nodded with enthusiasm.

'I have to tell you that today's preference – certainly in Britain – is to give birth in bed, to ensure ease of access to the mother and of course a presumed safer delivery of the child.' My students didn't look entirely convinced. 'And I agree with your dubious looks. While we don't have them here yet, I'll explain the use of stirrups on tomorrow's round. For the medical team it's a wondrous boon, especially if we need to use forceps, or turn the child – that sort of thing. However, I'm not sure the mothers would agree. Several mothers we delivered for in London who had laboured in wards for their first child chose home births for subsequent births so they could allow gravity to be their greatest assistance, rather than being urged into a bed, legs wide apart, feet in stirrups and expected to push out a child.'

They nodded their agreement. 'Please do not repeat this but I remain convinced that what is essentially pushing "uphill" can lead to lumbar strains, perineal tears and surgical involvement. But my instincts fly in the face of today's general practices that doctors – *male* doctors,' I qualified, and won smiles, 'seem determined to follow. I have expressed my concern at the highest levels that the pressure of the full uterus during labour might present problems for the mother's blood circulation. If the uterus presses on that all-important blood vessel, the vena cava – which permits what?'

'Vital blood flow to the placenta,' Yvonne answered.

'Yes. If that flow is constricted I believe there could be a risk of compromising oxygen to the baby with the mother on her back and pushing so hard. Make that homework. Think on it. We'll discuss tomorrow. Thank you all. Back to duties. Lily, can I have a word please?'

She followed me into my small office.

'I've been thinking,' I began, pouring a drink from the jug of regularly replenished safe water, 'about the women who aren't allowed to come to our outpatient clinic, or be confined in the hospital.' I gave her the glass, which she accepted and turned to pour another. 'Why don't we go to them?'

Lily coughed as she swallowed from her first sip, smiling as she patted her chest. 'Sorry.' I'd startled her obviously and I drank, watching her.

'Run a clinic outside the hospital?'

I put my glass down. 'Why not? Me, you, Dip, a couple of the others . . . once a week? Husbands and male family members couldn't possibly complain about an all-female team offering genuine medical help for their pregnant wives, sisters, nieces . . . surely? They could accompany them, and be sure it is only women who will see them undressed and in a fully enclosed tent.'

She drank some more; I knew it was to stall for time while she thought this through, so as I sat down and sighed, she sat opposite and turned her face upwards to the fan that stirred hot air around us, feigning a breeze but it felt more like hot breath. 'You mean just for the Muslim community?'

'I mean for every woman who needs our help. But if their faith demands all and only women, we're ready for them.'

'Well, over the last few years there have been lots of uprisings between Muslims and Hindus.' She shook her head in the Indian way that had so many meanings I'd come to learn. 'It was never like this. Suddenly, even the most trivial of quarrels can lead to riots and I know I'm generalising, Dr Fenwick, but it always seems to happen at festival time when passions are aroused. We have to be careful.'

'But we're not interested in any of that. We don't take sides.'

She wobbled her head again, pondering the idea. 'Of course it could work but they wouldn't just come with questions regarding pregnancy, as you'd imagine. Once they know we're available they'd ask us to look at their sores and boils, their broken limbs and twisted ankles, their running bellies or constipated bowels . . .'

I nodded, knowing instantly she was right in this presumption. 'All right. Two choices, then. We either make it a general clinic and have to extend the service we offer, or —' I paused as Lily shook her head.

'The only other female, Dr Powers, is going home next month. I heard on the jungle telegraph that they're replacing her with a male doctor, ex-military.'

I made a face of suffering. 'How reliable is that information?'

She shrugged. 'He knows Calcutta well; I think it's going to happen.'

'Right . . .' I bit my lip. 'Then we stick to gynaecological issues and obstetrics. We have all the right people and we can save some lives, perhaps get some better practices happening in the villages.'

'I suppose even if some of the other doctors offered a general clinic for the poor in the south of the city, you'd have more than enough work and could justify the special obstetrics clinic.'

'So do you think the women of the Muslim faith will be allowed to see us?'

Lily looked uncertain but smiled. 'We can only try and it's a wonderful effort to help if you can get the idea off the ground. I'm all for it but we have to be very careful, Dr Fenwick. Forgive me for the caution but this is an extremely tricky area because we're encroaching on faith.'

I rolled my eyes at her and felt badly about deriding a comment that was meant with the kindest of intentions.

'I'm sorry. I've had that advice rammed at me so many times but it feels more like an excuse, as though it negates all responsibility towards these women.'

She looked immediately concerned. 'Who else mentioned this, Dr Fenwick?'

I gave a groan. 'Among others, the intolerable Professor Vickery.'

Lily grinned. 'I thought of all people you'd enjoy him.'

'Why?' I looked back at her, aghast.

'Oh, I see similarities, even a common purpose.'

'Surely not?' I could hear how disconcerted I felt by this observation. 'He's the most unpleasant person I've met in my life!' I was exaggerating but the point was made.

She lifted a shoulder, unaffected by the belligerent tone. 'He's quite brilliant and I think with that brilliance comes a lack of patience and also a drive that doesn't let anyone or anything stand in his path.'

The way she offered her insight so carefully I could hear the blatant comparison. It made me blink, perplexed. Was I impatient?

Was I so determined I metaphorically drove over people? Perhaps she sensed my injury.

'I mean,' she said, quickly backtracking, 'these are qualities I can only admire. To be single-minded and committed, combined with such talent. Few of us can be so . . . so disciplined.'

'Is that what it is?' I said, clearly unconvinced. 'I personally think he's a boorish, protected, unrealistic male with early Victorian sensibilities who probably believes women are good for little else than child-raising and fundraising.' I hated the heat in my voice, burning through into feverish words.

I was impressed that she gamely pushed back. 'I don't see what you're seeing.'

'Dr Baird does – he warned me about him before I'd set foot in the hospital.'

'It's not for me to say, Dr Fenwick, but I do think Dr Baird is . . .' She blinked, perhaps thinking better of airing her opinion. I admired her control.

'No, come on. Spit it out. I'm not going to say anything to either of them.'

She looked embarrassed. 'Dr Baird often sounds jealous when he speaks of Professor Vickery. I suspect he's felt the sharp end of the professor's tongue but the professor doesn't suffer fools, as they say —'

'Are you calling Miles a fool?'

Lily gave me a look of horror. 'No, not at all. It was just an expression my father uses. Forgive me. I meant that I've overheard Dr Baird express his disgust quite openly that everyone praises the professor's work, barely notices his . . . and —' She stopped again abruptly.

'And what?'

She blushed. 'Dr Baird is, I think, envious of the attention Professor Vickery wins without even trying.'

'You mean the attention he receives from women?'

She nodded. 'All women.'

'Not this one!' I assured, trying to ignore the fact that I'd thought of no one else all of the previous evening and this morning and here I was, still talking about him into the afternoon. 'He was so rude to you yesterday and I heard he fairly terrified Dip this morning.'

She laughed. 'Dip is in awe of him, that's why. So am I. Most of the women who know him wish they could corner him in the supplies room and most of the male staff are jealous of him.' She waited for me to speak but I was embarrassed for both of us and Lily only giggled more. 'Perhaps if you saw him with his patients you might form a fresh opinion of him.'

'How so?' I didn't want to show more interest and yet I felt helpless.

'It is with sick people that he finds endless patience, gentle words, relentless energy. He never stops. That's why he looks hollow-eyed, always seems fractious and impatient. He is continuously trying to outrun death because his patients are never anything but critically ill.'

I swallowed some water to hide my shame but my hand tingled, reminding me of the slap and how I'd done a thorough job of humiliating myself yesterday. I could have heard his words and even if I didn't agree, I should have walked away when I had the chance. Now I felt small and, yes, histrionic, as he'd accused. I had never considered myself as someone who ever lost control and yet how could he reach any other conclusion? *I hit him!* I didn't appreciate his condescension but that was no excuse for my fishwife behaviour; I was better than that.

'He asked for my help,' I admitted.

'You should give it, Dr Fenwick. He's waging war against infectious disease; there are times I feel he's like a one-man army, crusading in an impossible battle.'

'It can be beaten. Infectious diseases will know their foe . . . and some will know their end.'

She shook her head at me as though she couldn't understand why I couldn't see what she did. 'Then help him. I've never heard him ask anyone for it before. He must see something in you.' There was a glint in her eye. It was silently asking a question.

I should have left it well alone. 'Lily! I am to be married!'

She stood to leave. 'I meant your talent with tropical disease, Dr Fenwick,' she qualified.

We both knew she was lying but we were interrupted by Matron. 'I can come back . . .' She waved a hand.

'No, Matron, I was just leaving,' Lily said and eased around the robust senior nurse. 'Dr Fenwick's going to run a special mobile clinic. I'll let her tell you about it but my suggestion if we go ahead is that we look at making the first clinic at the *bhusthie* of, er —' she looked my way '— that means shanty town.' Lily returned her attention to Matron. 'Behala, south of the city. They need a lot of help there.'

Matron looked at me, aghast. 'What is this all about?'

I sighed, gestured to a seat and Lily left me with a sympathetic grin.

Matron and I talked for another half an hour, back and forth. She wasn't charmed by my latest idea but I now felt obliged to press on with it. It's not that I particularly wanted to be controversial but I was increasingly recognising that I didn't like to be told I would likely fail at something. Matron was hinting strongly that such an innovation could lead to problems.

'The load would be too huge to bear, Dr Fenwick. We barely cope with the patients we have.'

'Then once a month. A chance for those women who are not permitted to come to the hospital to be reassured, perhaps receive some advice for when their confinement begins, some help with after-care for their babies.'

She looked back at me dubiously. 'I can't fault your endeavour; it occurs to me as you say this that we might be able to work with the Sisters of Loreto. They do brilliant work in the slums and perhaps together we can get your monthly clinic happening.' She raised a hand to stop my excitement gushing too fast across the desk. 'It would have to be restricted to check-ups for pregnant mothers. To take on anything else would be lunacy as we don't have the staff and we'd probably create more problems than solve. Although . . .' She frowned in thought.

'Although what, Matron?' I sounded hopeful because there was a chance I could broaden her view.

'Someone like Professor Vickery should be involved to widen the scope; his is such an important area.'

Inwardly I recoiled but kept my expression even.

'I spoke to him earlier; he said you shared a most convivial cup of chai on the lawns.'

'Er, yes, we did,' I lied, shamelessly convincing.

'I'm pleased. He's quite brilliant, you know.'

'So everyone keeps telling me,' I said, keeping my voice full of enthusiasm.

'I believe he senses brilliance in you too, my dear. To be candid, I haven't heard him speak so brightly of a colleague previously.'

That baffled me. I gave a demure smile to hide my bewilderment. 'He's being generous.'

'Not at all. In your short time, don't think we haven't noticed the loyalty you've engendered from the team of midwives and nurses under your care. They're a happy bunch and being led from the top by a wonderful role model. What's more, in just a matter of weeks you've reduced the deaths and complications in births by thirty per cent already.'

'I'd like to double that percentage in the next month or two.'

She smiled. 'I'm confident you will, Dr Fenwick, and the hospital administration is truly impressed. We would love it, of course, if you would lend your impressive knowledge and research into tropical disease once you feel you have the team working well in obstetrics.'

I felt my stomach clench again. No, I mustn't be tempted to break my oath. Fortunately, the thought of Professor Vickery helped me to stay resolute.

'I doubt I'll have time, not with the outreach clinic that I feel passionately about.'

She nodded. 'Yes, I understand. And I will help, but before you leave us I would consider it a personal triumph if you would lend your expertise to Professor Vickery at some stage. He's fighting what feels like an unwinnable battle and he's such a warrior.'

'I can tell you admire him.'

'His disposition can be abrasive, I'll admit, but watch him with the patients, get a feeling for his commitment, witness his extraordinary work and you'll perhaps enjoy being part of it. Just promise me you'll think about it.'

It was a compromise – not my strength – but wisdom was coming with age that I had to learn how to reach solutions that kept all parties happy. 'I'll do that as soon as I have the clinic in place,' I agreed.

It felt like a start and I could imagine how exciting it would be to leave Calcutta later in the year knowing I'd set up a monthly clinic that brought medical services and advice to women who previously had no access to it. It would feel satisfying to leave on such a positive and progressive note. I needed to refocus Matron on my work. 'Thank you. I'll look forward to hearing when you've spoken to the nuns?'

She smiled. 'Yes, leave that with me. I think we might even broaden the offering so we can garner more support and funding. When did you hope to begin?'

'Tomorrow?' I waited a beat or two before adding a grin to show her I was jesting. She let out her breath with relief. 'How about within a month?'

She lifted an eyebrow in consideration and then nodded. 'All right, then, Dr Fenwick. We shall talk as soon as I know more from the convent. Now, the reason I dropped in was actually to talk about a visit to the hospital by Her Excellency the Vicereine.'

I pulled a face. 'Oh no . . . when?'

She laughed. 'Oh yes! We need the support and exposure such a visit brings. The Viceroy is paying a visit from Delhi and his wife said she'd like to visit a hospital that provides for locals. We have been chosen. She'll be with us in early June. Her Excellency is apparently extremely interested in women and babies . . .' Matron dropped her voice. 'One of her two sons died during the Great War at just twenty-one, and she's been a solid campaigner for better conditions in India since they first arrived in the country in 1913.' She smiled broadly. 'Anyway, she's particularly focused on pushing better health care for women, especially against diseases that can be controlled through improved hygiene, and once again that forges your work with the professor's, which is why you're both being asked to attend a special soirée she's hosting.' Matron stood. 'I'll make sure all the details come through to you, Dr Fenwick, both of her visit next month and the event at Belvedere House.'

I sighed, knowing this was not a battle worth fighting. 'Yes, of course, thank you, Matron. I'll be glad to show her around.'

'You can tell her about your newly proposed outreach clinic. You never know where the help might come from.'

10

May came and went; I hardly noticed its passing, I was so immersed in my work. My world became so small I began to believe my shoes had the power to shift me between the flat and the hospital and around the wards without me having to think about the footsteps involved. If not for weekly letters from Jove, the odd note from my father and regular invitations from Miles, which I turned down, I could have been forgiven for believing I was in my own slipstream. It was as though I wasn't moving in beat with the rest of the hospital population but was instead in my private world. Life was punctuated by the groans of women in labour, the soothing sounds of midwives comforting those in pain, and the cries of new life – always so welcome.

I looked up to see Miles hovering once again at the doorway to my office. I was irritable from too little sleep and perhaps it showed.

'Bad time?'

A grudging smile formed itself. 'Tired . . . and hot!'

'You'll get used to it,' he quipped good-naturedly. 'I can think of a nice way to cool you down. How about tonight for that long-promised drink? You look like you could use a break.'

I'd been putting him off for weeks with vague excuses. I either needed to be blunt and risk offence or simply accept and make it clear we were no more than friendly colleagues. I hesitated in my decision as the former was tempting.

'I'm thinking a refreshing gimlet or a pink gin on the terrace of the Calcutta Club. You'll like it because the point of this particular gentlemen's club is not to be discriminatory. The first president was, in fact, a maharajah.'

'I'm impressed,' I said, nodding.

'Good. Then say yes and join me this evening.'

I was weary enough of this stuffy room that the thought of sipping something cold and alcoholic beneath an effective ceiling fan sounded suddenly attractive.

'All right, Miles.' He looked shocked and then covered it with a delighted smile and a sound to match. I wasn't thrilled by his rush of pleasure and looked at my watch to avoid having to share it. 'Er, so, I'll head home to change and I shall see you there at seven. Is that suitable?'

'Wouldn't you like me to pick you up?'

'No. Much faster this way. You're a member, I'm guessing?'

'Yes, of course.'

'Just leave my name at the door. That's fine.'

'Seven it is.' He beamed. 'What about dinner afterwards? The club does a great salmon in aspic and their beef Wellington is considered the best in Calcutta.'

I gave him a look of mock warning. 'A drink is fine.'

'I forgot you don't eat,' he said, risking an attempt at humour. This time my thin smile likely looked forced. 'Righto. See you later; can't wait,' he assured, tapping the door architrave twice as though the sound signified a task achieved.

Ugh. What had I done? Oh well, I had never led Miles in the wrong direction; interest was all one-sided and I'd certainly remind him of this should he overstep any invisible line. But the weeks of routine had caught up with me and I did feel like that drink and a change of scenery. I'd lived like a recluse for the past four months.

In the spirit of being more sociable, I packed up my desk immediately and was on my way home within fifteen minutes, emerging not much more than an hour later, dressed for the evening.

It felt odd to be so elegantly attired after my sensible skirts and blouses for work. As to wearing heels, if we had to stand, I doubted that I'd last the evening in the strappy sandals I'd packed, still new in their soft bag from London. I'd opted not to wear full evening satin but instead had chosen an appropriately floaty chiffon dress in a style that safely suggested late afternoon rather than evening. I didn't want to gives Miles any wrong signals.

The chiffon felt gossamer against me in its knife-pleated, pale-rose sheer silk. The fichu neckline gave it just the right feel for cocktails time, with its softly pleated waterfall collar, and I could wear a bolero to cover up until I reached the club. I'd washed and properly shaped my hair to look less like the helmet it had become when I didn't pay attention and more as it should, with gentle waves to frame my face. I checked myself in the cheval mirror before I stepped out and noted I'd lost weight. My eyes looked bigger than I recalled because my cheeks had hollowed somewhat. The dress fell off my frame as though it were hung on a wooden hanger; if I were honest, it looked better than it had when I'd bought it in London. Thin suited me but the bruising beneath my eyes and the redness within them didn't.

I feathered some mascara on my top lashes and, although I hadn't intended to wear much make-up, this was my first night out since my arrival. I felt I should make more of an effort so I added a hint of eyeliner beneath my lower lashes, tracing upwards from the tear duct, and finished with a very pale but smoky sweep of grey shadow. Soft dabs of foundation and some powder helped in a reasonable cover-up job of the dark circles. Jove said my eyes always seemed to have the magical ability to reflect colour around me and so tonight I suppose they became more grey than blue. I dabbed the barest hint of cream blush to brighten the apples of my cheeks and hide the hollows. I didn't want to wear much lipstick so I avoided the rich rubies of wintry London and chose instead a dusky pink. I glanced at my eyebrows and sighed at their untidiness. I didn't have time to pluck them and I certainly didn't want angry red brows either, so I neatened what I could and looked away. None of it mattered; it wasn't as though I was wanting to impress.

I arrived by taxi at one minute past seven, sweeping into the circular drive to be confronted by a double-storey neoclassical building, painted white. Arched, shuttered windows led straight to the grand portico entrance, while above it a bank of small squared windows of guest rooms glittered and glimmered their way to the central pediment of the building with its proud emblem, above which flew what was presumably the club flag.

Miles was waiting for me; he looked anxious as he skipped out of the shadows of the main entrance, emerging from behind the pillars to wave. I allowed him to help me from the car; he even paid the driver but his grimace told me something was up.

'You look gorgeous, Isla.'

I didn't want anything more made of this. 'Thank you,' I said as briefly as I could. 'This is pleasant.'

'Well, it would have been if Vickery hadn't turned up.'

'The professor's here?'

He nodded. 'Want to go somewhere else?'

'No . . . I've come to share a drink, some conversation, and I'm not at all troubled that one of our colleagues is likely doing the same. Why are you concerned?'

He groaned and shook his head. 'He just puts me on edge.'

'I warned you months ago, Miles, you're far too aware of him. Ignore him.' Good advice that I had personally not adhered to. Saxon Vickery had been stuck in my craw for weeks but as I hadn't come face to face with him since our best attempt to be friendly had failed so spectacularly, the memory of my horror had faded. 'Come on, show off your club to me,' I said.

I let Miles link my arm and guide me up three shallow marble stairs into the reception via the middle arch of a trio. The architecture had a strong Grecian quality, with Doric pillars downstairs, and I glimpsed Ionic pillars on the next level. But now that we were inside, the classical architecture was overwhelmed by the mood of the colonial tropics. A darkly polished staircase with ornate panelled balusters climbed away from us in a wide shallow curve of carpeted stairs to the first floor. My heels clicked on a marble floor with colourful inlay work upon which sat a huge *jardinière*. It was the central focus within walls that sported the hunting trophies of many a fine beast's head with enormous curling horns. Gold-leafed noticeboards reflected the names of past presidents while ceiling fans twisted gently above us as Miles escorted me to the reception. Here, dark-eyed, moustachioed men stared silently and gravely at me as Miles signed me in before I was guided towards the back of the building.

'This is the Crystal Room,' he said, pointing left, where I noted mainly couples were socialising quietly beneath a glittering series of chandeliers. I caught the whiff of tobacco fighting against the aromas of food emanating from the kitchens to our right. I looked across and through to a timber-panelled dining room with a few scattered early diners. 'And this is the main lounge,' he finished, sounding proud as he led me into an airy chamber.

It was louder here, the conversation more effervescent, with tinkling laughter and the deeper chuckles of men flirting with their guests. I felt my elbow grasped as Miles hurried me through a long room full of comfy chairs and clusters of people enjoying drinks and snacks. 'But I thought we'd have cocktails on the verandah,' he said, almost in an afterthought, I sensed. I looked at him without judgement but he added self-consciously, 'If that's all right with you?'

'Out here on the verandah is lovely,' I replied, although did he think I'd missed the smouldering presence of Saxon Vickery? I'd glimpsed the unfriendly professor, alone and reading a newspaper in one corner of the main lounge.

A waiter arrived and I let Miles order for us while I admired our surrounds. Cane chairs and tables sat against the sweep of the whitewashed wall of the verandah, which overlooked a manicured lawn and other buildings in the distance. Above us, moths and other insects zigzagged in the shadows, winking into existence when the verandah lighting suddenly illuminated gossamer wings. Conversations and laughter dulled to a general melody of human voices and became a comfortable hum. The drinks arrived.

It had vaguely irritated me that Miles hadn't asked what I might feel like drinking but it seemed trivial to make any mention. I smiled my thanks and the waiter placed a martini-shaped glass onto a coaster. From his tray the waiter also produced a bowl of large peanuts, which were lightly warmed, glossed with oil and flavoured with herbs and chilli, it looked like.

'You'll love these,' Miles assured as the waiter withdrew. 'Here's cheers, I'm thrilled you joined me finally,' he said, raising a glass, and I followed suit before taking a sip of the sweet Plymouth gin mixed with bitters. It was delicious and the fresh citrus of the lemon rind made me think of an English sunset; a bright curl of sunshine within the pinkish mix of alcohol. I sighed silently and relaxed into my chair as the cool alcohol gave me a perk I hadn't realised I'd been missing. I wanted to hold the chill of the glass, with its icy teardrops running down the outside, against my skin but I didn't want to give Miles any wrong signals.

'Do you like it?'

It wasn't my first pink gin but I let Miles have his pleasure. 'So delicious, thank you. What a wonderful spot this is. I can hardly believe there's a sprawling, choked city behind us.'

He nodded in agreement. 'I drop by here most nights. It keeps me sane, especially when the summer heats up. There are all manner of parties held on the lawn and there's a marvellous library here too.' I nodded to tell him I'd noticed it. 'They have their own bakery so there's always fresh cakes and breads on offer.' He was gushing, sounding nervous.

'It's a great escape,' I agreed. 'Don't you miss home, Miles?' I know I'd asked him this before but I was genuinely interested and hoped he felt no longer the strangers we were back then.

He made a scoffing sound. 'Scotland? No!' He took a deep sip of his cocktail.

I gave him a look of bafflement. 'You sound convinced.'

'Oh, I am. In India, I'm someone, Isla. I'm no one back there.'

What an odd sentiment. I didn't want to explore it with him. 'Have you heard about the special visit by the Viceroy's wife?'

Miles swallowed the contents of his glass. It had only taken him three swigs. He sighed as the gin hit the spot. 'Yes,' he answered in a weary tone. 'This happens from time to time. We just grin and bear it. Are you involved? I've not been asked in any official capacity.'

I nodded, unsure of what was best to say at his admission. 'Er, yes. Matron has asked me to give the Vicereine a tour of our maternity wing.' I chose not to mention Professor Vickery for fear of getting my companion charged with irritation but I didn't need to worry about my part in provoking that emotion for the man himself chose that moment to stroll up. I saw him coming but Miles had his back to him and I felt my gut tighten. I didn't want to admit to myself that I found his lopsided grin and slightly ungroomed appearance roguishly attractive against my companion's tightly knotted tie and precisely cut fiery hair, which accentuated the vulpine ears.

'Evening, colleagues,' he said as he approached, wearing an indifferent smile of high wattage. This was surely the most gregarious mood I could imagine him in.

Miles groaned and turned, slow-blinking at confirmation that it was indeed the professor I presumed he loved and loathed in equal measure.

'Hello, Professor.'

Our intruder waved a hand. 'Call me Vickery. We're off-duty, old chap. Isla, you look especially fetching tonight. I'm not used to seeing you out of your white coat and sensible linens.'

I smiled. 'You're not used to seeing me at all, but thank you. I'm enjoying this relaxing setting.'

'Well, while you do look relaxed, Isla, I'm afraid, dear Miles, I would suggest that gin is not agreeing with you. It makes your enormous ears go red. Swap to a Mary Pickford . . . the white rum and fresh pineapple have a lovely zing and the maraschino liqueur will match your hair.' He grinned lazily and I thought a bit cruelly. I felt instantly sorry for Miles.

'I'll have a gimlet with you, Miles, if you're ordering another,' I offered by way of consolation.

Miles cut me a smile of gratitude. 'Don't let us hold you up, Vickery.'

'You're not. I wanted to talk to Isla about the damned official visit that I'm being dragged into.'

I hated him in that moment for how he said my name. It unnerved me that he managed to give it a delicate Scottish lilt from where it came. Somehow he added sweetness and affection into those four letters and I sensed he meant me to hear this, which I didn't appreciate.

'What? Both of you are involved?' Miles frowned, sounding offended.

'Yes. Didn't you know? You normally make it your business to know everything that can further your profile.' Vickery looked at me. 'We're meant to be showing our special visitor around together like a double act apparently,' Vickery said, offhandedly. It was the first I'd heard that he was also included in the escort of the Vicereine around the hospital. I watched him lurch slightly behind Miles's shoulder but he seemed to catch himself. He didn't sound intoxicated but he could have been, for all I knew.

'I'm refusing to discuss work,' I replied, trying to soothe away the scowl from Miles's face. 'Off-duty, remember?'

The professor wagged a finger at me. 'Fair enough, fair Isla. But if you —'

I saw it before Miles did and was leaping to my feet as Vickery first staggered and then began to crumple. I grabbed him and within a blink or two Miles had his other arm.

'Whew! Steady on, old man. How much have you had?'

Saxon found his more common mood. 'Not enough!' he growled. 'Get off me, Miles.' He shook his subordinate free of his arm but I noted he didn't try to untangle himself from my grip. He turned to me and I was close enough that our faces were nearly touching. I smelled a vague whiff of alcohol, probably a Scotch, but not enough to convince me he was drunk.

'Forgive me,' he said, eyes looking into mine far too deeply for my comfort. 'I must remember to eat more often and not drink a good malt on an empty belly.' He gently unwrapped my fingers that clutched his arm, but didn't let go, and I felt the warmth of his skin against mine. He didn't take his gaze from me either, which was even more deeply unsettling because it felt as though he was searching through me, rummaging around in my thoughts to find something that didn't want to be found. 'Sorry for the nuisance.'

'You're not,' I said, feeling transfixed. I shook my head to free myself of his spell. 'Where's home?'

He grinned again. 'Why, Isla? Are you coming with me?'

I was clearly in a good mood because I found this amusing, although Miles didn't and his snort of disgust seemed to entertain the two of us even more. We must have looked like a couple because his fingers still held mine.

I chuckled. 'No, I want to make sure you get home safely. I don't like how unsteady you appear. Is it really because of lack of food?'

'Matron complains, my butler glares silently, my wife urges me from afar to take better care of myself. I'm sorry again for the intrusion. I don't have far to go . . . just upstairs, in fact.'

Hearing him mention a wife was more surprising than learning where he lived; she must be saint-like to put up with him and maybe that explained why she didn't live in India alongside the professor. 'You live at this club?'

'I do. Only transiently, though, since returning from England. I'm yet to find somewhere permanent, as I gave up my old flat on Park Road before I left. Miles grabbed it, didn't you?'

Miles nodded with an awkward smile and a glance back at me that was full of plea. I read into it that he wanted me to curtail conversation and help get rid of the professor.

'I think Miles would jump into my grave if I deserted it. He certainly wants my role at the hospital but that's another conversation for another time. Where was I?' He looked up to the ceiling, distracted. 'Ah yes,' he said. 'The other clubs are much too stuffy for my liking,' Vickery continued, clearly not in the same hurry as my escort. He coughed and it was slightly more prolonged than for someone clearing a throat or a dust mote.

'Professor?' I queried. I wasn't happy with how he sounded.

He grinned lopsidedly at me. 'Time to go. Dr Fenwick,' he began, suddenly more formal. 'I recall the last time we spoke,' he said, rubbing his cheek in some sort of silent signal to me that made me smile with guilt but also with amusement at his deft manner, 'you said you'd visit my department. I'm still waiting.'

'My recollection,' I replied, in a similarly lighthearted voice, 'is that you invited me. I am yet to take up the invitation.' The response had a soft bite but only Vickery would feel it; Miles did not need to know anything about our confrontation. I suppose time had helped to smooth over just how rough our previous meeting had been.

'Don't wait too long.' He spluttered again, apologising for it, and his breathing sounded momentarily erratic.

'I don't like the sound of that cough,' I mentioned. The clinician in me was alerted.

'Nothing to fuss about. This always happens around mid-year for me.'

I was sure I heard the lie but Miles had deepened his glare.

'Come on, then, Isla,' he said, shifting his weight as the cue to our intruder to leave. 'I think we should move on. You may like to see one of the other clubs . . . Tollygunge, perhaps? Goodnight, Vickery,' he added grudgingly. 'Hope you feel better tomorrow.'

'Miles belongs to all of the clubs,' Vickery said drily. 'Tally-ho, eh, Miles?'

'Have a good sleep,' Miles replied.

I was impressed with Miles's control that the professor, even in his slightly befuddled state, was making an extra special effort to topple.

Vickery had already looked away from Miles, fixing his penetrating gaze upon me. 'Good evening, Isla,' and then it seemed his legs could no longer bear the load and, like an old building being demolished, he folded on himself slowly, legs giving way before his torso followed. He clipped one of the cane chairs, toppling it as he fell. Once again I moved faster than Miles and bearers swooped from out of the shadows quicker than I imagined possible.

'Vickery!' I was cradling his head and it felt too hot. 'Just give him some air, please?' I said to the hovering men around us. 'Professor? Saxon?' At the utterance of his name he opened his eyes and gave me a smile that warmed me as though I'd stepped out of a frozen night to stand next to a bonfire. His gaze was turning glassy, though. 'I like how you say my name,' he said, either unaware or deliberately ignoring all the heads that peered over us.

I could feel the irritation of Miles building behind me as I squatted next to the man he loathed.

'Saxon, what's happening?'

He seemed to grasp through his blur that I needed a brief over-view of his medical status. 'Bit of fever,' he replied as casually as one might discuss the weather. But it confirmed what I suspected as he closed his eyes again and appeared to drift into sleep.

'All right. Let's get him up, please,' I said to the aides. 'An arm each. Just stand either side and be ready to catch him.'

Our commotion had caused other patrons to walk over, queries bouncing around the verandah. I noticed others craning necks from inside the long room to get a look at the activity. I turned to Miles. 'Please do the right thing and assure everyone. We don't need to turn this into a circus.'

'What are you going to do?' He sounded as bitter as a child who'd had his bag of sweets snatched away.

'I'm going to see the professor safely to his room.'

'I don't think that's appropriate.'

'Does it look like I am troubled by what you consider appro-priate right now, Miles?' I said.

He blinked quickly, stung.

'One of our own is ill. For heaven's sake. Help or leave. I'm going to make sure he's all right.'

'Right,' he said with a slow sigh of disdain. 'Leave him with me.'

'No.' I said this with such certainty, he stepped back, his face full of shocked query. 'You and the professor clash, that much is obvious,' I said.

'And you two are such good friends, you mean?'

There was no going back now. This episode would damage our loose friendship but my time here was short enough that it truly didn't matter to me. 'What I mean is that I have no history with the professor or feeling one way or the other.' I covered the lie with a firm voice.

'When it comes to medicine, you can be assured that I treat all my patients with the same level of care.'

'I'm not talking about your ability to care for a patient, Miles. I'm talking about our patient's desire to cooperate with you. I don't see it happening with the professor, do you? Whereas I think he will cooperate for me. Now, as I said, either help or don't, but let me see to him.'

'Well, then, I shall leave you to it. Good evening, Dr Fenwick.' He turned away, angry; he was right to feel humiliated in front of others, I suppose, but I didn't have an ounce of sympathy for his hurt feelings given the circumstances. I had no time for the furiously blushing doctor's dented ego and showed it by turning away and urging instructions to the bearers, who hefted Vickery to his feet. He looked dazed initially but recovered his wits.

'Up to his room, please. I presume someone knows which one?'

A senior man arrived wearing the uniform of the club. He told me his name but I couldn't pronounce it to even remember it so I simply nodded. 'I can take you to his rooms, madam. I have a key.'

'Good. Lead on, please.'

11

I barely looked around the spacious room but had the bearers seat my patient on the edge of the bed.

'My name is Dr Isla Fenwick,' I impressed so they didn't think I was breaking any club rules. 'Could you undress him, please?' I asked, turning my back on Vickery for modesty and to address the senior man. 'And could you have some lightly brewed tea sent up. No sugar or milk necessary, thank you.'

The man murmured some orders to his staff and then gave me a little bow. 'Please ring down if you need anything, Dr Fenwick.'

'Thank you.' I knew it to be highly unusual for a woman to be left in the room of a gentleman member but these were unusual circumstances. I kept my back to the men until I heard Vickery dismiss them.

He was covered by the sheet but only to the waist.

They withdrew silently.

'I'm near enough naked and defenceless, Isla. You can have your way with me,' he slurred, eyes closed.

I bent over to put a hand to his head, trying not to notice the broad chest that struck me as too thinly fleshed. Skin that I once imagined would catch the glow of sun so easily appeared slightly waxy in colour. 'Bit warm.'

'It's just a little fever.'

'Not concerned?'

'No. It will be gone by tomorrow. I've just been overdoing it.' His eyes snapped open. 'Thank you for your concern, though.' A smile broke across his face that reflected such pleasure it could be compared to climbing out of the sea to feel a summery sun on one's back. Healing.

I hadn't realised that I was holding myself tense. I let my shoulders drop and sighed softly. 'I've left this far too long but I do believe you're owed an apology for my behaviour the last time we spoke.' I couldn't even bring myself to refer fully to it.

He eyed me from his prone position, head tilted, hair greasy against his pillow. He'd been perspiring but now I noted him trembling slightly, although he was working hard to hide the shiver of a breaking fever.

'I earned it. I usually do.'

'So this happens regularly?'

'Not with quite such deadeye aim. Did you have brothers to teach you that hook?'

I laughed aloud now, helplessly amused. 'No,' I gusted. 'Just me and my pet rabbit, Horace.'

'A boxing rabbit? Perfect,' he said, slipping away from me, words slurring. I wanted to brush back the tuft of golden hair that fell forward as his head turned.

The soft tap at the door arrested any further notion of that. 'Come in,' I said, stepping back from the bed. The bearer tiptoed in. 'Thank you, just lay it out there and I'll pour.'

He was gone as quickly as he'd arrived. It was just the two of us again, with a choir of cicadas selling their suitability to females with their shrill mating call. I recall seeing a range of these winged insects in the British museum, some so brightly coloured they were as beautiful as any butterfly, but my mother taught me that the brightest of all was said to impersonate a toxic moth to dissuade predators.

It occurred to me in that odd moment of memory to wonder whether Vickery's toxic behaviour was contrived to ward off interest from predators . . . women in need of company. Was that because he was married? Was his wife the jealous kind? Perhaps she wasn't if she permitted him to live alone so far away? Or maybe she disliked him – that wasn't hard to counter – and yet I suspected it was none of this. Nor was it about permission, I admonished privately . . . it was about trust. In the same way that Jove trusted me to be away from him, Saxon's wife likely trusted her husband not to let her down while absent. I wanted to think the best of her as I watched her husband fighting fever so far away from her.

Maybe he sensed the burden of my gaze upon him because he stirred, turning his head back towards me, knowing eyes glinting, still a bit glasslike behind heavy lids. 'I'm feeling observed,' he confirmed.

'I don't deny it. Doctors observe, that's our job.'

'I see. Will you be observing me all night?'

'No.' I smiled. 'But I do want you to drink some of this tea, please. It will help to keep you hydrated and I always think tea is a great perker, isn't it?'

'Perker? Is that a word?'

I had to laugh. 'I'm sure you catch my drift.'

'All right. I shall drink some tea to perk myself.'

I was at his side quickly, helping to lift him. I was going to rearrange the pillows but it was faster and more expedient for me to sit behind him and let him lean against me. 'Do you mind?' I asked, concerned.

'Not at all. Who minds resting a weary head against a beautiful woman dressed in pink chiffon?'

'I'm impressed you know the fabric.'

'Oh, I know lots of womany things,' he confirmed.

'Womany? Is that a word?' I wondered, reaching for the china cup.

I felt his body bump against mine as his shoulders moved slightly in amusement. I would be lying if I denied this didn't feel curiously pleasant. I wouldn't call it erotic because this was a man who was ill but I could feel the feverish warmth of his skin through my flimsy dress, which he was crushing, and I could smell that skin. The vaguely acid tang of perspiration was blended against a spicy soap residue. It smelled manly – like walking into a barber's shop.

'Strange, walking dictionaries, us two,' he joked and I could tell he would be fine with some rest.

'I swear you have the fragrance of coconut about you.'

'You would be right. I have my soap made locally from coconut flesh. It's cooling, softening, and above all prevents prickly heat. Far better than gentian violet, don't you agree?'

I did. 'It smells spicily sweet, rather lovely, actually,' I admitted and cleared my throat. 'Here, drink it all. It's weak deliberately.'

'It's also Assam. I prefer Darjeeling.'

'You can tell the difference?'

'In a heartbeat,' he said, sipping obediently like a child. I held my hand beneath the cup to stop him dropping it, as I feared he was not paying enough attention to it. This meant that he was now essentially lying back in an embrace of sorts. I was glad that he didn't mention it and I certainly wasn't going to, so I pushed on with the discussion about tea to distract both of us.

'How?'

'Level of oxidisation,' he said in a tone as though it should be obvious to all. 'Assam is darker, more robust in flavour. Now, Darjeeling black tea . . . well, where to begin? It's fruity floral and of course the season in which it's picked is vital to the taste. If you want me to drink a weaker tea, then I'd recommend a first flush Darjeeling.'

I blinked with consternation, not that he could see this.

'Spring harvest,' he qualified for me.

'Is my patient a connoisseur of teas?'

He turned and for one terrible moment I thought he was going to kiss me. 'Does that surprise you?'

I nodded. 'A little. I prefer this feverish version of Professor Saxon Vickery than the entirely healthy one, to be honest.'

He turned away with a ghost of a smile curling briefly and drained the cup. Time to go. I replaced the cup in its saucer and eased myself out from beneath him, laying his head back on the pillow. I could feel a damp warmth from where our bodies touched, separated only by the thinnest of sheaths of pink fabric that now looked crumpled.

He noticed. 'I'm sorry to have crushed you like that.'

I lifted a hand as though it hadn't crossed my mind as I busied myself straightening the tea paraphernalia.

'I'm grateful to you, Isla, but I fear I've made an enemy for you of Miles.'

'Oh, I doubt it.'

'He's in love with you, that's his problem. Infatuation makes him unreasonable.'

'Don't be ridiculous,' I snorted, although I knew what he said was likely right. 'Anyway, I haven't encouraged him.'

'No, but that doesn't make it any easier for him to bear. If I were you, I'd set him straight.'

'But you are not me, Saxon.' I smiled again and answered him properly. 'Be assured that if Miles is in any doubt then his confusion is of his own making. I have been clear to him from the day I met him that I am betrothed to be married this November and I have no desire to compromise myself or disrupt those plans.'

He cut me a look that was deeper than made me comfortable. Although this time I was ready for him and it felt like an invisible tug of war, except we weren't pulling, we were pushing back . . . and it wasn't physical, it was all mental. I blinked first, I suppose, because I straightened but it didn't feel like I'd lost the challenge. He was smiling at me, however, as though we both knew something emotional had just occurred: an awakening of sorts. I needed to put genuine distance between us.

'So, I don't expect to see you at the hospital tomorrow. I'm going to order regular pots of tea to be brought up – Darjeeling, if you insist, first flower and all that —'

'First flush,' he corrected, sounding drowsy.

'I want you to drink and stay hydrated. Then drink the broth that I'll also order; solids by tomorrow evening. And I will be check-ing on you via spies – be assured of it. If you flout my arrangements, I will not go and visit your patients in your absence.'

Ah, now I had his attention fully on me. His head whipped back, his eyes snapped open. 'You will?' He sounded plaintive.

How could I resist it? 'Of course, because I know if I don't, you'll somehow drag your bony self in and just make it worse. Saxon, you have fever, which we'll discuss tomorrow. It needs to break. Until it does, you're a liability to everyone. What's more, you're no good to your patients if you genuinely collapse and are ill for days on end. If you trust me, this will pass quickly and you'll be back in your ward by the day after next. I'm guessing it's latent TB?' The question hung for a moment.

He nodded. 'I'd prefer not to share that. And I'll follow doctor's orders,' he promised.

'I'll . . . er . . . do you want me to call in tomorrow evening?'

My hesitation amused him. 'Only if you have nothing better to do.'

I felt my lips flatten in irritation. Now it was left to me to decide whether to look in on him. Somehow in my slightly rattled state I felt as though it would be a capitulation if I did . . . as though I'd become like one of the other women around the hospital who were so entranced by Vickery.

'We'll see,' I said, without commitment. 'Sleep soundly.'

He sighed, settling deeper into the bed, pulling the sheet up over his naked shoulders. 'Goodnight, fair Isla.'

I left quietly, tiptoeing down the parquet floors of the corridor of the first level to avoid my heels clacking. I passed a row of past presidents and the portraits continued to watch me as I finally made it to the carpeted stairs and all the way down to the lobby and into the reception area. I didn't expect to see Miles, nor was he waiting for me, which was a relief. I didn't feel like any further confrontation.

The uniformed man was waiting for me, though. I discovered his name to be Mr Johar.

'How is the Professor, Dr Fenwick?'

'Sleeping.' I smiled and discussed the refreshed pots of tea on the hour. 'A meaty but clear broth when he stirs fully, probably around mid-morning tomorrow is ideal . . . as much as he can take. Black tea all day – make that Darjeeling, please – and some solids tomorrow evening: something simple. Steamed fish, perhaps.'

'Very good.' He nodded. 'I shall see to this personally.'

'Thank you. I'll . . . er, I'll look in on him tomorrow night to see how he's doing.'

So there it was – I'd committed to returning without even giving myself a night to think it over. I convinced myself on the way home that this was purely in my professional capacity, but a tiny voice, echoing from an empty space somewhere deep, was warning me otherwise.

12

I arrived at Saxon's ward, anticipating an hour or two at most of checking on each patient's status and briefing his team. I hadn't imagined I'd look up at the clock and realise it was already dusk and that I'd been walking in his footsteps for ten hours. He'd gathered a good nursing team around him; to be honest, I'd barely noticed them but only because they were so well trained and took their instructions quickly and adroitly. They moved around me quietly, fulfilling every request so I could shift to the next patient as quickly as possible. And still we were immersed for hours on end. I could see the remains of an afternoon tea on his desk where I'd consulted paperwork and I do dimly remember nibbling on food around midday but only because I was pressed to do so by Matron, who'd called in. She hadn't seemed surprised to see me; in fact, she'd looked close to smug, as though she always knew it was just a matter of time before she saw me in this part of the hospital. Or perhaps that it was inevitable in the professor's absence that I would cover him.

It didn't matter. What did count was the feeling I was experiencing at being on this ward. Maternity was fun but here lived true reward for the clinician in me because these patients presented enormous challenge. I suspected only Saxon might understand if I explained that it was the tension of ever-present death that nourished my excitement. The anxiety of knowing time was never on our side with these sick folk drove me, so that I did not notice time passing or people talking to me, or did not think to pause and take on some fuel of food without being coerced. I was not tired, not even a little. If anything, I felt energised, as though I had boundless stamina, didn't need sleep, with a sense that I could be in several places at once, giving instructions.

The range of illness was profound and it was inevitable, I suppose, that I drifted unhappily but fully conscious now towards the isolation ward where TB sufferers dwelled. They would be my last patients of this gruelling yet exciting day. What I discovered would likely stay with me for the rest of my life and it was perhaps as I lifted the notes of Saxon's scribble on the first patient that I knew I was not only breaking my promise to my father and to Jove, but that I was doing so with relish and with a sense of arrival. I was finally where I wanted to be. The spangles of excitement to be walking a similar path to my mother's in her beloved India felt charged with high emotion but also a sense of rightness, as though I couldn't escape my destiny.

I looked up from the notes into the desperately disfigured face of a woman who might have been only a few years older than me. She was suffering from tuberculosis of the skin. Saxon had written down 'lupus'. In the cot next to her was a child, perhaps no more than twelve, suffering one of the most common incarnations of the disease. The old nickname for it was 'King's Evil' and it affected the lymphatic glands in the necks of young people. This girl was still in the ulceration stage and her neck was a mess of wet sores, with yellow curdy pus escaping the wounds. That poisonous material would be filling her glands, I knew; so did Vickery. He had planned – I could see from his notes – to operate on her today. The TB would heal with our treatment but I knew she would be left horribly scarred. I told the nurses to prepare this girl for surgery in the morning.

'She must fast from now. Nothing solid, only water.'

'Will Professor Vickery be returned, Doctor?'

'I can't answer that but this patient needs immediate treatment as per his plans. Each day matters with this disease. Whether he is well enough to attend or not, I will do the operation.'

She nodded, made a note on the page, and I had no doubt that my stern look forbade her from questioning me further.

Hobbling nearby was a hunchbacked man who led me into the ward of men. Apart from his misshapen body, I thought he looked hale. I learned from the nursing team that he helped out in the ward, having suffered the disease that attacked his bones as a child. His deformity meant he couldn't earn his keep, but rather than beg he preferred to help in the ward in exchange for food and being able to curl up and sleep in one of the corridors. Apparently Vickery permitted it. A man coughed, desperately gagging for air. Reading his notes, I learned this patient had been in a feverish state for nearly two years. At one time he'd had his own shop, been in a reasonable financial state, but had beggared himself in pursuit of a remedy that had not been found. He was too weak to work – too frail in this moment to do much more than lie down. He was so skeletal his skin looked as if it had been sprayed onto his frame in the thinnest of layers.

All the male patients in this ward had a similar appearance that marked the disease: sunken cheeks, deep hollows above the collarbones – especially those with consumption – and scraggy hair. One man knelt in a corner, too beleaguered to move.

'Why is this fellow here?'

'He is too sickly to be anywhere else.'

'Is he receiving treatment?' I frowned. I couldn't imagine a patient left in such a state.

'He is in final stages.' She didn't whisper this.

I could feel the sharp pain as I bit my lip. 'What about his family?'

The nurse shrugged. It wasn't meant unkindly or carelessly, I didn't believe. She was a realist, I decided, who'd seen her fair share of death from this disease and talked matter-of-factly. 'He is a burden; they cannot nurse him. He received treatment here but did not improve. We needed the bed and his family wouldn't have him home for fear of infecting others. He had nowhere to go. Matron thinks he's been sent home to die but Professor Vickery has asked us all to keep it secret and let him see out his days here. It won't be long.'

In that moment I could have admitted to feeling overwhelmed with a fleeting sense of wanting to run away. But I couldn't show any of that despair in my expression. Too many gazes were resting on me, waiting for instructions, waiting for answers. I thought of my mother and wondered how she got through each day; I couldn't imagine how Saxon faced this daily, for I'd already learned that for every patient he treated, there were another dozen or more awaiting a bed or medical help of some sort. Hospital stays for full-blown TB were usually lengthy anyway, often months of treatment with no promise of cure, or even respite.

'No other doctors here . . . ever?'

The senior nurse looked down. 'The professor prefers to work alone.'

She was loyal, I'll give her that, but it was obvious what she wasn't saying is that no one could work with him.

'Right. Well, the first change around here is that from tonight I want everyone wearing a mask. Fashion them as best you can.

All this coughing means sputum, and in that sputum are the minute *tubercle bacilli* that cause this disease.'

She blinked back at me, calm but clearly not grasping what I was saying.

I sighed, mimicking covering my mouth and nose with my hand. 'Masks on every single person who enters this ward, whether it's family visiting a patient, whether it's Matron, whether it's any of the nursing staff. No one – I repeat, no one – on this ward for any reason without a mask on.'

'Yes, doctor, but Prof—'

'Nancy, isn't it?'

She nodded.

'Well, Nancy, the professor is not here. And I don't see any other doctor except me, so that puts me in charge of these wards for now and everyone on the nursing team will just have to do as I instruct. This is how we're treating wards in Britain at the moment and it makes a whole lot of difference.'

She lowered her gaze. 'Yes, Dr Fenwick.'

'Thank you. Right, lead on and make sure that man is as comfortable as we can make him. Pillows and a sheet, please. I can tell even from here that he doesn't have days. He may only make it through one more night, so ensure it's one that ends with a smile and a kind word.'

———

I had thought twice about returning to the Calcutta Club. Fatigue had me in its grip and it was nearing ten at night, hardly an appropriate time to be paying a visit to a gentleman's room. Furthermore, all I could think of was a bath and bed. Food held no interest for me but I knew if I wasn't careful, I would go the same way as Saxon. I needed to stay well fuelled and so that too was nagging at the back of my mind.

Nevertheless, here I was, asking for Mr Johar at reception. He appeared, dour as I recalled, neither surprised nor impressed to see me.

'Dr Fenwick. How can I help you?' he said with a small bow.

'I've just come from a long day at the hospital but I feel I must check in on Professor Vickery. How has he been?'

'Brighter, Dr Fenwick, but not strong enough to leave his bed.'

I nodded. 'Yes, I imagined he would still feel weak today. Is it possible to see him? I wish to reassure myself about his condition.'

'Dr Baird has checked on him. He's only recently left.'

'Miles?'

The man didn't even blink. He held my gaze in that grave manner.

'I see. Has the professor eaten?'

'Tea throughout the night and all of today. He drank some broth at midday, as you instructed, and he took some rice and dhal at around seven this evening. I suspect he's sleeping at this time.' He glanced above to look at the clock and draw my attention that it was past ten p.m.

I drew the right message from that disapproving tone and glance. 'Well, then, let's not disturb him. Would you let him know I called in, should he wake?'

'Of course. May I call you a carriage?'

'Thank you.'

He rattled off urgent instructions to the young lad waiting nearby. 'Ranjit will see to it, Dr Fenwick. Perhaps you'd care to take a seat in the lobby?'

He clearly wanted me gone and I had no wish to linger, although by the time I was back in my flat, drying my showered hair with a towel and chewing on some of yesterday's meal reheated on the tiny bottled gas stove, I had the distinct impression that

I had been deliberately prevented from seeing Vickery. I couldn't fathom it but I suspected Miles was behind it.

———

The next day I moved far more swiftly on my rounds in my own ward and while I hoped the midwives didn't feel it, I was convinced I'd rushed them through today's lesson. The anticipation of getting back to the tropical diseases unit was thrilling. I was in a hurry to get to the TB ward in particular but when I arrived by midday – dare I admit already looking forward to surgery and another full day of care for desperately sick people – I found the professor back in charge.

He grinned at me on arrival. 'Masks?'

I nodded, trying not to look too surprised . . . or annoyed. 'It's no guarantee, but this is becoming routine in England.'

'It's good.'

'You look impossibly bright for someone who was flat on his back only yesterday.'

'And you sound cheated that I do.'

He'd caught me in open disappointment, clearly. There was no use in denying the truth and I covered my embarrassment with a shrug. 'I have a new respect for what you do here. In fact, all of these people are so very lucky to have a doctor as committed as you are. I have no idea how you keep up with all of them. There are so many, it felt beyond daunting yesterday.'

'And still you saw each one, I heard.' There he was again, pinioning me with that searching look of his.

'Well, who else was going to?'

He lifted a shoulder slightly. 'Exactly.'

'Er . . . shall I brief you?'

He grinned again, disconcerting me further. 'Why don't you?' The words belied his knowledge that I was desperate to get onto the ward and be with his patients. His tone was not mocking but it was in his gaze; there was understanding, as if he'd unlocked a door in me that only he could walk through. And now we were side by side, in a place only the two of us could fully appreciate.

'Does no one else offer help?' I queried.

'Oh, look, people do try but frankly I find them a nuisance.'

'So the help isn't genuine?'

'It is.' His mouth twisted and I liked the way the expression made him look boyish, trapped in awkwardness. 'How can I put this? They're either too much trouble or they're too ambitious and put themselves before the patients and become difficult to work with.'

Understanding dawned. 'Like Miles?'

He didn't look comfortable admitting it. 'Miles wants to run his own unit. I think he believes tropical diseases might offer him the right platform for broadening his standing in the medical community.'

I gave a soft snort. 'I see. I heard he visited last evening.'

'No doubt to dissuade you from lingering in a gentleman's bedroom.'

I didn't cover the sigh well. So I was right. Miles had prevented me from seeing Saxon under cover of attending to a sick colleague.

'Well, that's pathetic,' I murmured.

'No, Dr Fenwick, that's jealousy.' He grinned, making me wonder once again at his ability to recover quickly. 'Anyway, I'm not easy to work with, of course,' he said, referring us back to our original conversation as he picked up the first patient's notes to glance over them.

'Really?'

He snapped me a look and at my sheepish gaze he laughed . . . it was warm and genuine. 'I walked into that but I know to stand at arm's length from you, Isla.'

I didn't want to go into that territory again but I liked how he spoke my name. 'Do you always bounce back so fast?'

He knew immediately to what I was referring. 'I do. I wasn't lying to you; I hadn't been eating well or sleeping enough. I don't need a lot of either, to be honest, but the latent TB just loves that weakened situation. It only happens when my immune system is compromised but I'm able to recover swiftly.' The way his gaze rested upon me was unsettling; it was almost like a tender touch, stroking my cheek.

I became instantly businesslike and interested in the notes. 'It always intrigues me that the *tubercle bacillus* is a vegetable parasite and yet wreaks so much havoc on man.'

'If I could isolate all of my patients in dry, cool climes for a long period, I could help many of them recover.'

I nodded. 'My understanding is that outside the body, the germ is destroyed by sunlight. Apart from the obvious of close living and lack of hygiene as a spreader of the disease, how is it so easily spread in India with all the available sunlight?'

He lifted a finger. 'It can live for a very long time in the dark.'

'Right.' I frowned.

'More than that, my research has convinced me that when it dries it can be blown about in dust but still remain alive and capable of promoting disease.'

I looked back at him, astonished. 'I didn't know that.'

'I've been focusing my study in this area. The problem is that the germs are so minute they can readily float about in the air on particles of dust or moisture, which means the consumptive patient is so dangerous to other healthy people but especially in the close, cramped and often dark living conditions of a lot of the locals.'

'How do you know to work fast enough?'

He blew out his cheeks. 'That's one of the major obstacles. In India there's a tendency to attribute all obscure fever to malaria.

I insist on blood samples examined under the microscope with methylene blue staining.'

I nodded, fully conversant with the test that begins with washing and acid stripping cells before a dye is introduced that stains all material blue except the *tubercle bacillus*, which retains a red colour. I'd learned it couldn't be missed and is proof of the disease being present.

'I test every patient myself. I don't trust anyone to do it as diligently but I'm trying to set up the equipment and knowledge so it can be done all over the north, not just in these major cities.'

I sighed. 'Big task.'

'And never enough time. I'll be heading to a place called Siliguri soon. It's a growing town that services all the villages in the foothills below Darjeeling and those hill communities. But towns from all over the north in its region feed into it. I'm giving my energies to set up a solid working clinic there with proper blood-testing facilities. We can make a big difference.'

'Who pays for all this expansion?' I asked but he became distracted, calling out to one of the nurses, and didn't answer. I left it alone, although a suspicious thought suggested that he probably used his own resources.

When he returned, the thought had been lost. 'Where were we? Oh, yes. Well, I feel my role is to help everyone involved in fighting all disease to recognise TB at the earliest possible opportunity because it causes much suffering and pecuniary loss. It's a ubiquitous foe and we have to train the sick as much as those helping them. The sick must recognise their illness from the earliest symptom and know how not to endanger others. A ward like this,' he said, spreading an arm, 'is rare in India. It's more usual to have TB cases in general wards – even advanced cases – and adding more ruin to the already sickening. But more often than not I'm raging at deaf ears.'

'Is that why you're so angry all the time?'

He stared at me momentarily and I felt awkward silence surround us for just a heartbeat or two, before he smiled self-consciously. 'I am angry for many reasons but that's the major one, yes.' He laughed. 'Now, walk me through my patients and then we must discuss the arrival of the Vicereine – it's next week, I gather.'

We groaned in unison.

Later, leaning against a wall outside the back of his ward, we sipped chai in a far more convivial atmosphere than our previous effort, even though we stood near a drain and intermittently aides and bearers would come out with buckets to either refill or toss out dirty water. Despite the setting, I was feeling heart-warmed following more than an hour of earnest patient discussions in the area of medicine that I found so rewarding. Plus, I would be lying if I didn't admit to enjoying the company I kept. Seeing him in his familiar domain, I could fully understand the admiration that many held for him.

His bedside manner was the most tender of any doctor I'd ever met in my career. When he looked into the eyes of a patient to talk with them, even I felt isolated; his focus was riveted on that one patient to the exclusion of all others. The odd query he'd have for me or his aides was spoken over his shoulder, never taking his gaze from his patient. He exchanged words with them quietly, while holding their hands, not wearing the mask that I wished he would. He would help them to cough or spit into bowls, he would lay his palm against a fevered brow, or gently feel glands beneath their ears, and all the while offering a stream of soft, encouraging words in their own tongue.

I didn't think this possible from the man I had slapped weeks earlier. When it came to the children's ward, the skills he showed with his adult patients became all the more honed, as he aimed purely for comedy to make the little ones giggle. If they were able enough, they yelled his name in a united welcome. His obvious joy to be among the children made my eyes dampen as I watched him hilariously juggle three kidney dishes, before pretending to stick himself with a syringe and stumble into a mobile tray of instruments. He approached his young patients with tongue depressors sticking out of his ears or nostrils, or he deliberately got tangled in his stethoscope. At one point he involved one of the favourite young nurses in a slapstick routine that had the children clapping. But the greatest cheer was reserved for when Vickery balanced a bedpan on his nose and strolled the length of the ward while pulling an increasingly sour face, suggesting there was a terrible smell emanating from the vessel.

I wasn't prepared to be laughing aloud or to tear up while I watched Saxon Vickery. His sick youngsters, with their huge eyes and trusting expressions, were each a bundle of eagerness for him to arrive at their bedside. It was wondrous to witness and not only allowed me to glimpse where the real person behind the cold façade resided but to learn something that day about patient care.

'You make doctoring look effortless.'

He shook his head. 'Most of the adults aren't going to make it. Oh, they may go home but they're going to remain sick for years and then wither. When they're here I want them to know someone really cared . . . no, someone *white* really cared.'

The mention of skin colour made me blush.

'I'm sorry, but there are some doctors out here in India who are furthering their careers and knowledge without putting patients first. I prefer to do it the other way around. I feel a deep debt owed to the India we acquired for Mother England.'

I wanted to defend my position but he waved his fingers slightly. 'This isn't aimed at you or anyone in particular. It's all of us here. We do very well out of India but I worry that we take too much, don't give enough back to people who essentially live in abject poverty while we discuss the merits of a horse running at the spring carnival or whether it should be a gimlet or a gin fizz tonight.'

'This is not your entire burden, though, Vickery.'

'Sometimes I feel as though I'm the only one seeing India clearly.'

'You know that's not true.'

He sighed in acknowledgement.

'But you are brilliant with the patients, the children especially. I think we could all learn from you something important about patient care.'

He looked at me with such a soft gaze I felt like he needed my arms around him to hug those much-too-bony shoulders. I resisted. 'I am certainly going to leave India with a fierce intent for a more all-round care.'

'It's called holistic.'

I repeated his odd word, making it sound like a question.

'Coined in the mid-twenties by a military man, I believe, whose name I can't remember but it is based on the Greek root – *holos* – which means whole.'

I grinned. 'You're too clever for your own good. But yes, holistic, I like that. Well, what you perform is that whole therapy . . . you're taking care of their emotional health as well as physical.'

'It's vital, Isla, especially for children.' His passion felt infectious. 'People just presume because they're young that they bounce back and, yes, most of these children will recover because of good medical care but we have to make their time in hospital prompt as little fright as we can. Otherwise, we run the risk of them carrying those fears into their lives.' He shrugged. 'I believe all of us carry memories we aren't necessarily aware of and yet we respond to constantly . . . a fear of being alone, a fear of not being loved, a fear of failure. No one speaks of it and yet it comes visiting in your dreams, in dark times, when you feel scared. So, if I can make these little ones laugh, they won't be frightened of doctors or hospitals, and this generation will encourage their parents and their own children not to fear medicine either.'

'You do impress me.'

'Good,' he said. 'That's one of you, then.'

'Me and Matron . . . and most of my nursing team in the maternity ward. All the women love you, Saxon.'

He scratched his head. 'The women want to mother me. I'm grateful for it. It's flattering but I don't have the right personality to accept such kindness. I just need everyone to do their job and . . .'

'Do everything your way?'

'Yes! So much easier if everyone obliged.'

We both laughed and I sympathised because I suffered this attitude too – I just kept it hidden better than he did and I managed it far better than he ever could.

'So Siliguri? Why that place above others?' I asked, returning to our original discussion.

He smiled, as if to himself in memory. 'For all the reasons I mentioned but it holds a place in my childhood – a good place – of reward for surviving the journey down from the gardens without a single complaint. My brother and I were permitted chocolate and sweets, even a cake, if we kept our promise not to whinge.'

I probably looked baffled. 'The gardens?'

He sipped, watching me over the rim of his cup as if contemplating whether to explain. He obviously decided I could be trusted. 'Our family owns a tea plantation.'

'How marvellously romantic that sounds,' I gushed. 'So where are your tea gardens?'

He smiled, lost to good memories, no doubt. 'It's in Darjeeling, but to be accurate it's a couple of hours from Darjeeling town by a bumpy, unreliable road. It's the inaccessibility that I like, if I'm truthful.'

'Just you and the gardens?'

'Something like that. The estate is called Brackenridge . . . it's my mother's family name. Her family established the tea gardens in the previous century. My childhood home huddles above the valley overlooked by a king called Kangchenjunga.' At my frown he explained. 'Kangchenjunga is a mountain, third-highest in the world, in the west of the Himalaya. He overlooks the verdant tumble of tea bushes that carpet the valley. To me it's the most beautiful place in my world. I would like to die there, have my spirit lift into the majesty of the Himalaya and float around those snow-covered peaks.'

I was surprised at being allowed to glimpse behind his normally frosty exterior to the fiery passion that lived behind it. 'I'm guessing no one else knows?'

'I don't share my business with my colleagues.'

'Why me?'

'I don't know.' He looked vaguely embarrassed. 'Maybe because we've shared such intimacy.'

'Intimacy?' I repeated, perplexed by the idea.

Vickery nodded. 'You are someone highly trained in the ways of reserve. You know how to keep your expression even, your tone calm, your emotions in check. You'd make a pretty useless doctor in terms of patient care if you didn't have all of that under control.'

'And how does this relate to our supposed intimacy?'

'Well, you were clearly not in control a few weeks back when you lashed out with your anger.'

'I've apologised for that and I've tried to show my contrition by caring for you while you were sick.'

'You misunderstand. I'm using your sudden outburst to demonstrate that all of us walk a line somewhere between love and bitterness, anger and calm. Most of the time we can balance the emotions well enough. There is nothing more revealing about a person than when you glimpse their emotions in a raw way. And when you do, it adds an intimacy that cannot be reached unless you were there . . . unless you were part of it. Not only was I the reason for your fury but I was the recipient of it verbally, emotionally and physically. Skin on skin, Isla . . . don't tell me that's not intimate.'

I was so taken aback by his suggestion that all I could respond with initially was a gusting sound of surprise mixed with fresh embarrassment.

'Sorry. Is that too familiar of me?'

'I'll say.' I tried to sound disdainful but it came out as more self-conscious than ever. 'I mean, that's reaching, isn't it?'

His lips pursed slightly in an expression of doubt . . . or was it indifference? 'A woman's hand on a man's cheek. What's more intimate between relative strangers?'

'But the action was violent! Surely that can't be construed in this manner.'

'Ah, wait, but you are hearing the word intimate as meaning tender. Not in this instance, no. It was indeed violent, full of hurt and offence, but you were nonetheless intimate with me because you touched me, just as you were the night before last when you cradled my feverish head in your lap. I could feel your thighs through your thin frock.'

He had me trapped with reason. I couldn't deny the logic. He helped me out of my awkward silence.

'Anyway, that's why perhaps I've told you something no one else here knows. I feel we have a connection.'

I nodded, finding my equilibrium, and even smiled. 'All right, Saxon. I'll give you that. We are connected through my rage.'

He grinned, delighted by achieving his point.

'Who runs the plantation?'

'My brother.' He said it in a tone that clued me in to plenty that he didn't add.

'I'm presuming you don't see much of each other.'

'You could say we see nothing of each other. The last time was upon our mother's passing. That was more than a dozen years ago, and a dozen more years could pass and I doubt I'd think on him.'

'No love lost, clearly.'

'None. But the feeling's mutual and so it's an easy relationship, to be honest.' He drained the cup. 'We communicate via letter mostly but only for business reasons and usually via our bank or lawyers.'

'That's a pity.'

'Why?' He speared me with a glance of interest.

'Oh, I don't know. I'm an only child and often wished I had siblings.'

'It's not always fun. I think if our sister had survived, though, we might have been a different family.'

I blinked. His voice was achingly tender as he said this and I felt I was haplessly trespassing into an area of his life that hadn't been traversed in many years. 'I have spoken to no one of this, not even my wife,' he admitted with a sad snort that was half laugh, half despair.

'I'm sorry, I didn't mean to —'

'I know,' he said, his expression changing fast to a brief laugh of reassurance. It was warm and genuine, eyes wrinkling with pleasure.

'You should laugh more often.' It slipped out.

'I probably should but I need to be amused or in a state of pleasure to do so and I'm rarely either.'

'I've noticed,' I said. I looked into my empty cup. 'Well, shall we head back?'

'I think I'd like to show you the tea gardens sometime, Isla.'

I felt my breath become trapped in my chest. My throat gave a soft clicking sound that only I heard but I knew it to be the unmistakable siren of internal alarm. And this was not Saxon's fault for saying something so affectionate. It was my surprise at how instantly inflamed I felt. I was horrified by my own thrill at his offer. We both knew it was not going to happen – impossible to arrange, given our circumstances – but that he'd choose me of all people to share a secret with and to invite to such a private place kindled far more pleasure than it should.

'And I would certainly love to be able to return to England having seen a working tea plantation; we drink enough of the stuff and yet none of us know how it finds itself steeping in our teapots.' I was prattling. Could he hear the nervous pitch of my voice, or the vibration of my heart beating a little too fast?

If he did, he was gentleman enough not to show it. 'Yes, it's a pity because I think of all the people I've met in this place, it would be you who would derive the most interest and pleasure from it. It's a serene spot nestling in the foothills.' He gestured for us to walk and I fell in step. 'On a clear day, Isla, it feels as though you are moving among the gods. Above you sweeps the firmament of heaven, while below you the tiny lives of people unravel as they go about their daily work . . . and around you . . . oh, Isla, surrounding you is the humbling grandeur of the Himalayan peaks. Always wearing wraps of snow like the ermine-furred popes looking down upon the worshippers. It doesn't matter what season it is, Kangchenjunga is always dressed in virgin white.'

'Katch-chan?' I struggled to find the syllables he'd uttered.

'It's a Tibetan word that we've mangled to sound as close to it as we can get our lazy tongues around: *Kang-chen-junga*,' he repeated slowly. 'He bows to Everest but it's the highest peak in India. The people of Darjeeling and Sikkim call the various peaks of Kangchenjunga the Five Treasures of Snow.' His tone became wistful. 'I used to love waking up to that vista each morning. I never tired of it. I'd never have left it unless I had to.'

'To study, you mean?'

He cleared his throat. 'To grow up,' Saxon said. His voice now had a gritty quality to it and I heard only bitterness in his tone.

'So, you'll be running a clinic in Siliguri, you said?' I brought us back to the thread of our earlier conversation.

'Yes, as soon as duties for the Vicereine's visit are completed, I'll leave.'

'Saxon, are you sure you're well enough? It's only been —'

'And now you're mothering me, Isla,' he cautioned, but playfully.

I warded him off with my palms upraised. 'All right, all right. I'm holding a clinic of my own south of the city. There are some children there who could use some of your care and . . . happy antics.'

'Yes, Matron mentioned. One favour deserves another. Let my team know and I'll organise to attend.'

'It's the day after tomorrow,' I said with a wince, expecting him to take back the offer.

'Fine. I'll be there. Thank you again for taking care of me when I needed help and especially for . . .' He gestured into the main ward, unsure, I suppose, of how to convey his thanks wholly.

'I admit I enjoyed every moment.'

He winked at me and I wasn't sure what I was supposed to read into the action but I presumed my words were not well chosen or specific enough.

I turned away, making a furious promise to write to dear Jove tonight in a firm attempt to set myself back on course with my emotions. They were suddenly and alarmingly moving slightly beyond my control. I didn't appreciate the new affection filling the previously dark and empty corner that Professor Vickery had claimed in my life. Now it seemed to be bulging with admiration and laughter, with inspiration and something I dared not entirely confront but I knew was there, hiding in the shadows. I refused to let it come out of hiding but I knew it smiled softly at me from the depths. It wasn't mocking but it was daring me to confront an aspect to my life that perhaps just a few weeks ago I couldn't have thought possible, not even vaguely plausible.

I cautioned myself that what I needed to do immediately was school myself on how to enjoy Vickery professionally but not permit that dangerous stranger called affection to get any further grip on me. It must never show its smiling face from those shadows. Never.

I kept my promise and wrote to Jove. It was a happy letter, full of the challenges and triumphs of my work. The babies we'd safely delivered, the women we'd set on a new and better course for future pregnancies, how we'd reduced the death rate, and I came clean to him about what I called an emergency visit to tropical diseases because of one doctor being momentarily bedridden. I didn't elaborate on this, making it sound part of a chaotic week and not to be repeated. I was gilding the truth but my heart felt easier for telling that truth and for writing down Saxon's name in a letter to Jove. I spoke of my admiration for this doctor even though I found him prickly and difficult. I wanted no secrets between Jove and me. We'd agreed to be honest with each other in everything, and here I was breaking that promise.

As I stopped speaking of my work and wrote words of love to him, I found it easier to rationalise Saxon's shadow falling across the pages of my letter. I managed to convince myself that telling no direct lies constituted honesty, just as my Parker ran out of ink. It seemed somehow prophetic. The pen had been a gift from Jove on the day of my departure.

'Only released a few months ago,' he'd said, as I had opened the box and sighed with pleasure at the sight of the onyx-coloured fountain pen that glittered with gold finishes in its satin pillow. Jove was a modest man but I could hear his pride in this gift so carefully chosen: beautiful, practical, sentimental. And one only perhaps he could so easily afford to give. 'It's a vacuum filler.'

At my frown he had explained. 'No more messy top-ups with ink that runs down the side of the pen or staining your fingers.'

He watched me unscrew the pen with fascination. It felt heavy, yet marvellously weighted for my writing hand. 'I spent some time choosing what I hope is the right weight for you,' he said, as if he could listen to my thoughts. 'Ah, there,' he continued, delighted, 'that opaque sac allows you to see how much ink you have remaining. It also holds twice as much as traditional ink pens.'

'I love it, Jove,' I had breathed, genuine in my pleasure.

He had shrugged, suddenly bashful. 'Well, call me an old romantic but I decided the ink from this pen will connect us over thousands of miles through the words you'll write often to me. And I will kiss every page as though I'm kissing you, until your return.'

Recalling that scene now made me well up and I hurriedly dragged away the tears with the back of my hand and got on with refilling the pen from my bottle of Quink to finish the letter with some amusing anecdotes about the weather, a slightly runny belly I'd experienced and details of the Vicereine's visit. I sniffed as I sealed the letter, feeling a pain of disloyalty awaken through me, although I kept repeating in my mind that I had nothing to feel oncerned about.

I moistened the tissue-thin airmail envelope, licking lightly at the gum-edged triangle that would seal my words all the way to London, but my mouth was dry. Even the letter itself was mocking me for the treachery that was unwittingly building in my heart.

13

Our clinic was underway in Entally within central Calcutta. It was a mixed, depressed population of poor Christians, Hindus, Muslims and Chinese. Curiously, I noted that some Europeans resided in and around the Entally Post Office area but because the municipal slaughterhouse and the Chinese tanneries and piggeries were within Entally environs, it meant the wealthier Hindu population came nowhere near it.

The smell was powerful. It was an overwhelming stench of death that pervaded the day we operated from this village, one of nearly two score shanties of the region. I'd taught myself in the opening hour of day one how to breathe through my mouth and essentially hold my breath when I wasn't talking to a patient. Fortunately the queue for the clinic seemed to stretch well beyond the village and out into greater Calcutta – or so it seemed. Lily suggesting the tail was somewhere near Bangalore, in the south of the continent, made us smile, for there was little else to find amusement in.

While beautiful in its simple concept, my intention to run only an obstetrics clinic did not match the reality. It seemed that everyone – whether they had a weeping sore or a fever – was in that queue. I had persuaded several doctors to join me, donating their time, and was filled with silent pride to note that half-a-dozen had turned up. Miles was not among them and I think he likely would have been had we been on friendlier terms. I'd only seen him once since the incident at the Calcutta Club and he'd been polite but distinctly cool. I was not one to chase anyone's friendship and so I echoed his mood – cordial, professional, detached. I realise now that probably wasn't wise; it would only have taken a dedicated smile from me just for him, a message of friendship lurking within, to have healed some of whatever his personal rift with me was.

However, Saxon Vickery had kept his word and while I'd ensured any male doctors were kept a considerable distance from our female clinic tent, I was drawn to him, watching him examine a sick infant lying all but lifeless in her mother's arms. The child's gaze was glazed, unfocused, but what troubled me most was the woman's resignation. It occurred to me that she was already accepting that her daughter was going to die. I could tell from his body language that Saxon believed no such thing.

It impressed me once again how well he spoke the native tongue. He even had the gestures to go with his perfectly pitched instructions to make himself understood, often using those hand signals or a particular dip of his head that didn't require words at times but communicated plenty. And, as I suspected, if anyone could, Saxon could and did win a shy smile from the mother. He was urging her over something; I was smiling at the vignette, which looked as though it would have a happy ending, when Lily interrupted me.

'Dr Fenwick? I need your help with someone, please.'

'Of course.' I gave a final glance at the poignant scene of Saxon stroking the cheek of the sick child and was taken by surprise at the stirring within, like no feeling I'd experienced before. It was hard to describe. Although it was stemming from this new connection to Saxon, it really was more about the natural and gentle way this man laid a hand on the infant – healing and soothing, so full of tenderness. I would defy any woman not to be moved to see a man behaving so compassionately towards a baby. However, it was still more than that for me; it was, I now realise, the first time that I had felt the motivation and, indeed, inspiration to be a mother. I became acutely aware that I, too, wanted to have a child in my arms. Not a sick one, of course, but an infant who relied upon me, who laid her head back against my body in so trusting a manner, knowing within my arms she was safe. The love of a parent for a child had no equal. Love like this was honest and absolute.

I had to take a breath, force myself out of that moment of enlightenment and awakening and back to the squalid scene of queues of sick people.

'This way, Dr Fenwick.' Lily led me to one of the tents we'd set up for privacy. Inside was a young woman. Her eyes were strikingly uncommon in their colour and disconcerting in their pale watchfulness. 'This is Pratiti.'

'*Namaste*,' I said, to put her at ease, for she looked terrified. 'She looks healthy,' I murmured to Lily, who also seemed on edge. 'What's the problem?'

'She may be pregnant.'

'Ah.' It didn't sound problematic to me. 'How old is she?'

Lily translated my query into rapid Hindi. The girl answered, those startlingly bright eyes wide and fearful. I guessed fifteen, maybe sixteen.

'She's nearing nineteen.'

That gave some relief.

'Why is she frightened? Is her husband unhappy that she's here?'

Lily swallowed. 'She is not married, Dr Fenwick.'

In a heartbeat I had been drawn into the drama of this young woman's life. This, I knew, was now enormously problematic. Unmarried Hindu woman, pregnant, so young. I found I was unable to tear my gaze from her fragile beauty. Her eyes in the subdued light of the tent appeared of a hazel hue but I suspected could have been a grey. Rare either way, and her oval face and entirely symmetrical features made me realise she could hardly go unnoticed anywhere. Man or woman would glance a second time simply to appreciate the near perfection of that flawless complexion from which stared those scared windows. I could imagine she would have had to veil herself to avoid being seen here. She was dressed in a sage green and plum-coloured cotton sari that was help-lessly pretty to me but, I knew, would appear unremarkable as she moved through the crowds to get to our clinic.

I was stalling. Both awaited me. 'Er, all right. How long, does she think?'

Lily answered without having to check again. 'She hasn't bled on three occasions.'

I rubbed my eyes. Three months . . . maybe.

'Well, she's not showing and may not for another four or five weeks and even then only a slight bump – first child . . . so young, she's still tight as a drum. She can marry next week . . . tomorrow, even, and no one would be wiser. We can help. Deliver the child when the time comes – let's hope she's late as so many first mothers can be – and then we all behave as though her child has come early.' I was talking, making complete sense to myself but Lily, I could see, was unmoved, gaze darting elsewhere, already wanting to jump in and correct me. 'What is it?' I asked.

'She cannot marry the father.'

This only irritated me more. I felt the vexed thought bubble up that she should have thought about being inclined enough to marry him when she lay down with him three moons ago. I pursed my lips to prevent any such uncharitable advice escaping me. 'Why?' I said instead, as evenly as I could manage.

I could smell death from the slaughterhouse in the distance wafting through . . . fear, blood, gases . . . all of them leaking into the already fetid air of the tanneries creeping across the village. The atmosphere in the tent turned brittle as I waited for Lily's explanation.

'Pratiti is Kshatriya. She's their only daughter.'

I blinked.

'You remember me telling you about the Hindu caste system?'

I nodded. 'And he's not, I gather.'

She shook her head slowly. 'He's Vaishya.'

I let out a sigh. 'Explain quickly, Lily.'

'Pratiti's people are from the warrior caste . . . royals, even, of the past centuries. Naz . . . er, Nazmul, the father, is from the merchant and landowner class.'

'He's hardly a peasant, then.'

She looked down, embarrassed, though not for herself or Pratiti but for me. I was clearly like a blind man with a bludgeon in a room full of crystal.

'It makes no difference. Her family will demand that she marry and mother children from her own caste.'

'Or what?'

'They'll kill them.'

'Don't be absurd. They're hardly going to kill their only prized daughter.'

Pratiti began to weep silently.

'Dr Fenwick, they will kill him first and make her watch before they hack her to death with blades or stone her. It matters not the method of death, only that she dies for bringing the worst sort of shame that any girl could upon her family's honour. You must understand this. It is not how it is in England. There's shame but if you have broad shoulders, as they say, you can cope with it, or you can rely on your family to help, or forgive.'

I licked my lips in nervousness. It all sounded so barbaric and medieval. 'What does she want us to do?'

'She terrified. She's not asking for anything. She doesn't know what to do or where to go.'

Pratiti mumbled in weepy Bengali. I looked at Lily.

'She says they love each other.'

'Oh, for heaven's sake!' I felt a chill blanking out all that warmth of just minutes ago. Here was the true coalface . . . no, this was the cliff edge, the abyss below, because I had the skills to deliver a child, calm a fever, fix a broken limb, even detach that limb if I needed to. I could soothe a patient through a challenging disease and potentially bring them back from death's threshold but I could not fight ideology.

Religion. It ruled so strongly in India that a mother would rather see her daughter slaughtered by her own family's hand than risk the shame of the intermingling of castes. I knew I would be fighting a battle already lost to even suggest we try to talk to the parents.

'Dr Fenwick?'

'Where do her parents think she is now?'

Lily asked the question for me and then translated the reply. 'She works in one of the universities. She says she's too frightened to go home because she's now worried her eldest brother might suspect. She has five brothers.'

'Suspects what? That she's pregnant?' I felt sickened at the thought.

'No, not even that bad yet. He thinks she might be too friendly with Naz. If he knew the truth, the brothers would gang up and kill her tonight. We have to help her, Dr Fenwick. She won't make it, neither will Naz. I've seen this before. They cut them down in the street; their own families ambush them.'

I knew I wasn't thinking straight but we needed to act and both women before me were looking to me for leadership. I wanted to scream how unfair this was to rope me into such a knot of potential drama. Instead I straightened my shoulders. 'Right, get her back to the hospital and put her in a bed in an isolated ward.' Lily frowned. 'Pretend she's contagious. I need to work out what we're going to do.' I began to pace. 'Where is Naz?'

Pratiti seemed to catch my drift.

Lily translated. 'He's outside.'

'With her?' I sounded aghast.

'No. Watching from a distance. But she says he's fearful.'

Pratiti interrupted and spoke at length. I waited for Lily to tell me more. 'She says he's not worried for himself, already knows he'll die for this, but he wants to make sure that she and the baby are safe.'

'There will be no more talk of death. Where does Naz have to be?'

Lily didn't have to ask. 'He works in his father's shop.'

'Tell him to go to the hospital too – hide him.'

'Where?' She looked frightened herself now.

I shook my head. 'Anywhere!'

'No, the other Indians will tell if the family comes looking. We can definitely pretend with Pratiti because none of the nurses will spill the truth, but we can't trust the bearers or aides if we put Naz somewhere else, and he obviously can't be around maternity. What about Dr Baird?'

'Miles?'

'You're quite good friends, aren't you? Would he help?'

I shook my head. 'I doubt it.' I said no more as to why. 'Get Naz into a staff uniform.'

'As what?'

I looked at her with exasperation. 'Lily, you're going to have to think through some of this yourself. You've got me trapped in the problem and I'm going to try and work out a way to save these youngsters' lives. You must handle the hiding of them. The filing room is probably a good place. Give him some documents to push around. He is to remain there until he hears from one of us. If he's asked, he's doing a temporary job for me. He will have to muddle through with the fibs as best he can.'

'Until when?'

'I don't know!' I finally snapped. It wasn't her fault and yet I desperately wanted to blame Lily for disrupting my life with this problem; she'd made it mine, forced me to feel that unless I helped, I might as well land the first blow of the blade on Naz or Pratiti. I blew out my cheeks in an effort to find calm. 'I have to get on. Get these two away from here. I will cover for you.'

I left the tent and rejoined my team, losing myself in the work for a queue of patients that kept me challenged and distracted for the rest of the day. Sometime in the late afternoon the bell rang to end the clinic and I looked up to see that we'd looked after far more patients than I thought could be possible. Just a few stragglers left and none that were urgent, presumably because the nurses were now dealing with those.

The problem of the pregnant lovers came back to sit heavily on my shoulders. I went in search of the only person I trusted who might help us.

———

Saxon Vickery was kneeling by a boy when I found him. It appeared that he had been carried to our makeshift clinic by his parents on what looked to be a hammock of sorts fashioned from a couple of strong saris. Once again I was struck that the mother looked ready to accept the news that nothing could be done for her child. Presumably, it was the father – who squatted near the child's face, an anxious look speared towards Saxon – who had eyes only for the lad. He held his tiny hand and I could hear him speaking softly in Hindi. The patient was impassive, his expression slack, eyes vacant – they might as well have been two glass marbles pointed in Saxon's direction for their lack of response. The father pleaded. I didn't need to understand Hindi because body language was universal and this father was desperate.

Saxon glanced over his shoulder at one of the aides and said something I didn't catch and then he was straightening to his feet, the father's gaze capturing each subtle movement until Saxon towered over him in his white coat, pristinely starched, a foil for the man's raggish ensemble. My heart hurt for him and I wanted the mother to offer something to her family . . . but she remained as wooden and aloof as her helpless son. I watched Saxon cup both the father's hands in his in a gesture that urged courage and to keep faith. He gestured to the family to follow where the aide beckoned. They departed, their child slung between them, his weight dead, eyes already closed as if he'd given up the fight.

I took a deep, concerned breath, and while it inflated my lungs and then breathed itself out, I felt reassured that the boy was now in the best care of all. If anyone could save him, Saxon could . . . and would. He arched his back and lifted his golden, messy-haired head to the sun, letting its burning light fall fully across his features. In that moment of stillness I felt like an intruder; it was as though I was stealing this private moment from him by eavesdropping on it. Whatever private communion he was having, it was his alone and I suspected it was likely a supplication to the universe that helped him conquer the diseases he battled each day. I cleared my throat and pretended I'd just arrived.

'Saxon, there you are. Do you have a moment for me?'

He turned, with a grin crinkling his features. 'Just the one?'

'Do you know I struggle to tell whether you're being sardonic or flirtatious.'

He didn't answer, much to my relief. Instead he sighed. 'I need to drink something cold and sit down. Come with me,' he offered, not waiting for me to reply but taking my arm in a familiar but welcome way. 'Do you know where the word sardonic comes from?'

'No, but I'm filled with suspicion that I'm about to learn.'

'We can't have you leaving India without enriching your life somehow. It comes by way of a plant from Sardinia . . . you know, in Italy.'

'I know where Sardinia is. I have holidayed there.'

'Of course you have. Anyway, the plant, if eaten, reputedly poisons you but before you die you become convulsed with laughter.'

'Not a bad way to go,' I offered, trying to match his mood.

'Well done, Dr Fenwick. Don't you find language incredibly intriguing?'

'Perhaps not as much as you but I shall save your little gem and unleash it on my dinner guests sometime to impress.'

He smiled disarmingly. 'Think of me when you do.'

I nodded, afraid to commit aloud because I was thinking of him far too much already. The man I was convinced I abhorred had, without either of us perhaps fully realising it, become my friend; I was surprisingly at ease with him. He was the first person I could turn to with my dilemma. For all his hostile and ungentlemanly ways, I found him true. There were certainly no shadows to Saxon Vickery; like him or not, he didn't temper his manner for anyone. And while initially I was horrified by his ability to lose his equilibrium, I had probably begun to see what people like Matron saw in him or what they saw behind the bluster.

His emotions were honest, his ways with people genuine – whether he was yelling at them or tenderly promising to help their child, his laughter was rich and real. From what I could tell, there was no subtext with Saxon's actions or words. He meant everything he did, said, thought . . .

And so it was that I feigned a snicker to cover a pounding heart and the sharp, almost painful awakening that I found Saxon Vickery's gently flirtatious wickedness a highly desirable factor in this odd little life I was leading. I wanted to be immune to him, to the qualities that other women obviously had picked up on, but he'd most effectively worked his way past my thick-skinned defence. I liked him far too much in spite of the impatient, angry quality that showed itself without warning, but above this I respected and admired him. I think I was beginning to wish I, too, could be like him: careless of people's opinions, not looking for praise or physical reward, while quietly overcoming enormous hurdles, achieving success in medicine and taking all my reward from patients' humble thanks, their penniless but clutching, heartfelt relief that he had saved the life of someone they loved.

I heard him sigh as he folded his tall body into one of the camp chairs that had been set up for the staff, long legs stretching thinly like pencil pines to cross at the ankles. His boots shone to impress any parade.

'I'm guessing the spit and polish are not yours,' I said, nodding towards his feet.

He grinned lazily with a single shake of his head. 'The Club looks after our grooming needs. Another reason why so many men find it hard to go home to their small lives in England, where they might be required to shine up their own footwear.'

The bearers arrived with jugs of fresh lemonade they poured into pewter goblets and we both took a few moments to savour the delicious sensation of the chilled juice in parched throats. We drank greedily. Its tartness was balanced by a hefty amount of sugar syrup that banished the sluggish feel of weary bones. It wasn't just me; Saxon looked brighter for it too.

'How about you?'

'Mmm?' he replied absently.

'Will you find it hard to go home?'

'Home is not England, Isla. England is simply where I have a wife waiting for me,' he said, not looking my way. 'Home is India, where I was born.'

'That doesn't answer the question.'

'Well, let's just say I *will* be returning to England and I shall be polishing my own boots in the future.'

'Why not bring your wife out with you – wouldn't you be happier?'

'Because she doesn't want to leave her family, whom she's close to, and she doesn't want to live abroad. I think that's more than good enough reason and I'm not someone who would force anyone to do anything against their will.'

It didn't entirely answer my question but I decided it unwise to poke further.

'Saxon, I don't know who else to ask an enormous favour of.' I hadn't intended to open my topic so plaintively.

He turned to face me, suspicion in his eyes. 'All right. I'm sure I owe you, anyway.'

'You shouldn't feel obliged.'

'But I do. Let me pay my debt.'

'Don't be in such a hurry. Wait until you hear what it is.'

'Should I feel nervous?'

I blinked. *Don't string this out any longer*, I told myself and in a torrent I explained this morning's events. I tried to stop his interruption by talking without taking breath or pausing, hoping, perhaps, that my passion would get through to him, but I could see from his gathering rigidity that the opposite was occurring.

He sat up straighter. His eyes widened and that slumped, relaxed state of moments earlier disappeared so quickly I mourned it; it was replaced by tension, and a scowl chasing away the former humour.

'You did what?' he queried slowly in monotone.

I proceeded on the basis that this was a rhetorical question. 'I was cornered,' I replied.

'Rubbish, Isla! You're a doctor. You're the senior that staff look up to and I know for a painful fact that you don't let anyone corner you.'

Our shared happy mood had fled. The good Dr Jekyll had now been shoved aside by Mr Hyde, who had emerged from where he stood in the shadows to rage at me.

'I gave you one piece of advice,' he said, lean limbs now unfolding to stand so he could look down at me from his full height. 'One piece,' he repeated. 'And you've ignored it.'

'How am I supposed to walk away from that sort of desperate request?'

'You have to!' he snarled. 'Or you become yet another of those interfering do-gooders we spoke about, who believes our way is best and we can save the world from itself if only every culture follows ours.'

'Saxon,' I began as reasonably as I could, 'this is hardly —'

But he cut off my words when he bent suddenly, hands placed either side of my camp chair so that I became caged by the prison of his arms, his body; I could feel his polished boot toes touching mine in a soft kiss of unwelcome intimacy. He leaned closer still so I could see the roiling emotion etched into his features, his eyes intent with their stormy threat. 'Isla, you cannot save this couple. You cannot save every Hindu from his or her own centuries-old caste system. These youngsters knew the rules. They permeate every aspect of their lives, from the food they eat to the prayers they whisper . . . it's in every warm smile of their mothers and grandmothers. It's in every waggled finger of their fathers and grandfathers before them. It's in the earth they tread and the air they breathe. It is woven into the fabric of their life from birth; it is part of their souls. *The castes do not mix*.' He enunciated these last five words slowly as though I needed help understanding English. I tried to hush him, terrified of the consequences of being overheard, but he was oblivious to our surrounds, although he dropped his voice to barely above a whisper. 'Her own family will hunt her down.'

'Stop bloody lecturing me and help me! It's why I've come to you,' I said, shoving him back. He offered a hand and I took it angrily, allowed him to haul me to my feet. 'I don't trust anyone else but you.'

'I'm not flattered by that, Isla. I could hate you for it.' That hurt. He saw it too.

I wasn't able to corral my expression before it rearranged itself into one of dismay. 'Saxon?'

He glared at me, jaw grinding in that manner that was becoming familiar.

'Don't bother yourself,' I snarled. 'I know you prefer me not to meddle in the caste system but, Saxon, we've taken an oath to protect life and I don't care how you frame it, murder is murder. The fact that this is based in faith doesn't stop it being premeditated killing and I can't stand helplessly by and let that happen. Perhaps all of you well-adjusted Brits can turn away and rationalise it somehow but believe me that I won't be able to sleep again if I don't help this girl. So, I'll get them away without your help and then you needn't feel your snowy-white conscience is tarnished in any way.'

I stomped away, breathing out hard. I had no idea where I was walking to. And I hoped with all of my heart that no one was watching this vignette unfolding, especially once he had caught up with me in a few strides and had my elbow. He wasn't rough, his voice was low, but I felt a pinch at my arm where his large hand squeezed a little too hard. I winced. 'Leave me alone, Saxon. If you're not going to help, I have to sort this myself. There are lives at stake.'

'Too late to be thinking about that. You should have offered her an abortion, banished her lover, forbidden them to ever meet again and made it all go away.' He'd pulled me behind one of the tents, out of sight of public view.

'And what if she didn't want to have her child cut away from her?' I hissed.

'That's her problem. But now you've barged in and heroically made it mine.'

I shook my head. 'I don't want your help any more. It's grudging and it hurts too much to ask for it. Forget I mentioned it.'

'Again, too late. The hospital could be involved and that means we risk losing the trust of the people if we ignore the rules they live by. You may be departing after your brief sabbatical to play at doctor, but you risk leaving behind a trail that could be destructive.'

His barbs were hitting their mark; I was gushing invisible blood. 'I hate you.'

'Join the queue!'

I left him, holding my breath to stop myself saying more. As angry with myself as I was with Vickery, I did hate him on so many levels as I fumed my way back to the hospital – for toppling off the pedestal I had put him on, for puncturing the bubble of faith I'd invested in him, for that low blow about my time in India – but I had to be honest now. The fury that warmed my cheeks and tightened my throat, that made me feel as though blood was fizzing through my veins and my heart, normally silent, sounding its thump in my ears, was from knowing he was right about most of it. And while coming to the conclusion wasn't hard, accepting it with any grace didn't seem relevant because the problem was still waiting for me and now I knew I was on my own. At least if Saxon had agreed to help, I'd feel more confident of our chances.

Where was I to hide this irresponsible, dangerous pair? And for how long? And just how much trouble was I going to be in with the hospital board when they inevitably found out?

14

I decided I'd compose myself before I returned to the problem waiting for me at the hospital and detoured to the flat. I took my time
too. I was in no hurry to face the drama, or the dressing-down.
I didn't relish seeing those trusting faces that hoped I had the
answers and the clout to pull off what would have to be an escape
of sorts. It could all wait for a short period longer. I wanted to wash
away the day's grime and perspiration, as well as my growing guilt
at the rising awareness that Vickery's vision was not simply a threat.
What *could* happen probably would – that was the reality.

The notion that Naz and Pratiti were more likely than not
going to be murdered at the hands of her enraged brothers had
begun to feel like a sinking stone in the depths of my belly.

I sat in the bath, motionless, suds glistening the colours of the
spectrum around me, winking out of life as the once tepid water
cooled to urge the pimply gooseflesh on my exposed skin. I didn't
know if I was wiping away tears or simply drops of water from a
flannel but I was deflated in a way I'd not experienced before.
I knew I had to shake the self-pity because the worst that could
happen to me would be a reprimand, and then – as Vickery had

pointed out – I could head home, away from all of India's woes. But the worst that could happen to this young couple gave me a fresh crop of goosebumps.

I drew another mug of water from the pool around me and tipped it over my shoulders to rid myself of the residue of soap and salts, then stood up to catch sight of myself in the mirror. I'd lost more weight. I almost looked bony – something I might have celebrated in a different situation because I'd always thought of myself as well fleshed. But I took no pleasure in this because, frankly, I looked haggard. Jove was going to be standing at the docks to welcome home his bride-to-be and he might struggle to recognise the woman who now stared back at me from a slightly steamed-up mirror.

If anything ghastly happened to this ill-fated couple, I might as well add a few more years to that image. I wanted to blame Lily in the same way that Vickery blamed me, but there was no good coming out of that finger-pointing. What remained was for me to give up the personal pity and be decisive. The couple was in peril but I began to reason that if we could hold off the family wrath long enough, we might just give these two a chance at survival. I suspected their lives would be forever shadowed by the anxiety of discovery, isolation from those they loved, certainly poverty, I presumed, as neither of them could take anything with them. But my job now was to save their lives if I could.

I had no idea where they could go but standing in a foot of murky water with a towel clutched around me wasn't going to achieve anything. I moved with routine, from brushing my hair to dressing, emptying my mind of any thought for the time being . . . all of the regular activity felt like symbolic armour gathering about me before I went into battle. With no help forthcoming from the one friend I thought I had, I would rely on the women of the maternity unit but only those I fully trusted. I wondered about Matron.

Yes, I believed she would help. With that single tiny sliver of hope to light the way forward, I set my shoulders back, took a long, soothing breath and left for the hospital.

While the ward was calm, I sensed chaos about to erupt. The quiet atmosphere I arrived into was so taut it was not a matter of if but when it might break and shatter into disarray.

I found Lily, pinch-lipped and gloomy, tending to a mother in the early stages of her labour.

'Matron's looking for you, Doctor.'

'I expected as much,' I said, surprised how reasonable I sounded. 'Where is Pratiti?' I added in a whisper over our softly groaning mother-to-be. She had a much worse time coming but I patted her shoulder with a tight smile to encourage her.

Lily lifted a shoulder, embarrassed. 'I don't know.'

My expression turned to alarm.

She tried to explain quickly in a hissed voice. 'I left her in the library. She could fit in there easily enough without being noticed too readily.'

I nodded.

'But when I went to check on her about an hour ago, she'd gone.'

'To find Naz, probably, in the other wing . . . the filing room?' I said.

Lily shook her head. 'Naz has gone too.'

I covered my mouth to stop any expletives. 'Her brothers?' I barely breathed the words from behind my fingers.

She swallowed, blinking rapidly, with her anxiety finally allowed full rein. 'I don't think so. There was no turmoil, no warning. They just weren't where we left them.'

I ran my hands over my face as fretfulness knifed around in my belly like a clumsy surgeon. I needed to show a stronger, more disciplined front and yet the fear was getting to me too. I was a doctor, not a renegade. I had no experience to draw on for how to handle a situation like this and, to add to the angst, all I could see was Saxon shaking his head with disappointment. I couldn't hear the words *I told you so* but I knew they were circling the space around me like invisible vultures waiting to pick at the carcass of my regret.

'I'm sorry for the trouble I've caused.'

I nodded. The apology was necessary but Lily had found herself in an identical and impossible situation. I had to ease her anguish. 'Lily, how could you not help? I felt the same way. This is not your fault but I don't know how we make it better. Presumably, they've taken their chances and gone on the run.'

Lily sighed out her despair.

'Matron might have some answers,' I offered into our bleak whispering space. 'How did she find out, anyway?'

'Professor Vickery told her. I don't know how he knew; he probably found Naz hiding.'

'Bastard!'

She looked alarmed by my vulgarity but I refused to apologise for it.

'I told him in confidence,' I growled, whipping a curtain around our patient and leaning close to Lily so no one could eavesdrop. 'I didn't anticipate him splitting on us.' We were in far deeper trouble than I had anticipated.

Matron chose that moment to enter the ward. We both straightened, no doubt looking immediately guilty.

'Dr Fenwick. May I have a moment, please?'

'Yes, of course.'

Matron eyed Lily and I could feel her shrink beside me. 'You can stay on the ward, Lilian, although I shall be speaking with you later. My room, when your shift ends.'

'That's in ten m-minutes, Matron,' she stammered.

'I do know how to read the time, Lilian. See you at six. Dr Fenwick, shall we?'

I moved like a naughty child alongside her. 'I can explain,' I began.

'That will be helpful. You see, you've put us in a most fraught situation, Dr Fenwick.'

I cleared my throat, wanted to argue that it wasn't entirely my doing, but again it seemed redundant.

I followed her into my room, closing the door.

'Have a seat, Matron, please.'

She did, folding her arms, and waited for me as I let my own domain wrap its confidence around me.

I moved around the desk to sit down opposite. 'Where shall I begin?'

'Why don't I begin and save us both some breath?' she offered.

'Go ahead. Nothing you say can make me feel any worse than I do right now.'

'Really, Dr Fenwick? May I at least try?'

I swallowed hard, not prepared for her suddenly cutting tone. Her stare was terrifying.

I sat back and gestured for her to proceed.

'It's my understanding,' she began, and proceeded to tell me everything I already knew. I let her speak uninterrupted until she blinked, waiting for my response.

'All of this is true. But the facts hide the situation, or at least blur the reality. It's all very well in cold, hard reflection but in that moment I didn't know what I should do. Lily was dealing with a weeping, desperate, terrified woman who is pregnant and genuinely fearful for her life and that of her unborn child. Lily came to me, and the problem I never went searching for became mine.'

She nodded.

I pressed my point, perhaps unwisely. 'What would you have done, Matron?'

'I would have sent the girl home with the whispered advice that she needs to be immediately rid of her baby and her lover.'

I swallowed. 'You make it sound easy.'

'Nothing is easy in India. But experience teaches you that life here is mostly cruel and there are many threats to one's survival. The child, if born, is more likely to die than not. What you've done today is almost certainly sign off on its mother's and father's death warrants.'

'But that's not fair! Lily told me the couple would be murdered if I sent them away.'

'They are damned anyway, Dr Fenwick, that's the point. They both knew better but they didn't exercise that sensibility.'

'So let them be killed?'

She looked back at me evenly but said nothing. I suspected Matron, too, was torn.

'We have no choice in this,' she finally replied.

It's hard to describe the feeling that shuddered through my body at her words. Far too much adrenaline and other trauma hormones had just been spilled into my bloodstream, which would account for why I felt instantly shaky and glad I was seated. Strange pains erupted and rippled through me; there was no other way to explain them than that they felt like lightning rods. It wasn't heart failure but I could be forgiven for believing it was, and it took all my reserves not to clutch at my chest. Suddenly, air was hard to come by. It felt like all the oxygen in my room had been sucked and burned by Matron's accusation.

She could see I had nothing in response. I worried I was staring back at her slightly slack-jawed but, given my lips were numbed, I couldn't tell.

'I know that sounds dramatic, Dr Fenwick, but the Hindus can be astonishingly unreasonable and melodramatic when it comes to decisions around caste . . . especially if it is about flouting convention of that caste. It's a grave business and I have worked hard for all my nurses to respect the rules of their culture.' Her words were so precise it felt as though they were making small cuts all over me and yet all I could think of was the bigger picture and the sharpness of a machete being taken to Pratiti by a horde of zealous brothers.

I couldn't even swallow to wet my throat. *My fault*. I was the villain and the blame was already laid at my feet. I wasn't going to attempt to defend myself, as minds were made up.

'Where are they?' I said instead, astonished by how commanding I sounded.

'Safe, I hope.'

'I asked where they are, Matron. Please don't forget that I hold some rank here in the hospital.'

'Rank is given, Dr Fenwick. Respect is earned,' she said, standing. Then she looked down but opened her hands in a sort of gesture of hopelessness. 'Forgive me, but you'll find little sympathy in the hospital administration. I am fair in all my dealings, Doctor, but . . .' She lowered her shoulders with a sad sigh. 'This may not have a happy outcome.'

'You said they were safe.'

'I said I *hoped* they were safe. Someone else is cleaning up this mess, Dr Fenwick, but I'm not sure even he can pull off the wizardry that would be required to keep them hidden.'

It didn't take much to add up the arithmetic. 'Saxon?'

'Professor Vickery,' she corrected, 'has already left Calcutta with two new medical assistants.'

The guilt demons began having a party in my belly, except I felt the throb of their glee in my throat. 'He . . .' I sipped some water that was fortunately nearby. 'He's taken them?'

She nodded, lips flat and tight.

'Where?'

Matron shrugged and moved to the door. 'He refused to say, believing that the fewer people who shared the confidence, the less likelihood there was of blame to be slung around if things went badly. It meant no one would actually know where he was . . . and could put a hand on their heart and swear to that.' She blinked angrily, as though she was deliberately holding back on what she would like to say. 'He's protecting us . . . but especially *you*. I know the professor better than most; he's not nearly as heartless as his well-honed brusque demeanour suggests.' She gave a soft sniff. 'There are plenty of strutting peacocks around this hospital enjoying the life that the colony affords them. Not Professor Vickery; he's the most dedicated clinician I have ever had the privilege to work with, so forgive me if I seem a fraction biased, and not a little worried about what this will do to his health.'

She left me with that souring thought.

15

It was Miles who broke the news three days later. I was shocked to see him saunter up, never imagining our paths would cross at such an event as a fundraiser for a church school. My early acquaintance from the original journey to India, Elmay Bourne-Hughes, had sent countless invitations since my arrival, all of them politely turned down with genuine-sounding excuses. However, a mix of guilt at yet another kind invite glaring at me from my desk, and the realisation that much of my gloomy mindset was exacerbated by having no social life to speak of, prompted me to accept. I needed the distraction more than anything to dislocate me from the memory of Saxon's wrath and Matron's hard line.

It had seemed a harmless evening to attend and one I could escape quickly once I'd been seen. I didn't anticipate many others and I figured it was remote enough that most of the social climbers wouldn't be there and I could at least hug Elmay and generally have a brief interlude among other people's conversations, no matter how banal they might be.

My inexperience of the Calcutta social scene, of course, had left me unprepared for the fact that Elmay did nothing in half measures and it felt like most of the European community had crammed onto her lawns late on Sunday afternoon to help raise funds for the school. I'd barely paid attention to its name and perhaps most others were in a similar situation, coming along more for the socialising, with tossing a few pounds at the fundraising aspect a mere formality.

Elmay greeted me with the identical infectious warmth I recalled from our journey. 'Darling Isla, you look waif-thin, my dear. That hospital is killing you, surely?' she said, kissing me on both cheeks and holding me back to examine me. Then I was suddenly pulled to her bosom for another hug. 'Oh, my dear, but thin hangs well on you. You look wanly beautiful and dare I say only the merest hint of the sun kissing those exquisite cheekbones makes you look ethereal.'

'Elmay, really! You should be on the stage.'

She chuckled. 'It is lovely that you've finally come. Can I introduce you to some people?'

I didn't get a chance to respond; instead, she took me by the hand and led me to a group of military men and their wives and I was grateful to become lost in their discussion: at first serious-minded chatter about Mahatma Ghandi and his starvation protests before moving into the whole ugly business of terror attacks.

'Poor old Anderson's had so many attempts on his life now, I think he just takes it in his stride,' one fellow remarked about the Viceroy, his moustache ending in a needlepoint at each end of his thin lips. His listeners duly chuckled on cue.

'Even women are getting involved now,' one of the wives muttered to me. 'I was told two men were sentenced to death for attempting on the Governor's life and a woman sentenced to transportation for life. What could she be thinking!' A sip of her Bengal Moonshine – Elmay's specially prepared cocktail for the evening – was swallowed to help the alarm. 'Oh, gosh, this is good. Elmay's surpassed herself this time.' She grinned at me with sticky-looking lips that had been painted an engine red.

I smiled in a fake way. What else could I do? I sipped my Moonshine too and let them talk around me, fixing a look of interest onto my face, but my thoughts scattered to Saxon and the clean-up of 'my mess'.

Despite Elmay's high hopes, the Governor of Bengal would not be in attendance this evening, and our hostess looked downhearted when she made the announcement. Looking around, I couldn't imagine she would remain disappointed for long. The turnout was enormous. The church school would surely enjoy a most welcome injection of funds shortly.

I soon drifted from the main pack and wandered to the Bourne-Hughes's ostentatious fishpond that sat high above ground. It was away from the fairy lighting and the chamber music that accompanied the feathery conversations buzzing around the garden like fireflies, igniting into bursts of laughter from time to time.

I'd achieved it, I realised. Barely one hour from arriving at Elmay's home, I'd managed to isolate myself from the partygoers and stood now in the shadows like an interloper. A young woman startled me when she broke from the darkened area to my right.

'Oh!' she said. 'I think I've taken a wrong turn on my way back from the powder room.' She glanced back over her shoulder to a door from the end of the house and pointed. 'Yes, I came through there but should have walked back and out of there.'

I wasn't interested but schooled myself to be polite at least. 'Hello, I'm Isla Fenwick.'

'Florence Petherby.' We shook hands briefly, delicately even, in the way she just managed to touch fingertips lightly through gloved hands. 'Recently arrived,' she admitted.

'And how are you liking Calcutta?'

'Oh, it's marvellous,' she gushed, surprising me. 'So many parties and wonderful events to enjoy. I'd been warned that it's confronting but I've kept away from the streets outside . . . um, you know . . . sticking to the —'

'European settlement?' I offered. She did not hear the sarcasm because I buried it before it could grab my words and colour them.

'Yes,' she admitted. 'I'm not very good with squalid situations and I hear it's really very dirty and crowded outside of the city.'

'Wretched locals, eh?' I agreed in a saccharine voice. I didn't dislike her – how could I? I didn't know her – but I didn't want to spend any more time with this vacant girl who couldn't be more than twenty. She wasn't moving away, though.

'Um, are you married?' she enquired, large eyes glistening in the low light from a few candles burning nearby.

'No. But she shall be soon, won't you, Isla,' said a familiar voice, answering on my behalf. 'To a Mr Mandeville, wealthy MP and philanthropist in London?' Miles Baird slipped a proprietorial arm around my companion's waist.

She beamed at him, and then me. 'Oh, you know Miles Baird?' I nodded. 'And that he's a doctor?' my new friend offered in a breathy voice.

'Yes, Miles and I are colleagues,' I admitted. I frowned. 'Hello, Miles. Haven't seen you in a while?'

'I've been on a special project.' He put a finger to his chapped lips as though it was top secret. I wasn't even vaguely interested to know more.

'Oh, you're a nurse?' his new beau exclaimed, sounding impressed.

'No, Florrie,' he corrected. 'Isla is a doctor at my hospital.'

'A doctor?' She made it sound like an alien concept and needed to take another look at me to see that I was a woman and that she hadn't been mistaken.

I dismissed her ignorance, focusing on my fellow doctor. 'I'm surprised to see you here at this fundraiser.'

'Why?' He shrugged with nonchalance. 'It's a good cause for the school. My surname alone demands I do the right thing. Not all of us Scots are tight with our money.' He chuckled and Florence followed suit with a look of sugary adoration that worried me. What was she seeing in this man that I didn't?

I nodded. Of course. This was a fundraiser for the Scottish Church Collegiate School, one of the oldest in the country and founded by the first missionary from that church to India.

'Well, I think they'll raise a tidy sum,' I replied, lost for much else to say.

'Oh, Miles, there's Lucille. We came out on the boat together!' Florence said, more excited than I thought the sighting should prompt.

'Hurry along, then. I might lurk a little longer with Dr Fenwick. I need to speak with her. I'll catch up in a minute.'

I frowned; I wanted him gone, or for my normally reliable mind to deliver me a reason to excuse myself. But it was as vacant in that moment as Florence's smile when she wished me good evening.

'I hope we meet again, Dr Fenwick.'

I couldn't imagine we would and I chose to grin back at her with a polite nod. 'Enjoy your time here, Florence.'

She disappeared in a froth of expensive cotton lace, no doubt deemed ideal in some London store for the tropics, and I was alone with her escort for the evening.

'No need to remain here, Miles. There's only boredom in this spot,' I admitted, throwing in a self-effacing smile. 'I was actually about to make my excuses when your friend walked up.'

'Delightful creature, isn't she?'

'Er, yes, indeed. Are you fond of each other?'

'She's here to find a husband . . . one of the fishing fleet,' he quipped.

I had never heard the derogatory term before and felt immediately offended on Florence's behalf.

'So you're one of her suitors?' I sounded neither intrigued nor bored.

'The only one, I hope. She's pretty enough and has pedigree: very wealthy family.' He tapped his nose again. I wanted to punch it. 'I suspect many of the military men will be making a sharp angle to Miss Petherby, so I have staked my claim.'

'You have it all over them,' I said. It could be taken either way but Miles heard none of the sarcasm that I hid well for my own petty amusement.

'A doctor is a good catch for any fishing expedition, Isla. With a military husband she could be sent anywhere in this savage land. Have you heard I'm moving on?'

That was unexpected but of course he'd set out to catch me off-guard. I kept my voice even. 'I hadn't heard, no. Is it a happy move?'

'I haven't been fired, if that's what you mean,' he replied, only a small flash of irritation peeping through his controlled smile.

'I didn't mean that at all. I simply mean are you happy?'

'Yes. And if Miss Petherby works out as I hope, I may even be happier. It would be ideal to take a wife with me to Simla – er, that's the British summer capital – when the Delhi climate finally wears the European community down.'

It was an important posting so close to government and for Miles I could tell this was all about social climbing. Poor Florence Petherby, but then maybe their shallowness suited each other. 'I see. How lovely for you.' I didn't bother to ask what his new position was. I really didn't care.

'Yes, lots of frivolity and a need for more clinical practitioners up there in the Himalayan region above Delhi. It's really very beautiful too. English cottages, primroses growing wild and a whirl of fetes, balls, picnics, hunts, parties, polo and cricket.'

'Not to mention governance of India,' I added, keeping any tartness from my voice.

He tapped his nose yet again at my remark in that increasingly irritating way of his while grinning sardonically.

I began to wish I hadn't come tonight. Miles looked as though he was building to something, leading me, and yet I couldn't extricate myself easily. I didn't want to encourage his vendetta – I wanted my remaining time to be focused on work, not fending off a vengeful colleague. The maelstrom of potential functions I could have chosen to attend these last months was overwhelming and I'd dodged most of them with such sure-footedness I had begun to adopt a hidden smugness.

I was aware he was waiting on me. 'I'm pleased for you, Miles. I suspect you'll fit right in.' It was lukewarm congratulations at best and I didn't want him to think me envious, so I added, 'They're fortunate to find someone as skilled as you to up sticks and head to the mountains.'

He smiled, enjoying the compliment, taking time over lighting a cigarette. He offered me one but I shook my head. I smelled the naptha fuel as the lighter ignited and then the waft of burning tobacco overrode it. The glow from the cigarette as Miles inhaled lit his face and my instincts were surely right. There was something contrived about his expression; he was building to something. I felt like someone about to fall off a ladder, every muscle instantly tensed, insides feeling as though they were gripping but getting no purchase. The flare disappeared and his face was thrown into shadows. 'Pity about the Vicereine's cancellation,' he said, his tone lazy.

I sighed inwardly. Is that all it was? His chance to gloat about Saxon and me not getting to shake the Vicereine's hand?

He genuinely did not have my measure or he'd have known how little this mattered. 'Relief for me, to be honest. I don't go in for pomp and ceremony.'

'I meant it was a shame for the hospital.'

'Of course it was.' Where was this leading? I braced myself for whatever came next but made an attempt to leave. 'Anyway, Miles, I'm glad to see you and hear your good news. I'll be on my way, though, let you get back to the party and your delightful Miss Petherby. I do hope we'll hear news of an engagement short—'

It fell on deaf ears as Miles had begun to talk over me. 'You look exhausted, Isla. Pathetically thin too.'

I mustered a shrug. 'Don't worry about me, I'm a doctor.'

He grinned predictably. 'What you need is a pick-me-up and some distance from your routine life,' he said.

'I thought I was doing just that by attending this event.' I straightened my handbag over my arm. It was a clue I was about to bolt.

'This is hardly a tonic for the work we do.'

'You have just the thing, I'm guessing?'

'Well, now you mention it, I do. How about a nice cool gin at the Club?'

I looked back at him and I knew everything from my gaze to my tone seemed wearied. Faking it was not a strength of mine. 'And what about Miss Petherby?' It was the best I could do in the moment but I realised it sounded like encouragement rather than a definitive answer. I didn't wait for him to try. 'It's a lovely thought, Miles, and kind of you to think of me, but I am exhausted as you rightly note and I'm heading home for a bath and bed.'

He nodded, as though he'd fully anticipated the brush-off. 'Another time, perhaps?'

'Definitely,' I lied, not in the slightest guilty over it.

'See you anon,' he murmured, turning to leave. 'Oh!' he said, dramatically halting, clicking his thumb and forefinger as he turned back. I hadn't escaped. 'Damn, how remiss of me not to make condolences to you as soon as I arrived.'

I frowned, shaking my head. 'What about?'

'Your Hindu couple,' he prompted and I could hear the feigned sympathy in his voice.

I never lose my amazement at how rapidly the body can respond to fear; it's a primitive trigger but it is reliably powerful. My lips tingled instantly at his words. Numbness followed and I recognised that every ounce of me was now on alert, adrenaline flooding my bloodstream. 'What are you talking about?' It was obvious even to me that I was not covering my terror. My voice sounded thick and constricted. Why couldn't the vacuous Florrie Petherby feel a spike of jealousy and come back to link her arm around her horrible man and make her claim?

He was a smiling cat, torturing a mouse.

I waited for the kill.

Miles made a *tsk*ing sound of pity that infuriated me but I found my father's infinite calm. I took a step back, forcing my features to now give him a serene look that told him I was confounded. 'You're going to have to explain, Miles, because I'm too tired to play a guessing game.' I sounded impressively bored.

'Sure. I won't insult you with tact, then. I heard today that the family of your pregnant Hindu girl found her.'

It was no good; I couldn't contain the fright any longer and not beyond the fresh despair that this revelation delivered. 'You're lying!' My voice was small and accusatory. Was that really my finger poking Miles in the chest?

He wasn't at all unnerved. If anything he was taking a page from Saxon's book and going for the sardonic smile. I wondered in that ghastly moment of despair whether he had practised in a mirror, desperately trying to capture what came effortlessly to the professor. 'No jest, dear Isla, and no lie either. I'm so sorry for you . . . and for Vickery. This won't reflect happily on either of you.'

'What do you know?'

'I know all of it, but perhaps . . .' He shook his head with such a patronising smile he was fortunate I didn't respond with violence.

Nevertheless, despair had to find a way out and, like water finding a hole to leak through, it navigated towards my mouth. 'Go to hell, Miles!'

I'm still not sure who was the more shocked between us as the insult bounced in our near space off the trees, his chest, the stone that surrounded the pond. I didn't back down, though. In fact, I'd like to have cursed at him using the savoury language of a shipyard worker; this felt tame but it also felt as though a stopper had been released and all my pent-up tension was allowed to escape. It made me feel surprisingly strong. I gave him a final threatening sneer before stalking away deeper into the garden while his face was left a picture of reddening shock. My triumph only lasted seconds as Miles chased me into that quiet part of the garden.

'Well, well. Who'd have thought that Icy Isla would have such a fiery temper?'

Oh, how I hated this vicious man. I was waiting for him to grab my elbow or reach for my shoulder to give me an excuse to scream at him not to touch me and hopefully bring the fundraising crowd scuttling to my aid. He didn't, though; he was careful to simply stride alongside me.

'Really, Isla, I'm sure your fiancé wouldn't —'

I halted so abruptly he had to turn back. 'Listen to me. From now on you are to address me as Dr Fenwick. Furthermore, you are not to refer to my fiancé again. He is not known to you and you can't possibly judge what Mr Mandeville would or would not approve of. And also from now on, Dr Baird, unless our paths cross professionally and we need to discuss a patient or hospital practices, please be assured I have no desire whatsoever to share a moment of social time with you. I was lying when I said we can share a drink together another time and I did that to save you some humiliation, but frankly I don't care about you saving face, or your feelings any more, because you have so little regard for anyone else's. I have no intention of sharing another moment with you. I find you deeply unattractive because you are small-minded, weak, grasping, selfish, and you seem to suffer a permanent crisis of ego. I doubt you will ever measure up to Saxon Vickery as a doctor, as a decent person . . . or indeed as a man.' I could see how my final barb hurt him. Would I pay for that?

His composure was quick to reassemble itself. 'Dr Fenwick, I was simply being polite but that's no hardship that you don't wish to spend time with me. I'm about to be engaged, as you know.'

I wanted to walk away; I should not have allowed him another breath.

'I simply felt you should be apprised that it wasn't a happy-ever-after for your fairytale couple – they were doomed, as most of us would have surmised from the outset. The hospital directors have been briefed via the offended families at our intrusion. I learned earlier today from one of the secretaries of their astonishment that anyone from the hospital would meddle in the affairs of caste.'

'I don't want to know any more.'

'Why not? It was your doing.'

I looked back at him with disbelief.

'I didn't push them together!' I said and could hear how desperate I sounded, trying to distance myself.

'No, you did worse. You encouraged them to remain together. You made it possible for them to believe they could flee the wrath of their families and escape the vengeance that is demanded by centuries of their cultural rules. You lied to them. You're pretty heartless, Dr Fenwick, and you left others to clear up your mess. I could even feel a moment's sympathy for Vickery, who bore the brunt of their deaths.'

And with a small smile he turned and walked away from where the boxer lay on the ground after a knockout punch to her jaw.

16

Adding to my grim mood was monsoon season and we were in the thick of it. The odd pillows of cloud that had seemed to languish in the sky over Calcutta a few months back had begun to cluster into larger masses before those skies opened and monsoon broke viciously over the city. I told myself the heavens wept with me. Booming thunder had heralded the arrival of our wet season as though the gods were all pounding on drums to announce the long-awaited, life-giving rains that would cleanse the city, washing away its ills and miseries, grow its food and fill its waterways.

For most, however, it meant miserable inconvenience. It rained for hours at a time; I don't know why I thought monsoon season meant it would shower for a few minutes each day and disappear. Instead, it was a relentless torrent that lasted for half of each day. And when the skies briefly stopped their tears, the streets began to steam beneath the still unforgiving summer heat that turned the city into a sauna. Calcutta, I realised, had little defence, despite the centuries of knowledge of the inevitable months of being sodden. If life was tough in the heat, it now became intolerable in monsoon as traffic became bogged, trams slowed to a halt and roads were awash. It seemed at times as though only the tough, rangy rickshaw drivers, with their nimbleness and strength, could move, hauling cargo while calf-deep in the filthy water that coursed through Calcutta's narrower streets.

The rains were necessary, of course, or Calcutta would founder, but that didn't make the downpours or the gluey atmosphere they left behind each day any easier to bear. As thin as my cotton clothes were, they still stuck unhelpfully to every inch of skin they touched, and I had become one of those women who dabbed at their face and neck with a handkerchief, making swooning sounds. I'd considered myself a resilient person who didn't wilt fast under any sort of pressure, but this climate had my measure and I found myself beginning to yearn for an English winter. Perhaps that was life's way of pointing me in the direction of where I should be; that's what I told myself, anyway, as I lay damp on my bed, beneath a spinning ceiling fan, unable to grab much more than bursts of fitful sleep.

The hospital went on high alert from the first cloudburst and it was right to do so. My mind was jumbled over Miles's cruelly delivered revelation, and I constantly fretted over my involvement in the bleak outcome. Would I make peace with Saxon when I met him again? This thought was mercifully distracted by an outbreak of malaria, which seemed inevitable with this much stagnant water suddenly in our midst.

Female mosquitoes had waited for the moment of that first explosive torrent, busily hatching and injecting their human hosts with the sporozoites that would move through blood vessels to liver cells in order to reproduce. I was only too aware of how newly infected red blood cells produced hundreds of new infected cells, and how the human response to this war inside the body was fever, vomiting, liver dysfunction, chills, circulatory shock, jaundice . . . ultimately death if left unchecked.

There was no time to waste lingering on my bruised emotions. Not waiting for permission, I immediately relocated to Saxon's ward. Without him I was the next best defence, and it seemed the hospital administration agreed because it didn't even bother to query the shift but sent a note hoping I'd at least keep a supervisory eye on the maternity wing. As much as I could tell Lily wanted to come with me to tropical diseases, I left her mostly in charge of maternity, knowing she would keep it safe and ticking along without me.

Meanwhile, I not only found the isolation ward soothing but privately once again enjoyed the intensity that the infectious diseases wing presented. By the end of my first week I had every patient sleeping beneath a net that had been sprayed with a solution that was toxic to mosquitoes, poisoning most of them long before they could breach the net. Staff were surprised.

'You understand that the mosquito net is supposed to keep them out,' I explained to the nursing team. 'But the net is not one hundred per cent effective and it will only take one or two people to be infected here for our whole hospital to risk infection. Take the precaution. Be diligent in the treatment of the nets. You're saving lives simply by taking that extra care.' I dismissed them by looking away to the senior bearer and my next pet project. It would take every available hand, including mine, and I was not too proud to don a mask for this laborious task. 'Where is your team?'

'Ready, Doctor.'

'Good. They are to spray every surface around the entrances. Wherever water is gathering I want it coated in a light film of kerosene; we have to kill the young mosquitoes as they hatch. And this is to be done every two days because the fresh rains will dilute our efforts.'

He bowed and disappeared. I held faith in him to carry out my instructions carefully because I knew Saxon trusted him. I would join him soon in that battle. But first I turned my attention to our sickening patients before busying myself getting bulletins out to the other doctors in various departments offering guidance for their wards and how to keep the fevers away.

And all the while at the back of my mind he paced, like a ghost, a finger of shame pointed my way: Where was he? How was he?

Days passed in a blur of frantic activity as the entire hospital battled to stay on top of the disease, dispensing quinine at makeshift clinics on the streets of the most poverty-stricken neighbourhoods where malaria was raging. There were horror stories of dogs and other carrion eaters feeding on exhausted bodies that had slumped to die in doorways or on rubbish heaps. We were up against an invisible foe but the battle raged nonetheless.

It was Matron once again who returned my focus. She arrived one evening on the ward where I was momentarily alone, awaiting a shift change. I had leaned against a wall and haplessly, somewhat pathetically too, I allowed myself to slip down it until I sat on the floor, too weary to care, my knees pulled up tight to my chest. I didn't want to cry from exhaustion – that would be truly weak – but I just wanted the fear and frenzy to stop, even for a few hours, so I could sleep without guilt and forget the world . . . forget him.

'You know you alone can't save Calcutta from itself.' It was said kindly but there was a thin, sarcastic edge to the words that I knew was meant to shake me.

I looked up, startled, and then her sympathetic smile soothed me like rubbing oil into tired skin. 'I want to, though,' I replied.

She offered a hand and I took it. I was hauled to my feet and I sloughed off my fatigue as best I could with a small stretch. 'Thank you, Matron. I promise I wasn't feeling sorry for myself.'

I'm sure she knew it. 'No time for that. But I would urge you to congratulate yourself and your team for containing infection.

The hospital at the moment is holding its own. No new cases, as I understand it, which is unheard of during monsoon season.'

I nodded. 'None that we've taken in since this bad outbreak. Scores outside, of course.'

'Yes, but that's India, as cruel to some as she is bountiful to others. Don't make this about you.'

'I wish I could be that philosophical, Matron.'

'You take it all too personally, Dr Fenwick.' Although we'd been looking at one another, our gazes met awkwardly now as if our minds were sharing an identical thought. I had the horrible notion that I was about to blubber in front of her. Perhaps Matron sensed it too.

'I've ordered a pot of tea. Won't you join me?'

'I —'

She heard me reaching for an excuse. 'Let's talk, Dr Fenwick.'

I trailed behind her, nodding to the new nursing team, pausing briefly to issue them instructions. I caught up with Matron just as tea was delivered to her room. I noted there were two sets of cups and saucers already laid out; clearly she'd been expecting me.

'You don't look well, Dr Fenwick.'

'Just tired.' I shrugged. It wasn't a lie but it also wasn't all the truth.

She poured for us both. 'Well, you'll be amazed at what a good, strong Assam can achieve,' she said, handing me the rich, tarry brew. The mention of the tea made me think about whether Saxon was somewhere sipping a first flush Darjeeling. It only made me feel sadder. She pointed to a small jug on the tray.

I added some milk, watching its brief stream dive into the copper depths and eddy back up in whorls to turn the liquor an opaque amber. I smelled the tannin and relaxed into the first malty sip that provided an unexpected briskness as I swallowed . . . and sighed.

'Good, isn't it?' Matron said.

'Mmm.'

'Second flush,' she explained.

Did everyone but me understand tea? I wondered. 'I'm not that well versed with the varieties of tea but this is delicious.'

'Assam is robust. You'll certainly wake up with a cup of this. Darjeeling is more delicate.'

I smiled. 'It's nice to talk about something other than malaria.'

She returned my smile but then her features shifted her expression to serious. 'You've heard about the Hindu couple being found, I presume?'

I nodded. 'I haven't thought about much else for a week. I haven't even been able to write home because I can't muster a single jolly word while I worry about Pratiti and Naz . . . and of course Professor Vickery.'

'Is that why you're not sleeping?'

'I suspect so. Matron, I'm very sorry.'

'Dr Fenwick . . . Isla. I personally lay no blame. If I'm truthful with you, I would have considered it odd – knowing your ways – if you *had* turned a cold heart on the couple.'

That was a surprise. My gaze flashed over the rim of the cup I was sure I was hiding behind to meet hers.

She continued. 'Pratiti was beautiful, young, in love. I didn't meet her lover but apparently he was a gentle soul who worshipped her. He offered to stay behind and take the punishment, begged us to help Pratiti to safety.'

I realised I was shaking my head with pity and a sense of helplessness. 'I didn't want to involve the hospital – knew it was potentially dangerous – but it was the only refuge I could think of to buy some time.'

'Dangerous is probably overstating it. But troublesome certainly. It has put the hospital administration into . . . well —' she let out a breath '— shall we say a difficult position.'

Matron had obviously meant to have this very conversation. I sensed she was the messenger, no doubt sent on the unsavoury mission.

'So, they need to make an example of me?'

'No.' She sounded discomfited all the same. 'It's not like you have to wear a hair shirt.'

Neither of us smiled at her self-conscious jest.

'But I need to take the blame?'

'That's a harsh way of regarding it, but . . . yes, Isla. Someone must be seen to shoulder the responsibility.'

'I do shoulder it. It was my decision. I knew there might be repercussions but in the moment I felt I had no other choice. I've dedicated my working life to saving lives. Surrendering Pratiti or Naz for murder contravenes my Hippocratic oath and everything else I stand for.'

She nodded, and had the grace not to remind me that they were murdered in spite of me. 'Secretly . . . and I'll deny this if you repeat it, I might have attempted the same in your shoes, if that helps?'

I smiled for her benefit but I was angered by the hypocrisy that the hospital was not going to back me up; I just didn't have the strength to show it. 'What would the administration like from me? Is it resignation?'

Matron shifted in her chair. My candour had caught her by surprise. Knots of shock trilled through me. Was I about to be sacked from my position?

'Isla, hospitals can be highly political places . . .' She struggled to find the right words, shaking her head with obvious disgust at being the person charged to have this conversation.

I refused to let her speak whatever words were catching on invisible thorns in her throat.

'Matron, may I ask, have you heard from Professor Vickery?' It was the first thing I could think of to stop Matron having to say what she had presumably been sent to convey, but also it was the single topic that had occupied my mind outside of the malaria outbreak.

She looked momentarily relieved to be sidetracked. 'I have. He rang me.'

I waited, tongue-tied. But she left it there so it was up to me to probe.

'Is he all right?'

'No. He's devastated by how events have turned out. He witnessed both deaths, struggling to save Pratiti at the end, and got himself injured in the fray to help both of them. Ideology in the hands of the zealous can be brutal. There are no half measures in this instance, no forgiveness, no way back for those who trespass against clear rules they've known since they were old enough to understand language. Death is the price. Unfortunately, our Professor Vickery has been injured too and I fear for his life now as his old foe – the latent TB – may take advantage of his vulnerability.'

In shock I put the cup back into the saucer, trembling. I didn't think my shaking was obvious yet so I anchored my hands together in my lap and prayed my voice remained even. 'How badly hurt is Saxon?'

She sipped her tea calmly. 'Physically he'll recover from his injuries – some cuts, burns as I understand it. Emotionally, I suspect he's fragile. Like you, he takes life's bruises personally. My real concern, though, Isla, is the illness. I don't want it turning serious on him. He recovers quickly normally but he's injured now, and weak.'

I gaped at her and was ashamed how quickly I set aside the trauma of Pratiti and Naz. 'It's back?' My voice sounded as though it was squeezed out of me . . . tight and breathy.

'He's not saying as much but I'm guessing that's the truth. I've been nursing long enough to know the wheezing sound of someone with a chest infection.'

'He used the clinic at Siliguri to flee to with my couple, didn't he?'

Matron nodded; she looked impressed that I'd worked it out. 'And nearly got away with it. I've only just discovered this too. His plan was to move them into the foothills; when he bade me farewell he sounded confident they'd be able to disappear. It was inspired; it could have worked.' Her voice held only admiration. 'I wanted it to work . . . for both of you. I admired your fast thinking and action, I applauded his courage. We'd be having an entirely different conversation, of course, if they had escaped. You'd both be heroes.'

'So someone told the families, you're saying?'

She gave me a look that conveyed the opposite of what she next said. 'I didn't say that.'

I think I already knew who probably passed the word down the line and my belly heaved, bile surging to burn at my throat in that moment of realisation. Nevertheless, I felt obliged to qualify my suspicion. 'Who else might have worked out where the professor was going?'

'Professor Vickery's clinics are few and far between but they're routine. He always holds a clinic at least once a year at the foothills of the Himalaya.'

I had no concept of the foothills and my knowledge of the Himalaya stretched only to Mount Everest, having read somewhere of its extraordinary height of twenty-nine thousand feet, which I could barely conceive, and the drama surrounding the 1924 attempt to climb the northern route of the Tibetan side. I'm sure everyone in Britain knew they'd disappeared into the clouds on the eighth day of June that year, never to be seen again. My thoughts were wandering I was so worried.

'You should see those foothills before you leave India, Isla. There's no point in me trying to describe the drama of the Himalaya;

it must be your own spiritual experience. People say once you've seen it, you'll never be quite the same, as the Himalaya will have you in their thrall.'

I smiled. 'Maybe I shouldn't, then.'

'Maybe,' she concurred, her intense gaze urging differently.

'Matron . . . how sick do you think he is?'

'My instincts suggest dangerously so.'

I swallowed the bile, tasting the sourness. 'Will you let me know if you discover more?'

'If you wish. Thank you for stepping into his shoes in his absence. The hospital is grateful that you did.'

'Not that grateful, perhaps?' I couldn't resist cutting back to our original conversation.

She ignored the barb. 'You don't have much longer with us, do you, Isla?'

'My plan was to leave by the end of September but perhaps now . . .' I trailed off, unsure of my thoughts. I felt Matron was now guiding me somewhere.

'Well, given that there is only a month or so before you would have left us to return to your life in England anyway, and given that your expertise in TB could be put to good use elsewhere than in the hospital . . . and finally, given that it could be wise perhaps to distance yourself from the wards . . . er, just to give the administrators time to sort out a solution to our present dilemma, perhaps you might like to do some travel before your departure? The north is always better at this time of year.' She ended on a note of hopefulness as though desperate for me to hear beneath the words to what she was actually suggesting.

'So putting some space between me and the hospital right now is probably the best course?'

'In my opinion, yes. Sometimes issues that seem important in the moment have a way of losing their potency over time.

Memories can be surprisingly short, particularly if the source of interest is not easily seen. The hospital has far more pressing needs than taking steps against one of its prized recruits for following her raison d'être, shall we say? I feel if you're not as visible, then the families of the deceased, the politicians who may have something to say about it all, the hospital – anyone, in fact, with an opinion on the topic on the social scene of Calcutta – have no moving target.'

She was right. And I knew precisely where she was pushing me now. 'Then, Matron, if you are comfortable that we have the fevers relatively under control, and confident that the team can contain any new outbreak —'

'I am,' she cut across me. 'You've done a sterling job in setting up solid practices.' She blinked, urging me to say what I guessed she hoped.

'Then maybe I do need to see the Himalaya before I leave. Perhaps a few weeks' travel will aid my own health; I could certainly enjoy a break, as I realise I haven't had so much as an afternoon off in many weeks.'

'Working around the clock almost, week in, week out, is good for no one,' she agreed. 'Take that break. I'm sure when you return you'll find this issue we've discussed has cooled from warm to cold and no one will have a taste for it any longer.'

She was clearly urging me to take her advice so I could leave this post with my record unblemished.

'Should I put in formally for some leave time, Matron?'

'No, my dear. I can handle that. I came across you tonight physically drained, exhaustion threatening to make you ill, and I've suggested you take some time away to recover from a schedule that no doctor should be following. Heavens! The hospital is potentially at risk of being accused of negligence.' Her tone feigned growing indignance.

We shared a conspiratorial smile. I admired how she balanced a tightrope between management and staff. It seemed unfair that the Registrar steered clear of this reprimand and left it to Matron, who technically was not part of the chain of command for the clinicians. Nevertheless, her encouragement, which was feeling increasingly less subtle and more like a shove in the back, did make it seem as though a veil was being lifted from before me and I could suddenly see the obvious way forward. I had a debt to repay to a sickening man.

'I'd prefer no one knew where I was travelling, Matron —'

'That's fine, Dr Fenwick. I'm glad I left you before I realised I hadn't asked where you might head for your brief respite.' She nodded, making clear I needed to say no more. Matron stood and hugged me. 'Safe travels. Get some rest and my best advice is that you seek some fresh mountain air.'

There was no doubt that she knew where I was headed.

'Now, let me give you a hug of thanks,' she said, sounding deliberately brisk to hide the rising emotion I sensed we were both feeling. 'Just in case.'

I didn't ask what the *just in case* meant, but I could guess. Like me, she suspected I likely would not see Calcutta again. It made me glad I hadn't made any heartfelt connection to the city; my only emotional bond, curious as it seemed, was to a man – a relative stranger – sickening nearly four hundred miles away to our north.

17

As we set off from Sealdah Station in Calcutta, I was assured by my fellow passenger that our journey to Siliguri Town would be on a broad gauge for nearly one hundred and twenty miles. Then, my elderly train-buff friend confirmed, we'd take a ferry for many miles to a landing stage before we commenced our next part of the journey for another two hundred miles or so.

The gauges of the tracks and the history of the route held little interest for me, as in this instance the travel prompted no allure. Each passing shanty village, every mile of rattling track, plus our silent companion – the endlessly shifting River Ganges that rushed south as we chugged north – brought me closer to atonement.

That was all that was in my mind. The temptation to flee back to England strengthened after my conversation with Matron – I could simply pack up and leave. No one would complain. Who would grieve? I was not indispensable, just a transient clinician passing through with some fresh wisdom. I was certainly no longer even vital now that my maternity ward was ticking along smoothly and the malaria had been wrestled under some semblance of control.

My work was done, my time almost up anyway . . . These thoughts burst like tiny bubbles with glimmering sharpness in my mind, urging me to put my few belongings back into a trunk, close the apartment and head for Bombay and the tail end of a British summer. It began to seem romantic: back among the green of England, walking the great London parks with my father again, dinner and laughter with Jove. It even started to sound desirable, feasible too, to return early as a wonderful surprise. I would tell no one but barge into our home, slightly tanned and grinning, begging my father not to have a heart attack in shock. Then him inviting Jove to share a surprise with him. Me! What fun. It meant we could arrange the wedding breakfast together, I could linger over the design of my Eden Valentine gown, and while I was in no hurry to be travelling again, I could share the plans for an extended honeymoon into Europe. Christmas markets, roasting chestnuts – every clichéd wintry scene began to seduce me until Jove's letter arrived late the following afternoon.

I hoped with all of my heart that it gushed about how much he missed me to give me the final emotional excuse to follow the whim. Instead he gave me pause as I devoured the contents contained in the tissue-thin envelope stamped with the Royal Mail Ship.

Beloved Isla,

I trust this finds you in the peak of good health and coping with your first Indian monsoon. Hot as Hades, isn't it? Keep that beautiful, peachy English complexion of yours well covered against the harsh sun.

This letter is being written in the Cotswolds – I'm at my family's estate and it strikes me that I'd be hard-pressed to find a prettier place more suited to sit down and think of you. While you struggle through a tough summer, we are languishing through a gorgeous one of mild, dreamy days

*that seem to last forever. I am still walking our old Lab,
Winnie, as late as eight o'clock at night, not returning
much before nine, and still with time to sit out on the back
porch with a glass of port and marvel at the dusk . . . that
darkest time of twilight when you seem to be closest in
my thoughts.*

*I miss you, my darling, every day, every minute, but
I know with every passing hour you are another hour
closer to being home and in my arms. I keep trying to
imagine the novelty of seeing you moving around in my
world again, being able to hold you, kiss you, worship
you in the flesh rather than just in private thoughts. In
fact, the thought of striking out on a new life together
keeps me buoyant and wanting to run towards the future
and you in it.*

*But even as I think these selfish thoughts, it occurs
to me that you are likely in your busiest time now at
the hospital with no chance for similar romantic
musings or indeed the leisure for sipping something
delicious of an evening. I gather from your father –
who seemed hale enough but moving slower when
I saw him a fortnight ago – that you have a propensity
for becoming a prisoner of your work. I have no doubt
that the needs of your patients are demanding so this is
a quick letter to remind you to take very good care of
yourself, my darling, through your busiest of days. Not
long now before you become Mrs Mandeville – gosh,
that sounds wonderful – so I won't be selfish but will
patiently await your return. However, do remember to
eat well, sleep deep, let some of that sun kiss you and
keep you strong through the long hours that I know
you are putting into your patients. They are fortunate*

to have you and will never forget Dr Fenwick, I'm sure of it.

I thoroughly enjoyed your account in your last letter of the 'royal' visit that never occurred and can well imagine you at those wretched cocktail parties and endless social gatherings doing your best not to sneer. I have to do plenty of those myself and I feel blessed that I have found a kindred spirit in you.

Actually, darling Isla, the main reason for writing to you tonight is that I find myself in a pensive mood. I am not normally one prone to soul-searching but tonight . . . well, maybe it's because it's a full moon, or simply that dear old Winnie is walking slower than ever and might be on her last legs. Whatever it is, my thoughts are ruminative this evening and as always they flee to you.

I want you to know how proud I am. I haven't said this before and I'm sorry it's taken me so long to recognise that it's high time I shared my pride. I know I probably have no right to feel so conceited, as to be truthful we have only rediscovered one another so recently. Nevertheless, I am a fellow blessed that you are the person I will joyously share life with. When I think of how far away you are, the dangers you may have faced, the courage you've had to show in daily workings, the trials and the tribulations that have surely cropped up simply because it is India, it makes me applaud you. I privately despaired at your decision but I am long enough of tooth to know that you should never hold on to anyone too tightly as a possession. So while I could not say I am glad that you left me, I am navigating my way through the loneliness made sharper,

*more intense, by reminding myself of how lucky I am
that this fine, proud, smart, brave, driven, healing woman
has chosen me.*

*You are a rare creature, Isla Fenwick, and I suspect
you will be giving your all in Calcutta to the people
who work with you and the patients who count on you.
Stay bright, my beloved girl, and know in your heart
that I admire you and feel intense pride at your
achievement, especially that you followed through on
your dream. Help every last person you can out there
who needs you and then come home to me – all of you;
leave nothing behind. You are a marvellous role model
for young women and you may inspire a small legion of
girls to follow their hearts for a career. The world can
only benefit from women such as yourself pushing ahead
and bringing your sensitivities, gentler approaches and
creative ideas to all areas of industry as much as medicine
and the sciences.*

*Enough of my ramblings. The port is finished, night
has fallen and Winnie wants to head indoors. She hates the
gnats that buzz around us in summer.*

*I'm thinking of you, counting the days and hoping
you'll find some time before you leave to see something
of that grand continent you're living in, perhaps even
the Himalaya, which really aren't all that far away,
given that you're in Calcutta. Treat yourself!*

*Yours, very much in love and longing for your
return,*

J.

It was as though Jove was giving me permission to follow what was
in my heart. I'm sure if he knew my plans, he would caution me as

I was cautioning myself. I knew, though, if I didn't do this I would live with remorse in my life, and my father had taught me early on that no one should ever live a life that held regret.

'Not one, Isla, if you can help it. If there's a path you want to walk, walk it. If there's a person you want to know, take steps to meet them. If there's work to be done, do it immediately; don't leave it for another day. If there's bad blood between you and another, make it right. If there's unfinished business anywhere in your life, finish it.' His words haunted me now.

Unfinished business, bad blood, someone to meet, a path to be trod and work to be done . . . My father had summarised the range of grievances I had in my life connected to just one person. That's what this was with Saxon Vickery. I needed to repair us even though I couldn't undo what had been done. I had to face him, share his pain that was as much mine, after all. I felt I needed to atone, I suppose, for making my decision his trauma without seeking his counsel. And he was sick, potentially grievously ill, because of my actions. I needed to find him and ensure he was on the recovery path before I left.

Jove's timely letter, with all of its heartwarming affection and magnanimity, showed me the way forward. I would go to Saxon, I would give every ounce of my healing that I could, and I would make it right between us. And then I would leave India. There was nothing more here for me. I would obviously have preferred to depart on a high note; instead this felt like slinking away – but while my fantasy might indulge the celebration, the real me preferred no-fuss farewells and no looking back. Matron in her wisdom had already seen it and made her move to give me a hug. It had been a hard one, with much unspoken, but meaningful in that the squeeze lasted longer than a perfunctory embrace. It conveyed thanks and good wishes, forgiveness and, yes, even some pride in a fellow woman who wouldn't be cowed and didn't shy away from making decisions, especially ones that might lead to her own demise.

I shrugged in the knowledge that Matron would make all the right excuses for me if I didn't return. I had looked around my empty room after packing it up, feeling momentarily forlorn that I didn't have more to show for my time here. I had no trinkets, no mementos of my stay. I had gathered up no life-lasting friendships, I could remember few dishes that would colour my memories of India. In my thoughts were bone-wearying days and jewel-like colours mixing with filth and poverty. In my recollections I would taste gin and I would remember the languid twirl of ceiling fans and the smell of spicy coconut soap lifting off the feverish skin of a secretive, beguiling man.

My head banged against the window and I stirred from a sluggish half sleep.

'All right, my dear?' my elder passenger enquired. 'You drifted off there. Hope I wasn't boring you too much.'

'Not at all.' I sighed, straightened and stared back out of the glass to take my bearings. 'Where are we?'

'We should be in Siliguri Town in a few hours. They're serving afternoon tea in the dining car. Care to join me?'

———

I learned from my fellow travellers that Siliguri used to be little more than a gathering of folk – not even a true village – and had served as a transit point between Nepal and the hilly areas of Darjeeling, with traders from the old kingdom of Sikkim using the River Mahananda to move easily. Its development into a village and then a small town occurred when the British first occupied Darjeeling, from around 1835, and once places like Kalimpong became British-infested and the British East India Company introduced railways to north-east India, the lower-lying town had begun to thrive as the gateway into the hill stations.

'The railway opened up the whole of north-eastern India, Bhutan, Nepal and Bangladesh,' I was told by a fellow diner. 'They speak many languages here in the Chicken's Neck, as a result.'

'Chicken's Neck?' I enquired with a bemused look.

'The Siliguri Corridor. We call it the Chicken's Neck because it's so narrow and connects mainland India to its north-eastern states. It divides Nepal and Bangladesh, to be more precise.'

I couldn't admit how horrible I was at geography, especially as they'd discovered I was a doctor and no doubt presumed I was thus knowledgeable about all of academia. 'I'm staring at forest,' I admitted, gesturing to the thick vegetation we were meandering through.

'Oh, yes,' the train buff eagerly agreed. I decided he possessed a drinking problem from his telltale flushed face and the broken capillaries that spidered over his nose. 'And you'll have to be careful here, my dear. The town is prone to invasion by animals. Think nothing of a tiger or two, or congress of baboons, or whatever those damn cheeky monkeys are. They're fearless.'

I promised him I would remain vigilant as he signalled to the bearer to fill up his glass once again.

'Where are you staying?' one of the wives asked.

'I'm not sure yet. This is my first visit to this region.'

'Oh, my dear, then stick close to us,' she urged. 'We're moving straight up into the hills, of course. Anything to escape the heat. Come with us.'

'Thank you, but I must visit the hospital.'

'There is no hospital in Siliguri,' her husband added, frowning. I could smell he was drinking whiskey and it wasn't yet four; I began to imagine his clouded mind and groaning liver by seven.

'Um, there's a clinic, as I understand it. I must make contact with a colleague.'

'Well, come visit us in Mirik. My husband is a dentist for the region.'

I didn't baulk; I kept an admirably straight and interested expression to hear this nugget, despite beginning to imagine what his breath smelled like when he loomed near someone's mouth. 'When the British officers play their polo matches at Mirik, they get their teeth fixed too,' she chortled.

I smiled. 'That's so kind, thank you.'

I couldn't fault their generous manner and when they and the elderly gent I'd shared a compartment with gave me farewell hugs at Siliguri Railway Station as though we were the closest of friends, I felt grateful for the genuine welcome.

Outside the station I was greeted by a featureless town, still breathless from the monsoon season that had come early with angry thunderstorms but had ended abruptly. It clumped low and quiet on the edge of the plains of the north-east. However, I had been assured during my journey that around the moment of our arrival the mountains would breathe their cooling calm across this region, and the humidity, like the rains that gave birth to it, would dry. It was from here that I knew the climb into the Himalayan heights would begin. The land was no longer thirsting; life-giving rains had emptied their bounty onto the parched plains to turn it verdant green and the temperature was a comfortable seventy-seven degrees on the station barometer. I liked this place simply for that temperance, especially as I had wrongly anticipated heat to hit me with similar ferocity as I used to belt a rounders' ball with my bat at school.

A cycle rickshaw was to be my expedient mode of transport. Now familiar with the well-developed strength of its riders, I didn't worry about whether the rangy old man would be able to lift my luggage. It wasn't particularly heavy, not much more than a bag – I'd arranged to send all but a few garments and my handful of possessions onwards by ship back to Southampton. I'd tele-grammed Jove to ask him to arrange for its transport to London

FIONA McINTOSH

and unpacking to stop it becoming musty. He'd wasted no time telephoning me by return to share his joy that I was arriving home so much earlier than he'd anticipated. My plan to keep it a surprise had been set aside; albeit fun in my mind's eye, I didn't think it fair.

'So you're travelling?' he remarked, his voice accompanied by a series of curious noises that sounded like they were from outer space. I could also hear distantly other, indistinctive voices of people making and receiving their calls. I was struck, as we spoke, of how this contraption of science had suddenly made this vast world of ours so small. Thousands upon thousands of miles separated Jove and me, and yet here we were, talking as though we were next to each other.

'Taking your advice,' I said into the mouthpiece, perhaps too loudly but aware that we could lose the connection at any second. 'I'm going to the foothills in the north. I have a colleague who runs a clinic up there and he needs some help. A good chance to see some of the country as you suggested.'

'I can't hear you very well, darling, but I'm gathering you're going north. Good, good!' His voice had seemed to travel from me, turning more distant and small; it became muffled and I had a silly vision that he was speaking to me from beneath the ocean with a tin can.

'Jove, I can't hear you!' I said. Vacuous words. I needed to say it. 'I love you, my darling, see you soon.'

'I heard that!'

I could hear his pleasure even though the telephone had suddenly given his voice a metallic quality. 'Travel safe,' he called across the oceans. 'Enjoy yourself!'

His delight and all of his generosity lost their lightness to arrive as guilt, as burdensome as iron, in my heart. It didn't matter how I framed it in my mind, I was deluded if I didn't admit that I had feelings for Saxon Vickery. I had no explanation for them or even from where they erupted. I wanted to believe it was based on my admiration for his work, certainly for his courage in recent times at risk to his health, and his very life.

As I clambered into the rickshaw and gave the man our destination, written on a piece of paper, I wondered how Jove's and my love would weather this test.

We moved slowly on dirt roads, threading ourselves a curious path around even slower-moving cattle with sombre, patient expressions. Goats bleated and mules dragged their loads without so much as a whinny or hee-haw. Around the animals people pushed carts, pedalled bicycles or rode other rickshaws, avoiding holes in the makeshift road. As usual my gaze picked out the sharp punctuation of children in uniform and I wondered in awe yet again at how villagers kept their whites so arctic. A motley of homes clustered here and there in a raggle-taggle of village domesticity; I watched a woman toss out a pail of dirty water while another hung up saris on a line strung between trees; the garments looked like party streamers waiting for a breeze to lift them and flap them dry.

Shops that looked like back-shed kiosks sold everything from soap to cooking pots. They were so dark inside I couldn't see beyond the doorway and only what was hung at the entrance in the most basic form of advertising.

My rickshaw driver laboured on and this gave me some time to think about what I was going to say to Professor Vickery. I'd assumed over the course of the tedious journey to Siliguri that I might have formulated some sort of speech or introduction to my sudden arrival, but the reality was that I had nothing ready. I had not even the slightest notion of how to greet him. Would he be rude? Hostile? Would he simply refuse to meet me, leaving me with no option but to make the arduous journey back to Britain, unfulfilled, humiliated? And now the time was upon me. Minutes before we arrived, as the driver looked to be taking a turn towards a slightly larger than average dwelling, my thoughts treacherously emptied like water down a drain. The vessel of my mind was vacant and I would simply have to face him and cope with whatever he launched at me.

18

I'd entered what looked to be a makeshift chemist. Frankly, nothing about it could be termed a hospital; it was more a space where presumably cots could be lined up behind the counter where I now stood. I craned to see through the glass panel in the door behind the person manning the counter as to whether I could catch sight of Saxon striding around the beds.

'Good morning, madam?' the man offered, full of enquiry in his roundish face with features that were flatter than I was used to seeing in Calcutta. 'Have you just arrived off the train?'

The answer was obvious but still we both glanced at my hold-all that the rickshaw driver had placed on the ground, just inside the entrance. 'Yes.' I smiled. 'Such a long journey.'

'And you're not feeling well?' he said, sucking on teeth that were no longer there, I realised. He gave me a gummy smile.

'Er . . . I feel fine, thank you.'

He looked surprised and his bottom lip collapsed inwards, finding the gap where only gum remained. He stared at me through large, round black glasses that made his eyes appear bigger than they were.

'I should explain, sorry. I am here to meet . . . well, to see someone.'

He nodded. 'Who are you looking for, madam?'

His manners were as impeccable as his neat shelves, boiled white shirt buttoned at the top and a pharmacy that smelled of cloves. I guessed he'd been making up some tooth tincture recently.

'I was hoping to see Professor Vickery,' I offered, and couldn't hide the hope in my voice.

'Ah,' he said, nodding. I decided his looks had a sense of the Oriental about him, even though his manner of speaking was all Bengal, his English language reliable.

'Is he here?'

'He is.'

I blinked. 'May I see him, please?'

'No, madam.'

'So he's not here?' I craned my neck to look again.

'He is here, madam.'

This was becoming infuriating and painful. I remained patient, though, having learned these last few months about just how particular and thorough Indian bureaucracy could be. Men given even the slightest authority exercised it with dutiful attention. I presumed Vickery had yelled *No interruptions!* or something similar and the man was carrying out those instructions wholly, despite the fact that I'd clearly covered a daunting distance to be here.

'Mr . . . ?'

'Mr Bannerjee, madam. At your service.'

'Thank you, Mr Bannerjee.' I explained about the long journey I'd travelled. 'It is imperative I see him.'

'But he is dying, madam. His fever means —'

'Dying!' I said in a wheeze that sounded like all the air had rushed out of my lungs in that moment. 'What do you mean, *dying*?'

This was a man who took everything literally and I didn't want another conversation of me prodding to find the best way to access the answer. 'Where is he?' I demanded, coming around the counter. 'I am a doctor. Show me where he is, please.'

'You are a —'

'Yes, I'm Dr Fenwick, his colleague from Calcutta, and I need you to tell me where to find Professor Vickery immediately.' I stood taller than my companion. He frowned, not intimidated by me, but did seem impressed by me being a doctor.

'He is in isolation, Dr Fenwick.' He sucked at his gum. 'It is the TB that takes him.'

'Through here?' I laid a gloved hand on the door.

He nodded.

'What other diseases are in this ward?'

He blinked behind his thick lenses, looking momentarily confused by the question. I realised he was considering listing every complaint lying down behind that door, but no doubt my glare of impatience curtailed that inclination. 'Many diseases. The professor is in a small room at the back. Death is unavoidable, madam.'

I dug into my pocket and pulled out a handkerchief square; fashioning a makeshift mask with it, I tied it around my nose and mouth, much to the man's bemusement. 'Well, not if I can help it,' I replied with a fierce stare. 'Thank you, Mr Bannerjee.'

I opened the door and strode through the small, near airless, grey room. Patients, too sick to stir, were flanked by their families, keeping vigil. It was quiet, the loudest sound the squeak from an overhead fan and a soft, pressing cough from one of the ill. There was a sorrowful feeling of resignation but I passed through, despite the pinch at my conscience to pause, a brief check on each; maybe I could help? But for the moment my gaze was firmly on the locked door at the back. There was no glass to peer through. I knocked gently without reply. I could no longer care about protocol and opened the door just enough to slip into the room.

He was alone, his back to me, knees tucked up like a newborn emerged from the womb. I could see the knobbled curve of his spine, could count the ribs in relief beneath his skin, which was stretched too thin and too pale against his skeleton. His yellow hair was splayed out behind his head in matted streaks, giving the impression he was in motion: running away from this place . . . from his sickness. But as I tiptoed towards him, I could tell – even from a distance – that the professor was not outmanoeuvring the tuberculosis that was ravaging him.

'Professor?' I could smell staleness sitting around him like an invisible prison. 'Vickery?' I raised myself onto my toes to glance over and noted his eyes were open, fixed on the tiny louvred window that was positioned perhaps eight feet up. There was a desk fan creaking from the corner of the room, placed on a stool. It could barely stir the air hard enough to reach the prone man and the outside world could barely send a breath through that high, small window and its rusted louvres. Nevertheless, Vickery fixated on its threshold and I suspected I knew why; out there beyond his fever was life-giving fresh air – his only hope.

I risked touching his shoulder, trying not to look at his awkwardly bandaged arms, no doubt from his intervention with Pratiti's people. 'Saxon?' His skin was too warm and the staleness smelled to me like oncoming death. Mr Bannerjee was right. It was a matter of time, just like it was for the patients in the main ward too. Everyone in there was in a waiting room for Death's messenger to collect them.

He stirred, struggling to right himself onto his back. 'Frances?' he croaked, confused. His eyes had the glasslike quality of a doll's, staring but not seeing.

I shook him gently. 'No, it's me, Isla.'

His gaze cleared slightly, brow furrowing while he worked to concentrate, to find focus. 'Isla?' He still managed to imbue it with a romantic lilt and I felt the sting as tears welled.

'Yes,' I breathed.

'My Isla,' he murmured and despite all my training and ability to achieve dislocation from a patient, I couldn't help the spill of salted tracks that stained my cheeks. I let my pity flow. Bizarrely, the tears comforted me, reassuring that I was feeling more than the empty hurt that had sat inside since Miles had enjoyed delivering his cruel, hard piece of gossip.

I wanted to share my apology, promise to make amends, but all of that was redundant now. I had one task and that was to save Vickery's life – everything else, including putting my heartache at rest for the invisible blood on my hands – would have to queue and wait patiently.

I turned at the sound near the door, using the motion to swipe away tears and regret. 'Mr Bannerjee,' I began, thinking through this situation fast, 'I have to move Professor Vickery today.'

He looked startled. 'He will likely die today,' he replied. It was harsh but I preferred his directness; I doubted Mr Bannerjee was capable of a lie, even a white one to ease someone's troubles. Nevertheless, Vickery would not die today. I knew this disease too well and it liked to taunt its victims; it had plans to have fun at this patient's expense for a little while longer. And it was that glee I was going to exploit.

'Then he will die trying to live,' I snapped, making no sense, I realised, but the sentiment seemed to cut through to Bannerjee's heart.

'Where do you wish to remove him?'

I shook my head, racking my thoughts. 'I need somewhere that is cold, dry, plenty of clean air.'

He grinned in answer, giving me a glimpse of his gums as he pointed upwards. I frowned, predictably following his finger and looked to the ceiling. Mr Bannerjee forgot himself and tutted. This time he pointed beyond the walls.

'Kangchenjunga,' he breathed, sounding awed. 'Himalaya. Place of snow.'

Of course! I knew the foothills were just beyond this town but what was up there? Where could we stay? But Mr Bannerjee was ahead of me.

'Doctor, he may not live long enough, but Darjeeling is fifty miles away up into the hills.'

Fifty miles. That didn't sound so far. London to Brighton Pier was only fifty miles . . .

'Who will take me up there with the professor?'

He shook his head. 'Not easy. The distance is short, Doctor, but the journey is long.'

Now he sounded like a philosopher.

'Can I hire someone to drive us up there?' I enunciated, begging all the angels that guarded me to help me keep my patience intact.

'Drive? There are no cars. But perhaps a bullock and cart.'

I began to imagine just how quickly Saxon would give up the fight if he was laid out in the back of a grinding cart with a bullock or donkey to haul us those fifty miles uphill.

'But there is the train,' Mr Bannerjee continued conversationally.

I grabbed his arm with surprise. 'What train?'

'The Toy Train,' he said and I let go as I watched him wince. He resisted rubbing his arm. 'That's what we call it, anyway, because of the small engines. Again, not an easy journey but he would be more comfortable on the train . . . if he can stay alive.'

'Oh, he'll stay alive, all right,' I assured. 'Will you help me, Mr Bannerjee?'

———

I paid whatever was asked; I didn't care how much it cost or who needed to be part of my debt, leaving all of the organisation to my new friend, Mr Bannerjee, with a fistful of rupees for him to pay whoever needed paying. He dutifully made all arrangements and although it seemed to take all day, we were finally loaded onto the train leaving that late afternoon.

My idea was to head for Darjeeling, or perhaps even Kalimpong. The train could take us to both. I figured someone would help me to get Saxon into a guesthouse or hotel as Mr Bannerjee assured me the British had made themselves most comfortable up in the hill stations. I remembered the dentist and his wife had all but demanded I visit them in Kalimpong too, so even if they couldn't accommodate us, I was certain they would help me find somewhere to put Saxon and look after him.

Chai was being served through the windows as we waited for the stationmaster to give us leave to depart. I didn't want any, even though my belly was grumbling at how hungry it was. The last morsel I'd eaten was early that morning but I looked at Saxon's hollow frame and decided I couldn't eat anyway, not while he starved. But tea: tea would be good for him if I could get some down him . . . I just didn't want any of the warming effect of chai.

In my appalling Bengali that only a generous person could understand, I asked if there was any plain black tea. The little man with the darkest of skins split into an accommodating grin. He held up a finger to ask me to wait. I nodded. Within a minute or so he was back with a pot and I held out the cup that Mr Bannerjee had provided. It was filled with tea the colour of rich honey.

'Second flush,' he said as though they were the most natural words to say. 'Very good.'

Saxon was laid out on a makeshift stretcher bed on the floor of the carriage that I had hired for us. We were alone. I'd pulled down the blinds of the windows that faced onto the platform and he was hallucinating. Crouching beside him, I lifted his feverish head to tip some of this hopefully healing tea past his lips. I needed to keep him as cool as I could and as hydrated as possible.

He sipped greedily even though he was lost in his ramblings. But he seemed to smile through them.

'Second flush,' he whispered, and I was astonished at his repeat of the tea seller's words.

It was like a special language only they knew.

'Brackenridge,' he murmured as he drifted off.

I was instantly reminded of the day our new-fangled Toast-master gave me an electric shock and we never used it again despite my father's giddy excitement at a machine that could toast bread . . . and pop it up for convenience. That horrible sensation, first like a bee sting with no lasting pain, gave me a light tremor that remained for most of the day as though all of my nervous system was firing at once. That's what the utterance of *Brackenridge* did to me now. It was like a small electrical shock of dawning and my body was charged by a current of optimism. Of course – Brackenridge! Vickery's family home in the tea gardens of Darjeeling. We didn't have to ask for anyone's help; he didn't have to be anyone's burden or put ourselves or others into any awkward situation.

'Saxon,' I whispered. I shook him gently. 'Saxon, hang on, because I'm taking you home to Brackenridge.'

He said nothing but the smile that broke through the fever suggested to me the word was a balm to him. There was hope now and he would fight this fever with me; together we'd beat the enemy back.

———

The journey across the plain from Siliguri was short, and before I could empty the contents of the teacup into Saxon's mouth we'd begun the climb through forest. I was astounded to see a family of elephants lumbering among the foliage and could swear at one point that I glimpsed the slinking stripes of a tiger on the stalk.

Our train moved at the slow clip of the elephants but I must admit to feeling a certain swell of romance in my heart at this journey that mercifully set my anxiety over Saxon's illness at bay for a brief time. The train itself was a handsome blue, shone so highly that as we'd embarked I'd seen our reflections vaguely thrown back at us in its polished surface.

Saxon had drifted off once again and there was little more I could do for him until I could properly nurse him. For now the tea had worked a sort of magic of its own but so had being out of that airless room. His pallor, though hardly healthy, had lost that greyish tone of a death mask. And he slept in a more relaxed flop of limbs rather than that tight foetal position. It meant I could let the tension in my chest leak away for a while.

In quiet amazement I watched us pass by tiny stations that would not look out of place in rural Britain, one at a place called Sookna that would have sat comfortably in the countryside of the English counties. It reinforced to me that the Europeans, particularly the English, were doing their utmost to wrestle India into a miniature version of the home in their hearts. At a spot called Kurseong we took a long stop and passengers wandered the platform, with its low-roofed stationhouse, to stretch, change into warmer garments or take tea. During the climb into Kurseong the slopes were blanketed by white orchids that seemed to grow wild.

Hearing voices outside our first-class carriage, I stepped out into the corridor to strike up a conversation with a couple of gentlemen, elbows hung loosely on the open windows, enjoying their journey. More steam-train buffs, I presumed.

'Do you know the journey from Calcutta used to take nearly a week in the most uncomfortable of circumstances of steam-engine-pulled trains, then crossing the Ganges by steam ferry, not to mention a heinous journey by bullock cart and palanquins?' one fellow grumbled. 'Now it's just over two days of comfortable train rides and one thousand feet to Darjeeling,' he finished, with a flourish of his hand. 'Where are you staying?'

'I'm taking my . . . friend . . . who is rather ill at the moment, to another friend's home in the tea gardens.' I needed to remain vague.

'Oh? Which one?'

'It's called Brackenridge.'

Both men frowned now, searching their thoughts.

'Oh, wait, is that old man Vickery's place, near Singritan?' He nudged his friend while my breath caught. They knew it – which was going to be a great help.

The other fellow considered this and gave a grudging nod. 'You might be right, Harold. Fearsome old blackguard, wasn't he? My father never had a good word for Dougal Vickery.'

I blinked and cleared my throat.

They turned to regard me, remembering I was present, probably. 'Well, if it is the tea plantation we think it is, then you're best getting off at Ghum. It's from there that we make the famous U-turn to head for Nepal. In order to make our sharp ascent the engineers have put in a cunning series of loops and what are known as Z-reverses.'

I'd heard enough. 'Gentlemen, forgive me, I forgot to eat and I must admit to feeling a little faint.'

'Oh, my dear,' they chorused. The gents helped me back into my compartment and mercifully left me without any further reference to their giddy joy at the Z-reverses this journey was famous for, but they did suggest I hire a driver, cart and palanquin with bearers.

'It will take a day to get to that part of the hills. Worth the effort, of course. Apart from Darjeeling, it will take your breath away.'

'Thank you, gentlemen.'

I sat in our silent carriage, the swaying rumble of this train lulling me into a soothed headspace, and I plotted our next move, feeling comforted that I at least now had a plan.

19

I waited for help as we arrived at Ghum Station, glad to have the excuse to be the last to alight.

On its outskirts we were so close to the village life we passed through that I could have reached an arm out and plucked a piece of fruit or snatched any manner of goods from the makeshift shops that hugged the railway track. I looked into the dark space where shelves were cluttered with tins of goods and smiled at shy shop-keepers who eyed me with mistrust. Perhaps they weren't used to a pale-skinned person smiling so genuinely at them. I couldn't know; they were gone from my vision so fast.

The air had cooled considerably, which thrilled me; this was what was needed if Saxon was going to come back from this bout of his illness. I even pulled a shawl from my belongings, which down on the plains I couldn't imagine needing.

With the help of station officials, coolies were summoned, duly arrived, and mercifully the platform had virtually cleared by the time Saxon was unloaded. I noted that the train was being reloaded with fuel, and passengers bound for Darjeeling were stretching their legs outside the station, some taking chai, others pausing for a small picnic. I had Saxon taken into the waiting room, where there were no Europeans, only curious Indians watching our every move.

With the aid of a senior station staff member with exceptional English, I organised our next mode of transport, paying without query whatever was asked. While we waited, I watched the train rumble out again. Billows of steam, as though clouds had fallen from the sky to drift across the platform, were accompanied by an unearthly squeal of iron. The screech of the whistle forced me to cover my ears momentarily.

Saxon was loaded, together with my holdall, onto a cart pulled by a single mule that the station staff promised me was sure-footed, while I was urged to step inside the accompanying palanquin. Travelling by litter made me feel like I belonged in another century and yet I could tell there was no other way, for there was no room next to the cart driver and his helper. Nor would they permit me to sit in the back with Saxon; not only was there little room but it would become uncomfortable to the point of being potentially dangerous for me, I was told. There seemed no point in arguing. I wanted to get us moving as fast as we could, so I shrugged, smiled graciously at the four coolies who were to soon hoist me onto their shoulders and settled myself onto the cushion of the single seat of the palanquin covered by silk curtains. I could hear the station manager now giving rapid instructions and I understood it would take us the full day to make the journey of several miles back down the ascent I had taken on the train and into the tea gardens district.

At first I was sure I would topple out of the litter but my body began to move into the natural rhythm of the men carrying me and soon enough I was swaying in time with their steady walk. Their conversation was sporadic and so fast that I couldn't pick out even vague words to understand. Apart from craning time to time to check on my patient, who slept on, oblivious, I settled back, feeling like the Valide of an imperial Ottoman harem.

I must have dozed off because a jolt made me blink awake with alarm and I heard the equivalent of cursing. Perhaps one of the men stumbled, but we righted ourselves quickly and I was gladdened to have been so rudely awakened because what I saw past my silken framed window made me gasp audibly before holding my breath, as though if I so much as swallowed the vision might disappear.

We had entered an otherworld; there was no better way I can describe it. I couldn't imagine in that moment how I would ever put into words the beauty before me that had stolen not only my breath, but my language, my attention . . . I could swear my heart had stopped its steady pulse and I also knew in that moment that I was in paradise.

Strung like a glistening necklace above and around us was the Himalaya. I didn't know which particular mountains I was so awe-struck by but they looked back at me with a benign majesty. The jagged escarpments that I knew must exist on a mountain range, especially this high up in the world, were disguised by dreamlike, pillowy snow drifts. Was that my voice that was speaking? We must have paused, I must have got out, I must have finally started breathing again and my heart pumping once more because I found myself on the ground, away from the others, staring open-mouthed. Perhaps the coolies were used to this reaction from the first-time visitor because they kept their distance and allowed me the time to let this world in the sky fully sink into my consciousness. The towering mountains appeared weightless for I could not see their bulk . . . these lower parts were engulfed by a purplish mist and only their snowy peaks soared into the ocean of sky, which appeared a uniform colour: no patches, no clouds, no draining of the hue. A single, sprawling, achingly rich lapis lazuli that stretched beyond my vision.

I was staring at the roof of Earth; beyond this fragile dome was the moon, the stars, the sun, all those planets we're told about. The

Himalaya was the sentinel that guarded us. And these imperial guards of Earth linked hands and watched over a tumbling valley stepped by verdant gardens, studded by clusters of fiery-coloured poppies that grew wild among the tea plantations of Darjeeling.

I heard a choked voice. 'Brackenridge . . .' and looked across in fresh alarm to see Saxon straining to glimpse above the rim of the cart. He couldn't see much from his prone position but I suspected he could smell the air, no doubt feel the presence of the mountains of his youth that were to his back. Suddenly I envied him his child-hood in this enchanted landscape.

I found my composure, pulling myself down from the shock of speechless awe, and called over. 'Saxon, be still. We'll be there . . . ?' I looked over to the leader of the men who were escorting us. He pointed to a house in the distance. I nodded. 'We'll be at Brackenridge in minutes. Lie down.' Waving away my litter, I asked the same man to help me into the back of the cart, explaining that I knew it would be uncomfortable but it was only for a brief time.

'I shall be very careful,' I promised.

I'm glad I hadn't tried to make this journey all the way in the cart but I would be lying if I didn't admit to a private feeling of exhilaration to hold Saxon's hand and ride next to him, while I drank in the view like a person emerging from a desert. Actually, I think anyone who never has the fortune to witness this scenery probably does live in a desert. London, Paris, Rome – with all of their history and romantic architecture of centuries past – cannot compare to Nature's greatest amphitheatre. Saxon was dazed but he turned his head to glance at me in what was perhaps a moment of clarity. While still holding his hand, I touched my heart, eyes helplessly welling with tears at the emotion of being allowed to share this special place of his.

He smiled, I hope in understanding, and lost consciousness.

The house looked out across the tea gardens that belonged to it with what I could only describe as a glow of authority as the setting of the sun painted it with a radiance. Crepuscular light turned the windows to mirrors and the ivory-painted bungalow into a golden place as though we were approaching a throne . . . where royalty resided, answering only to those distant gods that towered above it.

As I alighted from the cart with help, a bow-legged man with spectacles and a solemn gaze emerged to greet us. He had not come from the house but he climbed onto the front steps as if he felt compelled to offer an official welcome. The man was attired in the traditional Bengali dress of *dhoti* and long white shirt – both so white and crisply ironed, his brightness almost hurt the eyes in this sublime, gentle light of afternoon. I wanted to admire the surrounds, look again at those peaks floating in the distance, but he was looking at me with bewilderment and also a measure of respect. I knew he wanted to fire off questions to the men around me but he waited for me to speak first.

'Good afternoon.'

'Madam.' He bowed low and I was thrilled he spoke English.

'I am Dr Isla Fenwick, a colleague of Professor Vickery, who —'

'Master Saxon?' he interrupted, forgetting himself.

It was then that Saxon roused and his golden head peeked above the rim of the cart as though the king had returned to this palace. I heard the old man give a soft gasp of surprise and delight. Saxon couldn't hold up his weight and flopped back down.

'He's very unwell,' I said, somewhat redundantly. 'Can you help me, please? I've brought him home. It's the only place I could think of . . .'

The man didn't wait for me to say more. He was giving orders like a general marshalling his troops. Men were in motion again under his instructions and as tired as they were, they rallied and Saxon was borne away with his family's servant beckoning and harrying them along.

I didn't know my place here and didn't feel it appropriate to arrogantly follow them in and take over. I waited for guidance and it was surprisingly not more than a few moments before all the men were back.

'Dr Fenwick?'

I was pleased he remembered. 'Yes.'

'I am Adri.'

'Thank you. Are you . . . ?'

'I work in the tea gardens,' he said with a small bow. 'Third generation of my family to do so.'

'Oh,' I said, taken aback. 'So no one is in the house?'

He looked confused, then shook his head. 'No one from the family has been here for many years but Mr Vickery senior runs it from England. He uses managers – I am one of them.'

I was lost for what to say. There was little point in asking any more about the dwelling, although some obvious queries leapt to mind. 'There's running water?'

He nodded. 'But I am guessing that the boiler will be contrary, madam. I'll check on it immediately.'

'Right.' We were going to need hot water at some point but for now I was happy to thank the stars that we had a roof, some safety from the elements . . . but no food, presumably. 'I'd better check on him,' I said, trying to prioritise.

'Please,' he said, gesturing towards the stairs that led to the entrance of the house. As I followed I explained quickly about where Saxon and I worked together and, without too much detail, why I found myself here.

He paused at the main door. 'You have come from Calcutta?' His accent was rich with Indian nuance but I could tell his English was reliable. I would not have to restrict my words or speak slowly.

'Yes. I found him in Siliguri too sick to even move and I had to make an immediate decision. It's tuberculosis and he needs this cold, clear air if he has a chance to be well again.'

He nodded. 'It is the right decision, Dr Fenwick. He will rally fast here.'

I smiled. 'Should I telegram someone?'

He looked back at me with a grave stare and slight frown. Then he shook his head. 'It has been a decade, Dr Fenwick, since anyone has lived here.' He said this in the resigned tone of someone realising he hadn't made himself clear the first time. 'I am charged to unlock and air it from year to year, make sure no stray dogs are roaming around or monkeys finding their way in to cause mischief, but I am the tea manager. I have nothing formal to do with the house or its contents, other than knowing where the key is kept.'

He added more with a tone of sympathy. 'I have worked for the family since I was a child and my father was head of the garden's servants, as his father was before him.' Brackenridge seemed to shift behind us, as though waking up to people within it. 'The house is content to have one of its own back.' He smiled gently at the creaking sound as it settled. 'I'm sorry there are no servants but we can find some people to help when you need.' He pointed into the shadows. 'Down that corridor to the end wing,' he said, gesturing, 'that's Master Saxon's.'

I sensed he wasn't going to escort me there, as if he didn't feel it was his place to be inside the house. 'Thank you. Er, may I open the shutters?'

'Of course, madam. The house is now in your charge.'

I pulled off my shawl and began opening the louvres to reveal the windows of a house that had not looked outwards for years.

Instead it had held its memories close, the sounds of the family it had raised, their joys, their secrets kept intact. Instead of feeling comforted by this, I was saddened slightly that this house I'd heard Saxon refer to briefly but with such affection had not been permitted to age as its family had. It was trapped in the invisible vault of time. It prompted me to think of my mother's bedroom and I made a promise that I would dismantle that chamber, in which we tried to imprison her for our own comfort, upon my return. Was it the clarity of this empyrean world I found myself in, among the tallest structure of our planet, that made me see the only way for my father and me to move forward?

My mother was holding us back but the mistake was ours. I was trying to avenge her death, still believing that if I walked in her footsteps, I would honour her. That was her life, though. As I walked down dark floorboards that had gathered the dust of untrodden years, I felt understanding sigh into my awareness. I had to let her go. I had to let her research be her mission, not mine. It was time to make my own path.

Opening the house onto the gods felt empowering and I experienced a prick of envy that Saxon had this special place among the heavens to run away to. Except he chose not to, it seemed. Another secret that Brackenridge held close, perhaps?

As its windows threw light into former shadows, I gathered that this was a most airy bungalow, much larger than I first imagined. A new sense of space was created through the abundance of glass and French doors, plus there was the wide verandah that encircled the house, sweeping like a protective embrace around the family that had grown up here. I looked forward to exploring its grounds but right now I had to stay focused on Saxon as I tiptoed to where I'd been directed. I knocked on the door out of politeness and anticipated no answer, got none, so I stepped first into an anteroom – a sort of sitting room with a gallery of windows that had been unshuttered, presumably by Adri as they'd brought Saxon in. The view looked directly out over the purplish valley that the plantation ran into. Tearing my gaze from that vista, I moved to the inner door that was open. I could see him lying on a high bed that was dressed in white linen with a faded, puffed eiderdown of old roses, which struck me as charming in a man's room. A mosquito net fell like a wispy cage around his four-poster bed and Saxon looked like a misted sketch behind it.

I decided the time for awkward politeness had passed. I lifted the net and perched on the bed beside him, reaching for his face. He was warm but not burning and he was statue-still, which was reassuring. I had been fearing that he would be in the grip of tremor or hallucinations.

Adri arrived to stand at the door, looking unsure; clearly he felt like a trespasser.

I tried to set my companion at ease. 'I'm a doctor who has long believed that ill people feel so much better at home and recovery can be hastened if we can treat them from their own beds.' I glanced at Adri, who stood, shoulders squared, hands behind his back and fully attentive. 'I have now proven that theory true. I haven't given him a single sip of medication and yet he seems to be pulling himself back to us through sheer force of willpower.'

'He was always a wilful boy,' Adri remarked and I heard only affection in the remark.

Our gazes met and I smiled and shook my head. 'May I stay and help him to recover?'

'Dr Fenwick, none of us has your expertise so I am very grateful for you being here. It's wonderful to have Master Saxon back after far too long.'

I could believe it, looking around Saxon's vast room, which was in desperate need of a clean. I wanted to sneeze and fought the eye-watering pricks of desire to do just that.

Adri caught on to my thoughts quickly. 'I will send in some people tomorrow to clean and dust. We always hope one of the boys might visit but it has been a long time.'

'He hasn't spoken with any detail of his brother to me, other than to mention there is one and that he runs the plantation,' I remarked, trying not to pry but hoping for some information.

The servant was as reticent as the master was to discuss personal information. 'I'm sure Master Saxon will tell you about his family. Right now, you must be very tired, Dr Fenwick.'

I chuckled. 'I'm so tired, Adri, I'm past feeling it. But the sight of the mountains was like a life-giving tonic. All fatigue disappeared when I saw them.'

'Kangchenjunga,' he murmured in soft awe and nodded.

'You or Master Saxon is going to have to teach me how to say that.'

He turned around, speaking to someone I couldn't see. 'Dr Fenwick, I have asked my niece to make tea. Can we offer you some?'

'That would be most welcome, thank you.'

He beckoned and a shy young woman appeared at the door.

'Please,' he said, taking a cup and saucer and handing it to me. 'You must keep your strength up too.'

I recognised the Limoges design from one identical in my grandmother's collection; it was painted in fragile, exquisitely rendered violets. I could almost smell them off the gentle fragrance of the tea. 'If you say first flush, I'm going to scream,' I joked.

Adri actually smiled, getting the jest, I was relieved to note. 'Tea is our life, Dr Fenwick. Master Saxon knows all about it; he can teach you. This is our *second* flush, picked during the warm days of summer now behind us. All the flavours of the best tea in the world are concentrated into this brew.'

I had decided I could listen to men talk about this subject

all day; I'd witnessed Saxon go misty-eyed when explaining tea, as though he was reminiscing over an old and wonderful romance. And here was Adri, with that same tone of whimsy, discussing the summer pick. I hoped I would learn more. Jove would be impressed by my knowledge.

Jove. I needed to contact him. I frowned. What about Saxon's wife? She would want to know where he was, surely? But then I recalled Saxon's despair at my meddling and I was torn. He would waken soon and I would ask him to make that decision. 'Adri, do we have access to a telegram office here?'

'Er, no, madam,' he said, shooing away his niece, who had arrived and departed in silence, and with no eye contact for me but a glance at the person prone in the bed. 'The closest telegram office is Darjeeling.'

I thought of the road back up the hill; to say it was bumpy was to understate in a way that was almost comic. Coming down it was hard, fraught with potential accidents. How those men carried me down even half the way without losing their footing was beyond me. The ascent could only be fairly described as a mountainous trek, so I had no inclination to make that journey again immediately.

'I see. Is there any way of getting a message to England?'

He considered this. 'If you write the message, perhaps I can make sure it is taken into Darjeeling to be sent, although when I cannot promise, but certainly in the coming few days.'

'That's more than acceptable, thank you, Adri. I'll do that. My family will wonder where I am.'

He nodded, understanding.

'Will you help me to get some tea into Saxon?'

'Of course, madam. And I shall have my family make up a mutton broth for later too.'

'Excellent. If we continue the fluids and he keeps his willpower strong, then we might pull him past this,' I said, my voice full of optimism. I believed it too. I sipped the tea, which was strong and delicious. Bizarrely, while it woke my tastebuds it also clued me in to how exhausted I was. I must have slumped in relief.

'Madam . . . Dr Fenwick? If I may?'

I nodded.

'You are deeply tired. The journey alone from Calcutta is fatiguing. The train ride from Siliguri is a challenge, but nothing can fully prepare a gentlewoman for the descent into the tea gardens by cart and mule . . .'

'Or palanquin,' I added with a sigh.

He nodded. 'Please, take a rest. I will watch over Master Saxon without leaving his side. I will ply him with tea, as you ask, and I will fetch you if he wakes. Both of you need rest to get strong. I am no doctor so I would wish you bright and rested to show me how to get Master Saxon fit again. Please sleep . . . just for a few hours.'

He was right. I was no good to anyone if I couldn't hold myself erect, and I was feeling heavy-lidded and sluggish now that the novelty and sparkle of arrival had dissipated slightly. The other side of Saxon's bed looked inviting. I could almost picture myself lying my head onto that pillow and sneaking beneath the faded eiderdown next to him.

'While you've been here, my family have made up a room next door. It is small, not properly prepared, of course, but I thought you would want to be nearby.'

'I would. I don't mind how unprepared it is. To lie down for a brief while would be wise and I'll be strong in an hour or two to take over. Er, how many children do you have, Adri?'

He grinned. 'All my relatives work for the Vickery family in the gardens. We belong to them.' It sounded oddly proprietorial and yet I could feel his pride reaching out. 'Please rest. Bathe. I shall see you in a few hours. I promise to keep vigil. Come, let me show you.'

I cast a glance towards my patient, who slept now with a relaxed cast to his face, like a child tucked in safely by loving parents.

20

It took me several seconds to realise where I was when I opened my eyes, without alarm, to the sound of women's laughter. Unlikely they were household servants, for the voices were too distant. Tea pickers, perhaps? I became aware of the scented air that I'd noticed on arrival and looked up as a fan circled lazily above my bed. I stretched and wondered if that earthy, cut-grass scent on the wind was the tea bushes, the fragrance of the soil or the forested region nearby.

I lifted my lids fully to take in the new surrounds through a lens made gauzy by the mosquito net that had been draped around the bed. I could swear I'd just surfaced from the best sleep of my adult life and, although the various worries pressing on me arrived one after another like eager sparrows onto a freshly tossed piece of bread, I could truthfully say my heart felt lighter in that moment.

The room that Adri had provided for me and described as small appeared bigger than mine in London. Perhaps it was the timber ceiling painted a rich white against the dark polished boards of the floor, or maybe it was because two sides of the room boasted picture windows, one with French doors that opened onto a balcony and the other a bay window that created an alcove where a day bed, plump with cushions, looked inviting. Ivory-coloured muslin curtains hung around this alcove and were embroidered with leaves depicting tea, I guessed. The drapes filtered the sunlight, which danced against the whitewashed walls and glinted off the brass handles of the chocolate-coloured furniture, gold picture frames and a carriage clock that looked as though it had likely not been wound in decades.

I reached for my wristwatch and was astonished to see it was nearing seven. Unforgivably I had slept through to morning, seemingly without stirring. And, as if Adri possessed the talent of a seer, there was a light tap at the door.

'Madam? Dr Fenwick?'

'Yes, Adri? I'm awake.'

'We have prepared some food for you. It is a lovely morning,' he said from behind the door.

'Er, I'll dress and be out,' I said, looking at the clothes I'd dropped in a haphazard pile yesterday.

'Please do not hurry yourself. All is well with the patient. Bathe and your breakfast will be served when you're ready. Er, madam?'

'Yes?'

'We can have your clothes laundered.'

I'd used all of the clothes I'd brought in my holdall and the idea of them being laundered was enticing. 'But what shall I wear in the meantime?'

'My daughter found some clothes in the house. She has left something in the wardrobe for you to wear until your own clothes are prepared.'

'Thank you,' I called.

So I was right. I frowned; I had indeed entered an otherworld and somehow the problems seemed to feel as though they were not nearly so dramatic as I had sketched them in my mind. It was not as though I was ready to start humming a jolly tune to myself, but the mere fact that I lingered in this safe, comforting cloud beneath the mosquito net, and didn't feel stung into leaping to stutter an apology and get busy, made me realise I had clearly left my ordinary world. The Isla of just days ago would be filled with recrimination for not demonstrating that I was beyond the normal human frailty of fatigue, that I could simply keep going, always outperform and out-think people around me. Maybe this was the overachieving, perhaps even arrogant, quality that Matron had referred to when she had warned me not to personalise everything. Had I really made every aspect of my time in India a reflection of myself?

As I lay here in a petticoat, feeling stripped emotionally as much as physically, her cautionary words made sense. I was merely one of the unwitting players in the story of Naz and Pratiti. And there would still be sick people in India long after I'd left – not every ill patient was my duty, my responsibility. My thoughts became more lucid and I realised I'd been on a personal mission since arriving in India and that I had indeed made it all about me; I was no different to horrible Miles! Even Miles's passive remarks I had challenged rather than shrugging them off as Saxon had. I hadn't yet found the wisdom to allow for people in my orbit to be contrary, to act emotionally or irresponsibly sometimes. I think I understood now that what I liked most about Saxon was that he was such an island. To him people made choices, good or bad, and he dealt with the result; he did his best not to engage or participate. He stayed true to himself by always giving his all, even when it could bring injury and grief upon himself. This was what Matron was getting at. Saxon cared about the world beyond his life, his needs, his ego; meanwhile, I internalised too much and viewed life from a highly subjective perspective, considering how everything from the weather to the decisions of others affected me. Humiliated that it was so clear to me now, I felt a prick of shame that I was too self-absorbed in work, my role, my own vision for my life, perhaps, to see any of this previously.

Audibly clearing my throat, I ducked under the net and steered my thoughts elsewhere. Adri sounded bright; maybe there was good news awaiting me with Saxon. I squared my shoulders, determined not to be introspective. He'd insisted I take my time and so, in the spirit of not trying to control everything, I drew a bath. Someone had tiptoed in through the hours I slept and left not only clothes, as Adri mentioned, but some toiletries. I lingered long enough to scrub away the days of travel, unknotting hair that had been tied up for too long, and luxuriated in the slippery feel of soapy bubbles against my skin.

I did pause to congratulate myself, as it seemed – even in my tired stupor of yesterday late afternoon – that I'd had the presence of mind to wash and hang up my underwear, which was now only a fraction damp. It would do. However, I couldn't imagine myself wearing a sari or the pantaloons and long shirt that Bengali women favoured for practicality. As reluctantly as I had left my bed, I now half-heartedly stepped from the bath onto the crisp pattern of black-and-white tiles and towelled myself dry before tiptoeing back into the bedroom and turning the key of the wardrobe. Inside, greeted by the scent of cloves, I saw a simple calf-length European-style dress of starched cotton. Relief made me sigh. Peering into the depths, I noted a fine net pouch containing chips of wood and leaves studded by cloves. There was the source of the pungent peppery anise fragrance. Although I was immediately reminded of toothache tincture, it was certainly an improvement on the ghastly smell of naphthalene.

Grimacing at the momentary clammy feel of the damp lace against my skin, I pulled on my French knickers and tried not to jump at the touch of the cold satin of my bra against my flesh. I pulled on the dress that was essentially a shift with a sheer top layer.

While it was neither my size nor to my modern taste, I felt immediately prettier in it. It was large for my frame but, given it was a drop waist of the previous decade, it would fit. I remembered wearing a dress of this styling in my teenage years. The pintucked skirt had pale embroidery at its hem and the dress tied sweetly just below the throat. It would do just fine.

I combed out my wet hair and emerged from my room to where the same young woman who had brought the tea stood barefoot and bowing as I stepped over the threshold.

'Good morning.'

'Morning, madam,' she said in a quiet voice.

'Er, thank you,' I said, running a hand over my hip. 'The dress is lovely.'

'My uncle is on the verandah,' the girl said, her voice so soft I had to strain.

I desperately wanted to turn right and visit Saxon, but Adri had already spotted me and lifted a hand in greeting, so I moved towards the kind man who had welcomed me so generously.

Once again the sight of the Himalayan mountains imprisoned me. They were misted today: more of an impression of what I saw yesterday, as though they'd been haphazardly picked out in watercolour this morning. But their power was like a magnet to every cell of iron in my body. I had to tear my gaze away again.

'Good morning, Dr Fenwick.'

'And to you. I had a wonderful sleep,' I admitted before he asked.

'I am so pleased to hear it. The mist has only arrived in the last ten minutes. It will pass, though. We must get back to the sheds, madam, but I have cooked some porridge as I was taught as a child by Master Saxon's grandfather.'

He pointed to the table, laid out ready for me. 'And, of course, tea.' He noticed me shiver and reached for a soft stole he had already laid out on the back of the chair. 'This is from Kashmir.' He touched his chin. 'From the softest wool of the goat's beard.'

I smiled in thanks and allowed him to wrap the pale sheath of woven wool around my shoulders. It was whisper-thin but its warmth was immediate and surprisingly complete. I would have to hunt down one of these to buy before I left.

'How is Professor Vickery?'

'It seems home is the great healer, Dr Fenwick. Would you believe me if I told you that Master Saxon drank a pot of tea on his own?'

I know my mouth gaped. 'Truly?'

He nodded, smiling benignly.

'He's sitting up?' I couldn't hide my incredulity and he enjoyed it.

'Briefly. Sleeping now, which is why I didn't disturb you. The fever began to break through the night. I stayed with him, as I promised you I would. I watched the shivering arrive and then I watched him become still and sleep properly. He is covered now against chill.'

'He'll be weak.'

'He already is.'

'There's a false recovery . . .' I began, even though I sensed Adri already knew this. He had the grace not to stop me. 'Saxon will recognise it but he'll also ignore what he knows about the strange sense of wellness that doesn't last so we must be firm with him.'

Adri nodded.

'Anyway, that is news to give me an appetite.'

Adri beamed. 'Excellent.' He waved a finger and two other people arrived, young men this time.

'Are these your nephews, Adri?'

'One son, one nephew. We all work in the gardens, madam, although I oversee the processing of the leaves. Please forgive us that you will be alone. I can look in tonight?'

'Adri, we shall be fine. Can you send up some fresh food . . . perhaps some eggs, that broth?'

He nodded. 'This I will do. Enjoy the tea while it is hot.'

'Brackenridge Estate?'

'We only serve our own tea here,' he assured. He touched the pot with pride. 'Our latest monsoon flush,' he explained. 'The leaves were plucked in mid-July midst the lashing rains and humidity of the valley. After anyone's long journey up the hill from Siliguri this is the ideal "pick-me-up", as you British say. May I?'

I nodded and then gave an involuntary sound of surprise at the colour as he poured. 'Looks like it's been brewed from the bark of trees,' I admitted.

He looked impressed by this notion. 'Nothing delicate about it, Dr Fenwick.'

'People tell me Assam tea is the hearty one.'

He lifted an eyebrow. 'But Assam tea is for the world to enjoy. Darjeeling is for royalty.' He smiled and handed me a cup of tea that was a richly red-brown. 'Milk?'

'I shouldn't, should I?' I asked but he could hear in my voice how much I wanted milk in my tea.

'Just a dash.' He smiled and obliged. 'There is a bell on the verandah.' He pointed. 'If you need help, Dr Fenwick, with anything, ring that bell. Someone will run up.' Now he gestured to the sheds down the hill in the distance. 'That's where I work. It's also where we dry the leaves and they become tea. You must visit.'

'I shall.' I smiled.

'Remember the bell,' he reminded. 'You will be alone all day.'

I nodded with confidence, adding, 'Don't worry.' I watched him leave with his niece and nephew. They fell in step behind him and headed down the hill.

The porridge was thick enough to cut with a spoon – just how I liked it, I thought, feeling like Goldilocks in that moment.

Rich milk was lifting the solid mass from beneath while its surface was daubed with honey that glistened a burnt toffee colour, looking like molten gold with the morning sun's light firing it. Seated here, on the verandah, overlooking the steppes that dropped away gradually and took on a hummocked appearance due to the round bushes of tea and the purplish haze of mountains in the background, I was tempted to pinch my skin, be sure I was here. I ate deliberately, chewing carefully to savour each mouthful, to fix this special scene, this new experience into my memories for when I was returned to grey London and city life.

As I sipped my tea the low cloud began clearing and Darjeeling's protectors were no longer shadows in the mists. I smiled, full of helpless admiration as the kings of the skies emerged from the veil of vapour. 'How does anyone ever leave here unchanged?' I asked them.

A zephyr trembled through the tea bushes in answer and I swore I could hear Kangchenjunga whisper that no one ever does.

I stood at the doorway to Saxon's chamber. I was now on unfamiliar ground; it felt like each footstep I made took me closer to quicksand, although I didn't know where exactly the sinking sands were or even what they were. It was as though I was now participating in a stage play and an invisible director was calling the moves from the wings of the theatre. It wasn't that I felt like a puppet so much as someone no longer in control; I think I'd handed that control to Fate, or some force outside of myself.

I was looking into the room that was sparsely furnished but with the clutter of childhood evident, although only the items that must still have been meaningful to him. There were no paintings or artworks by his hand, from what I could tell, and yet there was a clay model that had captured the ugly hunch of a toad with a ridiculously wide, smiling mouth that made it a handsome piece.

Fresh meadow flowers, presumably put in that morning, looked at ease in that mouth.

I thought he was deeply asleep but his head turned at the sound of a floorboard creak.

'Did I disturb you?' I said, embarrassed to be caught on tiptoe. It was a redundant question but I was compelled to achieve some sort of introductory talk between us. I felt the gap between us was littered with invisible obstacles, like broken glass shards waiting to cut me and remind me that my actions – no matter how blameless I might be – did cause him suffering.

'No.' His voice was croaky and even from halfway across the room I could see his eyes were shot through with bloodied capillaries. 'No one ever could get across this floor without sounding the creak; only I know how to avoid it.'

I smiled at his memory. 'Well . . .' I began as breezily as I dared. 'Aren't you an amazing patient? I thought we'd be days in anxiety but you've surprised us all.'

He stared up at me through eyes of a colour that still struck me as being the cobalt used for expensive ceramics. I'd arrived at his bedside. 'May I?' I asked, gesturing at the bed as there was no single chair nearby.

'You may,' he said, his voice scratchy but his tone hard to judge. He glanced at the water nearby.

'Oh, let me help you.' I reached for the beaker and he surprised me by pulling himself to his elbows. I watched his arms shake from the effort but, even so, I was impressed with his recovery. 'Saxon. You mustn't exert yourself.'

'You do realise I'm a doctor,' he said, swallowing and cutting his gaze over the beaker to me.

'And doctors make the worst patients and even worse at self-diagnoses.' I took the beaker, striving to sound bright. 'Adri is sending up broth and tea, some other fresh food.'

He let his head drop back to the pillow. As impressive as his recovery was, it was also obvious how weakened he remained. 'Why did you come?'

'I . . . I had to.'

'That's no answer.' He faced away from the view and all that was lovely about this place. He chose a blank whitewashed wall instead, with a single shelf of books and some childhood clutter. And this was because of me.

I took a breath. 'I heard you were sick. Matron said the TB was back. I was the most qualified to help.'

'The hospital would not have sent you.'

'I came of my own accord.'

'I don't need you, Dr Fenwick.'

'Oh really? You prefer a shivering, hallucinatory state in Siliguri?'

'It wasn't a conscious choice.'

'Precisely. If I hadn't arrived when I did you could well have died there.'

'Better to die here, you think?'

He was twisting my words. But I was better prepared for the bite of his sarcasm, even ready with a swift, acerbic response. 'Yes. Except once again you've made one of your miraculous and fast recoveries. Obviously a habit.'

I watched him shift with effort to turn even more of his back to me. I studied it, concentrating on the two large contusions that were only just beginning to leak blood . . . or *extravasate*, I corrected in my mind, into the surrounding tissue. Considering the damage in this clinical way helped me to keep a distance, keep my emotion withheld; if I didn't think of it as Saxon's flesh, bruised from a blunt trauma, I could stay in control. He'd presumably leaned his cheek onto the fold of his elbow but all I could see were fingers curling from beneath the bandaging on his burnt hand around where his scruffy hair flicked. 'Leave me, please,' he said.

'I can't do that, Saxon.'

'Hippocratic oath?' His voice sounded muffled.

I made a decision to be conciliatory. We would reach no middle ground if I continued to match his hostility. Revealing my true motive forced me to take a slow breath first. 'Listen, Saxon, I couldn't forgive myself if —'

He ignored me and my peaceable efforts. 'But you've forgiven yourself for the death of two young people?'

It was the return slap, long overdue. Tears shockingly sprang with the speed that blood flows from a deep cut and I had to accept I was most certainly not in control.

'No,' I answered in not much more than a whisper.

'Thank you for not trying to justify your actions,' he said to the wall. 'I watched them both die, Isla.'

'I know.'

'But you can't know how it felt. I was helpless. None of my doctoring skills could save them.'

'Don't torture yourself,' I pleaded.

'Why not? They were tortured. The killers found us so fast. We were still in Siliguri, making arrangements,' he said, his voice not much above a croak. 'They chased Naz and Pratiti out of the clinic, where I thought they were safely hidden for a couple of hours – chased them into the street like dogs, yelling and shoving them. No one intervened other than me but I was one against six men and they beat me back too. They used clubs to deliver crushing, heavy blows, and they used thinner bamboo to whip Pratiti's face until it was swollen and bleeding beyond recognition. And still she struggled to help Naz as he tried to cover their child with his body. It was the most pitiful scene anyone could have the horror to witness. Yet bystanders watched with a ghoulish, uninvested interest. Despite what I already knew about the wrath of the castes, I was ashamed and appalled by the audience's collective lack of sympathy. To those watching it was a killing rooted in honour and thus justified and they would bear witness – that's all . . . which is more than I can say for us. We did so much more. We meddled and two young people paid the price.'

I was not trying to hide my tears. I no longer cared if he minded my touch. I moved to lean against the bed and pull his shoulder around. I needed to look upon him. He was too weakened to resist me but his gaze was fierce, unflinching and full of accusation. It felt like another blow being landed. Even so, I tried again. 'They would have been killed anyway. I was assured of this.'

'No one is sure of anything in life. I could have got them back to Calcutta.'

'No, Saxon, they were —'

'Regretting their actions!' he snapped and the effort drained him. 'If only we'd left them alone they'd have reached the same conclusion that their lives were too precious. We should have counselled them instead of hiding them in the hospital and encouraging them in their madness. And then it was too late – I was put in the impossible position of having to get them away. I hoped I'd put enough time between us and their pursuers that I could somehow disappear with them into the foothills, make a more assured attempt to keep them safe. Even so I was glad they were convinced about returning home while we were on the train.'

I looked surprised through my silent tears.

He nodded. 'Pratiti made the decision to rid herself of the baby.'

I gasped and he sneered at me.

'They were scared, Isla. They didn't want to die. They loved one another – yes – but they didn't want to die for a love that might end in each other's murder or alienation from everything they knew, everything they loved. They needed time and an adult around them to make them think clearly, see their true situation in sharp relief. They arrived at the conclusion that running was simply putting off the inevitable.'

'But how could they have saved themselves?'

'Got rid of the baby. If you'd asked me to help with that they might well have returned to their families and their lives.'

'And forgotten about each other?'

'Not forgotten. You don't forget a love that is true. But you can live with its memory. You can still make a good life even if you're not with that person you truly love.'

'You believe that?'

'Of course I do! Isla, wake up. All over the world there are people married to people they like well enough – or not at all – and all over the world those same people might well hold another love secret and close to their hearts. It may be a love from youth, it may be their first love, it may be true love found too late. Whatever it is, they feel it transcends their everyday lives and nourishes them . . . even if only as a memory. Naz and Pratiti found their realism on that train while in fear for their lives. We'd agreed to take the next train back and perhaps their families didn't ever need to know the truth. We fashioned lies for their absences that could have worked.' He balled his fists in redundant fury. 'It could have worked!'

'I'm sorry.' It was such a useless offering against his trauma.

'Sorry couldn't save them. I was sorry, they were sorry . . . we're all sorry. Perhaps even Pratiti's father, who was among the enraged relatives, filled with blind, killing righteousness, is sorry now that he's calmed down. But Pratiti is dead. Murdered by her own family, by his hand, on his orders.'

I gulped back a sob but he wasn't taking any pity on me. His glare had found a fresh energy to gleam with his own style of righteous rage. 'They made her watch them kill Naz first. I don't suppose anyone mentioned that, did they?'

I shook my head, staring at the faded floral eiderdown through a watery lens as tears leaked in heavy droplets onto its fabric. 'After beating him senseless, they roused him with a pail of water so that he was aware enough when they hacked at him with machetes. His feet were taken first.'

I began to tremble. 'Saxon, don't —' I pleaded.

'Five sharp blades. Again and again they dropped upon him until what remained looked like meat instead of a person. I couldn't stop them. I tried.'

Imagining the cuts from those same blades beneath the bandages on his arms I stood up, almost covering my ears like a child.

'Hear it! And understand it, so you are never tempted to meddle again in affairs that are not yours. After forcing her to bear witness to her lover's execution, they picked up another pail, the contents of which they poured over her. The mob that had gathered stepped back when they smelled petrol.'

I knew what was coming then in this horror story but I also knew it was hopeless to try to stop this torrent of pain Saxon was inflicting. It was a toxin within him and no doubt adding to his illness. It needed to be released, vomited out with all the pus in his mind so that he had some chance to heal.

'I yelled, cajoled, I begged. In fact, Isla – and I think Miles would have loved it – I pleaded, on my knees, to the men of her family to spare her. They didn't even know about the baby. If they had, I suspect they would have cut it from her belly before they lit the match that ignited her.'

I looked at his bandaged hands and arms, would have to re-dress them soon, and yet didn't want to confront the wounds that would likely remain as scars and a reminder forever of deaths he couldn't prevent.

'She lit instantly like a small bonfire; the whooshing sound of erupting into flames I will hear in my nightmares forevermore.

I could no longer get close by then and if I ran for water, I couldn't have saved her. The doctor in me knew it was better now for her to die quickly than to hope she could recover from burns. It would have meant unspeakable suffering and so, like the villagers, I bore witness instead despite her screams for mercy. I watched her long glossy hair shrivel while her head charred; the fire consumed her in minutes. You know I'm surprised how fast a human burns and yet it felt like it took my whole life to watch Pratiti wither beneath those flames that were supposedly to cleanse.'

'Saxon, stop . . .' I sobbed.

He refused. 'Finally the kneeling, melted mass toppled backwards; the flames began to die back once the fuel had consumed itself and her life. At last, once she fell, I was allowed to pull off my jacket and cover her smoking, twisted, blackened corpse. Her relatives cried then. Now they could keen over the loss of their daughter, sister, niece, cousin . . .' He took a slow breath, coughing it out, refusing my help or a sip of water.

When he stopped coughing and his breath came in a ghastly wheeze, he pressed on with his tale. 'People moved away and I lost track. I roused from my stupor to find nothing but a sticky stain on the street as testimony that Pratiti and her unborn child had once lived and died there. The flames had even burned away Naz's spilled blood. I have no idea where his body had been taken or dumped. As my helpers from the clinic moved me, I stared at the discolouration on the street but already humanity was filling the space, while cattle, none the wiser, plodded through Pratiti's shadow. But it doesn't matter how far away I run, or how many years I put between myself and this horror, Isla, I will never rid myself of the smell of burning mother and child from my memory. My only consolation – and it is so small to be near negligible – is that the doctor in me believes that that beautiful young woman died within a minute from asphyxiation. Fortunately, the fire was fierce and the smoke great.'

I thought he was done but he needed to deliver one final blow with the precision of a surgeon. 'I'm not sure you have any consolation, though.'

We sat in a heavy silence as though our lives were suspended in time. He'd said his piece and had gladly shifted part of his pain to me. I had nothing to offer; even my tears had dried, making it worse . . . as though even that emotional crutch was being denied. Through the open windows of his room I could hear every other sound around us with such tight clarity it felt like a spring was being coiled within. Birds chirruped with annoying jollity like unwelcome guests and the distant voices of the tea pickers carried up the slopes of the gardens; the burst of laughter between women that should have made me smile instead felt mocking.

I had to say something. I couldn't just stand, straighten my skirts and leave. Besides, I knew he needed some proper medical care for a little longer. Looking for an answer, my mind fled to my wise father and I could all but hear him speaking one of his favourite sayings along the lines that you cannot prevent the birds of sorrow from flying over your head, but you can prevent them building nests in your hair.

'Ancient Oriental proverb, darling . . . one I live by.' Another favourite abstract item of wisdom was that of not being able to put blossom back on the trees. I think my father had read Chinese philosophy at some stage and that reasoning resonated with me now.

'Saxon.'

'Still here?' It was meanly spoken but he was in a cruel mood.

'I failed them but not because I didn't try to help them. I helped them but in the wrong way; I see that now. I won't trouble you with the whys or wherefores other than to say I, too, was put into an impossible position in the moment and I reacted the only way I knew how. If I could undo it and make a different decision knowing what I know now, I would.' *You can't put blossom back on trees.*

'I can't bring them back but I can fix the mess.' I sniffed for fear of a leaking nose that would only make me look and feel more pathetic.

My patient turned and sighed at me. 'There's a handkerchief in the drawer over there,' he said, pointing with his chin.

I shook my head. 'I'll be fine. You've given me enough. Look, Saxon, let me help you to get well and —'

'I don't need —'

'You do,' I said, more firmly than I thought I was capable of at that moment. 'You need someone who knows what they're doing to undress and re-dress the wounds or the skin on your arms is going to stiffen and lead to all sorts of problems for your work in the future.' Despite his blank expression I could see that he agreed but was finding it hard to admit. 'So let me just help you get well . . . at least on your way to a proper recovery so I can leave you knowing your burn is healing, that the TB is arrested.'

He shook his head.

'Why? Why won't you let me do this for you?' I had thrown my hands wide in despair and my voice cracked. I hated to hear the weakness.

I think he did too. It made him angry. 'It's not about Naz and Pratiti. You can't fix that mess – neither can I; no one can. I just can't have you around me in this weakened state. All right?'

I could feel my forehead wrinkling, my mouth forming a twist of confusion. 'Why?'

'For a clever woman you're awfully dim, Dr Fenwick.'

Now all I could do was stare at him, perplexed. I shook my head with bewilderment and he stared at me as though I was simple. Clearly it was because I couldn't catch his meaning. 'You can't have a doctor around you because you're weak and need doctoring?'

He glared but pressed on. 'Not *a* doctor. *You*. I find it risky to have you near when I lack my usual strength. It was dangerous in the Calcutta Club and it's only going to be worse here where there are no prying eyes.'

It dawned on me finally. Heavens, I was slow. A treacherous and nervous half laugh erupted from me as though I was a child caught with her hand in the sweetie jar. I clamped my mouth over the inappropriate bluster and stared back at him in surprise. The warming sensation of embarrassment began to creep up from my throat.

'Uncharacteristically silent, Dr Fenwick, but you did push me and I'm hardly the gold-star performer for subtlety. So, all right, then. Do we at least agree that I have not asked for your help nor have I encouraged you to remain here?'

I was still choked for what to say and was glad he gave me the path forward so I could utter something helpful and leave. 'Quite the opposite,' I confirmed in a contrived, brisk tone. 'Now rest. I'll be back with supplies and food.'

I don't even know what I meant by that but it sounded crisply professional, every inch a doctor . . . before I turned on my heel and strode out of the room, closing the door behind me to shut him out of my immediate space. I leaned back against the wall, appalled at how undone I felt, my breath trapped in my chest.

Breathe, I demanded, suddenly and acutely aware of my heartbeat, and furious that it was pounding.

I realised I had stopped directly behind where he lay and even if it were in my imagination, I swear I could feel the heat of him through those thick walls. This is what he was warning me about . . . warning both of us away from.

I knew I should go. Not just go from his rooms but this house. In fact, I should leave Darjeeling. Run from India . . . flee back to England and the arms of Jove. Unfortunately, the untidiness of my behaviour these last few weeks had reached far deeper than I thought. And Saxon's warning did nothing more than blunt my

good judgement, it seemed, because I pushed off the wall, straightened my shoulders and made the pact with myself that no matter
what happened, I intended to see him well and on his path to
recovery before I left him.

He said it was 'risky'; used the word 'dangerous'. But I was
convinced I had no weakness in this regard and all the right armour
in place.

21

It was late afternoon and Adri had returned, this time badgering a troupe of people who had followed him up the hill with his sharp instructions. I gathered they'd brought food and other supplies. Saxon was much brighter in himself. Some colour had returned to his complexion and he conversed easily with Adri in the local language; I stood silently at the doorway to his room and watched them share a fond smile that spoke of a warm history between these two.

I walked Adri out, offering to pay for the food, but he waved my protest away and said Master Saxon would sort it out. I wished him and his folk farewell with thanks, and now once more we were alone, but I sensed a shift of mood in my patient when I returned to check on him. Perhaps it was Adri's influence? Whatever had been exchanged it felt to me as though Saxon had grudgingly decided that, as I was clearly not leaving, he would tolerate my presence with a more grateful attitude.

'It's obvious that Adri is incredibly fond of you,' I began into the silence as I unnecessarily fussed with his bedclothes, tucking in corners that were already neatly tucked.

He swallowed the remnants of some broth and replaced the mug on the bedside table. 'His family has been with us for decades.'

'So I understand.' I stood at the bottom of his bed, unsure of my next move.

'It's how it is up here. Generations of tea growers, pickers, driers and processors . . . alongside generations of plantation owners.'

I looked out of his windows with a sigh, past the patio I could see to where the land dropped away to the valley. 'To describe this place as beautiful is inadequate. It's paradise and even that phrasing is overused and seems not to fully sum it up.'

He fixed my gaze to his. 'I'm glad it strikes you this way.'

'Who wouldn't be awed?'

He shook his head with a shrug as if to suggest he knew of these very people.

'I know it's your home,' I continued, 'but what do you love most about it?' I needed him talking so I could hear how he sounded as he breathed, and also to help get us away from those sinking sands of recrimination that surely wanted to swallow me.

He didn't hesitate at my question. 'Its simplicity. Everything about life is clear, uncomplicated.'

'Right.'

'You don't think so?' He gestured to the seat that he'd asked Adri to bring in for me.

I moved to sit in it now, facing him, and leaned an elbow on the bed. I chanced a grin. 'Those mountains change. One moment they dominate the landscape, and then in a few heartbeats the mist shades them away. Sometimes they're purple, right now almost glacial blue. I think that makes them complex . . . full of intrigue.'

He smiled. 'Yes, but they are there, have been for millennia, and you can count on that never changing. They're reliable.'

I felt he was using them as a metaphor. 'Not like people, you mean?' Oh, what was wrong with me, leading myself straight back to the marshlands?

'Indeed. All I can hear is the birdsong of the hills. That is healing in itself.'

I wasn't prepared for him to cover my hand with his. His fingers loosely wrapped beneath my palm and I was sure I could feel each fingertip's pressure against my skin. 'Anger has made me remiss. Isla, I do need to thank you for bringing me here.'

I didn't move my fingers; I held his gaze and aimed for a doctor's controlled response. 'You were curled up in fever but I noticed you were staring towards a tiny window high on the wall of that clinic you run.'

He frowned. 'I don't remember that.'

'I believe you were willing yourself towards the outdoors, the fresher air . . . probably the mountains. It's how I got the idea. It was from you. You showed me the way: what you wanted, what was needed.'

The pressure around my hand became slightly harder. It was only a small shift but now his fingers touched the most sensitive part of my hand.

'Then we share something very special, if we can communicate without words,' he continued.

'What about your wife?'

'What about her?' His tone was even but I sensed suspicion.

'Do you want me to let her know you're unwell, that you're here at Brackenridge? Perhaps —'

'I do not. But thank you. She doesn't need to be unnecessarily worried.'

It was clear he did not like me referring to his wife; either that or he didn't like me speaking of his other life . . . the one away from the India that he loved. I took his message to steer away from that topic for now. 'What about some more tea?' I offered, and could hear the self-conscious tone.

'Let's talk . . . while we can.'

'What do you mean?' I reacted, thinking he was referring to a potential relapse or worse.

A crooked grin lifted one side of his mouth. 'I mean, before we begin arguing; it's our usual pathway.'

'Let's aim not to while you're sick.'

'Twice now you've cared for me in illness. You do know there's an old superstition that if you make it to three times, you have to stay?'

It was good to laugh with him again. I even covered his hand with mine now, feeling immediately less tense. 'You're making that up.'

'No,' he said, feigning indignation. 'It's an old saying from Bhutan.'

I doubted it but it was amusing. 'Well, I refuse to let you be sick a third time.'

'Pity,' he murmured. We looked at each other and I surprised myself at not being embarrassed to enjoy the subtext of that remark.

'Let me look at the burn, change the dressing while we chat. What would you like to talk about?' I said, even though I would have liked to remain in that jokey mood of innuendo. His gaze held me like an addiction. I found it took genuine willpower to look away. I began to unravel the bandage.

'Will you let me go outside, Doctor?'

I cut him a look of worry. 'Oh, is that wise?'

'Fresh, chilly mountain air. Nothing like it for TB.'

I nodded. 'Yes, of course that's true and we can try, but, Saxon, if you stagger or fall, I'm not strong enough to hold you,' I warned.

'Then let me fall,' he said, making it sound so simple. 'Being out there will do wonders.'

'Now?'

He shrugged. 'In the next hour the temperature is going to drop dramatically. Now is best.'

'Let me sort your hand first.' The burn was angry and moist. 'Second degree, in my opinion.'

He nodded.

'Pain?'

'Plenty.'

'Right. I've brought some painkiller for you to inhale. We'll change the dressing twice a day and use cold flannels. Debriding, perhaps, when the blisters begin to dry?'

He nodded.

I soaked off wherever the dressing had stuck to his wound and spent another ten minutes, frustrating him while I fussed over the wound care, before finally using fresh strips of bedsheet that Adri had cut and boiled through the night as my bandaging.

Getting him out of bed and into socks, slippers, a dressing-gown and a rug thrown about him all but exhausted him.

'Wait here,' I said, leaving him seated on the edge of his bed, wheezing. 'Give me two minutes.'

I skipped down the corridor, gathering rugs and cushions from my room before setting up a day bed fit for a maharajah on the verandah. Surveying my work, feeling it would do, I was shocked to see him limp into the open, but witnessing the genuine pleasure in his expression and how it creased his face into smiles pushed away my irritation. It looked as though every muscle of his face was all about joy. His eyes shone brighter as he looked upon what I could well imagine was his favourite vista.

'Saxon, really, you do test one's patience. I asked you to wait.'

He ignored me but put out an arm. I let him lean his weight against me as we manoeuvred him onto the day bed and then I was all about briskly snuggling him in as one might a child against winter's elements. The dying afternoon was still mild but the wind could cut, I'd noticed.

'Ah, I can smell it's August,' he said, his long legs stretched out, but he insisted on sitting up.

'How?'

'Imprinted on *le grand lobe lymbique*,' he said, touching his temple.

'I too have read Broca's work. I thought the French physician was mostly associated with speech and language processing.'

'It is, but he gave us more insight into the mysterious paleo-mammalian brain that's triggered new research. Doesn't that whole area of memory, emotion, motivation, intrigue you?'

'It does.'

He shook his head in soft awe. 'That small soft matter at the base of my brain is responsible for me inherently knowing it's August through sense alone . . . how it feels, how the air tastes,' he said, sticking out his tongue and wiggling it for effect to make me smile helplessly. He inhaled, lids lowered. 'How the landscape smells,' he said, sounding dreamy.

'How does it smell?'

He opened his eyes. 'You tell me. Give me a word.'

I played along. 'Grassy.'

'Good. How about wet leaves?'

'That's two words,' I corrected and he gave a look of amuse-ment that conceded my point.

With eyes closed he inhaled his favourite world again. 'I can smell the tea from the withering troughs,' he continued, 'and I know the difference in bouquet between first flush and monsoon flush so I know what time of year it is from the most prehistoric sense I own.'

'Withering troughs?'

'When I'm strong enough I'll take you down there and explain the process of tea from the bush to the teapot.'

I nodded. 'I'll look forward to that. Speaking of which, how about a pot?'

'Of tea?'

'No, I was thinking wine.'

He gave me a look of disdain. 'You're going to make it?'

'I see no one else who will. You know something, Saxon? I think you've spent too long around people who wait on you.'

'And you don't have any help at home?'

'In London we have a housekeeper who comes in to keep us tidy but I do cook for my father and myself most evenings.'

'Really?'

I nodded, surprised that he envisaged me as being waited on. 'I even clean my own boots, you know. I catch a bus to work, or I ride my bicycle in the summer.'

'Should I be giving you an award?'

I grinned. 'No, but you should refrain from making judgements. I don't know about the women you mix with in England but I'm today's London girl, who doesn't wait for a man or anyone else to do . . .' I couldn't find a word that felt neutral, so I plumped for a meaningless one. 'Things for her.'

'How does your fiancé feel about your fierce independence?'

I shrugged. 'Technically he's not my fiancé, although I am returning to marry him. Even so, you'll note Jove's not here directing my life, is he?' I turned to walk back into the house, affecting a sort of cheeky spin on my heels, hoping that my response hit the right note of brazen without sounding contemptuous of Jove, but as the deeper hallway swallowed me I wondered to myself what I had hoped to convey to Saxon with that comment. I thought of myself as someone who didn't make empty remarks. Had I just opened up the doors of my life to Saxon Vickery, suggesting I could do whatever I wanted? And within that frame, did that move from beyond *I can think how I choose* to *I will behave how I want* without fearing repercussion? I blamed Saxon. It didn't matter if we were having an out-and-out disagreement that stretched to raised voices and yes, even violence, or whether we were friendly, as we were now; I behaved differently around him.

I looked into rooms, their furniture covered with dust sheets, and ultimately found my way to a kitchen. It was small, I thought, for a house of this size but it was still bigger than our kitchen in London. The room smelt musty and while I could tell Adri's folks had wiped down the surfaces, I could see their barefoot prints in the layer of dust on the floor as though ghosts had stepped here. I began opening cupboards, forcing them to yield the air they'd held tight for years. All the implements required for tea were left neatly on a counter.

More of the broth and a small helping of rice, plus some curried meat, were also left on the stove. Fresh eggs, milk, boiled water and oats for porridge had been provisioned as well. I still needed to do some food shopping, I suspected, so I could get some variety into Saxon's diet, particularly some vegetables and fruit.

A small wood fire had been lit in the oven, and was merrily smouldering. I fed it with some kindling and then tossed in a couple of logs. With a spirit lamp, the brass kettle felt as though it took a full year to come to the boil but I spent the time putting together a tray and then amusing myself drifting through the unlocked rooms in the house. I didn't touch anything. I didn't open their shutters, although I wanted to; instead I let my eyes adjust to the distilled soft afternoon sunlight that stole through the angled louvres and I watched the dust motes I'd disturbed dance in muted light before they settled back down to rest.

I tried to imagine the house echoing with childhood squeals and laughter of the brothers, with their mother shooshing them, a father smiling with a pipe nearby. Instinctively I decided that was not how Saxon's family had lived; it was as though

Brackenridge was setting me right about the presumption. No, this was not a house of much laughter but there was no doubting it loved its family and sat here beneath its dust covers, ever ready to welcome its members back. In my wanderings I fetched the painkiller for Saxon; though he was not asking for it, I suspected he needed it.

I returned to the kitchen, opening the two safes easily although the keys hung from both locks and I presumed in days gone by one kept meat, the other dairy, and were locked up against thieving. I had entered a bygone world in this kitchen; it was thoroughly English in its layout and all the pots and pans were familiar to me now, including the aluminium *degshis* that the locals favoured cooking in, but it did feel as though it was trapped in my grandmother's Victorian era. That thought prompted me to remember the chamber pots that would need to be emptied regularly. Given we would likely be here for a week or more, we were going to need some staples. I would have to speak to Adri about purchasing those goods.

I made the tea, pouring boiling water over three scoops of leaves: one for each drinker and one for the pot, I heard my granny say in my mind. I covered it with a discoloured old cosy that someone had made and embroidered with a fine eye for detail and a keen needle. I wondered if it was Saxon's mother who'd put love into it.

And then I was drifting back down the lonely corridor but smiling to myself, feeling suddenly domestic after months of spending most waking hours in a hospital ward. The mildness of just twenty minutes or so earlier had stolen away, replaced by the pinch of chill as I stepped back out onto the verandah. I gave a soft gasp and shivered, glad that I'd urged Saxon to make himself comfy in the end portion of the verandah where it had been glazed, like a tiny conservatory.

'You look pleased with yourself,' he remarked as I set the tray down.

'I was just thinking that I haven't so much as cooked myself a slice of toast since arriving in India.'

He cut me an ironic grin. 'And there you have part of the secret as to why so many Brits love living here and never want to leave India. Some of the men who would conduct lives of little consequence in menial desk jobs back home can live like kings out here, with a retinue of servants to wait on their every whim.'

I shook my head. 'Haughty wives, no doubt, giving a lazy savage a good clip around the ear, eh?'

He smiled sadly. 'Not all but too many.'

I handed him the inhaler, making sure he breathed in some low-level morphine. 'How about the lady of the house here?' I asked, keen to learn more. I settled into a wicker chair next to him, against plump cushions whose colours had faded in the sunlight.

He regarded me, sighing out from the inhalation. 'My mother, you mean?'

I nodded. 'Tell me about the family while the tea brews.'

I watched him shiver a little and wasn't sure if it was the dropping temperature, his illness, pain relief, or my mention of his family.

'I don't think we're that different from many other families. I suppose the best way to describe my mother is cold.' His frankness caught me off-guard but he didn't notice my wince as he was staring into the distance, remembering. 'I think love was an alien concept for her. I didn't know my grandparents well but I think as they raised four boys, the single girl in their midst was confusing and they treated her as something strangely separate. They didn't allow for her emotions, which I suppose she in turn learned to damp down until they hardly ever appeared. Meanwhile, my father was about as distant a character as you could imagine. It was almost like the angels that arrange the chess pieces of life decided to have some fun and bring together two remote people who were starved of affection and any knowledge of how to give it. That they worked out how to have children is remarkable,' he added, with a helpless trill of sarcasm edging the words, 'and we were raised in an atmosphere of right and wrong – no grey areas.' He shrugged.

'That's it?'

'What else would you like to know? Perhaps that I didn't like my parents and I sense they felt much the same way about me?'

'Oh, Saxon, why? How could they not love you?' I sounded devastated but felt instantly stupid for the patronising tone; I didn't know them so why should I care?

He gave me another of his withering looks. 'Isn't that tea brewed?'

'Half a minute more,' I said. Determined to hear it, I risked pushing. 'Tell me about them and you, your brother.' I didn't dare trespass on the memory of a dead sister.

He impressed me by continuing. 'Well, they liked Rex in their own way, and because I'm the antithesis of my brother – he was the right and I was the wrong – they found me to be the imposition I always felt.'

I resisted offering any sympathy. 'How are you boys so different?'

He sighed, wearying of my curiosity. 'Rex aimed to ingratiate. He wanted their love and pride . . . earned it the hard way by pleasing them in every way he could. I suppose from very young I must have decided that, as their son, I was owed their love and didn't feel obliged to prove myself worthy of it.'

I turned the pot and ignored his gentle scoff. 'My granny insisted,' I said. 'Three times.'

'Be careful not to turn it widdershins or you may invite the devil here,' he cautioned.

I grinned, looking out. 'Not with those sentinels guarding us.'

He returned my smile. 'That's how I regard Kangchenjunga too. He and his friends are my guardians.'

I nodded. 'Well, they loved you, even if your parents didn't.'

'My parents tolerated me. I was a male Vickery – I got that bit right.'

I poured the tea in a gentle torrent of amber light, the liquid curling around the inside of the cups to spin gently. 'No milk for you yet, and no sugar even if we wanted,' I warned.

'None needed.' He took the cup I offered and blew on the steam through lips that looked like they'd whistle when he was happy. I wished I could see him happy. He gave a low sigh. 'Not bad, Dr Fenwick.'

'How about you and Rex? You said you don't communicate much.'

'Barely,' he said, in a hard tone. 'He lives in Hampshire somewhere. I'm sure I mentioned that we have nothing in common.'

'You have Brackenridge in common.'

He remained silent with that remark for longer than felt comfortable. Then he shifted, swallowed the tea and I immediately poured him a second; the more he drank of this, the better. 'We had Brackenridge and our childhoods in common, that's all. He doesn't get on with me.'

I resisted a sarcastic remark along the lines of *I wonder why*. Instead I said: 'Is he married?'

'Yes. Three children.'

'What does Rex do?'

'He's a solicitor. He isn't a happy man.'

'How come?'

'He was one for the easy path: not terribly good at anything, including the law, but mostly because he was lazy rather than

307

lacking in intelligence. Instead of applying himself he decided to marry well.'

'For money, you mean?'

He nodded. 'Rex chose with great care – but not too long after the wedding his wife's family suffered terrible losses financially. I don't know the cause. They were involved in mining at home and abroad in Africa and I have a suspicion they were involved with the *Titanic* and lost plenty on that. Anyway, the wife he thought would be an heiress became a near pauper overnight.'

I lifted a shoulder in confusion. 'Why does that affect you . . . your relationship with him, I mean?'

'Because I also married well. My wife inherited handsomely from her grandparents and from her father – a modern man who believed that the daughter he loved as much as his son deserved equality. Anyway, for Frances, her fortune remains intact.'

I felt as though something invisible and mean had just clawed my throat. So far while dwelling on Saxon I had managed to keep thoughts of his wife apart. He barely referred to her, so it had been easy to convince myself she didn't exist. And I suppose until the tea gardens I'd never felt the investment in him as strongly as I did now. Ownership felt like an ugly word, and I wouldn't permit myself to regard him that way, and somehow friendship was, under the circumstances, a little too vague. We were more than friends but less than lovers; a wife and fiancé hadn't needed serious consideration but suddenly I felt I was deliberately blinkering myself. And I knew this because at the mention of her name stings accompanied my swallow and I realised it was jealousy; suddenly she was a real person standing beside us. I tried to drink away those green thorns.

Oblivious, he continued, pressing those invisible but painfully sharp needles into me. 'She is a generous woman, educated, a will of iron and boundless confidence that comes from wealth. However, her affection for me, I've come to realise, is equally boundless, as is her tolerance of my needs.'

'Your needs?' I choked out.

'To be here and not there with her,' he explained and his voice suddenly sounded raw.

I backed away from seeing him so naked. 'And Rex envies you your wife, you mean?'

'Not the person. His wife is beautiful, you see, but he envies me my wife's money and her affection for me, which is why he punishes me.'

'In what way?'

He had finished the second cup of tea and I'd only sipped my first. He looked wearied from the talking, or was it the remembering? 'After my father died, everything was left to Mother. And when she died, everything, including Brackenridge, was left to Rex.'

I showed the shock – it wrote itself across my face with astonishment and the cup of tea held halfway to my mouth paused in dismay. 'That doesn't sound fair.'

'I agree, but they were never fair parents so I was not as shocked as others were on my behalf. However, Rex always hated life at Brackenridge, while I never really wanted to be anywhere else. I've offered to buy it off him many times.'

'But he refuses out of spite because of your wife's fortune?'

'Something like that,' he conceded and returned a gaze to me that despite his dismissive tone held grief.

'So what will happen?'

'To Brackenridge?'

I nodded.

'He keeps it ticking over for the income it gives him, although he takes no interest in the tea industry or the potential of these tea gardens or the enrichment, education, housing and medical care of the families who look after it. He does the bare minimum required. Worse, he lets the house idle here without any regard for it. It will gradually disintegrate or he may sell it off as a guesthouse, or most likely he'll unload the whole concern to a hotel group. The tea business is growing but we need to invest in the plant and equipment, bring in more expertise as well. Rex could easily run it himself but his wife refuses to so much as visit and frankly he hates India. He needs the city noise and buzz around him; makes him feel important in his pinstripes and London address.'

'Would you like to run it?'

He blinked as if cut by the question. 'Of course I would.'

'Could you give up medicine?'

'I wouldn't have to. I could set up a clinic in Darjeeling and service the whole of the foothills.'

'And would Frances be prepared to live here?' My throat wanted to close at speaking her name aloud.

He looked away again. 'I doubt it.'

'Will you tell me more about her?' I had so many questions.

'No,' he replied in that flat way of his.

'Why?'

'Because there's no reason to know anything more than I've already mentioned.'

'I'd like to, though.'

'Why?'

'Insight?'

'Into me? Or is it just curiosity about the woman in my life?'

I swallowed. 'Please yourself,' I said in a breezy, dismissive tone, although the thorns pushed deeper.

'I usually do.' He waited a few beats. 'To answer your query, there's just not enough to keep her interested here – she's a woman of the world.'

'I see.'

'Do you?' He regarded me again with a spearing look that caused me pain in my chest.

I took a deep breath and smiled. 'Of course. India is hard work. Up here, beautiful or not, it is likely even tougher and I suspect isolating, if you aren't a loner like yourself.'

'Or you,' he added and he watched me now.

I opened my mouth to reply but realised I had nothing to say, for he knew me too well. I nodded and stood, began to clear away the cups as I formulated something bland to respond with. 'Yes, except I have responsibilities, although I hope to return to India sometime.'

'As a married woman?'

'Yes,' I said quickly. 'Jove's a great explorer of other lands and is determined to take me travelling. His favourites, I gather, are Australia and the Levant. India feels far enough away so I can't imagine how long it will take us to sail to the underneath of our planet.' I wanted to show him I wasn't guarded about Jove. I could speak about him without feeling awkward or guilty.

'Sounds like you both have plenty in common.'

'I hope so. I've known Jove since I was a child – adored him as that child.' I frowned. 'The oddity is I don't know much about him but I know how I feel when I'm with him.'

'And how is that?'

I left myself open to that question and I wasn't sure how to reply to it. 'I can't explain. Different to how I feel when I'm with you.' I was sidestepping the question.

'And how is that?' he asked, a keener edge to his tone now; clearly it was his turn to interrogate and I was obliged to answer.

I looked back at him but picked up the tray so I had an excuse to leave. 'Awkward most of the time,' and I added a smile so he couldn't take offence but also to give me something to hide the truth behind. 'I think you should head back inside, please. Do you want some help?'

'No. I thought I might stay a little longer.' He sounded as if asking for approval.

I couldn't give it. 'Perhaps tomorrow. Cool, fresh air is vital for your recovery but getting too cold is not helpful . . . as you well know.'

And yet as our gazes found each other awkwardly all my treacherous body could feel was heat.

22

The following day after changing bandages, delivering more pain-killer and getting Saxon back off to sleep, I found myself climbing a hill. I'd gamely suggested to Adri that I didn't need him to fetch food supplies and that I would enjoy stretching my legs and walking with a niece of his to one of the villages above us. I understood now why Adri gave me a look that was a mix of pity as much as concern. He knew what I didn't.

'It's a trek and will take you a long time,' he pressed.

I had shrugged. 'Our patient needs rest, not company, right now and I'll enjoy the exercise and getting higher to look out towards the plains.'

He had already tried to dissuade me twice so at that point had simply nodded. 'My niece speaks only a little English but I have told her where to take you.' He had looked at my shoes doubtfully. 'Wear your stoutest shoes, Doctor,' he offered, as clearly my soft cream leather lace-ups were inappropriate.

So here I was, regretting my casual confidence that ascending a hill of this challenging nature, in the woodlands of the Himalayan foothills, was something this city girl could take in her stride. I felt breathless within an embarrassingly short time, whereas the fourteen-year-old, who was no longer at my side but several yards ahead, looked to me as if she were strolling with no effort required for the sudden gradient we were facing. I told myself it was the age difference but that was a lie. The realisation was that I was not nearly as fit as I had presumed and that this journey was not to be one of pleasurable discovery but a stamina-sucking grind up what was feeling like a mountain rather than a hill.

Her innocent smile came easily as she looked over her shoulder. 'Are you all right, Auntie?'

I'd got used to this term in Calcutta. It was arresting at first because it always sounded too familiar and as though I was some ancient biddy, but I came to understand this was merely a term accorded to all women, strangers or known, if someone wanted to give respect.

I put a hand to my chest and showed her the struggle.

She grinned kindly. 'Nice and slow,' she reiterated, recalling the words she'd heard Adri say to her as we left, although I was sure he'd impressed this in their own language too.

I checked my watch. We'd been moving up the hill for twenty minutes. She offered me a chance to pause, passed me the water flask, which I gratefully swallowed from. We both accepted there was no point in trying to converse as we didn't understand each other sufficiently to have any meaningful exchange and so through sign language we proceeded. Her name was Shanti and, like any youngster, she skipped, flitted around, intrigued by an insect or a bird; she pointed out flowers to me, giving them names I couldn't get my tongue around, but I conveyed my pleasure with a smile. We fell into a slow, steady climb and I found losing myself in my thoughts was the best way to conquer the desire to simply stop. I didn't want to be so weak and, with no view at this stage to admire due to the thick forest our track cut through, I distracted myself by pondering Saxon's comments of the previous day.

I was glad to be away from him; distance was needed after yesterday's intimate conversation. It hadn't occurred to me but now, like a shadow following me, it nagged in my mind. 'Dangerous' was his word. Melodramatic? Yes, I thought, ridiculously so, but the shadow taunted me as it dodged the trees and hanging vines, reminding me that there was no melodrama about Saxon Vickery; he was painfully direct and with a starkly straightforward view of life and people. I was sure, as I stared at my thick-soled brown boots, that he was simply being candid with me. Honesty takes courage, especially when it bares one's true feelings, and he had made himself naked with that confession of not wanting to feel vulnerable around me, so I should be wary of dismissing it as hyperbolic. I still believed, firmly, that I was on my way home to London and only here in Darjeeling because I was exploring a part of the world I would likely never return to and because a friend was sick and needed my help. It seemed a perfectly sound explanation for my presence and still the shadow mocked from the trees. I could swear I heard laughter.

Shanti was pointing with a grin. I came out of my thoughts to follow her line of sight and noted a family of monkeys foraging. I paused to watch them, wanting to pinch myself that I was alongside these wild creatures in their natural living space. I discerned they were macaques, recalling their brown bodies and pinkish faces from the London Zoo. I smiled, watching them licking dewdrops from the low-slung foliage. One mother, with a baby on her back, pulled down a branch to give her youngster a drink. They seemed untroubled by our passing, cooing and grunting contentedly, although Shanti returned to my side and gestured towards a large single monkey that was watching us with the same intensity as we were watching its companions.

Shanti beat her chest and I grinned, understanding. This was their dominant male. She pulled at my sleeve to urge me forward and I presumed she believed we had outstayed our welcome. The male macaque confirmed this with a low shriek and we moved on.

The sounds of the forest lulled me and I became used to the calls of the macaques, the glimpses of birds and their accompanying cries. Perhaps the most striking was a small bird that was scarlet with a black head and markings, easy to pick out. I was astonished by the bright punctuation of colour and presumed that naturally this had to be a male, with its flamboyant colouring. We climbed on, my thoughts drifting back to Saxon and the real reason I was on this journey. I couldn't hide from it any longer. The shadow had stepped closer, emerging from the woodland of larch and elder, birch and chestnut to join with mine as we headed towards noon and my shadow shortened.

The fact was today I was running away from Saxon and the very danger he alluded to. I didn't even farewell him, instead cowardly leaving a bright note as he slept that I was going to explore the area and find us some food. I impressed that I was in the company of Adri's family so he was not to send out a search party. I added that he should rest and I would see him this evening.

———

With my bowl of clean water and fresh bandages, late that afternoon, I found him seated on the wall of a patio that I didn't know was there until Shanti, having packed away all that we had bought, walked me to the edge of the house's drive and directed my attention below. She waved goodbye and skipped away. Saxon cut a lonely yet romantic figure seated on his walled perch high above the valley. He had dragged a blanket around himself and looked to be lost in its folds as much as in thought. I pulled a shawl around my shoulders, not at all fooled by the mild temperature; it could drop in a few moments as the sun dipped and a breeze whirled up the hillside. I took the steps slowly.

'Still here?' He repeated his words from yesterday.

'Can't get rid of me, I'm afraid,' I answered. 'Besides, it's time to change those dressings on your arm.' I arrived to stand beside him. 'You have good colour in your face.'

He nodded absently. 'The mountains heal. I've only recently stepped out from the house, before you complain. Just had a shower, in fact – brushed my teeth, even shaved.'

'I can see,' I replied, noting damp hair.

'How was your day?'

I began unbandaging his arm, placing it on the towel on my lap and trying not to blush at the intimacy of his action. His fingers were all but curled around my thigh.

'Shanti took me up to one of the markets in the hills. Nearly killed me but she's as agile as a mountain goat.' I grinned. 'I managed to get some good fresh food. Those markets were fun. You shall eat like a king now.'

'They must have thought a movie starlet had come into their midst . . . not that they'd know what one is.'

I laughed. 'I was followed around by an ever-growing troupe of children and in the end had to buy a pile of sweets to distract them. The women all wanted to touch my hair and cheeks.'

He reached to finger the garland of hill flowers I wore, bending forward to inhale their heavy scent. 'This is a special gift of respect they've bestowed upon you. Flowers of this quality could be sold for a lot of money.'

I nodded, feeling guilty that I hadn't paid sufficient attention to that, instead enjoying the rush of charm at being hooped by flowers. I didn't dare mention this was one of half-a-dozen . . . the others I'd donated to Shanti for her family shrine.

'I didn't recognise half of the vegetables,' I admitted and he grinned knowingly. 'But Shanti chose for us.'

He looked up to regard me. His eyes were much clearer than yesterday and their gaze rested upon me more gently today. 'Had you better let someone back home know where you are?'

I shrugged. 'I've let the right people know I'm travelling in the north. Adri sent a telegram too for me.'

'When do you plan to head back?'

'I have to be home during September. I gave my word.'

'Keep it.'

'I intend to, Saxon, but I need to know you're fine.'

He surprised me by shifting closer, turning his back to the arresting view and fixing me with a firm look.

'Have you finished?' he said.

I tied off the bandage. 'Yes.'

He removed his hand and I keenly felt its absence against my leg. 'How many different ways can I suggest you leave me be? It seems you're prepared to risk what I've warned against.'

There was no point in pretending I didn't know to what he alluded. I busied myself folding up the towel, throwing the used rags into the dish.

'You talk as if I have no say in this . . . or any control. You genuinely believe that I am suffering from your weaknesses.'

He laughed. 'At least I'm honest.' He was clearly suggesting by the remark that I was not.

'No, you're relentlessly brutish and this is why you have no friends.'

'I don't need them.'

'Nor family who loves you.'

That caught him out. I saw his eyes widen fractionally as though he'd felt me land a blow. 'That's unkind.'

'I'm sorry.' I felt smaller for attacking him in this way.

'Being vicious doesn't suit you. It needs my sort of personality to pull it off, Isla.'

I knew he was right and he was enjoying watching me bristle. I should have left it there but he had my ire up now. 'What I'm trying to say is that you might be prey to certain whims but don't tar me with that same brush.'

His smile widened and in that moment I felt soppy enough to believe that perhaps it was worth getting angry with him just to see its brilliance. 'Really? You being here is wholly about doctoring?'

'What else do you think it is?' I demanded, frowning, covering the guilt. I hated myself right now for the attempted deception, not just of Saxon, but of myself.

He said nothing for a few moments in which I could swear the world stilled. There was no sound, no movement, just Saxon's stare, filled with accusation. I felt consumed by the blue . . . his eyes, the dome of sky that I suddenly felt weightless within, the stripe on the pyjamas he wore. All that compelling blueness conspiring against me, drawing me under a spell.

'You're a useless liar, Isla.'

Before I could speak again he had leaned forward and in doing so had claimed my space as his. Now he was so close I could taste the sugary flavour on his breath from his tooth dentifrice, and still he paused, embarrassingly near, disgustingly confident, and I remained horrifyingly excited.

'Worried about my illness being this close?'

'I know what you have is not contagious.'

He grinned and I knew he'd said that to give me one final excuse. But now it was too late. Saxon thieved the tatters of my conscience and without mercy stole the kiss that I had promised myself over and over in my mind I would never relinquish to him. I had thought myself barricaded against such weakness, believed I possessed self-control that temptation could not penetrate. I was spoken for, another man's property. I loved Jove. *Didn't I?*

And yet all Saxon Vickery had to do was lean forward close enough and pause a heartbeat before my permission was given. Once his lips had closed over mine it sealed something intensely private between us. It wasn't a case of unlocking those feelings. Those feelings lived around me, within me, were me. I had just been moving through my days on the pretence they did not exist.

But they were living, breathing, passionate feelings. These secret moments belonged only to us and none of the world's sights or sounds, smells or creatures could penetrate our locked embrace. As I kissed him back so recklessly, I opened myself up entirely. This man aroused me – not only physically but emotionally – so that I could feel rage and raw desire in the same heartbeat. Sadly, I wasn't thinking about Jove. I also flattered myself that he wasn't thinking about his wife.

For me there was only 'us' and I was dizzied by kissing the man I'd longed to kiss, was forbidden to kiss, and it made me feel weightless, floating in a cloud of delicious need. In spite of how powerless I knew I'd become beneath his loving, there was also empowerment. I don't think in those passionate moments I'd ever felt more in touch with myself, my desires, or who I truly was. And worse, I was consumed by a possessiveness that frightened me; it roared up like a monster and became a greed for him.

I couldn't let him go so I pulled him closer and the seal strengthened; our lips moved in a silent conversation that conveyed thought, emotion and more feeling than any words could. Is there anything more intimate than a deep kiss? I think not. I think Saxon and I were more naked in that moment to each other than we might ever be again. The honesty of it made me weepy and when we finally broke apart, dismantling the spell, I had nothing but my tears to give, all of them falling for my easy betrayal of Jove.

Saxon looked down into my lap where we had laced fingers, anchoring hands, perhaps, so that we couldn't be tempted to venture further down this precipitous path. I dared not look into his lap. He was trembling from the slight breeze that was picking up, shaking his frailty, and also no doubt from the pounding desire he was controlling . . . as he controlled everything about his life.

'Besides, what you say isn't wholly true about not being loved,' he murmured, his voice grittier than usual. He spoke as if we had been in the midst of a discussion and then I realised we had been, and he was referring to my cutting remark that no family loved him. 'My wife loves me,' he said.

'Jove loves me,' I whispered, chasing his confession.

'And yet here we are.' He mocked our treachery.

I untangled my hand from his. 'Oh, I hate myself!' I sniffed.

'I did warn you.'

I nodded. 'I wanted to prove myself above your smug belief.'

'It was as much, if not more so, a warning to myself.' And in typical Saxon style his voice turned tender and I heard only affection. 'Isla, I've been married for four years, most of that time spent here in India. It doesn't matter how unpleasant I am, women continue to flirt, some of them go further and have tried quite ferociously to get beneath my defences. But I haven't once been unfaithful to my wife.'

'Until now,' I qualified.

He sighed, nodding once.

'But I haven't flirted or tried to catch your attention,' I added. It was as though I was trying to make this all his fault.

'No, you haven't but you also won't leave me alone.' I wanted to dispute this but my actions defied any protest. He placed his hand on mine again, gently though, so the gesture was not at all possessive. '*You* haven't done anything wrong, Isla.'

'Are you saying this is all your fault, then?'

'Yes. Your conduct to the outside world could not be misconstrued.'

'Except this isn't the outside world, Saxon. No one is here but us,' I said, looking around. 'This is our world that we've created and in this world I don't think I can misinterpret the plain truth that I have just kissed you and I did so with longing and with passion.'

'I'm sorry.'

'What for? I'm not a child. I didn't have to kiss you back. I could have pushed you away at the first sign of indiscretion. No, Saxon, obviously whether I was conscious about it or not, I wanted this to happen.' I watched him shiver. 'Come on, let's head back. There's a million steps to climb and I can't carry you.'

'There are twenty-one steps,' he said, easing himself off the wall and allowing me to link his arm through mine. I wasn't sure if I was offering support or simply wanting to keep touching him while I sorted through my anguished thoughts.

Fortunately, he was exhausted by the time we reached his bedroom and I was able to fuss like a good nurse in getting him settled into bed and tucked in. I offered more painkiller, although he pushed it away, preferring to cope without the drug.

I busied myself, talking all the while about nothing in particular while I checked his temperature, which was still up but not too high. I refilled his water jug, flannelled his face, and pointed to the vessel, should he need to spend a penny, and he gave me one of his withering looks to suggest he was not an idiot.

And then he mocked me by pulling away the layers of distance I had been trying to create. 'You can run all you like from it, Dr Fenwick, but you must face the reality of what happened today.'

'I'm not running away. I'm here, aren't I?'

He seemed to change his mind on challenging me. I could see his body loosening into the limpness of weariness. 'As you wish.'

'I'm going to make up some food.'

'I'm not hungry.'

'I don't care. Your body is. Rest. I'll be back in an hour.'

I scurried away before he could say any more, which left me and my guilt to confront one another. I moved around the kitchen in a slight stupor but it was helpful to have my hands busied, knowing what they had to do as they chopped and stirred until I had a chicken soup simmering. In it I had vegetables, diced tiny for easy digestion, and was pleased with myself Saxon would get a good dose of protein and vegetable. And while I stared at my small pot of golden healing liquid and began the repetitive chore of skimming the surface to take away as much fat as I could from the meal, I let my mind wander now into the dangerous area I had been avoiding.

What was I doing with Saxon? Where did I think it might lead? What were my hopes for this recklessness? I had no satisfactory answers; in fact, nothing more than mere bleats seemed to bubble up. I was dealing with an itch I had been trying not to scratch for months. It would lead only to misery. I had only the hope that I could resist him until I left this place knowing he was well down his pathway of recovery. Could I turn away from him? Yes! That was my only definitive response. Why? Because I was too scared of the consequences if I did not.

I carried a tray I had taken much care in preparing, including the small bunch of wildflowers, back down the corridors, retracing my steps. Evening was settling across the landscape and I was feeling more in control. I had kissed him. That was an error but the itch was now scratched. I would live with that brief mistake, bury it deep, never confront it again, and I knew in years, even in a few months' time, the reality of this slip-up would dim. The guilt would lessen. Yes, I'm promised but not married – I'm sure lots of engaged people experience similar crises and are able to make sense of them and pack them away. I had sampled what was forbidden and I needed never taste it again. There! I felt strong and composed standing outside his door. I knocked.

'Still here?' he called out. Obviously this was to be an ongoing amusement for him.

I balanced the tray expertly and let myself in. 'Afraid so,' I said, smiling but in a professional way, I thought.

His pyjama top was open and his hair damp.

'Did you bathe?' What a stupid and obvious question.

'I've cooled my temperature.'

'Well, you shouldn't do that alone,' I said, trying to regain some ground. I checked his bandage, which was intact and dry.

'So I'm to call you when I'm naked, am I? I'm to act helpless and as though I don't understand my own physiology?'

'Saxon, stop being contrary and do as you're told – just for once.' He knew how to vex simply by grinning at me. 'Well, a shower has perked you up, that's for sure.' He had colour in his face again that was not fever.

'What have you been up to?'

'This is a poached chicken soup. Lots of good healing in here.'

'It smells good, thank you.'

My hackles smoothed. 'I used tea to help in the poaching and give that deep colour.'

'Tea? Goodness, I'm impressed.'

'Whatever are you doing?' I asked, frowning to see his hands moving expertly with paper. Even bandaging halfway up one hand couldn't make him look clumsy.

'Have you heard of origami?'

I frowned and shook my head.

'Ah, so you don't know everything, Dr Fenwick.'

I gave him a look of exasperation as I set the tray down and sat politely on the edge of the bed, careful not to touch him. I kept my eyes firmly on his and what was in his hands, although my gaze fought me, wanting to glance at the taut belly, the broad chest, but I watched his fingers finish folding paper into something small and intricate. He made a final neat manoeuvre, tucking a tiny triangle of paper within one of the concertina-like folds. He held it in the palm of his hand and waited.

'A bird?' I said, genuinely delighted.

'Not just any bird. This is my best interpretation of a Himalayan green magpie.'

'It's exquisite.'

'Thank you. And before you ask, we had a house guest who came for three months and stayed thirteen years. He was Japanese and an old master at the art of origami.' Saxon said this word in a special way, fast and rolling his 'r'. 'He taught me over a decade of growing up how to fold a square of paper into anything I wanted.'

I stared at the beautiful little creature made of paper. 'And Himalayan green magpie sounds very specific.'

'It is. This little thing is trying to capture the spirit of Jade, my pet bird of childhood. She was young, injured and I found her one day while trekking. Everyone else was all for wringing her neck and being done with it but I put her into my shirt next to my heart so she was warm and, I hoped, reassured. She survived, and then couldn't go back to the wild so she lived with me for years and was tame. I used to walk around with Jade on my shoulder. She was a luminescent, vivid green . . . she was truly extraordinary and whistled beautifully.' I loved to hear this wistfulness in him because it rarely sounded as if Saxon had many happy memories but this was clearly one. 'When she died, strangely she turned blue, the colour of glaciers.' The colour of your eyes, I thought. 'I was inconsolable for about a year and I used to make these little icons of her most days.'

'What a precious relationship,' I murmured, enchanted by the story.

'Which is why this is for you, Isla.' He offered the paper bird and I accepted it, thrilled. 'I think our relationship is precious,' he added and I wished he hadn't. 'I think I love you as much as I loved Jade.'

Because that was all it took. The right words in an affectionate tone that was rarely heard from Saxon, I suspected. The words themselves seemed like the most tender of caresses.

I swallowed. 'Our friendship means a lot to me too.' It was a poor attempt at deflection.

'I know you're trying to protect yourself but being disingenuous is not helpful. I've been fighting against a tide of desire and yearning since you first slapped me.'

My gaze snapped up to him to see if he was teasing me but he was earnest this time. 'No one's ever fought back like you. Oh, my parents and I fought but they didn't care. You fought with me because you did.'

'And your wife?' There it was, the invidious claw of jealousy, bubbling up. I'd put ownership on him even though I knew I couldn't have him or he me, so I hated that she could legitimately call him hers.

He didn't seem to notice me inwardly gag at my indiscretion, and made an effort at a candid answer. 'I married to please everyone but not myself. I never set much store by the notion of love; I'd never experienced it at home so I had no real sense of it for life; the closest I got was Jade. I loved that bird more than anything. When she died after a long, good life, it hurt terribly. And I probably decided that loving something too much was painful, so perhaps

I decided not to love anyone ever and closed myself off to it.' He lifted a shoulder, clearly self-conscious of this deeply revealing fact. 'But my wife loves me with all of her heart. There's nothing fake about how she feels.'

In that moment my jealousy fled and was replaced by interest. 'But, Saxon, surely Frances deserves more than passing admiration for putting up with you?' I was trying to be so objective but her very name sounded 'green' in my head, as I fought the jealousy monster.

'Yes, she does. She's a lovely person, tolerant of me, seems to accept – even if she doesn't understand – all the horrible parts about me, and there are plenty of those,' he qualified. 'She's the counterbalance, you could say, because everything about Frances is fine and I am deeply fond of her. I question what she's doing with me.'

'Unfortunately it's your thoroughly brusque, often indifferent, attitude that makes you interesting to women.'

'I don't understand it.' His admission appeared genuine.

'And then there's how you look. You can pretend, Saxon, but you can't hide from it. You were blessed and that makes you hard to miss in a crowd.'

He waved my rationale away, clearly tired of being reminded.

'Only those kissed by gods can be that dismissive. There are men —'

'Miles, for instance,' he said, a wickedness in his tone.

'Yes, poor carrot-haired, freckle-faced, gangly-limbed Miles, who surely suffered terrible acne as a child and an ugly disposition to boot.'

'He deserves all the bumps in the road that he meets on his journey. Miles lacks empathy and for a doctor that's unforgivable in my book – certainly a doctor out here. Sometimes empathy is what keeps the whole circus going.'

I nodded. 'It's not a vocation for him, no calling. He simply had the brainpower and opportunity . . . he used both. He's getting married, by the way, to a beautiful, seemingly empty-headed creature just arrived off the boat. I admire his resolve.'

He cut me a sharp glance of confusion.

'But I don't admire him. Anyway, you neatly manoeuvred me off my topic.'

'Which is?'

'Frances. Surely she wants you home.' I tried not to make it a question but it hung between us. He didn't answer, staring at the paper bird I twirled restlessly. 'So do you love her?' I pressed, knowing he'd already answered that question but I needed him to clarify it.

He looked slightly bewildered. 'She is my wife, I shall remain fond of and care for her until there's no more breath within me.'

There was the truth of their relationship; he would let nothing affect their status as man and wife. I shouldn't have been surprised, yet his admission cut as surgically as a scalpel through skin, straight to my aching heart. I begged myself not to say it but out it came like a train emerging from a tunnel, steam exploding from the mouth that had held it. 'What about me?' There it was, my deepest insecurity aired. I loathed my weakness.

He raised his gaze to look upon me and his expression was bruised. He shook his head and my throat felt constricted by the certainty of the gesture. 'Our love is irrelevant,' he murmured, and while I'd misread his response, its negativity nevertheless stung. 'We're not allowed to have "us" beyond here,' he qualified quickly, waving a hand through the air to signify Brackenridge. 'But let me say this, Isla, how you affect me transcends any relationship I've had with anyone. I don't know what this is that we have, but . . .' His words trailed away.

I needed him to be specific. 'But what?' I urged, desperate for him to help me understand how I could betray the man I loved for someone who clearly didn't want me to love him.

'I've done everything within my power to resist the gravitational pull towards you, but the universe insists on drawing us together so presumably it wants something from us.'

I frowned. 'Don't go vague. What's your point?'

'I think it wants honesty. It wants me to admit to understanding that what I feel for you is the love I've been denied and that I have denied others. And if you'll forgive the presumption, I think it wants you to admit that you've settled for the man you've agreed to marry before fully exploring the potential for love that actually hurts when you can't have it any more.'

'That is presumptuous,' I said, barely controlling my breathing. I could see my chest expanding with fury but I suppose part of me knew that Saxon saw the truth of me. He saw beyond the carefully composed exterior and the perfect, neatly organised life I'd built around myself. Jove was the safe marriage decision but I did love him.

'I don't mean for a moment that you don't care enormously for him, Isla, or perhaps if we hadn't met, that you wouldn't consider it true love. But, if we turned it into a numerical formula, I think ninety per cent of you is committed to the man you're pledged to but you've held a small fraction back. And while you didn't know why then, you do know why now. No one's listening. So be honest. If you could be with me permanently without hurting anyone or letting someone down, would you choose it?'

I swallowed softly. 'Yes.'

He nodded. 'And so would I choose the same. Isla, I've never loved nor will I love anyone as I do you but we've met in the wrong time so in this moment of the year 1933 it feels wrong and potentially destructive.'

Our fingers laced across his bedspread.

It hurt to know he was right. How could I disagree? 'Saxon, when we kissed, were you thinking about Frances?'

'No.' It came out as a harsh sound. 'And I'm not even embarrassed to admit it, nor am I thinking about her now.'

'Meanwhile, I *am* embarrassed to admit that I didn't think of Jove until later.'

'They amount to the same, as far as I'm concerned.'

'Does that mean we can separate ourselves?'

'Buddhism, the main religion in this part of the world, encourages detachment from material things. I'm unconvinced we can apply it specifically to ourselves but up here in the lap of the gods I'm sure you'll admit that you feel aloof from the world you know.'

I couldn't deny it. 'It's as though I'm on a different planet.'

He gave a shrug of helplessness. 'I always see my life through a lens of clarity here. I'm certain Brackenridge does sit between worlds.'

I liked this concept. Somewhere in those words permission was being given.

'And so the world we come from can't touch us?'

His gaze rested heavily upon me now; I could feel the weight of consideration.

'Are you looking for sanction, Isla?'

'I'm looking for a way to spend a little forbidden time with you before I must return to my life and the world I know and belong to.'

I watched the blue eyes narrow. 'You want to be guilt-free? Impossible. Guilt is the companion of all lovers because there's almost always someone being hurt within the equation of that relationship.'

I made a decision that shocked me with its speed. 'Then I shall confront my guilt later, on my own when I feel like it. But right now I want to love you. I've never felt like this about anyone and before I commit myself to being only with one man for the rest of my life and giving him my absolute all when I take a holy vow to love and honour him, which I shall never break, I want a short selfish moment in spinsterhood of being permitted to love with abandon that doesn't hurt anyone who doesn't know about it.' I'd never felt more certain about anything.

His eyes glittered. 'That's a dangerous concept, Isla.'

'Even so,' I pressed, appalled and yet somehow undaunted by this path of reckless behaviour, 'how else can I learn about loving Jove until I have something to compare it to? I will not give him up; you will not turn away from Frances. So we are safe in the knowledge that the people we are committed to shall be untouched by this special bond we share.'

'And then you'll ruthlessly walk away from it?' He sounded surprised for once.

'Yes.' I was unequivocal and it felt true. I genuinely believed that what I shared with Saxon was entirely separate to how I felt about Jove but that I would walk on with Jove and leave Saxon and whatever we had now well and truly behind.

'I think we both need to sleep on that,' he said, a note of bewilderment in his voice that even caught him off-guard. I was shaken that we weren't acting upon my decisiveness immediately. It felt like I was the one with a fever, my body warming with each passing minute that we talked so openly about making love.

But I could hear the sense of his suggestion. Just like Jove, he seemed to possess a wisdom or a perspective that I didn't yet have. I trusted his instinct as I had trusted Jove's the previous year. I nodded and began to shift to depart his room, but he lifted his coverlet. 'Don't leave me. Lie down next to me and let's sleep.'

Without questioning it further, and fully clothed, I gently eased myself into his bed, my back turned to him as he fitted his long body along the length of mine. We moulded together as though we'd been carved that way. And with a paper bird cupped gently in my hand and chicken soup cooling alongside us, we drifted into silent thought and ultimately into sleep within that embrace.

23

I stirred from a dream in which I was flying among snow-capped mountains. It was peaceful, as though I was my spirit trapped within a bird. I was aware that I was dreaming, drifting between nearly awake and still asleep, and I was content. I tried to hold on to it but the calming dream began to fade with the new awareness that I was not alone.

I heard a crack of bones.

Eyes slitted open, I spied Saxon standing at the open window, unaware that I'd woken. He was gloriously naked; his back to me, he was stretching tall with fingers laced high above his head. His flesh was lean across his frame but he looked strong despite the toll of his illness. The mere fact that he could be this physical was testimony to the departure of fever. He would improve quickly now, I suspected, with the cool mountain air, good food and plenty of rest. He'd beaten his weakness into submission again. Latent TB was such an oddity, often showing some consumptive-like symptoms, but with rest and care it was like recovering from a flu. I think my father always hoped – prayed, even – that my mother's version in the early days was latent, and perhaps it even was.

I'd discovered in my study that a small percentage of sufferers would develop active TB and suffer the full range of its debilitation, often including death. My mother was one of the unlucky ones, and Saxon clearly one of those blessed by resistance, although I wondered how later in life, as he aged, he might fight off that lack of contagion switching to active TB. I didn't want to dwell on it as I watched him in all of his naked beauty.

Saxon held that pose for a full minute, I estimated, before he shocked me by reaching backwards and bending himself in half to grip his calves. It looked like an impossible position, one I was sure would snap me in two if I tried, and yet he seemed to find this position with ease, and he held it for another weighty minute.

Fascinated, I watched him move through a series of moves, each seemingly more complex and challenging than the previous. My favourite was without doubt the final one – he effected a handstand in a sinuous movement so fluid he could have been a dancer or acrobat. The burn did not seem to trouble him through these movements. He was healing well. Dust motes floated about him like adoring sparkles that seemed to add to the lustre of the moment. His golden hair flopped heavily like a mop poised to sweep across the floorboards and the sunlight caught its natural glints and, together with the dancing dust, turned him into a sort of angelic presence, suspended in stillness for me to admire.

I presumed he followed this routine daily as his eyes were closed and he seemed to be entirely within himself. It did, of course, give me the irresistible opportunity to let my gaze roam every inch of his athletic, if still rather shrunken, body and I realised that it was this daily exercise that kept him so fit and strong. It also answered my private query as to how he made swift recoveries.

Saxon was beautiful. I could not deny that watching him was a pleasurable indulgence. His uninhibited nudity stirred something else within me too. I was used to naked bodies but they were usually desperately ill and my mind was only focused on healing, not seeing their individuality. But I was seeing all the masculine joy of Saxon, the man, in this moment, and I would be lying if I didn't admit I wanted to feel his body against mine.

He snapped his eyes open and caught me watching him intently. The upside-down grin stretched.

'Still here?'

I smiled.

'Don't move.' In a single, brisk action he had flipped himself neatly to his feet and I was almost sad to see him reach for his loose pyjama trousers and cover his bottom half.

He came to sit beside me and I could see how much improved he was. 'Good morning.'

'What time is it?'

He shrugged. 'About six, I suppose. The fever has passed.'

'You can't —'

'Trust it, I know, I know. But I feel vastly improved. My wrist and forearm feel less tender, drying too. It must be your soup.'

I shifted to glance over to the tray and back at him, slightly perplexed.

'Even cold, it's delicious. I ate both bowls. Now I feel strong.' He flexed his biceps to make a point, which I found amusing. I was not used to Saxon Vickery being playful, unless he was drunk, of course. He grinned wider. 'Feeling awkward?' he wondered, looking at me clothed and fully buttoned.

My hands were gripping the sheet close to my neck. 'Er, no, perfectly at ease.' Irony bounced off my assurance and it prompted a delicious bellow of laughter.

'You are such a dreadful liar, Isla Fenwick. Heaven help you when you say to your new husband that your trip to Darjeeling was uneventful. Run while you can.'

'Or what?'

'Or I shall have to undress and ravage you. You cannot be in my bed and not anticipate that I would —'

I squealed and leapt up and away as he pretended to grab for me. We were both laughing.

'What a tease you are,' he accused and then his features straightened, I suppose at my uncomfortable expression. 'I'm only joking, Isla. I don't expect —'

'I know, I know.' I did feel awkward. Thoughts of Jove and promises made crowded around me.

'Let me run a bath for you,' he said. 'Life always feels easier from the perspective of a deep tub.'

I grinned. 'It's not like you to be this carefree, Saxon.'

'I don't think you know me that well to make such an observation,' he countered. 'In Brackenridge life is carefree.' He disappeared into his bathroom and I heard him clattering around, water splashing into the tub, and I smiled sadly. There was no escaping the fact that I wanted him: to hold him, to kiss him again. I wanted to be naked beside him, to feel his skin against mine, to feel him all around me and within me. It felt empowering to be this honest with myself . . . I set guilt to one side with the rest of the invisible critics to glare at me but its potency had dulled while allowing truth to become my shield.

This, I now knew, was what wise Jove had been talking about on that cold evening in London when he had aired his conditions of our betrothal. How sad then that I had borne out his fear; I was predictable and capricious, two qualities I never thought could be levelled at me.

Saxon returned to the room where I stood near a bed that looked rumpled from lovemaking but was innocent of that charge . . . for now.

He sighed. 'You look pensive.'

'Guilty conscience,' I admitted.

'Over a bath?' I know he was teasing me but also trying to lighten my load. 'I won't look.'

'Now who's a terrible liar?' I couldn't resist him. I couldn't turn away from this moment or I would yearn for it for the rest of my life. 'How is your conscience?'

'Untroubled. Men have affairs and most of them never leave their wives.'

'Bastards. Jove wouldn't see another woman.'

'You can't be *that* sure of anyone, Isla, but let's say he is as pure as you suggest, then you will be one of the luckiest brides who walks the planet and he is worth feeling guilty over. Whereas I'm not. So ruthlessly take what you feel like from me and then equally ruthlessly turn your back and go home.' Saxon pointed over his shoulder. 'I'm getting in. Whatever you decide, I can live with, even if you steal away now and we don't lay eyes on each other again.' He disappeared into the bathroom and I heard the soft splash as he lowered himself into the warmth with a sigh.

I remained where I was, taking another few precious moments in contemplation. I was not married. I was not even officially engaged. I was promised to someone in November . . . in England. So if I joined Saxon in the next room, I was not being unfaithful to anything, because it was still August 1933. Jove had all but suggested this might happen and virtually given permission by insisting I not wear his ring or commit us publicly until I was home again and could physically become his fiancée. Could I make that slippery rationale feel strong enough in my mind to live with?

I paused on the threshold of what I knew was potentially the biggest decision of my life.

―――――

'Still here?' He didn't open his eyes as the ephemeral colours of bath bubbles glistened and popped around him in dozens of tiny explosions at once. Whatever was about to begin between us would be as evanescent as those spheres . . . unique and short-lived but real.

I undressed silently, leaving my clothes in a pile around my ankles, and I paused to watch him. He had not stolen a peek; his head was leaned against a rolled towel and his injured arm lay across the bath's edge. The rest of his body was submerged and statue-like. Steam drifted off the mostly still surface, which shifted only barely to the rhythm of his breathing. Curiously, my heartbeat had slowed and my breath came gently and steadily. More reason to trust my decision.

'May I?' I said, but without waiting for further permission I lowered myself into the water to sit on top of Saxon's long legs, his feet braced against the end of the bath as I lay back against his chest. I think I let out a low, slow sigh at the soothing warmth as though I were trapped in one of those bubbles, and then there was the new, thrilling feel of his frame beneath me.

We exchanged nothing for what felt like several minutes; time had surely slowed but the sensation of our skins touching intimately for that period was all that mattered. And then, as if I'd given silent permission, Saxon's arm reached around me to hold me in a hug that felt so secure I turned passive, yielding entirely to him.

Because we were naked, when he finally spoke, I felt his voice as an echo from his chest to mine.

'If such a state is possible, then in this moment I have arrived at perfect contentment,' he said. There was nothing mocking or even vaguely amorous in his words.

I felt much the same. When I hadn't replied after another protracted period, he shifted slightly. 'Isla? Are you dead?'

I wanted to laugh, stop him making fun of me, but I was feeling such a surge of emotion I wanted him to know it. 'The French have a phrase – *au courant* – which means to be entirely cognisant.'

'Fully aware,' he murmured.

'Yes, literally . . . *in the current*. That's how I'm feeling . . . like a light bulb has been switched on for the first time.'

He squeezed, holding me closer, but I was enjoying his restraint in not rushing me into anything more physical. 'That's nice. I'm your electricity.'

I chuckled. 'I don't know what you are, Saxon, but you've unwittingly changed my life.'

'Is that a good thing?'

'Probably not, but I can't shift it back now, nor do I want to. This is precisely what Jove warned me might happen.'

'An affair?' he queried, sounding bewildered.

'No, but he wanted us to be promised rather than make a public engagement or for me to wear the exquisite ring he gave me. I thought it harsh at the time.'

Saxon wrapped his legs around me, shifting how he held me so he could reach beneath my arms to hold my breasts. A tremor shook through me but if he felt it, he didn't react. 'Except now you understand this was his generosity shining through?' It was odd discovering how ungrudging he was towards Jove, or was it simply ambivalence? I couldn't pin it down.

I nodded. 'Travel would change me, he insisted. It would open me up to new experiences, new people. While I accepted his advice, I didn't understand back then to what he was referring.'

'Your Jove sounds like a wise man, although I would guess that his precaution might be protection, perhaps, for his fragile heart as much as for your freedom.'

Whorls of steam lifted from the water's surface, scenting the air around us with a woody smell of bath salts that I would always remember as the scent of Saxon Vickery. Mysore sandalwood, in particular, with vetiver and then an onslaught of warm, peppery notes, perhaps some cardamom and ginger.

'It's distressing to realise that he knew I might be vulnerable to romance, even though I had claimed I was impervious to other advances.'

I watched Saxon reach for the soap. 'There have been no advances. I think you're being unfair on yourself. I'm guessing here but I doubt something as intangible, invisible or as life-altering as love – which you know I don't claim to understand – can be planned for when it just steals into your life like a wraith.' He couldn't see it but I smiled sadly at the word *love* suddenly being discussed, watching him soap his hands, loving the golden-haired arms that moved beneath my breasts as he did so. 'Come on, let's not be maudlin. Our time is limited.' I thought he meant here at Brackenridge, but as usual with Saxon there was jest. 'This bathwater won't stay hot for long.'

Fresh tendrils of steam lifted from the surface as he shifted. 'Trust me, this will relax you.' And without asking, he pushed me gently forward into a sitting position, then pulled at the pins that held my hair in a loose bun and sighed as my hair dropped in loose waves.

Saxon began to soap me gently, starting at my shoulders. He used the slipperiness of those suds to begin massaging my muscles, first gently and without hurry at my neck, then more insistently down my spine. As I relaxed, I felt his attention turn more amorous. I closed my eyes and let his sensuality stroke me however he chose. With patience but ultimately with need, his fingers moved around and I felt, for the first time, his touch become demanding. The control he innately possessed was banished to desire. Now everything about where our skin met was hard; full of need. There was nothing shy about how he caressed my breasts, soaping them, fondling them in a way that was so teasingly erotic I gave a strangulated sound of pleasurable anguish.

And then we were both au courant. Except now it was a lightning current that only we were creating and travelling together.

I surrendered, following his urge to clamber out of the bath. He cocooned us in a towel while greedy lips sought and found each other, and there it was, that special seal that fastened us together. Did he lift me with one good arm? He must have and there was fleeting anxiety in my thoughts for his health and strength, but it was chased away when I was laid back against his bed. The chill of being out of the water and feeling the soft mountain breeze against my skin coaxed a shiver of delight and fresh desire until I was reaching for him like a person famished. Saxon took a few moments, though, resisting his own urges, to gaze at me, damp, naked, desperate for him.

His normally rakish smile had a tentative quality to it; was it regret? Second thoughts? I'll never know.

He lowered himself onto the bed and, still exerting a last reserve of control, he paused. 'Are you sure?'

I'd touched his body as a doctor, even as a nurse, but now I touched him as a lover. I held his face and kissed him for my answer. I kissed him more deeply than I had ever permitted a kiss to be and then I began to kiss all of him. I pushed him back against the pillows. There would be nothing submissive about me in this activity; I was choosing it, I was permitting it, I was leading it.

He understood, relaxed as best as I imagined he could under my ministrations, making do with burying his hands in my hair as I lost myself to the full exploration of my hunger for Saxon Vickery.

Not long after I heard his gasp and then when he found his voice again he couldn't help the gentle mockery. 'Dr Fenwick, I'm going to have to recommend your type of medical therapy to all my male patients.'

He heard my shaking laughter from where I lay across his belly while he stroked my breasts.

'My, my,' he continued, his tone impressed. 'I think I shall have to submit a journal piece to the *Lancet* for consideration as groundbreaking new treatment for TB.'

A part of me was annoyed that he was teasing me like this at a moment when I wanted only intimacy; but I was helplessly amused, knowing it was also his way of assisting me to come to terms with our recklessness.

'Now,' he said, moving swiftly to change our positions. 'Let me show you the more intrusive Vickery way. It's your turn to lie back and think of England.' He frowned. 'Are we safe?'

I understood immediately and nodded. 'Fortunately, yes, but we shall take greater precaution next time.'

'Next time?' he said, lifting an eyebrow. 'Well, I'd better hold something back, then,' he quipped.

'Don't. I want all of you. I'm selfish and starved and I can't think of next time because right now is all that matters —'

Saxon cut off my words, lowering himself for a searching kiss that I could swear lasted for hours. And, silenced, I abandoned myself to him again, momentarily frightened by how defenceless it made me feel to be making love with someone I desired too much. There was no sense of control left within me; my surrender was whole.

24

I discovered my limbs sprawled proprietorially across Saxon's body. He was breathing peacefully in sleep, unaware that I had woken and was now watching him resting with a sense of wonder.

Given my longstanding ardour for Jove, I knew the lines of his face almost as well as my own. I'd studied him from afar, from up close, in photographs, from behind bushes. Jove had always been handsome but he'd softened a little over the last couple of decades. Gravity had begun to pull on that once tightly stretched skin so that the line of his chin had blurred slightly as he headed towards fifty.

Looking upon Saxon, his jaw was still starkly drawn and the only lines spoke of that rare laughter and much frowning. Midway through his fourth decade they still remained the only clues to where age would write more of its years and its experiences upon him.

I wondered if Frances had ever splayed her arms and legs over his body in this same manner? She didn't have to, I suppose. She was Mrs Frances Vickery and had claim to him. I was the interloper . . . I was the thief, stealing from her. I swallowed at the ugly title, feeling my pulse quicken.

'Hello, fair Isla.'

I grinned, banishing demons. 'I had no idea we fell asleep.'

'What time is it?'

Warmth and the heaviness of slumber had moulded our bodies to one another. Reluctantly, I left the comfort of our union to reach for my wristwatch from the bedside table. 'Good grief, nearing midday. How ridiculous.'

'Nothing ridiculous about exhausting sexual liaisons.'

'I've not stayed in bed this late since I was ten and too ill to leave it.'

'Then you should have had a lot more lovers in your time.' He waggled a finger.

'You don't mean that.'

'No, I don't. I'd be jealous of all of them. Come on, have a shower and dress. Today I'm going to teach you about tea, although we could have a quick —'

I squealed, laughing and tumbling out of bed as he grabbed my hips to swing me back into his embrace.

'I don't want to be responsible for any relapse of your health.'

'But what a way to go, Isla. Death by lovemaking.'

'Don't jest. I need you well.'

'So you can leave me?'

Our expressions lost all amusement and our gazes met across the room and rested sombre and heavy, like gravestones marking sorrow. We both knew death of a sort was coming at us. This little window into a different life could only ever be short-lived.

'I have to leave,' I murmured.

'I know.'

I gave a small shrug. 'But not before I learn about tea and life up here in the hills. Come on, show me it all . . . if you're up to it.' I glanced at his crotch and he feigned despair at me as I guffawed and headed for the bathroom.

———

We emerged with flushed faces, polished and gleaming not just from our ablutions but I suspect from pure vigour of what life had just given to us. We touched each other constantly, whether it was a squeeze of the shoulder as we stepped past one another or a proper pause so he could twirl around his finger a strand of my hair that had dropped from its loose fastening.

Arm in arm we wandered down the hill from the house. I'd never seen Saxon dressed so casually; he wore cream linen trousers and an open-necked white cotton shirt that caught the soft breeze and allowed me an erotic glimpse at his body beneath every now and then. I'd become the child again, feeling besotted. We'd taken off his bandage so his wound could breathe now. It was more superficial than I'd first thought and healing well. He probably wouldn't be scarred . . . not externally, anyway.

'First into the gardens themselves,' he said.

I noted that all the nearby workers' faces had a distinctly different look from the more angular lines of the Bengalis in Calcutta. Here they generally had the flatter, rounder Mongolian features of people who had found their way here from Bhutan and Nepal. They were squat, appeared strong-limbed, their fingers short, nails gnarled from the work. But they were dressed in colourful clothes and their singing was melodic and pretty. I mentioned what I was thinking.

'They're called Lepchas but I won't give you an academic lecture about their history or culture. Suffice to say they're originally from Nepal, some from Bhutan and indeed Tibet.'

He waved to the women and spoke to them in their local language. I watched them giggle and reply shyly.

'They think you are very beautiful,' he translated.

'Do they also think I'm your wife?' I sighed.

He gave an expression of not caring what they thought. We stood awhile to observe them at their work and as they relaxed again into it, they began to sing softly among the bushes.

'So, if you watch the pickers,' he spoke quietly, 'they don't pull the leaves off the bush so much as pinch them off. Do you see?' He made a twisting gesture in the air with his thumb and forefinger. 'It's harder than it looks,' he assured.

I didn't need to be told. I could already imagine it as I observed their wondrous fluidity and economy of motion as the workers didn't just pluck a leaf but moved their fingers across the top of the bush like a human version of locusts. They harvested at speed, both hands moving on separate sections but in synchrony, somehow in the same manoeuvre gathering the leaves into pliable palms. When hands were full, without looking but simply knowing precisely how hard to throw, they tossed their bundles of leaves behind their shoulders into conical baskets that ran the length of their backs. The baskets were miraculously held in place by a band of plaited rope around each woman's head. Some wore hats, while others veiled themselves from the sun with prettily woven shawls.

'The pickers carefully take only double-headed leaves.'

'What? You mean they're being precise at this speed?'

He laughed. 'Yes, my word. It's years of experience that teaches them what to pick and when. Can you see that woman over there is leaving that bush next to her?'

I nodded.

'It's not ready.'

I shook my head with awe. 'Show me what they're picking.'

He moved across and spoke to one of the workers. She smiled, then gestured that he was to go ahead. I watched him point to a particular pair of leaves and she nodded. He pinched it off and brought it over to me. Long, waxy-looking leaves of the richest green were placed in my hand, each with razor-shaped sides.

'They're essentially shoots. Right now the women know to take only the tender first two leaves with a curled bud.'

'That's sounds mathematical!'

'They know what they're doing. Their mothers did so, and their mothers before them. They've learned from tiny children around the skirts of those grandparents and parents.'

'These late summer pickings mean larger leaves, lots of silvery tips.' He pointed. 'This is our pride. It makes a coppery-coloured tea with the special gilding of a muscatel flavour that only this region can produce, plus the insects make all the difference.'

'Insects?'

He nodded, frowning. 'They would look to you like tiny grasshoppers but they're known as green flies. They arrive just for a couple of weeks and feed on the leaves, sucking at the moisture, which, can you believe, is beneficial as it shrivels the leaf, stunts growth and intensifies the flavour.'

'Well, I never. How many leaves to a tin of tea, then?' I wondered. It wasn't a genuine question but Saxon pondered.

'It varies from flush to flush but I would say probably well over ten thousand shoots to about a pound of the best tea for first flush.' He pointed at the tiny leaves in my hand. 'Darjeeling's finest,' he assured. 'All the way to our royals. Gold to the Brits.'

'Can't live without it.' I grinned back. 'Solves all of life's crises.'

'Suffice to say that what you see being picked here will fetch a fine price . . . but these poor workers will see only a few rupees for their day's labour. In fact, that pound of tea is equivalent to probably a month of their wages and I suspect I'm underestimating that.'

I didn't want to get into a conversation about social issues, although I could hear the current of disappointment in his tone. This was presumably an old argument . . . a constant claw of contention between the brothers.

'Do they live on site?' I asked, trying to shift the direction of the conversation.

He took the tea-leaves back and flung them into one of the women's baskets. 'Up in the nearby villages. They all have families to care for. Many work with the new babies strapped to their front. Some of those babies might only be a few days old.'

I was not prepared to take on Saxon's guilt; I had plenty of my own to work through so I ruthlessly moved him off-topic, making a sighing sound. 'It's so romantic, really, isn't it?'

'The tea gardens?'

'Tea itself, and especially the gardens.'

'Well, like all good romances, it nearly didn't happen,' he said, giving me a wink. 'Let's walk on. We can stroll through the bushes.'

I followed, waving my thanks to the women.

'There's much legend surrounding tea and the people around here like to believe it was a fairytale story of a wandering Buddhist monk who was one day boiling water and had a gust of wind blow a tea-leaf into his pot. When our monk drank the liquid, he felt enlivened.'

'Nice,' I agreed.

'Except tea goes back a couple of thousand centuries and then some to the mountains around south-western China. Leaves from tea bushes were steeped, drunk and enjoyed for their flavour. It was only much later that brewing tea refined itself into an art form and part of the culture of China. It became a ritual, with firm etiquette surrounding the tea, its pot, the place of the brew.' He held my hand to help me around a particularly dense part of the gardens. 'Like everything bitter, it was considered medicinal. Chocolate, for instance, until it was lightened with milk and sweetened.'

I grinned.

'In its earliest form for the Europeans it was considered a not-so-pleasant-tasting beverage for detoxification and virility.' He pumped the muscles in his arms.

'Can we thank the British for adding milk and sugar, then?'

'Indeed,' he said theatrically, jumping over a small tea bush to make me laugh.

I was more astonished by his vigour and sense of fun than about the tea story, to be honest. This was not Professor Vickery of Calcutta but the hidden Saxon Vickery of Darjeeling.

'I don't think any people embraced a drink so wholly as the folk of the British Isles – easily their favourite beverage by 1800 and the popularity hasn't waned. In fact,' he said, waggling a forefinger, 'I think we're dependent upon it for our daily existence.'

'Hear, hear!' I said.

Saxon pointed us towards the series of low sheds. 'Fancy a potted history of tea?'

'It would be churlish of me to refuse you.'

He laughed. 'I'll keep it brief. It's wrapped up with the Opium Wars. It was the Dutch traders who added small amounts of opium and arsenic to their tobacco. Soon enough the Chinese had tossed tobacco in favour of smoking opium in its lethal pure form, most of it coming from India. Despite Chinese diplomacy to slow the export, the East India Company was only too aware that the opium trade was vital to its cash flow. It became the penultimate revenue source for British India.'

'Truly?'

'No word of a lie. The Chinese Emperor was determined to stop this blight, though, and destroyed something like twenty thousand chests of opium in the port warehouses. Britain responded with war. Nevertheless, the East India Company began searching for other ways to source Britain's national addiction.'

'India,' I said, with dawning.

'Precisely. It needed a place where it could control not only the price but every stage of production. Tea had been growing in India for decades but now this most powerful of British institutions went hunting for it, no longer prepared to trade for it.' He pointed.

'We're nearly there so let me jump forward many years. Victorians became tea planters. Assam was the key place and vast tracts of jungle were cleared for it and many died for it – not just disease but wild creatures attacking them, from big cats to snakes. Elephants had to be trapped, tamed, taught to help clear the trees, roads, et cetera, and of course the great railways that you've experienced had to be cut into mountains. By the mid-1830s tea was grown commercially and companies like Twinings & Co were leaping aboard. By the Great War India was producing enough to brew about fifty billion cups of tea!'

I roared with delight. 'You're making up those figures.'

He raised his hands. 'I swear I'm not. Quantity, however, does not equate to quality.'

'So I'm guessing this is where Darjeeling enters the story.'

'Follow me, Dr Fenwick,' he said, and led me into the first of the sheds. 'Darjeeling *is* the difference. Assam's teas are generally malty.'

'And strong, yes, I've noticed.'

I liked the way the edges of his eyes creased with his smile. 'In the tea industry they'd prefer you to use the word *bracing*. But, true, it's a roughish tea, with perhaps a slight barkishness to its flavour.'

I marvelled privately at his clever descriptions.

We'd arrived into a long structure of wooden floors that were smooth from wear with a pitched roof of corrugated tin and plenty of windows to let in light. I felt a sense of great airiness in here even though I'd seen from the outside that it was three storeys high. I noticed several workers hard at sweeping.

'The brooms are made from native grasses,' he commented. 'We like to keep the processing area tidy of fallen leaves. It's hardly sterile but we don't like dust in our fine tea.'

I really wasn't used to him being so chatty and it was obvious that he guessed my thoughts.

'Am I banging on too much?'

'No! I'm enjoying myself hugely. I just can't believe what a difference a kiss makes.'

'Or indeed a right róyal —'

'Saxon!' I cut in before he said anything more revealing because a man was arriving behind him.

He winked at me. 'Where were we?'

'Bracing Assam tea,' I obliged.

'Right. So now what was needed was some finesse; producers wanted more of that delicate, floral flavour they knew grew in the hills of China. A tea thief was sent, out from the Chelsea Physic Garden in London to Hong Kong and then Shanghai before he traversed another thousand miles to the Yellow Mountains in the north. He wore robes, shaved his head and had sewn on a long plaited hair tail, learned to wield chopsticks and marked himself a pale-skinned Chinaman as he journeyed to acquire plants and seeds. And, before you ask, that's no lie. His name was Robert Fortune.'

I was entranced and he could tell. 'How thrilling.'

'Not for the Chinese, who guarded their tea secrets zealously. Anyway, the shorter version of this story is that Fortune is the father of tea in this country – he spent years wandering China not only gathering up the botanic jewels that he would sail to Calcutta, but also bringing with him a team of Chinese tea plant-ers and pickers. A new industry began in northern India and some of it inevitably found its way here to Darjeeling and ultimately to my family. I've simplified just how hard Fortune's role was, of course.'

'Gosh. I'd love to know more.'

'You can read about him back in London.' He led me up a small flight of wooden stairs. 'Anyway, here we are at the withering loft and the troughs I spoke of.'

Vessels not unlike horse drinking troughs were filled with leaves, from fresh green through to a dried sage colour, curled from lack of moisture.

'Now, making quality tea is an exercise in control,' he continued.

I loved the way he naturally reached for my hand: it was filled with both enthusiasm and affection, as though he'd never shared this knowledge with a woman previously. 'Saxon, have you told your stories and explained your love of tea to Frances?'

He shook his head. 'No. When I'm in England, I'm not encouraged to talk about India. My wife prefers me to be focused on life at home. She prefers Assam too.'

I took pleasure at being allowed into this private world of his, which I suspected only I might ever glimpse.

I refocused my attention to his sweeping gesture at the troughs that were, at my guess, about seventy feet in length but narrow enough that they were only the width of one of my arms. 'Each step – from the moment the leaves arrive from the gardens into these sheds – is critical. Everything we do can affect the final flavour. The steps are withering, maybe toasting, then rolling, fermenting, drying and finally grading and sorting before packing.'

I looked into the first trough, where the most recent basket of leaves had been tipped.

'We spread them out to dry and we need to be quick because piled up in the baskets the leaves generate heat. We spread them to about eight inches deep.'

I watched him dip both hands into leaves up past his wrist and move the tea around. I noted a wire-meshed bottom to the trough as he did so and I realised how the air could penetrate the mass that was regularly stirred, no doubt in the same way that Saxon was moving them around now.

'How long do they remain like this?'

He frowned. 'Just over half a day usually does it, although it's not exact – experience teaches you when they're ready. After about sixteen hours most of the moisture has been extracted from each leaf.'

'What about in monsoon?'

'Very good, Dr Fenwick. When it's rainy and humid we help things along with a coal fire to make the leaves wither and it's extremely carefully monitored.'

I nodded.

'After withering, this trough will be barely knuckle deep.' He pointed to another trough. 'Over there, they're ready.' He sounded so confident I had to look for myself.

The tea-leaves had lost their brilliance and they'd curled; become limp. Their edges had browned and most had changed to a murkier green.

'They're pliable now, so they can be rolled,' Saxon said, strolling up to put an arm affectionately around my waist. He kissed my neck, although I twisted away, shameful of how quickly my body responded to his touch. I knew if he led me back to the house in this moment, I likely couldn't resist him or his bed once we got there.

'So you know from how they feel?'

He let go of me to scoop up a handful of the withered leaves. 'How they look, how they feel and this . . .' He buried his face into the leaves. I thought he was simply being comical but I heard him inhale before dropping the leaves. 'And by that bouquet, I do know. Go on, do the same and use both hands.'

I lifted a double-handed load of leaves and buried my nose into them as he had and smelled, closing my eyes as the slightly musty fragrance arose.

'Describe it.'

'Well,' I began, inhaling again before I looked up. 'It's like a Somerset apple shed in autumn that I remember from childhood.'

He beamed at me and then flung down his leaves and clapped once. 'Isla,' he said, fuelling his voice with affection. 'I couldn't have said it more eloquently, poetically or indeed perfectly than that.'

I grinned back, pleased with myself.

'Of course, the experienced team here know from how the leaves appear in the troughs . . .' He grabbed a handful again and squeezed. 'There's a certain way those leaves look as they open when you relax your fist,' he said, opening his hand, watching the leaves unfurl from the tight ball, 'and they can estimate the percentage of moisture gone. What they don't want to see is that they're too dry.'

'Why? I thought getting rid of moisture was what this was all about?'

'We still have to roll. If the leaves are too brittle, they'll break. We want them pliable.'

'Ah,' I answered, understanding.

He pointed. 'We drop them down that cloth chute when ready and in the earliest days workers would roll leaves by hand.' He gestured rolling with both hands on a flat surface, pointing halfway up his underarm. 'All the way to here was used against wooden tables. Now we have a rolling machine.'

I peered down to the heavy equipment with a central rotary action that mimicked the way Saxon had demonstrated. 'We want the leaves twisted into long curls – not broken – that easily unfold when rehydrated with boiled water.'

'And green tea?'

'Allowed to wither less. White tea is even more delicate.'

'All from one type of tea bush?'

'*Camellia sinesis*,' he replied. 'The different teas arise based on how you treat the leaves, what soil the bushes grow in, climate, and which characteristics we want to enhance.'

I couldn't help it, I had to kiss him.

When I released him, he blinked. 'I'm boring you, aren't I?'

'No, I wanted to thank you for this.' I sighed.

'I've barely begun. Don't get me started on terminology. You have to kiss me again to stop me.'

I did, first checking that no one watched us, although Saxon made sure of it by pulling me behind a screen. As if I had no care in the world, I pulled him close and kissed him long and deeply, trying to imprint on my memory how it felt to kiss him.

I finally let him go.

'Here's the cupping room, which is where the tea is tasted for quality.' He pointed, leading me to a small enclosure with a long bench and a clutter of white china implements that looked like small pitchers without handles. Saxon referred to them as infusion pots. There was a kettle and a few other items but otherwise it was clean and mostly empty, leaving room for men to gather and sip the various brews. 'Exact measures of dry leaf are steeped for five minutes using an hourglass,' he explained. 'Weight, time of day of picking, time of day of tasting, all of these factors are important. Consistency is paramount,' he impressed.

Finally he took me to a room that was surprisingly busy with endeavour, including a circle of women squatting on tiny stools. Their mouths and noses covered, they spoke quietly to each other, while sifting tea-leaves through large round sieves into pyramids on sacking at their feet, dust dancing in the shaft of airy sunlight around them.

At my look of query, Saxon explained. 'Sorting happens here. We make sure at this point any twigs or stalks are cleared. There's whole leaves, broken leaves, fannings – smaller leaves to you – and finally what we call dust, which gets swept up and used, of course.'

'What's the finest quality?'

'Well, highest quality in terms of the leaf rather than flavour – because flavour is subjective – is called Fine Tippy Golden Flowering Orange Pekoe.'

'Don't fib!'

He grinned. 'Would I dare? Tippy means there's a considerable level of the highly desirable whole-leaf tips, and orange pekoe describes a large-leafed tea, which is also preferred. Now, Isla, I think I've crammed your brain sufficiently. Have you seen enough?'

Arousal was showing itself in various ways but especially in the roughness of his voice suddenly. I nodded.

'Good, because I'm taking you back to bed, and tomorrow, if the good doctor will permit me to leave the house, I'd like to take you up into Darjeeling. You should see the town.'

We walked back to the house, arm in arm, he no doubt anticipating an afternoon of lovemaking but I reckoned he'd be ready to sleep before we could undress.

I was right. He tore off his clothes and flopped on the bed while I took care to re-dress his arm for fear of him reinjuring that wound during his ardour. However, by the time I'd finished, after slapping away his exploring fingers, he was gently snoring and I left him that way, climbing in behind to put my arms around him, cupping my body to his for a short while as afternoon came in. While I didn't sleep, I wouldn't permit myself to think on Jove, England, even doctoring. Right now, nothing outside Brackenridge could invade until I let it.

25

Hours later Saxon found me on the verandah, sipping tea, staring out at Kangchenjunga, no longer feeling like a thief. I'd made my peace with the gods on earth. *Just a few more days*, I'd begged them. *Then I'll leave and I will never see him again, never interrupt his life or allow him to disrupt mine.*

'I'm still here,' I said brightly, before he could ask. He leaned over the top of me and kissed me upside down. I laughed, tasting mint once again, and I sensed even better health than yesterday or even this morning. 'Let me look at you.'

He walked around, blocking my view. 'Never felt better,' he quipped, but a forced tone tripped me up in my happy mood; I pretended I hadn't heard it.

'Liar. But you do surprise me; you appear surprisingly hale.'

'I feel it, Isla,' he said more seriously and I knew I couldn't avoid what was about to descend. It was like a change in weather – a cold wind blowing in.

'Good. But what does that expression mean?'

He didn't look away, spearing me with that disconcerting stare. 'It means it's time for you to go,' he said.

I felt like he'd not spoken but instead answered me by punching me fully fisted into an unclenched belly. Barely hours ago we'd spoken of love, but that naked, emotional Saxon had retreated and I knew I was now staring at the professor, his strength returned, his barricades against emotion in place.

'I know how you're feeling,' he said.

'Do you?' I said.

He squatted before me, reached for my hand, but I pulled it away, feeling stung and suddenly injured. I was also frightened that he was about to take away something special and shiny that I had only just been admiring privately.

He reached again, firmly this time, and wouldn't permit me to pull back. He clasped both of my hands in his larger ones. 'Isla, please look at me.'

Unhappily I obliged and all of a sudden it hurt to gaze upon the man whom I had no right to be feeling this way about. It didn't matter that I felt a surge of love. The universe had chosen for us before we'd met.

'No matter what you tell yourself I suspect you're even more conflicted than I feel right now.' I didn't reply. I didn't believe I could convince him about making my peace so I let him continue. 'And I woke up understanding that I was being desperately selfish and unfair to you.'

'And I have no say?'

He shook his head. 'No, because you won't make the harsh decision that I can. I need you to go. Go before anyone finds out about this . . . this tryst.'

'It's not a tryst. We didn't arrange to meet here,' I replied, no longer able to conceal the hurt.

'Call it whatever you want. It's still clandestine, it's still sneaking behind the backs of people we care about and don't wish to hurt. And mostly I don't want to hurt *you*. What's more, I don't want you being enmeshed in scandal.' He raised a hand to stop me leaning into his pause, snarling back at him. 'Isla, listen to me. You have something magnificent to go back to. And although my situation is different to yours, I won't leave Frances.'

'I know that!' I snapped. 'I don't remember asking you to and I have no intention of not marrying Jove.'

Was I lying? If he asked me to stay here forever with him, would I be weak, think only of myself? I hoped not, but it seemed I'd never know because he clearly had no inclination to offer me anything but the hardest journey of all.

'Why now?'

He stood, turning his back to me to become a tall outline against the sky. The lowering sun forced me to shade my eyes and look at him as a shadow. Apollo was floating in the fiery firmament of his heavenly home, I thought.

'Because, Isla, it compromises you. You're a good, fine doctor with so much to look forward to, and you're risking too much. And it's not all about you. I know you want to hear this so I'll say it, because maybe this is what you take away with you. You weaken me. You're going to leave and each day you stay, you will make me love you a little more. As much as your doctoring can make me well, *you* are killing me.'

He was back crouching in front of me; he took my hands once again and placed them against his cheeks. 'Take your wonderful healing hands away. Leave, while I still have the strength to push you away.'

He was right; I did need to hear these words of love and they softened me immediately. I traced the outline of his face, consciously committing every part of him to my memory.

'I have to be selfish,' he reinforced, 'defend myself against you. This hasn't happened before; I will not let it happen again, and because you can't stay, I insist you leave . . .'

'When?'

'Tomorrow morning, first thing. I've already made arrangements for you to be picked up.'

'Saxon, no! I'm not ready to —'

'If you won't leave, I'll leave you.'

I could see he meant it. 'You really can be very cold.'

He shook his head. 'So they say. I'm doing this for both of us . . . today, tomorrow, next week – what does it matter, Isla? We *can't* be together!' His voice cracked on his final words and at least I glimpsed that this was as desperately hard for him as it was for me.

'What about Darjeeling?' I could hear the plaintive note in my voice.

He shook his head. 'A dream. Too many nosey people up there. It's a hotbed of gossip; they've got nothing else to do all day except prattle on about each other. I would be fair game and our family, though long departed from here, is nevertheless well known and respected. They'd love to get some dirt on my brother. I won't give it. I may not like Rex but I won't have his name tarnished because of my impropriety and I know you wouldn't want Jove hearing of us dancing arm in arm at the Gymkhana Club or the Planters Club.'

'No,' I said, dropping my gaze. 'That would be heartless but I'd hoped for a few more days . . .'

'Those extra days will only make it worse. You'll return to England to be swept up in marriage plans, a honeymoon, rediscovering Jove, making children, travelling the world . . . I return to Calcutta and cholera, tuberculosis, malaria and death.'

'Have you forgiven me?'

He knew what I meant. 'No. That's for you to seek atonement in your own heart. But I am entirely under your spell, and viciously in love with you.'

I smiled through watering eyes. 'I liked the idea of dancing arm in arm with you.'

He nodded. 'I know and we shall . . . tonight. We have a few more hours together. I can smell you've cooked a meal, so I shall dress appropriately, put on some music, find some wine that hasn't gone off in my father's cellar . . . and we shall dance all night until the sun rises on a new day when you will leave me and go home to a much better man.'

I covered my mouth to prevent a sob escaping. He smiled at me to reassure. 'We'll always have the tea gardens in our memory. Our secret. No one hurt and perhaps your conscience can find a way to clear itself – you're not officially engaged, you wear no one's ring, but I can't see you again after I kiss you goodbye. Don't write, don't come back to India to see me, don't seek me out ever and I will give you the same respect. It's our only defence.'

I nodded, crying openly now, and deep inside, where some sensibility still resided, I knew this was for the best.

So this was it. We had only hours left together.

'Come on. Bathe, dress. I'll find a tuxedo. We'll make a night of it that we can always remember.'

I sank into self-pity while I took my bath, preferring the grittiness of Epsom salts to the soft rose and geranium scented foam bubbles that had been so perky and colourful this morning. Someone, long ago, it seemed, had infused the salts with dried lavender and, although it took a while, by the time its slightly smoky, minted, herbal fragrance began to rise on the steam, its sweetness started soothing away my melancholic mood.

This bond that had developed between us could never have been a happy one, I reminded myself. It felt like a delicious madness this morning, where nothing else mattered except us and we locked out life, but reality was always going to find us. I looked at the folded paper bird that sat on the windowsill and finally accepted it was right for me to fly away before we got any deeper into this dangerous relationship.

I sat up and buried my face in a hot flannel, remembering our lovemaking – that's all we'd ever have, one morning of tenderness, but one that would surely haunt me. *Be jolly, be grateful you've had these special moments that no other woman in the world has enjoyed with this man.* 'And then set them aside,' I added. I could admire the memory from time to time but it must always be held as a secret, private pleasure . . . never to be aired, never to be rekindled. Each of us surely has one secret love in our lives . . .

By the time I was patting myself dry I felt strong again. Maybe Epsom salts do have magical therapeutic powers, I thought, with a hint of irony. I was surprised to find a new garment had been left for me in the wardrobe. Perhaps they'd left it during the day, thinking I'd need something for the evening. Once again, it was a throwback to the previous decade, but it was nonetheless exquisite. I didn't hesitate to pull it on and immediately adored the slightly drop-waisted line that accentuated the hip. My new hollow shape and flatter breasts suited this jazz-age frock that combined a sheer, powder grey-blue chiffon over what I suppose could only be described as a 'shrimp pink' crepe shift. Opaque matching pink beaded embroidery added dazzle and some superb grey-blue satin embroidered flowers intermingled with dazzling effect. The broad neckline was softly embroidered too and a glowing shrimp-coloured silk satin bow tied off at the hip, with its tail dropping almost to the length of the narrow gown.

It felt suddenly symbolic. I was instantly as much in love with the dress as the man I was wearing it for, but I now had every intention of taking off that dress and leaving it behind as I left him behind. My skin was bronzed slightly from the sun it had caught on the trek up the hill and I needed little more than a light sweep of soft peach lipstick. I don't think I'd ever looked better but I needed to feel stronger than any previous time because I knew it would require all my resolve to walk away from Saxon Vickery in the morning.

I'd roasted a chicken, serving it with a few root vegetables that I'd thrown into the dish alongside. Simple, healthy fare for Saxon. The bird had been resting since I climbed into the bath and everything was browned to perfection. We'd eat when we felt inclined – no rush – and I could hear the clink of glasses and smiled, walking through to the front of the house, where I noted Saxon had been busy. He'd turned off all lights and instead lit candles around the porch to give this special last night a twinkling quality. He was making up a gin cocktail of sorts but his sharp hearing made him swing around at my soft footfall on the chequered grey-green tiles of his family's verandah.

He gasped at the sight of me. 'You look ravishing.'

'Then ravish me,' I quipped, glad I'd found the right mood to help us enjoy this last night.

I watched his expression crease into that wicked smile I loved, which felt like the sun had just emerged from behind clouds. He looked quite the rake in a white tuxedo and black trousers, although he clearly couldn't be bothered to tie up the bow tie so he had still managed to make himself appear raffishly handsome with his shirt open at the collar.

'Whomever this dress belongs to, she has delicious taste,' I mentioned, spinning for him and feeling the chiffon, light as a breath, lift on that soft twirl.

He returned to pouring our drinks. 'My mother's, I suppose, although I never saw her wear it. She was an elegant woman with fine taste.'

'She hadn't worn it. The Parisian shop tag was pinned to the sash.' I showed him where I'd concealed it.

'Oh, unpin that!'

I shook my head and laughed. 'I don't mind – it's not mine, after all. Besides, it can wait here for your next affair.'

He gave me a slit-eyed warning but I sensed he took my jest in the bright way it was delivered. Saxon handed me a glass with curled bright-green lime peel twisting within. 'You should know before you sip that I make the perfect gimlet, Dr Fenwick.'

I thanked him with a wry smile, took the glass and clinked it against his. 'To tea,' I offered.

He tapped his glass once again against mine. 'And when we drink it, we shall always think of each other.'

I leaned in and kissed him softly before I sipped, wanting him to know my humour was restored and that I would not let him down by being maudlin. 'I can never drink a cup of tea again without thinking about all the effort, science and indeed the mystique behind it . . . and you leaping over tea bushes.'

I could smell the zesty spritz of lime ahead of the fume of alcohol. Its bright, sharp tang cheered me further. The bitterness of gin and the sparkle of the soda seemed to refresh my spirits. 'Mmm, delicious, Saxon, thank you.'

'No, thank you, Isla. For your generosity as much as your calm. We've probably only had the sum total of a week in each other's presence since you came to India and I have to say, not a moment of it has been dull. And I do find almost every woman I meet a bit . . . well, arid . . .' He shrugged.

'Jove said something similar.' I told him Jove's views and why he'd taken so long to agree to marriage.

'The more I hear of him, the more I like him,' Saxon said. 'To you and Jove. I hope you find abundant happiness together and I suspect you will because you aren't boring and he sounds witty and wise.'

'He is. Thank you. And you must promise me to stay well but also to go home and make time for Frances. I know what it is to love someone desperately and for them to not understand how it aches to not have a response.'

He looked at me with a perplexed expression. 'Tell me more.'

I did. I told him everything I could remember about my child-hood crush on Jove. I found it excellent therapy to remind myself of how crazily in love I'd been with him as a youngster. Saxon had cut to the heart of it – how distance had made it too easy to overlook how I'd felt when we'd been reunited as adults; how he made me laugh with such abandon on the day he proposed; how firm he could be . . . how kind and generous he was.

'Isla. You speak with such fondness. You know you've made a brilliant decision to marry him.'

I nodded and it felt more right than it had ever felt before.

'Would you be offended if we didn't sleep together tonight?' I couldn't believe I was asking this. 'I think the weaning from you needs to begin, especially now that I've got Jove so strongly in mind.'

Saxon pulled me close and kissed the top of my head in answer. We said nothing for a moment as we contemplated the starvation of not being able to enjoy the night as fully as we'd intended.

'Again, right decision. But I promised you dancing, did I not? I think that's permitted.'

'It is,' I said, relieved and brightened. I watched him move to the gramophone and blow on the needle before he let it drop to crackle and grate softly before Rudy Vallée's memorable song of the previous decade rang out across the verandah. The lyrics spoke of romance being a game of chance. He'd chosen well.

'Shall we?' Saxon asked, his good hand outstretched.

I took another sip of my gimlet, put down the chilled glass and made a jest of twirling into his arms. At first we danced politely, not speaking, but the way he held my gaze spoke plenty and I was sure I was communicating similar regret and longing. By the time the first chorus had come along, though, we were holding each other close, my head leaning on his shoulder. I didn't feel forlorn, I just wanted to remind myself, in readiness for leaving, as to how it felt to hold Saxon Vickery so completely: the broad, hard sweep of his body, the soft curls of golden hair that flicked carelessly at his neck, the smell of his lavender-scented Potter & Moore shaving soap I'd seen in his bathroom and whose fragrance clung so faintly to his freshly shaved jaw. But especially I cherished laying a soft, fleeting kiss against his bared neck and felt my lips kissed back by a strong, healthy pulse.

This was our silent goodbye: our bodies farewelling one another as Vallée also wound up his song of tender surrender, moonlight and love. We'd stopped dancing halfway through the song and had simply let our melded bodies sway to the music. Now, with the tune finished, we continued to sway to the scratching sound of the needle, neither, it seemed, wanting to let go because we both sensed this was the last time we'd touch intimately.

26

Of all the voices to pierce our affectionate bubble, I would never have imagined it to be the one I heard. The tone of that familiar brogue made the sense of butterflies in my heart turn to wasps. What on earth was Miles Baird doing here?

'Well, now, isn't this just so romantic?'

Saxon and I let go of each other as though we'd both been stung. Neither of us said anything, perhaps waiting for the other to make the first sound, but even Saxon had no cutting remark. Instead, he let go of me and walked slowly across to the gramophone and gently lifted the arm so the needle would stop bumping on its uneven, scratching revolutions. He threw me a tender glance of apology.

Our night was instantly in tatters; there really was nothing to say, so Miles filled the heavy, expectant silence.

'Should I apologise for interrupting this sweet, intimate scene?'

Still we gave him no response.

'Nothing to say?' he wondered gleefully, and in a show of poor manners reached for the gimlet at the occasional table and drank from Saxon's glass. 'Oh, I say. That's seriously good, Vickery. You always could make a damn fine gimlet.'

'Cut the Hooray Henry accent, Baird, and revert to your uncouth Aberdeen upbringing, why don't you? Everyone knows you fake it because you're such a desperate social climber.'

I expected Miles to bristle or quake. He laughed instead.

'And what were you hoping to climb aboard this evening, Vickery?'

'You really are repulsive, Miles,' I joined in, turning away.

'Be very careful,' Saxon warned. 'If you insult Isla again, there'll be no time for apology.'

'And risk those surgeon's hands?' He feigned sympathy. 'Oh, pity about the burn.'

Saxon returned an unblinking, glacial stare. 'Risk your clumsy ones, more like. What the hell do you want, anyway? Why are you even here? How did you find us?'

'All will be revealed,' he said in a mocking tone. Oh, he was surely enjoying himself and our shock. 'I'm actually on an errand of mercy,' Miles said, glee in his voice. 'Quite a job getting here, though, isn't it? I'm surprised you didn't see the torches of the coolies who got me here, or perhaps you were too lost in your embrace to even notice the light or smoke?'

Saxon had told me the locals deliberately burned off forest at night; perhaps he had seen the flames and thought nothing more of them. It didn't seem worth enquiring about. I for one had not been looking out of windows this evening but I wasn't going to fuel his pleasure by asking questions or even answering them if I could help it.

'Anyway, you're looking surprisingly well, Vickery,' he continued. 'I had been told by Matron that you were knocking at death's door but I can see Dr Fenwick's special sort of ministrations have coaxed you into almost shining health – you certainly look happy with yourself.'

I saw Saxon's fist form; Miles was flirting with the notion of a physical fight. I didn't think Saxon would give him another warning.

Nor was he as prepared as I was to wait for Miles to explain. 'Why are you here, Baird? I can't imagine you came all this way from Calcutta to look in on my recuperation.'

'You're right, I didn't. Mmm, that roast smells good. I don't suppose —'

'No!' we both said together and I didn't feel a moment's remorse at being so harsh.

'Well, I'll need a bed, old chap,' he snivelled with an open-palmed look of appeal, and then he dug a deeper hole. 'Perhaps I can sleep in yours, as I suspect you've got a far warmer cot to tuck yourself into tonight.'

Saxon moved but I was ready for the explosion and grabbed him equally quickly. The wrench on my arm tore the small cap sleeve of his mother's exquisite dress. We all heard the horrible ripping sound and fortunately it halted Saxon from launching himself fully at Miles, who'd predictably leapt back fearfully. I didn't think it was achievable to think less of him, but I did in that moment of cowardice.

Saxon unclenched his fists and ran a hand through still-damp hair, which he'd combed for my benefit into a slicked-back style that only enhanced his looks.

'Miles,' I said, finally feeling obliged to take charge, 'you are unwelcome here. The last time we spoke I thought I'd made my position extremely clear. I don't know why you're here but whatever message you have presumably brought, deliver it and then you can sleep on the day bed over there —'

'He can sleep in the sheds!' Saxon growled.

I threw Saxon a look of censure. 'You can leave in the morning the same way you came. You said you had coolies carry you down?'

Miles grinned back lazily. 'I did, at great expense,' he jested. 'And I suspect you might want to leave with me, Isla,' he said, unable to hide the mischief in the Scottish accent.

'I'll leave here when I'm ready and certainly not alongside you.'

'Really?' he mocked. 'One last night of rutting, eh, before you head home with that butter-wouldn't-melt-in-your-mouth smile for your husband?'

'I don't have a husband, Miles.' I held up my hand, pointing to my ring finger. 'And I don't wear an engagement ring, either.'

'Well, now you don't have a father any more,' he sniped.

Silence claimed us as though a huge switch that controlled all the creatures of the land – including the chatting crickets – was thrown and we all fell dumb.

My lips tingled with the fear that raced through me, like a thousand watts of electricity had just arced into my body. 'What does that mean?' My voice sounded as though it was coming from the other side of the room.

'What does it sound like to you? Your father's dead, Isla. Heart attack, apparently. It's why I'm here at your filthy place of orgy with a married man – shame on you, Vickery. Your poor wife must never know, eh?' He carried on as though we were making small talk at a party. 'Your good fortune is that I just happened to be in Darjeeling, visiting my fiancée and her friends, when the news came through to the telegraph station from Matron. Naturally, they found me as I am personally known to you as a colleague.' He sounded bored explaining to us. 'I offered to bring it down on the grounds that I could soften the blow . . . something like that, anyway.' He smiled and I saw that the vulpine ears I'd once mentally accused him of possessing suited him perfectly. A crafty fox lived within Miles Baird.

Saxon moved to me. 'You bastard, Miles.'

I was still staring at him with my numb lips and perhaps a slack-jawed look of disbelief, trying to discern the meaning of what he'd just said. My father was dead from a heart attack . . . That was the phrasing and yet the words were like pebbles falling on flagstones, harsh and bouncing away. I tried to grab at them, make sense of them, but it wasn't until I felt familiar arms around me that I collapsed into full understanding.

'Isla, I'm so sorry,' Saxon murmured, holding me tight, and all but carried me to a seat.

'Listen, you two, I've got —'

'Shut up, Miles!' Saxon snapped.

'Well, there's gratitude for you,' he said, flicking the envelope towards us, which presumably the telegraph office had given him. Saxon picked it up and gave it to me. I read it through a film of tears that rapidly dispersed in two silent streams. He was still talking through my horror. 'I'm the one who took my life in my hands to come here in the dark and . . .'

I set Saxon's reassuring hands aside, pushing the telegram into them, and while Miles bleated I stood and took a deep breath. I didn't know what I was going to do. I thought I might just swing the punch that Saxon longed to deliver but instead I walked right up to Miles, who maybe thought I was about to fall into his arms for solace – or perhaps hug him – but he stopped talking and looked at me with wonder that I'd disentangled myself from Saxon and appeared to be choosing him. What he didn't factor in was the fluid grab of my barely touched gimlet and with dead-eyed accuracy I hurled the contents of my glass into Miles's face. It hit him in the left cheek, stinging his eye and splashing all over him. 'You've used my father as your excuse to come here and gloat at my expense, and into my grief, you perfectly revolting toad of a man. You will not sleep at this house. You will have no food, no drink or hospitality from me and I know Saxon couldn't care less if you fell off the edge of the world. Walk off into the dark. There's a shed over there. And there's a lamp by the step that will light your path. I will not accompany you anywhere, ever. Remember me telling you to go to hell? I haven't changed that attitude. I hope I never have to look upon you again.' I had to stop talking because the emotion was too powerful; it was rage and despair, it was fear, anger and loathing, all of it wrapped into a huge dark ball of pain sitting in my belly, and it had begun to unwind to start tying my insides into knots.

But Saxon was there behind me and he held me, keeping me strong and upright. 'You heard her, Miles. Do the world a favour and scuttle off and, I don't know, die somewhere, won't you.'

'You deserve each other,' Miles snarled. 'And you deserve the pain of knowing that while you were fu—'

This time nothing was going to stop Saxon, although much later I would recall his restraint – no doubt for my benefit again. With his punching arm injured, he instead shoved Miles, who sprawled across the verandah, taking chairs with him as he fell. 'Get out! You're lucky I don't throw you off the whole property. Don't let me so much as glimpse your ugly head tomorrow or I really will make good on the threat.' He loomed over the fallen doctor.

'You'll pay for that, Vickery,' Miles simpered.

'Really? I can't wait.'

We watched Miles get to his knees, then his feet; he angrily grabbed the lantern and the box of matches and walked off into the dark to light it somewhere else – we didn't care where. I didn't give him another thought but I began to tremble. 'I have to go.'

'Adri has already made arrangements for you to leave at first light. Here, let me pour you a stiff drink. You need a brandy.' I waited until he brought it to me. I sipped it in silence and Saxon made sure I drank it all. 'Was your father ill?'

I nodded. 'Heart problems. I think we both knew it could happen at any time.'

'*Massive heart attack* is written in the telegram. That means he wouldn't have known, and you could have been anywhere when it happened . . . on your honeymoon, shopping in London, or even just in the garden – you still couldn't have helped him.'

I nodded.

'Then perhaps there's something to be said for your last memory being of your father looking well, looking proud, smiling, waving to you.'

Did he always have to say the right things? He was more like Jove than he could ever know.

'As it is, it says that he died in his sleep so he didn't suffer and you haven't suffered finding him, or the despair of trying to revive him and failing. No one will ever take that far happier memory from you and it's a good one to lock away.'

I nodded but I'd never felt further from home than I did in that moment. It was cunning timing for this news. Maybe it was my father's final way of ensuring I kept faith with my promise to return and marry the man he approved of. 'I want to be on the first available train to Bombay.'

'Ghum first and then down to Siliguri. Let me see that telegram again.' He reached for it and read it once more silently. I looked away, never wanting to read those harsh black letters that formed horrible words of pain again. 'Jove says he's booked your passage home from Bombay. You've got three days to get there – more than enough time.'

I heard Saxon ringing the bell on the verandah as I served two small plates of food. We ate, standing up with only forks, waiting for the sighting of Adri. I didn't taste a morsel but I knew if I didn't go through the motions of eating, Saxon wouldn't either and I couldn't bear to worry about him relapsing.

'There he is.' Saxon pointed and I saw the first glimmer of a torch, swinging its way through the black of the forest around us. 'I'll go meet him and let him know we'll need him to fetch you in a few hours with men and a palanquin,' he said and handed me his unfinished plate of food. He looked at me sadly and touched my cheek. 'Everything about us is unfinished, isn't it?'

I held back tears for our sorrows – it felt inappropriate to have selfish needs in the midst of grieving for my father. 'I'll go pack.'

We went our separate ways. I deliberately forced my mind blank so that I wouldn't have to think on my father; I wanted to be alone when I did so, and it was a blessing because it meant I thought about nothing. I didn't switch on a light, but instead moved like a marionette around my darkened room, as though someone else was working the strings and I simply obeyed. There wasn't much to do – I was already in neat shape with all my clothes freshly laundered and easily thrown into the holdall again. I slipped out of my beautiful frock, wincing again at the tear in the sleeve that the moonlight highlighted. The ripped seam appeared to sum up my life just now as I split company with important parts of my life.

Saxon and I were over.

My father's life was over.

India was over.

Go home, Isla, I whispered. *And make it work.*

I hung the beautiful gown back in the sweet-smelling wardrobe and closed the door in a final, deliberate gesture.

———

I think there was so much sadness suddenly walking with me that I disappeared within, gathering up my pain and neatly tucking it away. I had a long trip ahead; I had to be composed and Jove was at the end of it. I could give away nothing of my all-too-brief affair with Saxon.

I now had a few weeks of journeying across continents and oceans again to also put Saxon away, deep and secret, where Jove's sharply attuned perceptions couldn't reach. Perhaps I could box him up into that part of me where Jove had lived all these years and essentially been forgotten about until that day last year when my father had spoken his name again. Could I forget Saxon? No, but I had to distance myself – not just physically – if I was not going to let him impact on Jove's and my future.

All the candles had been extinguished by the time I arrived on the verandah again. It was as dark as a coffin out there. No moonlight either but I sensed Kangchenjunga watching us. Saxon melted out of the shadows.

'How are you doing?'

'I don't really know. Numb.'

'Adri will return at dawn as promised. Everything's in place and we can leave as soon as we can see our feet in front of us.'

'Thank you.' I hesitated but then said it. 'Saxon, I don't want you to come.'

There was a weighty pause. 'I won't ask why. But if you change your mind, for any reason, I would prefer to see you onto the train myself.'

I leaned back against him, closing my eyes at the reassuring feel of his body. 'I know, but I'd rather leave you here . . . where you belong, where I'll always think of you, laughing and happy. Will you return to Calcutta?'

I felt him nod. 'Of course. I'll likely see out the year back in Calcutta. I have research to finish at the hospital and then back to England I must go. I promised Frances.'

'I didn't realise you'd be gone that soon. I didn't even ask.'

'Do you wish to be alone?'

'No. That's the last thing I want. I'd like to sit in your arms and watch the sunrise together.'

He gathered up blankets and we moved to the furthest part of the verandah. A large, worn sofa slumped in this corner and had obviously been used for watching the dawn by various Vickerys. It creaked a sigh of surprise, as though delighted to have one of its own back in its embrace, and I snuggled down, allowing Saxon to wrap me protectively in his arms and beneath the blanket. Safe and quiet we remained. There was nothing more to say, although our silent touch said enough. I may have dozed and if I did, or he did, I wasn't aware of it. I knew only peace in this cool elevation of the tea gardens, where I'd learned the buds grow slower than other regions, allowing their flavours to develop a deeper intensity. I let my mind drift over today and what I'd learned – it was an escape – marvelling mostly that because the region was so dramatically hilly, each of the tea gardens of the area could have their own particular climate.

'From tropical to temperate, and some alpine,' Saxon had said, astonishing me. 'Some shadier, some moister, some where the sun hits fiercely and different ripening periods. While some of the higher-altitude gardens are reaching first flush, others well below might be developing their second flush teas.' I imagined explaining all of this to Jove, who would watch me, delighted by my enthusiasm. I reminded myself of his handsome face with its wise lines and the kindness it expressed each time his gaze rested upon mine.

Even the short telegram was kindly crafted. Jove had used those few words to explain the news in a gentle way. I felt a new, important surge of affection and understood that this was what I had to harness now and hold on to. I had to do everything within my power to save Jove any pain over this, which had lasted just three days. One day in fever caring for the man I'd fallen for, one day in loving him, and a last one in saying goodbye. It was hardly torrid but it was nonetheless a betrayal and the only defence I could cling to was my spinster status.

I must have turned that thought over in my mind for hours because night passed and I sensed a soft lightening of the sky behind us. I hadn't realised Saxon was awake; his breathing was so rhythmic, I'd presumed him asleep. But he shifted to point.

'There they are,' he said with awe. And I saw the peaks begin to emerge . . . five sentinels with their ermine stoles watching over us. 'The sun rises behind Darjeeling Town so it hits the summit of Kangchenjunga before it lights the valley,' he explained.

'Where's Everest?' I wondered.

'About one hundred and fifty miles from here; you can sometimes see it on a very clear day from the top of Darjeeling. Watch now as those peaks begin to blush,' he murmured.

I remained silent and observed precisely that. The sun's first kiss was feathery light, waking up the gods, and they stirred with an orange glow, but then the heavenly light whispered words of teasing affection, as almost shyly each of the peaks began to wake properly and flush a luminous peachy pink. It was dazzling as they continued to brighten, the light creeping downwards to their hillsides until they fully mirrored the golden joy of the sun, reflecting it off their jagged surfaces while the sky joined in, swooning from the pink of a baby girl's ribbon to the rich blue of a schoolboy's blazer.

So much beauty.

'Time to go, Isla,' he whispered. I could hear the shuffling of feet, men and animals, and soft voices.

'Saxon!'

'Ssh,' he hushed, and helped me to unfold myself from the comfort of his embrace and from the cocoon we'd created. Stiff from being in one position and cool despite our heavy, warm blanketing, I stretched out my spine and straightened my resolve.

He wouldn't look at me, immediately greeting Adri and company so that all intimacy was banished.

Adri bowed as I came around the verandah. 'Morning,' I whispered. It didn't seem right to speak loudly. 'I'll just fetch my bag.' Before anyone could offer, I'd disappeared into the house to my room. I used the bathroom – this would be the last time for many hours that I'd have such decent facilities – and I washed my face, splashing the coldest of water so I was shocked awake. I brushed my teeth and, with each small ablution, I swallowed the lump of emotion that had threatened to spill. *He was never mine.*

I returned, surprised at how in control I felt. If we just kept avoiding looking at each other, I could leave and then it would be too late to look upon him again. We went through the motions of loading up my holdall, plumping the cushions within the litter and rearranging a blanket for the cool morning. There was a strange sensation that I could only describe as fizzing in my mind and my throat was tight. I tried to breathe but the air felt shallow.

And then the moment arrived. 'Are you sure you want to go on alone?'

'I'm sure,' I squeezed out, lying to myself and him, not meeting his glance.

He offered his hand to help me into my chair. I had to raise my gaze to his. We had an audience, which in a curious way I was glad for because it helped us to remain as aloof as possible. He was grinding his jaw and I suppose I found it reassuring that he was experiencing a similar struggle. He deliberately mentioned Miles, perhaps to keep my emotion keen. 'Is Dr Baird still around, Adri?'

'No, sir. He left just before dawn with his own group.'

He looked at me. 'You'll be following them up the hill.'

I nodded.

'Tell the men to keep a distance. I don't want Dr Baird any-where near Dr Fenwick.'

'I shall instruct them.' Adri left us.

We were still holding hands. 'Be safe, Isla.'

Time to swallow. 'And you take care of yourself.'

He gave a sad grin.

'I mean it, Saxon. Promise me. Your hand needs care and —'

'Be still. I'll drink a lot of tea and think of how much I love you.'

'I want to kiss you,' I admitted in a voice barely above a whisper.

He shook his head slightly. 'Save your kisses for Jove. He deserves them.' He leaned down and kissed my hand instead and I had to swallow a rising sob.

'Farewell, fair Isla.' He let go. 'Move on!' he called out, sound-ing almost angry, but I knew what it was taking for him to be this strong for us. He gave a sharp whistle and the palanquin jerked into motion.

I pulled the curtains aside so I could watch him. And now I did cry, because no one but the Himalayan peaks could see me weep. I saw him ruthlessly turn his broad-shouldered back on me and hoped he was crying too but I suspected that was an empty wish. I watched him lope toward the ridge and he kept his back to us as we began to ascend the narrow, uneven path. Soon we'd turn and I would be pointing the wrong way; I wouldn't be able to see him . . . the sensation was akin to panic and I leaned out of the chair, forcing my bearers to adjust quickly or risk toppling, but I didn't care. One last look, one last moment of stolen love . . .

There he was. He had turned to watch us. I waved. He lifted his injured hand in farewell and dared to blow me a kiss. And now the sob did escape and I didn't care if the men heard. I had one final glimpse over the top of the rocky terrain we were now navigating and it was of Saxon, bathed in a fiery morning light, standing at the top of the world, in the bosom of Brackenridge where he belonged – strong, golden, protected by mountains that hugged the tea gardens – and I wept openly.

Epilogue

We didn't exchange a word or seek news of each other in more than two years. It's now autumn of 1935 and I returned home on the first day of Autumn, 1933, to bury my father and to keep my promise to Jove to be home for our wedding. Out of respect, we held off on our marriage until a frozen winter wedding took place at the end of February, and I admit to quiet contentment in my life as Mrs Jovian Mandeville.

I teach now and find it far more rewarding than I imagined it could be. I am still consulted from time to time for clinical work, but I've kept my word and make sure that Jove and our life comes first, although the new Mothers and Babies Institute I've championed and chair could demand every moment of my life if I let it . . . I won't, of course. I had no idea how busy it would be as the wife of a popular member of parliament and given that we move between the house in Mayfair that we now call home and his family manor in the Cotswolds, there is always entertaining to be done. What I thought would be tedious is nothing of the sort, as Jove's friends – the ones he is genuinely close to – are all interesting people, and I've found a few of the wives to be colourful, including a writer, an artist and a woman who is an expert on herbs; she's teaching me more about natural medicines, which I find irresistible.

Our wedding present to each other was the purchase of a four-storeyed seaside home on Brunswick Terrace. We plan to slowly renovate and decorate to our taste but we hope to spend a spring and an autumn down there within a couple of years.

All of this has helped to anchor me to life as Mrs Mandeville but the struggle of keeping the memory of Saxon Vickery tied down is my burden. It's a daily chore, worst first thing in the morning as I tend to wake and rise at dawn; it's a delicate time for me as memories crowd. As the day wears on it all gets easier and by evening I could honestly admit that he has no impact. It's the fragile hours when I'm at my most vulnerable, but the truth is that time's passing eases most burdens . . . the grief of losing my father is, these days, a soft pain and now I have reassured myself that it is a case of time: waiting it out for the ache of leaving Saxon Vickery to slide into the sunset of my past.

All of that thinking held firm until this very moment, the moment when Saxon Vickery appeared like an apparition before me and Jove, here in the middle of Hyde Park. Until a few minutes ago I had thought time and I were in concert, but confronting him again just now was harder than leaving him. Oh, why did this have to happen? Us Mandevilles arm in arm, gently debating the colour we would paint our drawing room, which overlooked Hove beach on the seafront, nearly stepping into the path of Saxon and Frances Vickery.

'Oh, do forgive us,' I said, not realising at first because I looked absently at the elegant woman pushing the wheelchair.

She was dressed in a calf-length fur and soft felt hat. Her pencil-thin eyebrows framed dark, almond-shaped eyes and the bow of her lips was painted a soft cherry, while auburn hair was fashioned in a curly bob. Slim, like a mannequin, she walked with confidence and a long stride. She struck me as terribly beautiful, all her actions graceful, whether it was pulling the fur coat more snugly around herself or reaching to touch her hair. Naturally I glanced down, really just to offer a polite smile to her companion, but let out a gasp to see the familiar beloved face ravaged once again by illness.

'Saxon!' It came out as a whisper. Breathing was suddenly hard.

'Good grief,' I heard Jove remark. 'Is this the professor you speak of?'

The bundle in the wheelchair sighed and the small child on his lap grinned up at me before offering a sticky lick of her lollipop. Shock upon shock.

Jove rescued me, taking it upon himself to introduce us all. Handshakes and polite greetings were exchanged and the inevitable awkwardness of what to say next arrived.

'Well, isn't this daughter of yours a cherub?' Jove offered.

'She was christened Rosamunde. But we call her Rosie,' Frances Vickery said in a cultured accent; her voice was smoky, rather compelling.

'It suits her,' I said, looking at the happy, apple-cheeked child with golden curls. I needed to pull my anguished gaze from him and say something. 'Er, Frances, I've heard so much about you. It's lovely to meet you at last. Rosie's beautiful.'

'Thank you,' she said, not gushy as I'd always thought she would be; instead composed and slightly cool. I watched her lay a hand on her husband's shoulder, then stroke his cheek as if she could check his temperature through her ecru suede glove. A message was being communicated, not so subtle, either. 'Not too chilled, darling?'

'I'm fine,' he said, his stare from those familiar, beloved eyes belying his words. His gaze reminded me of the gelid air that swept off the Himalayan peaks and roared through the valleys to drop the temperature dramatically.

'Rosie.' It was Jove again, helping me out. 'Would you like to see the ducks? I suspect your father and Isla here would like to exchange news of India.' He beamed at the adults as Rosie licked her lollipop. 'Care to take a look, Frances? It's just a few steps away.'

'Oh, I think Rosie would love it, thank you.'

And they were gone.

Saxon hadn't stopped staring. 'That wasn't very adroit, was it? They've obviously planned this "accidental" meet.'

I felt unnerved, unsure of what to say. 'Surely not?' My words were pure reaction trying to deny what already began to feel plausible. 'It's true that Jove knows I'm extremely fond of you. I've told him everything that can't hurt him. I don't understand, though. What's to be gained if you're right and they have arranged this meet?'

He gave a light shrug, the action so familiar it felt like a pinch, waking me up to all those other small gestures I'd fallen in love with but learned to keep in a darkened, sleeping place deep within. 'Perhaps you've revealed too much, or why else would we be standing here? I suspect Jove's decided to confront a problem rather than worry about it. My wife, on the other hand, doesn't know anything about you – not from me, anyway.'

'Are you suggesting Jove has told her?' I moved us on, my cheeks burning with shame.

'Well, why else am I here? This is not one of our familiar walking routes.'

I began to feel my well-ordered world fraying, like a thread coming loose with the potential to unravel the whole. 'How long have you been back?' I asked, helplessly calculating Rosie's age.

'I came home for Rosie's birth in February last year,' he replied, as if he knew what I was doing, and then to make sure I understood, he added, 'She was conceived on my last visit home, before you arrived in India.'

I begged myself not to flush further with jealousy. He had never promised me anything. He had tried to discourage me. I had, in all fairness, forced us together. I cleared my throat. 'Last February's when Jove and I married – a little later than planned but still a winter wedding.' I hated myself for sounding so clumsy. I shifted to the safer ground of medicine. At least I could sound professional. 'When did it strike again?'

'Recently. English winters can be harsh. I'll be fine.'

'You look terrible.' In spite of it, you can't hide those features, I thought.

He took no insult. 'You look happily married.'

'I am.'

'Isla, I know it was you behind the purchase of Brackenridge.' Straight to the point, as always.

'I . . . er . . . I don't know —'

'Don't. Jove hid his tracks well but I'm not a complete fool, you know. Neither's my wife. That's probably how they've connected – she may have put two and two together.'

I hesitated and then came clean. 'After seeing you there and how much you care about it, I wanted you to have it. I gather Rex couldn't get rid of it fast enough.'

He nodded.

'Does he know?'

'Not yet. But I do want to thank you; I've been wanting to thank you since the sale but I also wanted to keep the promise we made about not making contact, so I didn't know how to show my gratitude. Without the cloak-and-dagger stuff, Rex would never have sold it direct to me.'

'Is Frances fine with it?'

'Yes, surprisingly so, and given that it's her money mostly, I'm grateful to her as well, although I think your husband has superb skills of persuasion. No doubt a very slick politician. I'm guessing he convinced her that to buy Brackenridge would stop me being so wistful about it. I suspect now that they've met during the negotiations and yes, it's feasible that they've likely discussed our marriages and hatched this rather uncomfortable meet.' He gave me another doleful stare of accusation.

I smiled crookedly. 'Will Frances . . . er . . . will she join you?'

'She's agreeable to making a semi-permanent visit soon and to stay until Rosie is three. I suspect she is no longer prepared to live alone now that a child is in our midst. Anyway, by then she hopes we'll have another.' He cleared his throat as if to rid us of the awkwardness of that last statement. 'Meanwhile, I've agreed I won't live there all the time. We'll split up each year as best we can, bring us all home annually for three or four months.' He looked unsure, frowning. 'We'll work it out. I'm happy for Rosie and whoever else comes along that it remains in the family.'

'I'm glad for you, really I am. How's your arm?'

'Healed as best it could, thank you.'

Anguish that ghosted in his face dissipated. He smiled and I glimpsed the Saxon who'd entirely seduced me.

'You look wonderful,' he said unexpectedly, his voice too soft. It would undo me if I didn't get away from him. He continued. 'I've . . . well, let's just say, you're missed. Oh, one piece of news – take it how you will. Miles Baird is dead.'

'What?'

He nodded. 'A hunting accident up in Simla; he died from his injuries. Showing off, no doubt. The tiger apparently turned and attacked. I never did hear all the gruesome details, nor did I care to.'

Sad, I suppose, but I had not forgiven Miles his trespass and while I didn't celebrate his death, I didn't mourn him either. 'Saxon, I'd ask you both over for dinner but —'

'Please don't,' he interrupted. 'Isla, you are not to take this the wrong way but I'm sorry we've met.'

'I understand. I feel the same way.' I glanced up. 'Here they come, our two plotters.'

He gave a brave smile, coughed, and with his back to them they couldn't see the way he took my hand tenderly. As I pulled away softly, our fingers lingered, intertwined. It was unbearable. 'I miss your special healing, Isla.'

I pretended I hadn't heard him, as the life I thought I'd set up so well once again threatened to unwind. 'Hello, again,' I said loudly. 'Did Rosie enjoy the ducks?'

Both Jove and Frances beamed. She arrived at the handles of the wheelchair and that was my cue to move next to Jove.

'She did. Bit scared of the swans, though. Right, well, darling,' Frances said firmly, 'we'd better get a move on and you out of the draught.'

I watched her fuss at his scarf and knew he'd hate that as much as the blanket covering his legs. I wanted to touch the wayward lock of hair that had escaped its combing; I noted he kept his hair tidily trimmed these days; no disobedient flicks at the back that I had loved. I wanted to kiss him goodbye, but then I'd always be wanting to kiss him one last time.

Jove linked his arm into mine and I hoped I hadn't sagged with relief. 'Good to finally meet you, Vickery.' He shook Saxon's hand. 'Sorry we can't stay longer.'

'We must be going,' Frances said, a fraction too quickly.

I just wanted to run.

'Goodbye,' I said, a cursory glance at the beautiful wife and a stolen but lingering look at Saxon. 'Be well soon, Saxon. Bye, Rosie.'

And we walked on, they in the other direction. Just like that, he was gone again, wheeled away like an invalid by his wife, who was perhaps all too aware of his attractiveness to other women. Smarting from the meeting and unable to say much, I was relieved when the banker had conveniently happened along.

'I thought that was you, Jove. Ah, Mrs Mandeville, hello.' He removed his hat and gave me a short bow. I dug up a smile, forcing myself not to look back over my shoulder. 'I wonder, may I borrow your husband for a tick? I promise not to keep him too long.'

Jove began to make an excuse but I jumped in. 'Of course. I'll visit the ducks myself,' I think I said, giving Jove a gentle shove. 'Go on. I won't go far.'

And so here I find myself, no longer trembling, I'm glad to note, but feeling the numbing hardness of the park bench after nearly a half-hour of calming my breathing and slowing my pulse and thinking back upon the period that brought me to this point. Was I past the shock of seeing the person I had been trying so hard to forget?

Nearly. Past the immediate fright, having sat here contemplating our story, but I would have to start the process again of trying to no longer hear his voice, to bury the affectionate words just spoken to me and not listen for their echo, to blur the features of his face until —

'Here I am,' Jove said, taking me slightly unawares. I felt the timber slats bounce up as he landed next to me. 'Sorry, took a little longer. All right here?'

'Yes, yes, just fine,' I said brightly. 'Getting cold, perhaps.' I touched my cheeks, embarrassed they were burning with guilt.

'Let's get you home, then. I'll run you a bath and pour us a sherry. Must have been good to see your old companion again?'

'It was a shock. Bit overwhelming to see him looking so unwell.'

'I'll bet. It's curious, isn't it, Isla, that someone you speak about as such a close and trusted colleague and confidante is someone you never write to, you never see, and you don't even know is back in the country.'

I cleared my throat silently before cutting him a look of offence. 'What are you getting at, Jove?'

'We said no lies.' He took my gloved hand and squeezed it.

'We did.' I sounded suspicious.

'Meeting Vickery and his wife wasn't a coincidence.'

I looked down, nauseous. 'So you arranged it.'

'I did. As I arranged the purchase of Brackenridge and then the sale of it to your good friend, the professor.'

'And was this meeting contrived with his wife's sanction?'

'Frances wanted it as much as I did. She knows her husband hasn't fully come back to her from India. And she admitted to me that it was no longer just his work or the country that hurt him to be away from.'

I gave him a glance of pure injury. 'Why did you do this, Jove?'

'Well, to use a medical analogy that might appeal to you, I thought it could help lance a boil.' He gave me a sad smile. 'I thought it important that you and Vickery laid eyes on the people who love you both; the ones who are your partners in life, who worry about you, look after you.'

I felt desperately sad to realise I hadn't kept my pain from Jove at all.

'Isla, when you travelled to India you were still something of an indulged child; when you returned, you couldn't put my ring on your finger fast enough. There was a sort of frenzy about you on your return, as though I couldn't pin you down . . . couldn't find you in here.' He touched the side of my head. 'The woman I loved had gone missing even though she was in my presence again.'

He was right, of course. When he'd proposed I was the girl. In India I became the woman and I was alarmed to discover that my life was made less purposeful by finding such dangerous love in Saxon; I was no longer impenetrable and I discovered, to my despair, that love does not strengthen; it weakens. It's a drug that loosens one's hold on the sensibilities and responsibilities of life. A new person emerges from under the influence of love. A fragile, more vulnerable version, and yet one sufficiently beguiled who believes that even the seemingly impossible might be achieved. In the end, the reality is that one is entirely weakened – sleeping, in fact – removed from the real world under the influence of the addictive drug that love is.

'Is Isla back? Is she mine?'

'Oh, Jove, don't,' I pleaded.

He gave an affectionate shrug. 'I'm glad we're talking about it. I realised I had to give you time – I have the patience of a crocodile, you know.' He grinned kindly. 'I knew something had happened and I could guess what that might be. I forced myself to accept that you were a single woman while it occurred. It was one of the reasons I'd made my conditions. But it seemed you'd chosen me; you were home and you were in my arms, determined to marry, so I decided not to fight it.'

Tears leaked and I sniffed.

'I reassured myself that you were happy to be my wife and since that moment you've never given me cause to doubt your sincerity of that.'

Despite the chill I pulled off my gloves. I took his hand, pulled off his glove so we could feel our skin against each other before I kissed the palm that caressed me so often, and so affectionately.

'Don't doubt it, my love. I never want to be anything but Mrs Jovian Mandeville.'

'The thing is, Isla, returning to the condition of us getting married . . . you do remember?' He pulled out his handkerchief and gave it to me. I nodded thanks. I knew he was waiting.

After dabbing at my eyes and nose, I answered. 'Of course I do.'

'You made a promise that when you returned I got to have all of you, that nothing would be left behind in India.' He paused, spearing me with a solemn gaze. 'That goes for your heart, my darling. I can't have it belonging to someone else.'

Oh, how I'd hurt him and still he was being generous . . . 'It doesn't, Jove. It's yours. I love you and that's not going to change. I told you how ill he was – you can see today how that disease can rob him of his health without warning.'

He nodded.

'I had to help him.'

'Of course.'

I sensed he had more to say, wanted to hear more from me, but I was thunderstruck by how long he'd held this knowledge from me and also by what was perhaps an admission by me. He seemed to dither on the precipice of pushing me to say more and then in his wise way, he pulled back. 'I think it's a bit of a struggle for her with him and the baby. I think she, too, needed to see for herself that nothing more existed between you both.'

Nothing more. Jove, in his wisdom, was allowing for whatever occurred while I was single to be just that – events from the past when as a spinster I could make my own decisions about whom I spent time with.

'Nothing does exist. We talked about Miles Baird dying.' He raised an eyebrow at this because I'd told him about the behaviour of Miles. 'We talked about Rosie, the fact that they wanted more children, when they were moving to India together, and we talked about you.'

He smiled gently. 'Listen to the jealous old fool I've become.'

I shook my head.

'So we don't need to have them over or anything?'

'Jove, I never need to see either of them again.' I meant it.

He held my gaze. 'I love you with all of my heart, Isla, and do you know what?'

'What?'

'Seeing that gorgeous child, Rosie, has given me an idea.'

I sniffed as I laughed, determined to shift our mood, determined in that frantic moment of nearly losing him to shake off my hunger; to let go of my need for a man who no longer existed. Saxon Vickery of Brackenridge was like a ghost . . . he didn't exist out of the tea gardens of Darjeeling. Perhaps no other living person had experienced that Saxon other than me. He was only *Saxon of Darjeeling* when he was with me, and we were not together. We never could be . . . we never would be. I remembered something he said: *You don't forget a love that is true. But you can live with its memory.* Well, I would live with that memory but I was going to lock it away now because it had no place in my present life; today was an epiphany as I glimpsed the horror of losing Jove.

Until this second I'd never feared it but I realise now what Jove needed was for me to choose.

But this time to choose without secrets.

'What do you say, Isla? Is it time we thought about children?'

I stood, held out my hand and he took it. 'Come on. Take me home and let's see if we can't make a Rosie of our own.'

He stood and hugged me tightly; we held the embrace long enough that people began to notice but I couldn't care. I felt the change coming over me and perhaps seeing Saxon today with his wife and daughter was the best situation that could have occurred.

Perhaps Jove's cunning move had achieved everything he'd hoped . . . It's not that I would ever stop loving Saxon, but the reality of his life was laid out before me in such a stark way. It's one thing to talk about a wife on the other side of the world, quite a different feeling to meet the living, breathing, jealous version who had simmering emotions and a fiery, consuming love for him that I couldn't match. Her love was angry, full of ownership, while I loved him from afar and knew he could never be mine. I didn't relish the conversation they might be having but that was their life, not mine.

Now I wanted release from the torment. No more lost hours, no further soft regret, no more replaying of our brief, brightly burning but ultimately extinguished relationship. I dipped into my coat pocket for the talisman that had been my companion since I left India; it was never far from me but now perhaps it was time to let it go, fly free. As Jove raised an arm to wave to an acquaintance that he recognised across the lawns, I dropped the tiny origami magpie that Saxon had folded for me beneath a hawthorn tree we passed, which I knew would provide nectar next spring and food for the birds during this autumn. It was an ideal new home for Saxon's magpie . . . wild and beautiful – like him, like our love. But I was letting go and it felt right.

I had someone real, someone loyal, who near enough worshipped me but wouldn't share me and that was how it should be. I was done with wanting to be two women, I was ashamed at my weakness, and I would set everything right with Jove.

Kangchenjunga would not see me again and the tea gardens of Brackenridge would raise a new family of Vickerys, in which I had no place, no role.

'Never doubt me again. I do love you, Jove,' I urged as we walked away from the hawthorn, arm in arm, back towards Mayfair where we called home.

'I know, my darling,' Jove said as he kissed my hand and I held back tears, grateful for this man I'd known was right for me from my early teens, as did the Lady Palmist on Palace Pier. I decided to trust the oracle and the pledge that we'd made as we stood on that invisible, magical line between land and water and agreed to honour each other in marriage.

And hundreds of miles away at another magical line where heaven and earth kiss, a mountain looked down benignly upon the world and scattered into its mists the memory of a couple who had touched a brief but extraordinary healing love among the tea gardens.

Acknowledgements

My mother only remembered to tell me after I'd completed all the research and written the first draft of this novel that a member of our family had a tea plantation in Darjeeling! I wanted to scratch at my face in frustration when I heard. Having made the long, often challenging journey to discover as much as I could 'on the ground' in Calcutta and the foothills of the Himalayas around Darjeeling, it would have been a special experience to walk among the tea bushes whose planting by our family can be traced back 100 years or more.

It was a coincidence that I chose to write a story set in and around this region of the foothills of the Himalayas, the same neighbourhood in which my grandmother and my mother taught orphans in the 1950s at Dr Graham's Homes. I had hoped to take Isla Fenwick into Kalimpong, but as it turned out there was too much story in and around the tea gardens to do so. Nevertheless, it felt satisfying to walk in the footsteps of the important women in my life and I am wishing Dr Graham's Homes another hundred years of care and education for the children who live in these scattered foothills.

There are always people to thank who make the journey of the book easier and who contribute a part of themselves to the story. These include the wonderful historian Alex Hutchinson. Together we got thrown out of the British Library's Asia Reading Room because our whispers were getting far too excited for the boffins around us as we read and discovered how the story might unfold. Alex has now collaborated on the research for three of my novels and I can't see her interest waning, for which I'm enormously grateful.

A lovely gentlemen, Ken Staynor in England, answered my plea for help with the history of trains in India. What a wealth of knowledge he has. Since we had to ruthlessly edit this big book into a more manageable size, a lot of the train journeying was lost. However, it wasn't lost in my heart and without first learning it from Ken, I might never have fully understood Isla's journey from Calcutta into Darjeeling. I was lucky enough to ride on the world-famous Darjeeling Himalayan Railway known as the 'Toy Train' between Ghum – the highest railway station in India – and Darjeeling. This is a UNESCO World Heritage Site and truly the most extraordinary feat of engineering in any era, but given it was built before the turn of the previous century, it leaves you slack-jawed. Ride it if you ever get the chance.

At my side, keeping me safe and making all my varied travel connections, is Ian. No book is ever written without him in the background handling all the planning that goes into one of these enormous research trips, which usually cover a remarkable amount of geography with endless flights, buses, trains, accommodation, professional guides, etc. to be found, organised and dovetailed into a workable itinerary. Meanwhile, I just turn up and hope he's organised train seats that don't point backwards and plane seats that offer a quick getaway for this impatient soul. He's also my first and most ruthless reader. I'm sure I never thank him enough.

My other stalwart is Pip Klimentou; she has travelled every book's journey with me and is always ready to drop her tasks to read quickly and offer that first, all-important feedback on the early drafts that I count on. Her thumbs-up means plenty.

Big thanks to Ali Watts – my publisher, editor and my friend – who is so generous and supportive, as well as the other talented people who are intrinsic to making my job enjoyable, including Saskia Adams and especially Lou Ryan. Thank you to the team at Penguin Random House . . . so many hands touch the story at some point and in such a variety of capacities. You know who you are and I hope you also know how grateful I am.

Booksellers and librarians are often unsung heroes in the face of all sorts of ups and downs in our industry, but look at you now . . . brilliant, flourishing, ever supportive. Thank you for always looking after my books with such generosity.

Finally, and especially, all of you readers out there in every corner of the world . . . you are the most important to thank and celebrate. Without you, what's the point?

Fx

Almond, sweet cherry and Darjeeling tea cake

This is getting close to our family's favourite slice to go with an afternoon cuppa and nothing pairs better than a light and sparkling pot of golden Darjeeling. It also feels sentimental; if you're a baby boomer, then this is the sort of cake your grandmother baked.

Hunt around and find the Amarena cherries – these are black cherries, originally from Bologna, that have a wildly sweet and intensely genuine flavour. Don't buy them in syrup. You want the slightly candied variety. They're sold in delicatessens and really good supermarkets. I'm trying to avoid you buying the fire-engine-red glacé cherries that also come in green when you want a Christmas theme… but if you have to buy glacé cherries, go to a delicatessen and buy the very best. You'll thank me and so will this cake.

Ingredients
250g Amarena cherries, cut in half and lightly floured to stop them being sticky and to prevent them from sinking to the bottom of your cake.
250g self-raising flour (2 cups)
220g unsalted butter, room temperature

185g caster sugar (¾ cup)
3 extra large eggs
120g ground almonds (I use unrefined, 1 cup)
pure almond essence to taste
3 tablespoons single cream
½ cup cooled Darjeeling tea

Method
Bake this in a standard-sized loaf pan. I like to use those loaf pan liners for easy turn out but take the precaution to butter and line the tin if you don't have a non-stick tin and a loaf liner.

Get your oven up to around 170°C.

Cream the butter and sugar. Now, I have a stand mixer and so I just get it on and walk away for about ten minutes until the sugar and butter have turned extremely pale and are fluffily combined. But you do what you prefer. The main thing is cream the mixture well.

I then whiz my eggs with a fork in a cup or jug and then gradually pour the egg as my beater is going. Do this slowly or you'll end up with glug . . . the patience ensures the eggs are incorporated fully into a mixture that just desperately wants to curdle on you. But it won't if you go slow. Add in your almond essence to taste. I won't give an amount because when it comes to vanilla or almond essence, I always want to pour six times as much as most recipes want, so you do it to suit your palate.

Mix the almond meal and flour together and then gently, in perhaps four loads, fold these dry ingredients into the cake mix. It's going to feel thick but keep a light hand. Now, add the halved and floured cherries you prepared. You're not going to think it will work but it will, especially now when you add three tablespoons of single pure cream (or full cream milk if you prefer) and then another three tablespoons of cold Darjeeling tea.

Then into the tin it goes. Smooth the top and pop it into the oven for an hour at least. I've always found this cake takes longer than I expect so keep checking and then let it cool fully in the tin before you tip it out. Then, dust with icing sugar, flounce with some fresh flowers and serve it with a fresh and steaming pot of Darjeeling.

Enjoy the explosions of cherry flavour in your mouth that go with the tea in a delicious manner!

Book Club Discussion Notes

1. Is *The Tea Gardens* a story of true love or devastating betrayal?

2. Do you think Jove was kind, clever or cunning when he allowed Isla to follow her heart to India? Could you appreciate his motives?

3. As a physician, Isla is driven by an intense need to save others. In what ways does she learn that this is not always possible?

4. Matron tells Isla that rank is given but respect is earned. Do you think Isla earns respect during her time in India?

5. Do you agree that faith is far stronger than medicine?

6. In his letter, Jove tells Isla to 'leave nothing behind' in India. Was this good advice, in your view?

7. 'No one ever leaves Kangchenjunga unchanged.' Discuss.

8. What is the significance of the book's remote location?

9. Identify some of the many different ways in which tea is used throughout the novel.

10. Do you agree with Saxon when he says, 'You can still make a good life even if you're not with the person you truly love'?

11. How did Isla change through her experiences?

12. Do you find Saxon the hero or the villain of this story?

13. Is this a book about people maintaining control of their emotions – or losing control of them?

14. If you were Isla, would you have chosen Saxon or Jove?